MAX ABADDON AND THE DARK CARNIVAL

Book 4 of the Max Abaddon Series

Justin S. Leslie

J.S.L

Paperback ISBN: 978-1-7353035-9-8
E-book ISBN: 978-1-7353035-8-1

Contact Information
Email: Abaddonbooks@hotmail.com
Facebook: @Maxabaddonbooks

Website: www.JustinLeslie.com

Copyediting by Happily Ever Proofreading LLC

"Curse ruthless time! Curse our mortality. How cruelly short is the allotted span for all we must cram into it!"

WINSTON CHURCHILL

PROLOGUE

"Will it hold?" Tom asked Hades as they both stared at the angled rock wall.

"For now, yes. But we can only keep the Fallen for so long. The power it would take to do so permanently is not found here," Hades replied curtly.

As the two men turned, Tom nodded his head approvingly.

Tom and the god of the Underworld stared at the frozen body of Mengele. He was suspended in a clear glass-like substance inlaid on the side of a stone wall. This part of Hades personal prison was hundreds of feet tall, with several other encased figures all stored away for safekeeping. The rest of his domain was another story.

The irony that the gods of Olympus basically all had jobs was not lost on Tom. After the great celestial wars, it had been the Olympians' responsibility to do things such as ensure safe travel, have basic oversight of the elements, or as Hades, oversee the entryway to the Underworld, also known as the Everwhere.

In all fairness, while he reported to Devin on paper, it was more of a dotted line relationship for the two immortals. The Devil, or as most people knew him, Devin, and Hades worked in tandem to secure the Underworld, including all that dwelled in it.

Mengele's body looked like an insect trapped in amber from prehistoric times, just like one would see in a movie about dinosaurs. His eyes were open and aware as an expression of confused hate sat frozen in time on his face.

"Well, enough of that," Hades bellowed, leading the way out of the room, the clank of his armor echoing.

"I'll make sure we figure out a way to handle him long-term," Tom assured as the two entered another smaller room with several fireplaces and chairs. A loud thump reverberated, shaking the room as if someone had dropped a ton of bricks.

"Ah, Cerberus is back. He's been a busy boy lately," Hades said, handing Tom a glass of red wine.

"We almost got to play fetch a few weeks ago," Tom replied, taking a sip.

"So I've heard. Tell me, what is it you're up to?" Hades sighed.

"I'm trying to figure out why the Plane is shifting and how to stop it," Tom answered as Hades sank into the largest of the chairs.

"While that doesn't affect me, I can see why it would be a concern for all you Earthbound types," Hades said, shaking his head.

"It will come knocking on your door at some point. You know this. Oh, and Lilith is going to help," Tom said cautiously.

Hades spit out his wine, sitting up straight. Electricity danced in his eyes as the sounds of a rather big dog started echoing from outside the room.

CHAPTER 1

Head Games

"Just calm down," I said as the car let off the brakes, nudging me to move faster. Looking up, the outline of a giant, rather pissed spider came into view over the moving tree line.

The ten-foot jump I had decided to take had not treated the vehicle well. Even though I was driving a 1970 enchanted Cadillac DeVille in the Everwhere, it still needed to have the batteries hooked up to work. Shocker, I know.

"Boss, that thing is really pissed this time," Petro said, flying overhead and keeping a bird's-eye view on the chaos that had ensued.

Three days prior, we had finally discovered the location of Jamison's body. His head, which was yelling at me to *get my ass moving*, also just happened to be on the dash. I'll never quite figure out how a bodyless head could yell.

My hands fumbled as I turned the old wrench, connecting the last of the battery wires. The drop and not-so-graceful landing had launched the batteries out of their holder, disconnecting the soul-powering energizers.

The horn blared as the headlights flashed, letting me know it was time to move. "Petro, go time!" I exclaimed as he came flying down out of the cool purple sky. I slammed the transmission into drive as the engine screamed to life, telling me the car also knew its ass was on the line.

Without warning, the massive steel beast lurched forward at impossible speeds just as the spiked front leg of a forty-foot-tall spider slammed into the road. Chunks of asphalt and pitch-black dirt sprayed the back of the car. The mix of the purple, endless dark sky and red headlights made the scene even more chaotic.

"Take it easy!" Jamison barked accusingly as I grabbed him by the hair, slinging him to the back seat. His body caught the head as Petro just mouthed "*WTF . . .*" looking up at me from the cigarette ashtray.

While we had found his body, we hadn't done the whole put-Humpty-Dumpty-back-together-again thing. We would have to leave that up to Jenny.

Over the past several months, we had kept Jamison's head in a sort of bag with straps on it. While not the most pleasant way to talk to someone, it had sufficed.

"Phil, you there?" I asked over the communicator.

"Aye, I'm here. Is that you making all that racket?" Phil asked, standing in the driveway of the Everwhere version of the Atheneum. Due to current circumstances, we had had to leave him behind, just in case. Lana, the keeper of the local area in the Everwhere, had decided to take a little break. This meant anytime we gated into the Everwhere from the Postern, someone had to stay behind until we could put the wards back up.

"Yup, and hey, man, I hate to tell you this." I paused, knowing Phil's utter phobia of spiders. To be fair, I didn't know anyone who would not shit themselves after seeing what was chasing us. "Big spider."

"Is it following you? And, uh . . . just exactly how big, bruther?" Phil asked in rapid succession.

"Too big, coming in hot. We may have two or three minutes tops before it gets here. Get by the door; I'm going to swing by as fast as I can. The car will be fine; she's a good girl," I spit out, growling the last part about our ride. The car gave a little extra push after hearing my compliment. She was temperamental that way.

The purple sky and flowing shadows made it hard to focus. Apparitional beings came into focus, only to be left behind in the red glow of taillights.

"Hey, boss. Jamison's body is doing something funny back there," Petro said. I glanced back to see his body trying to place its head back on, only for it to slide off with a resounding thud. This, of course, was followed by a flurry of curse words courtesy of Jamison.

"Stop it, you twit," Jamison barked, but it was clear his body had other plans.

"Shut up, you two, or whatever you are now. Petro, is that thing still behind us?" I yelled, looking in the rearview mirror.

"I don't see it. Wait a minute . . ." Petro drawled out before screaming. "Left, turn left!"

Without thinking, I slammed the car left as the engine roared. Two large hairy legs slammed into the pitch-black road directly where the car had been.

Taking a deep, calming breath, I patted the dashboard. "So, are there any tricks that you can do to get us out of here?"

"Right!" Petro yelled as I again swerved, the tires screaming like a young girl in the front row at a boy band concert.

"Trust me. I'm fresh out of led for my foot," I said as the hazards came on. The loud ticking from the lights was different from that of the newer cars on the road. These were old, clanking tick-tocks.

"What's she doing, boss?" Petro asked from the back

window, still working to gauge our next move.

"I don't knooooo—" I gasped as the car shot into the air, wobbling slightly. The motion slammed me into the seat, putting a permanent imprint of my ass in the leather. A wet thump came from the back seat as Jamison's head, again letting out a flurry of curse words, bounced around like a pinball. His unguided body reached blindly, grabbing at Petro.

"Let me go, you big bag of bones!" Petro exclaimed before jamming his small sword through the body's palm.

After a minute of shuffling, Petro flew to the front, letting off a trail of dust, his reinforced metal wing clicking lightly. This often happened when his wing was slightly bent. Casey would, of course, set it right when we got back. If we got back.

"What the hell is that?" I asked, staring at a building floating several hundred feet in the air.

The sky, as well as everything else in the Everwhere, was in a state of eternal night. Trees and buildings, as well as shadows, danced in the grim, deep purple darkness of the in-between.

Before Petro could reply, lightning spidered across the sky. I turned the wheel, but quickly figured out the car was in charge when driving, or whatever it was doing, in the murky air.

After a few seconds, I finally gave up as Petro just shook his head before replying. "If I were taking a guess, long-ago buildings. You know, torn down?"

Squinting my eyes, the age and desolated look of the structures confirmed Petro's statement. What I wasn't planning on seeing were the glowing red eyes coming from the buildings. We both unfortunately saw them at the same time.

"What is it?!" Jamison demanded as Petro and I exhaled, "Shit . . ." at the same time.

Dozens of what looked like zombie birds came flying out of the floating, abandoned structures like schools of fish fleeing from a whale's mouth.

"Gods and graves. Who the hell did we piss off?" I said under my breath as I patted the dashboard, pointing to the glowing red dots moving closer.

Taking my queue, the Cadillac shot toward the shifting ground as even Jamison's body gasped, letting out some type of farty noise.

Directly below was the spider. It was looking at us as its two front legs rose into the air, the jaws of the creature opening wide as its fangs lifted.

"Boss?" Petro asked.

"Car?" I asked, continuing the trail of questions. "It's going to eat us!" I yelled as the vehicle went into ludicrous speed, using our downward momentum, flinging us toward the creature faster.

"What the shit are you doing, bruthers?" Phil's confused voice asked over the communicators.

"Don't ask . . ." was the last thing I said before the metal Cadillac of death slammed into the mouth of the spider.

Let me tell you. The outside of spiders, especially large ones, is scary enough. The inside doesn't get much better.

The car had launched itself fast enough to bypass any chewing, going straight to what looked like a stomach. The fact that I had my eyes closed for the initial impact would probably save me a few sleepless nights.

The three of us took stock of our bodies and the car. The car was intact, as were the windows. We sat there as "Fire Water Burn" by The Bloodhound Gang came over the radio.

Just as the first verse started, I realized the car had set us directly in the middle of the spider and wanted me to burn, baby, burn.

"Boss," Petro slowly drawled, pointing out the window at the smaller spiders that were drifting down from the roof, or whatever the hell you called it.

"Yeah, I see that. This spider is so big it has a cave of smaller spiders inside. Take a picture. I'm going to make sure Phil sees this shit for not being here."

Petro let out a snicker, knowing it would make Phil uncomfortable; there was a reason why he was not here by now.

"Car?" I asked, reaching into the back and placing Jamison's head in the seat. He had a lollipop stuck to his forehead, as well as some dirt and a clump of hair. He must have picked it up on the floorboard while rolling around. I had no clue where it had all come from.

The vehicle let out a little rev, letting me know she was listening. "If I light it up, will you guys be good?" I asked, getting a clear picture of our only way out.

The cigarette lighter popped out of the dash, telling me all I needed to know. It was time to give this thing some heartburn. As if knowing we had concocted a plan, the spider began moving, shifting us around.

Petro started singing, "We don't need no water, let the mother . . ." echoing the song coming out of the radio.

I shook my head, taking a deep breath. After a few seconds of emptying my pockets, I was ready. Much like Spinal Tap's amps, I was about to turn the furnace up to eleven. It had been roughly three years of training and learning new tricks, and for today's little ditty, I was going to do what Jenny and Ed called a burnout.

This involved me stripping naked and basically letting my entire body push out every bit of will and power I had in one brief flash of hellfire. I would even have to remove my castor. The power I had stored in the device would be used to get us back home if needed.

The click of little spider legs started making themselves known on the car's metal hood and roof.

"Petro, it's been a hell of a ride," I said, grinning at him.

In reality, I had no clue what was about to happen. The one thing I did know was that, as time progressed, the other parts which made me who I was kept getting stronger. The demon part of my blood took center stage in helping my reflexes, while the Mage piece combined gave me the ability to project magic at a higher level than most.

The issue with this was that we didn't really know the limitations of my body. I could just as easily burn myself to ashes. This one, however, was a trick I had worked on.

Petro smiled back. "Can you cover that thing up?" he complained, looking away. I was naked. The car opened the door just as quickly in an attempt, I assumed, to get my bare ass off its sticky leather seats.

The car followed by honking the horn, furthering its point and drawing the attention of thousands of small spiders now sliding down on silk webs directly toward me.

"Dammit, I hope I never have to write a report about this," I said before crouching down, pulling all my will into my core.

I stood up, taking a deep breath, yelling, "*IGNIS!*" Hellfire erupted from my body in all directions, swallowing the entire cavity in a flash of violent red light. Before I passed out, I heard the roar of the creature, followed by a dropping sensation in my stomach as I, well, dropped to the ground.

Did I forget to mention I was supposed to have a date with Kim later tonight?

CHAPTER 2

Dinner Is Served

"Y ou ass. You could have at least called me or let me know you were going to be late. Or better yet, how about this: let me know you are going to the Everwhere to get Jamison's body!" Kim barked as I sat there taking the well-deserved scolding.

While I was good at many things, letting others know what I was up to was not one of them. Over the past year, Kim and I had been steadily dating. We had even discussed moving in together at some point in the spring. It was a good relationship, but as with most couples in the line of work we were in, it was strained at times. Schedules rarely lined up, and travel had taken a fair amount of Kim's time lately.

"Things just started moving, and I lost track of time. Look, I'm not making any excuses, but—" I started, trying to atone for my transgressions.

Kim cut me off. "No buts; we talked about this. If we are going to make this work, we need to know the other is safe, or at least okay. I'm a little upset you didn't pull me in. This just keeps happening; me waiting around for you, then getting a call that you are naked, covered in gore or something, in some strange, distant land. It's just . . . I can't keep doing this," Kim said, the tiredness coming through in her voice.

"What are you saying?" I asked, furrowing my brow. Was she about to break up with me?

"I just need a break." Kim sniffed lightly as she took a pull from her wine.

"From?" I asked, fishing for more.

"This, everything . . . I mean, you know I care for you. I just need some time. Maybe a vacation; hell, who knows. I'm just asking for you to think about this, and if you want to make things work long term, we need to figure something out," she finished, laying it all out.

My heart sank as I looked at her. It wasn't just me but everything else she had been dealing with catching up to her. In her new role as director of the OTN division of the marshal's office, she had been on call the entire time.

The phrase *long term* danced around my thoughts as I sat there, shaking my head. I reached out my hand to grab hers. We smiled at each other, and as if ordained by the gods themselves, Aslynn walked in right then, seeing me. Since I was facing the door, she hadn't seen Kim sitting with me.

"By the gods! I'm a lucky girl tonight!" she shouted, walking up and finally realizing Kim was sitting there. I had a feeling she had made that entrance on purpose.

It's hard to explain the look a woman can give when conveying death. It's a mix of hatred, intelligence, and unethical plotting all at the same time. You know the look . . .

I would compare it to the stare you give a coworker when they get a big promotion and/or raise when you, in fact, know you have been carrying them for the past several years, and they have somehow taken credit for all your hard work. You get a nice email the next day from upper management saying thank you and giving you a 25-cent raise. Looking out, you see the same ass that used you pulling up to the front row in their new company-paid BMW.

That person then proceeds to walk into your office and tell you that you're fired after getting the 25-cent raise. The look you give that person would be comparative to the laser-like flames Kim was burning through Aslynn.

I hadn't seen Aslynn in a little under a year. Jenny must have called her to come into town as she put Jamison, her brother, back together again.

"I, uh, hello. Do you mind if—" I started, wanting more uninterrupted time with Kim.

"Of course I'll join you! I just need to use the ladies' room first," Aslynn interrupted, not giving me a chance to finish my sentence.

"Well," Kim said as Aslynn walked off, "looks like you have other plans for the night."

"She's in town to check on her brother. I'll get her to leave. Jesus Christ, just talk to me. It's been a long day." I sighed, shaking my head.

"I've got to go. We can talk later," Kim tightly replied, standing up.

"Just—"

Kim stopped me by holding up her hand. "I need to think things over. Let me know how Jamison is doing," Kim finished before she walked out of FA's, leaving a twenty on the table.

I sat there staring at her empty seat until Aslynn sat down in her chair. Our uneaten food was now sitting there cold. Aslynn was, as always, dressed to the nines, looking amazing. It was deliberate, and she knew what she had done.

"Oh, relax. She still likes you," Aslynn said, seeing the expression on my face.

"It's not a good time," I answered, noticing Trish had not brought her a drink yet. I was betting she had witnessed the entire episode and didn't want to serve Aslynn.

"Is it ever. You need to put your big boy pants on and either get serious or move on. There are other fish in the sea, you know," Aslynn replied smiling, running her hands through her straight red hair.

"Yeah, I know. Listen, your brother should be ready for company in the morning. I'll meet you at the Atheneum then." I slammed what was left of my beer before motioning Trish over for the tab.

"Well, okay then, party pooper. I thought I was about to have a fun night and catch up on old times." She was shaking her head, obviously not happy with me blowing her off.

"I'm just busy," I said, the conversation with Kim still swimming in my head.

"You going to be free enough to see Planes Drifter? You do know they're coming into town in a few days for a five-day music festival and carnival, right?" Aslynn asked, pursing her lips in a suggestive manner. That caught my attention. I had grown to know the band members, and was surprised they hadn't contacted me about coming to town. Hell, the fact that I hadn't realized they were coming explained exactly how Kim was feeling. I wasn't just ignoring her, but myself as well.

"Dammit," I sighed, shaking my head again. The motion was becoming as second nature as breathing. "I'm going to call it a night."

After a few minutes of useless banter, Aslynn left. Trish had taken her time with the bill.

"Max, I'll get your change," Trish said as I looked up from my phone, typing a message to Kim that I would more than likely not send.

"Keep it," I replied as a cool breeze filled the air. Trish stopped, looking at the tall, long-haired man who had walked in and sat down at the far end of the bar. She glanced up hesitantly.

"Is there a problem?" I asked, seeing her expression.

"I'm not sure. Wait here for a minute."

She walked over to the new arrival.

After a few minutes of me writing and deleting more text messages, Trish came back, nodding her head toward the man sitting at the bar.

"Looks like you caught someone's attention. Next time, be careful who you mention," Trish said, handing me back all the money I had left for the tab. "Keep it. Promise me you will stop by and see Amon. He asked about you."

"I'll stop by this week and see him. I have a question about something I saw in the Everwhere. Who is that?" I finally asked, eyeing the rather bland-dressed man sitting at the bar while drinking a Vamp Amber.

"Oh, you're in for a treat," was all Trish said as she walked off, taking her spot behind the bar. Sarah, her new employee, had taken to also staying behind the bar. I had yet to see her leave its confines.

I stood up, walking toward the gentleman wanting to talk. The man dressed as if he had been thrown up from a JCPenney's suit collection catalog. He had on ugly brown loafers, and khaki slacks with a pronounced crease stitched into them being held by one of those ugly weave leather belts from the '90s. The button-up, short sleeve work shirt was crinkled around his waist where he had tucked it in. The man was basically dressed like Dwight Schrute.

"Hey, Trish said you wanted to talk to me. I'm about to head out, so . . ."

The man turned, his blazing blue eyes catching me off guard.

"Max, how's it going, buddy?" the man asked in a calm voice which immediately put me at ease. I quickly realized it was deliberate.

"Good, and you are?" I asked, having flashbacks of the last weirdo I'd met in FA's.

"That's not important. Let's just say I'm a friend; I'm pretty sure by now you've figured out that Trish would have told you otherwise. It's so good to see her and her staff doing well. You had a chance to meet the cook yet?" the man asked, handing me a Vamp Amber that neither Sarah nor Trish had brought over.

"How do you know about Amon?" I asked, picking up the beer. While I was still tired, something was compelling me to talk to this odd-looking man. In all fairness, it wasn't that he was odd looking physically. It was his mix of clothes, light beard, and long hair that made him so.

"Oh, I used to get him to send me pizzas all the time. You know, before they were a big thing. Did you know he actually invented them?" the man said as he polished off his beer, only to have another one appear in front of him when I glanced away.

"Look, I get it. Trish thinks it's cute not telling me who you are. Though I have a feeling we've met before, I'll say that much," I said as I used my preternatural sight to zone in on his subtle movements. He didn't have any. The man was stoic and solid as a rock. His eyes didn't even shift when he talked. He was not human. Or Mage, for that matter.

"We've met. Just not in person. Anyway, I just wanted to stop and say hello. Oh, and give you some advice." He paused, drinking his beer in one impressive pull. By the time I blinked, another beer had appeared in front of the two of us.

I wasn't shocked; rather, I was impressed. "Does this advice include how to make beer magically appear?" I asked, chuckling lightly as the man joined in on the joke.

"I wish, but no. That's my little trick; I'm kind of known for it," he informed me before continuing. "Here it goes. When you love something, sometimes you have to let it go. Not all the way, but enough to allow it to breathe and let it blossom. This may pertain to more than your girlfriend. You never know; you may not like what blooms."

I started to cut him off, not being comfortable with strangers knowing about my personal life. Before I could, he raised a finger, stopping me. It wasn't forced; it just felt like the right thing to do. Sit there and listen.

"Anyway, I see a lot of people make good choices and bad choices. Sometimes, you have to do both. What most people don't realize is that it's perfectly fine, at least on my side of the fence." The man took a clearing breath, looking down at his watch. "Look at the time. I have to get going."

"What in the ever-living hell does any of that mean?" I asked, confused by the awkward advice.

"Oh, I have a feeling you'll find out soon enough. Peace be with you," the man said calmly. I blinked, looking over at Trish, only to see her shrug. A cool breeze hit my neck as I turned around to find the man gone.

"Trish, who the hell was that?"

"Wrong direction there, sunshine." Trish pointed up, not giving away anything, still smiling.

CHAPTER 3

Humpty Dumpty

"That was it," I finished, trailing off as Phil and Petro stared intently at me. Both of them were sitting with spoons full of Golden Grahams dripping milk on the table.

The two busted out laughing as Phil's spoonful of cereal flew at me. "Hahah . . . bruther, so you're saying that Kim wants to take a break, Aslynn showed up looking all hotty toddy, then J-man appeared all in the span of ten minutes, and you didn't call us to see this shit show?" Phil bellowed, making fun of my prior evening.

We were all sitting at the kitchen table eating breakfast while Casey was out of town for a few days. Phil had on a bright red bathrobe; Petro and I, being more conservative, opted for the matching Scooby-Doo pajamas Casey had made us over the summer. The crime-fighting team was one of Petro's favorite cartoons. It wasn't lost on me that Pixies didn't understand adults generally opted not to wear cartoon character pajamas. However, the craftsmanship of the clothing was second to none, making them my go-to when no one was watching.

"So you're saying that was really Jesu—" I was cut off, as always.

"Don't say it, bruther!" Phil exclaimed. "He'll pop in and

drink all our beers and tell us feel-good stories, giving us advice that makes no sense."

I let out a breath, flicking a spoonful of cereal back at Phil. "That sounds like the guy I met. Except he just kept making beers appear."

"Hey, boss, look at you. The ladies are all fighting over you," Petro bragged, doing his hip gyration thingy, which always led to me flicking him like a bug. He didn't like that, but it was the routine.

"I wish, buddy. Hey, what's really important is that PD is coming to town. You guys know anything about that?" I asked as Petro and Phil looked at each other, obviously not able to hold the secret any longer.

"Surprise!" Phil bellowed as Petro zipped out of the room and back faster than I could blink, carrying three laminated VIP passes.

"How could you guys not tell me?" I asked, shaking my head.

"Well, boss, you've been all busy helping Jamison out, and when Abby Normal called, you were out doing something. So we decided it would be a surprise," Petro answered, pride in keeping the secret evident in his voice.

"Hell," Phil chimed in. "We were surprised you didn't already know. That just told us you had your head up your arse, even if you were doing something good or whatever."

"Anyway, the kicker is that they are calling it the Dark Carnival Festival. Back in the 1920s, the Vs and a few not-so-nice Mages ran what was called the Dark Carnival. It got shut down for some nefarious reason. A bunch of folks are excited to see them bringing it back, even if just for nostalgic entertainment."

I looked at Phil, squinting my eyes. "That's the thing that gets me with all this old-timey stuff. I would bet most of the folks involved back then are still around. What was so crazy about it anyway?"

Phil just shrugged. The rest of our little morning meeting was spent with the three of us making our plans to party like rock stars.

***

Ed walked into the recently updated medical bay. The east wing of the Atheneum was now full, bustling with workers looking as if they had more important things to do than everyone else. When I had first walked into the building, this section had been sealed and unused, much like a long-forgotten book.

"Right. How are you feeling?" Ed asked Jamison while Aslynn, Jenny, Phil, Petro, and I stood at the end of the bed.

Jamison flexed the muscles and bones on his face, something that was apparently not easy to do when you didn't have a body.

"Relax, your muscles and nervous system are trying to work things out," Jenny informed him, setting a clipboard down on the table next to Jamison's bed.

We all took a step back as he slowly raised his arms, spinning his wrists making a fist.

"Would you look at that," Phil said, grinning. "At least he won't have any more lonely nights."

Other than myself and Phil letting out a light chuckle, the rest of the group didn't get the joke. Aslynn walked closer, putting her hand gently on Jamison's forearm.

"Can you feel my hand?" she asked as Jamison started to grin.

"It's just like it used to be." The joy in Jamison's voice was front and center. "I feel like I can get up and carry on with my day."

"I wouldn't recommend that." Jenny tried to stop him as Jamison slung his legs over the edge of the bed, trying to stand up. Luckily for him, Aslynn and Jenny were on either side as he started to fall face-first onto the hard checkered laminated floor.

"Right, I think you should take the good doctor's advice. From what I understand, the muscles in your body have changed, getting used to doing things on their own and not as you direct, for the past year," Ed said as Jenny nodded in confirmation.

Jamison gave Ed an understanding salute. Not too long ago, Ed himself had been paralyzed. It'd taken them over a year to get his motor functions back to where they should be, and since then, he had almost made a complete recovery.

"I'm just glad to see Humpty Dumpty back together again," I joked. "Not to mention, I was kind of tired of carrying your head around."

"Jamison is going to need some rest now. We should be able to get him up and moving around a little bit tomorrow. I think we all need to head upstairs," Jenny told us with finality. "Aslynn, you're welcome to stay for a while if you would like."

Aslynn walked over and hugged me, holding the gesture a few seconds longer than normal. As if the gods knew I was once again in a compromising position, Kim walked through the door with a fruit basket. The look on her face made it clear she was getting tired of these kinds of run-ins.

"Well, it looks like everything is normal here," she said, setting the basket down on the table. "This is from the marshals upstairs."

"Thanks. You guys proved yourselves to be true friends. Not only to me but to my family as well," Jamison said reflectively, squeezing his sister's hand. "Max, what you've accomplished . . . it's more than anyone has ever done for me. I don't know if I can ever repay you."

"Like I said, not dragging your head around anymore is payment enough. Get better, and when we get some time, we will go out and knock a couple back," I told him while smiling pensively at Kim.

"I actually need to speak with you all, if you have a few minutes," Aslynn said in a professional tone I had not heard from her.

Ed raised an eyebrow, also taken aback by the tone. "Sure, we all need to let Jamison rest anyway."

"I feel fine. Matter of fac . . . t . . ." Jamison zoned out as Jenny held up her hand, pouring a green, radiating glow over his body, forcing him to sleep.

"That's settled. Let's head up to the dining room," Jenny commanded, bumping into Ed playfully.

"Hey, boss," Petro whispered in my ear. We were the last ones to walk out of the room. "If Kim's heart rate goes up any more, she's going to explode. You got some ass-kissing to do. Need some tips for the bedroom?"

"The last thing I need is sex advice from a Pixie. Plus, I know I need to spend some time with her. Hopefully, the two won't go at it." I sighed. "Aslynn knows what she's doing; that's what I can't figure out. And I know she's Fae, but I bet Kim would be up for the challenge," I said proudly, standing up for her. Too bad she wasn't there to hear it.

Aslynn and I had a moderately sordid past. She was the daughter of my prior sponsor, Ned, and on-again, off-again late-night bar-hopping companion. This, of course, was all before Kim and I became serious last year, if that's what you called it.

Arriving at the dining room, the familiar glow of the lights and smell of warm, rich foods calmed my nerves, making me feel at home. The Atheneum had a perfectly good conference room, but the dining room was used for private meetings. It was the most secure spot in the facility for discussing sensitive subjects.

Leshya, the craft that worked with Tom, had chosen to keep up with the fantastic cooking after his decision to play dead a second time. Gramps had played a prank on everyone throughout the years by convincing her to serve them lousy food; something about a bet and Ed not altogether paying up. Her food was, in fact, on par with Amon's, FA's chef extraordinaire.

"Hey, Leshya," I greeted as she pointed at the cream cheese and cucumber sandwich sitting in front of my old seat.

"Max, I need to talk to you later," Leshya said in her lofty, calm voice, not giving me a chance to reply.

She, as always, just lurked back into the shadows of the hall toward the kitchen. Something had changed in her. She was more than the average craft. Leshya was something more, something real, something alive.

Phil was already making a ridiculous amount of noise slurping chicken wings. He still hadn't grown his beard out after having it mostly burnt off. Instead, he had opted to let it grow just enough to cover his jawline.

"This is the one damn thing I miss about living here. Leshya's cooking," Phil said with a mouth full of food, a light streak of wing sauce dripping from his mouth.

"Too bad we didn't get to experience it till last year," Ed added.

Aslynn stood up, holding a small wooden box. "Excuse me, everyone. This will only take a minute or two. I need to get going. The queen directed me to bring this gift for Max's service to Faerie. Free of obligation."

Petro lightly dusted the table as Ed and Jenny looked stunned. "Which queen?" Ed asked, obviously knowing more than I did.

"Titania, of course. Oh, and it's free and clear of any obligation, as mentioned."

Ed and the others relaxed. Petro was still looking antsy and started hovering over my shoulder.

"I guess this is supposed to mean something?" I asked, having heard the name on a handful of occasions.

"Bruther, that's two fairly important people with your name in their thoughts recently. She's the queen of all Faerie, basically meaning the Plane, and someone you want to be on the good side of," Phil explained, actually wiping his fingers off with a napkin instead of licking them clean.

"Two people?" Ed asked.

"Yeah, I apparently had beers with Jesu—" I abruptly stopped myself, getting my point across by pointing toward the sky.

Petro was still hovering over my shoulder, not talking. This was rare for him.

"I'll need to hear about that one later," Ed said, shrugging his shoulders.

Turning to Aslynn, I said, "I accept," not seeing the need for anyone else's approval.

She walked over, handing me the small wooden box, pausing as I held it. Petro landed on the table, dust still lightly coming off his clicking wings.

"Open it, boss. I don't think the queen would give you anything bad," he encouraged, looking up sharply at Aslynn. I caught the brief interaction, knowing them both being from the Plane had a better understanding of the gifts importance.

"Well, since no one is moving, I guess that means I need to open it now."

Aslynn looked down. It was clear she didn't know what was in the container.

The box was warded and set to only open for its intended recipient; I had grown used to the feel of this type of magic by now. I snapped open the intricate lock as it clicked with deliberate authority. A light pop of ozone wafted through the air, disrupting the smell of food.

Inside, wrapped in a green velvet cloth, was a key. My immediate assumption was that it had to be the key to another one of the Postern gates. Ed picked up on the thought, nodding his head in agreement. While he couldn't always read my thoughts, Ed could still pick up on my mood and somehow translate it into a clear understanding.

"Shit," was all I said, letting out a huff.

"You daft? That's a gift from the queen!" Phil exclaimed, chuckling at my sudden shift in mood.

"You ever met her?" I asked as the room turned to look at Phil.

"Well, no, but . . ." Phil started before shutting up for once.

"You see, gang—if you don't mind me calling you all that —every time I get a new key to that damn room, all hell breaks loose." My point landed like a new smartphone on concrete with no screen protector. Cue the chorused moan as the group agreed.

Phil put an unlit cigarette in his mouth, getting the usual death stare from Jenny.

"Well, this has been lots of fun," Aslynn cut through the reflective silence, "but I need to get going. Things to do, people to see, and all that."

The room watched as she leaned over, planting a kiss on my cheek. I could feel the heat radiating from the death stare Kim was now giving me. Again, Aslynn was doing this on purpose.

"So, no clue on what gate the key is for?" I asked, still

MAX ABADDON AND THE DARK CARNIVAL

blushing lightly. Not due to the kiss, but from Kim's stare.

Aslynn just shrugged as she walked out the door. I looked around the room. "She's European or something," I said as Phil and Petro started laughing. Kim, finally coming around, joined in the laugh at my expense, seeing how flustered I indeed was.

"Right. Max, a gift from the queen is not something to be taken lightly. While it came at no cost, she will have something to gain from that key, mark my words," Ed warned. Jenny started slamming the keyboard on her laptop as if she was a DJ and the computer was her turntable.

"Why would you say that?" I asked, the nostalgic feeling of having the group all together flooding back as I looked around the room, trying to hold back a smile.

"Well, for starters, why else would she have the key? On top of that, she knew exactly who to give it to. I'll even take it one step further by stating that she knew this was an opportunity to give it to you without seeming out of place," Ed responded as Petro inspected the box.

"I guess. Just another thing to add to my list," I huffed, taking a deep breath.

James chose that moment to knock on the door. "Nice little spread. So glad I was invited," he chided, shaking his head, walking in.

James was a trusted marshal and one of the group's satellite members, much like Dr. Freeman and Jamison.

"Ah, James. Grab a seat. I was about to call you," Kim said. She respected James after the past two years, and had mentioned giving him a field promotion in the near future.

"What's up, man?" I greeted after taking a bite of my sandwich, the sentence coming out sounding like, "*Uts ham.*"

"Max, you have guests getting checked in. Abby Normal and Jim Smith are here." As in Abby, the Mage lead singer, and

Jim, the Vampire drummer, for Planes Drifter.

Jim was one of the new age Vs who preferred a bland hip name, much like Frank. I crammed the rest of the sandwich in my mouth as I stood up, grabbing the box.

"Calm down there, boss. Your makeup looks fine," Petro joked, chuckling.

Abby and Jim walked in as a group of other marshals and general Mage workers crowded the main entrance hall.

"Hello, hello, everybody," Abby greeted in the coolest possible rock star tone he could muster. Jim just rolled his eyes, grinning, one of his fangs longer than the other.

"Abby," Jenny said, standing up gracefully.

"Oh my. Well, if Ed here doesn't work out, you know where to find me," Abby flirted as he spun Jenny around by her hand.

I felt that if it had been anyone other than Abby saying that, they would be picking their minds out from under the ocean.

"Still a smooth talker, I see," Ed said, chuckling as he walked over to Abby, followed by the lead singer giving him a brotherly type hug. It was clear they had all once been close friends, and the banter was to be expected.

"Abby," I greeted, walking over.

"Max, my main man. Just the cat we wanted to see," he said, waving at Phil while placing his hand palm up for Petro.

Rock stars . . . they continuously knew how to make an entrance. As always, Abby was dressed in an eclectic manner, combining an angry wizard with a hippie from the '60s. Jim was more put together, wearing a contemporary black suit. Come to think of it, Jim was hitting the easy button, telling everyone he was a V through his moody clothing.

Petro flew over, landing on Abby's palm. "What's up, big

guy," Petro said, getting a small fist bump in.

"Oh, you know. A little of this, a little of that, and a whole lot of everything in between," Abby replied as Petro smoothed his beard.

"Right on!" the little guy exclaimed, flying back over to the table.

The door closed as Angel, one of my favorite Vs, walked in. I was fairly sure she was a member of the Night Stalkers, an elite Vampire military squad that I had worked with on several occasions. They valued their privacy. She also happened to be one of the most drop-dead—in the literal sense—women I had ever laid eyes on. I had to keep reminding people she could, in fact, kick their ass.

"Well, looks like we're getting the band back together," I quipped, actually landing a joke for once.

Abby sat in an empty seat as Jim stood beside Angel, the two whispering.

"I just wanted to stop by and make sure you are all coming to the show. We are setting up today and will hit the strings tomorrow night. Max, when you guys get situated, stop by the backstage entrance behind the VIP tent and show them this," Abby said, giving me a gold, glowing wristband.

Phil pounded the table, the bowl of ranch in front of him splashing onto his shirt. "Hell yeah, bruther!"

"I don't know what to say," I told him, standing there with a grin.

"How about 'thank you,'" Angel suggested, chuffing.

"Yes, right, thanks. This is just unexpected. I've been tied up lately," I explained, walking back to my seat as Petro took the bracelet out of my hand to inspect it.

"So I've heard. It's my understanding that I can stop by and see Jamison at some point. His father and I went back to the old days," Abby said, pulling out a flask, pouring its contents into a coffee mug.

"He should be fine tomorrow for more visitors. If everything holds, he will be on his feet and moving around," Jenny replied. "He might even be able to catch one of your sets, since you are playing several days in a row."

Abby grinned, showing a mouthful of perfectly manicured teeth.

"Perfect," Jim said in an odd tone.

"Yes, no headbanging for him," the singer joked, the timing perfect. Phil, who had been about to cram another wing into his mouth, snorted, the wing shooting from his fingers landing across the table in front of Jenny, where the chicken appendage smacked the back of her laptop.

Phil grimaced, hunching his shoulders, waiting for some type of death ray to be slung in his general direction.

"Hold up," I said after Phil regained his composure. "Why are you all of a sudden interested in Jamison? I talked to you guys a few months ago while I was carting around his head; he would have been more than glad to talk your ear off then."

The issue for me was the odd timing of Abby's visit and that he specifically wanted to talk to Jamison. While I was starstruck as always around PD, the conversation had taken too much of a quick turn toward Jamison for me not to notice.

Letting his guard down, Abby started nodding his head. "Just like your grandfather and father back in the day. Able to cut through the bullshit. I am here to discuss another matter as well. Ed, were you aware the Dark Carnival has been spun back up as some type of promotional stunt to get everyone out to the festival?" He turned back to face me. "Oh, and Max, to answer your question. Ned was one of the Council members who shut the Dark Carnival down. Jamison was part of that. It may be nothing."

Ed paused longer than usual. He was reflecting, putting long-buried memories in place. Ed had once explained to me that his memory was much like a filing system due to his ability to read minds and Ed needing to clear up space while still not forgetting important things. It confused the hell out of me.

I could barely remember if I had worn the same underwear the day prior. There were times when I was scared to verify their cleanliness and just flipped a coin. On a positive note, since I had been dating Kim, I had taken better care to avoid wearing dirty underwear. To be clear, I had a bin full of dirty drawers, and a pile of new underwear I just kept buying. At some point, I would need to address that.

"No, I wasn't. There's no way this is some revival," Ed said, leaving his statement open for Abby to finish.

"Well, that's the thing; it just kind of happened. Some regular in charge of the festival's marketing campaign saw the name in some history book and thought it was cool. Next thing you know, they are reaching out to a few people who were involved in the damn thing. I doubt it's going to be anything like it was, but I have yet to meet any of the people or things they have working on it. It may be a marketing stunt, but . . ." Abby trailed off. There was more to his statement than I could pull out.

"You're saying they are having an actual carnival? If memory serves, there were some bad folks involved," Ed said before pausing to think for a second. "I doubt there's any need to worry," he concluded as Abby smiled.

"You're probably right. I just have some bad memories of those times. What I'm asking is for your team to check it out if you have time tomorrow," Abby conceded.

"It's no big deal. We don't usually get involved in festival planning, and this new hybrid music scene is still uncharted waters," Jim added. "It's cool as hell, but still, we would like to have a friendly set of eyes we trust making sure everything is cool, you know. This is, after all, our first co-regular show. We just wanted to ask Jamison about the carnival," he finished.

My fanboy mode took over the conversation then, ignoring pretty much everything else that had just been said. "So what are you going to play during your set? Any guest appearances?" I asked as Petro echoed my question.

"Yeah, guest appearances," he chirped under his breath.

"Well, we are playing five days straight, so we plan on hitting most of our old stuff the first few nights, then the new album the last two. We are opening with 'The Gate to Everwhere,'" Abby said as I jumped up.

The high-octane single, "The Gate to Everwhere," was a crushing track about a man who sacrificed his life to save the Earth from Hell. Abby had called me earlier in the year, after Belm's death, and while most of the operation was considered secret, I had been able to at least relay enough information for Abby to write a song about his heroics. The general population may not know the truth about Belm's sacrifice, but we did.

"I knew it!" I exclaimed as Ed looked at me, motioning for me to calm down.

"Max lasted longer than I thought he would this time," he said, referring to my outburst and how I'd waited a full five minutes before caving. "Right," he continued, getting back on track. "We will keep an eye out. These three geniuses have passes and can check it out."

I noticed after Ed's comment that Kim had been stoically quiet the entire time. While Ed didn't truly dictate what I did and did not do, I respected him enough to let him speak for me. Plus, he knew I would help anyway. "Abby, do you think we can get one more pass for Kim?"

Kim looked up, actually cracking a smile, before pulling out her laminated VIP pass and bracelet. She already had one and hadn't mentioned it to me. Either she was that pissed off at me and things were as bad as they seemed, or she was part of the surprise and Aslynn's actions had changed her mind. I was leaning on the latter.

CHAPTER 4

The Dark Carnival

"I'm not going to be able to make it tonight," Kim said in a strictly professional tone on the other end of the phone. Last night, after our meeting with Abby and Jim, we had all decided to meet up today to go check out the festival downtown. You know, for professional reasons. Not to mention that I could now officially expense the concert.

"What's up? Something going on?" I asked as Petro and Phil stared at me from the couch in the apartment's upstairs living room. The smell of stale beer, cigar smoke, and rich, aged wood permeated the space.

Over the past year, we had all landed on an eclectic mix of furniture, including an old, worn, U-shaped brown leather couch and several bookshelves with, you guessed it, books. Hanging on the walls were a new flat screen TV and several vintage horror movie posters from the 1950s. Those belonged to Phil, as well as the beat-up coffee table that was chipped and worn around the edges from, of course, years of having booted feet propped on its rich mahogany top.

The best way to describe the space was if the movie sets for *Indiana Jones* and *Harry Potter* threw up in the main living room set for the old sitcom *Friends*.

"Something's come up downtown. It looks pretty messy.

The local police called our office in. I gave James a shout just in case it's something he can handle, and if everything looks normal, I'll head over to the stadium and meet you guys," Kim said before hanging up the phone with a resounding click.

Over the past year, the regular police force had grown wary of labeling cases OTN, or Other Than Natural. The logic behind this decision was to avoid the federal marshals' and teams'—such as the one stationed at the Atheneum—getting involved. Their inclusion often generated a significant amount of paperwork and more media attention than most local law enforcement groups wanted on their operation.

As with most music festivals in town, this one was set up by the football stadium on the east side. We had opted on gating into the area just in case we had too much to drink. While the plan was for us to look around, the majority of that strategy involved us having a good time.

"What did she say, bruther?" Phil asked as Petro took a pull of rum from the small cap sitting in front of him.

"It looks like Kim's getting called in to take a look at a murder scene. By the sounds of it, things are pretty messy, and they want a second set of eyes on it just in case," I answered, taking a pull of my beer.

"Well, at least we don't have to watch you two play kissy face or listen to you try and solve all your relationship problems tonight," Petro said as he lifted a finger, shooting a fake gun at Phil.

"Aye," was all Phil replied as he took down his Vamp Amber in one long pull, letting out a slow, reverberating belch.

"I need to go to my room to grab a few things real fast." I figured I should at least bring a few things just in case.

Looking in my nightstand, I grabbed the most logical items. The short staff which happened to be the first blended item I'd ever worked on, a stone from the Evergate, and lastly, my Council badge and service pistol, better known as my get-out-of-jail-free card. The Council badge had gotten me out of trouble more times than I could count on both hands.

The short staff had five distinct slots for spells, each loaded for a specific and different purpose. The combination was fairly straightforward. It included a stunning, levitation, and tracking spell, a magical version of a flashbang, and last but not least, a shield. All of the spells, while very strong, only had one go at it. Meaning, if I used the stunning spell, until I reloaded the staff—which could take several days—it was out of the fight.

"Hey, guys, you about ready to leave?" I asked while Phil and Petro snickered about something. Since Phil had moved in, the two had spent a fair amount of time gossiping about not only my love life, but that of everyone else's. They were like two gossiping grannies.

"Hey, boss," Petro started, taking off from the table, leaving a light trail of dust blowing in the air. "I just talked to Casey on the phone. I'm good to go."

"Bruther, same here. I see you grabbed a few things. I've had substantially more than I was supposed to drink, so I'll leave all the up-and-up copper stuff for you to do. That is, if there is anything to worry about," Phil said standing up as he wiped crumbs from some type of snack off his pants.

"Yeah, I think it's just a bunch of old-timers worried about people digging up the past. I'm excited to check it out. I looked at the schedule, and we will have plenty of time to check out the rest of the carnival before Planes Drifter hits the stage. Meaning, once we're done checking it out, it's time to hit the bar," I said, reaching into my trench coat, pulling out a long flask.

There was something about concerts, even as an adult. I could absolutely afford to buy drinks at the festival, especially with the VIP package, but I always felt like a bit of a rebel sneaking in a little bit of booze to a show. It was a tradition, one as old as the dawn of man, and almost as important as the radio test with friends and new lovers. It had been a long time since I had felt this young and excited.

We gated into an area slightly south of the stadium, next to the local public radio and TV stations. A good portion of the festival spilled over in the fields beside it, as well as all the parking. That was one good thing about being a Mage in charge of a room of gates. I never had to pay for parking.

"Damn," Phil said as we stepped out the gate, closing it behind us. "This place is slap full."

"You're not kidding," I agreed, looking around at the waves of people by the road walking toward the entrances. "Good thing we have VIP passes."

"You think there are going to be any other Pixies, boss?" Petro asked, darting overhead.

"I'm pretty sure if Planes Drifter is playing, there's gotta be plenty of Pixies flying around," I replied. Petro's words got me thinking. How did something like a concert accommodate Pixies? They could, after all, just fly in.

"Yeah, you're probably right. I can tell you one thing: the whole place is warded. No ticket, no gety iny," Petro said in some type of Southern drawl I'd never heard before.

Looking for the VIP entrance, we kept walking in front of the crowds, and several people hurled insults at us. The funny thing about having a Pixie and an overly tattooed, prominent Irish Mage was that people tended to shut up after you turned around and looked at them.

While Petro had mostly stayed out of sight after the second round of insults from the angry regular people in line, he finally made his presence known. Having a Pixie land on someone's shoulder unexpectedly did precisely what it needed to do.

Someone tapped on my shoulder as I turned around to

see a young woman. "Sarah, I didn't expect to see you here," I said, giving the young woman a light hug.

Sarah worked at the Fallen Angel, and happened to be the first person who had talked to me about joining the magical community. She and Gramps had some type of special relationship; not the awkward kind of a young woman and an older man, but more along the lines of a distant relative or promise made to a dying friend to take care of the offspring. I still hadn't gotten the full story from her, and figured I never would. She had even joined our circle of friends, starting to date James last year.

"Well, lass. It looks like you're on the take today," Phil said, pointing at her laminated badge and VIP tag snuggly attached to her black-and-gold shirt.

"Guilty as charged. Trish is helping cater to the magical bands, and agreed to set up a VIP experience for regulars to try true Ethereal alcohol. This thing has turned out to be a cash cow already. If things work out, we might just be able to get a pool table at FA's," Sarah said, motioning for us to follow her. Her voice always struck me as odd, having a slight, barely noticeable British tang to it. If you weren't looking, you would never pick up on it. It at times reminded me of people who had spent too much time in England or who had gone to school there coming back with a slight drawl.

"So you're here to escort us into the festival?" I asked as the three of us got in step behind her.

"Yup. Amon is cooking food in a trailer, discreetly staying out of the public eye. I walked over to check in on him, and he told me you guys were wandering around like a bunch of Neanderthals," Sarah explained as we walked up to the gate clearly labeled VIP. There was no one in that line, and I looked back, seeing thousands of people waiting to gain entry into the festival.

I'm not going to lie. I still had an ego, and I'd be lying to myself if I said it didn't make me feel good.

After getting our tickets scanned and putting on our wristbands, Sarah pulled us over to the side. "The carnival's on the far end by the water. I talked to Ed earlier today, and he told me to make sure you guys stayed sober long enough to walk down there at least."

Sarah eyed Phil suspiciously while he just grinned.

"We're good for it. Hey, is there anything you can tell us about the people working down there?" I asked as our group started walking toward the Dark Carnival tents, several labeled arrows pointing in their general direction.

"Nothing out of the ordinary. Well, of course, that depends on what you consider ordinary." She pointed to the crowd of people dressed in various costumes heading toward the Dark Carnival tents.

Several groups of regulars had on odd costumes. Some dressed like wizards had obviously never met a real Mage, and the typical group of gothed-out teens trying to make themselves look like Vampires was also present. I would love to introduce the little shits to Davros. That would change their opinion of Vampires. Frank, no; Davros, yes.

"Have any other Council stooges been running around?" Petro asked, making a great point.

"A few. I think they are here more to see Planes Drifter than anything. You know, sons and daughters of powerful Council members, yada, yada," Sarah replied before she abruptly stopped. "Well, this is where I leave you, gentlemen. When you get done with your official business, I'll see you guys in the VIP tent."

"Check it out!" Phil exclaimed after she left, his face lighting up. In front of us was a massive tent, the type and size the big circuses used, but this one looked dark and ominous. On the path leading to the front entrance, staked into the ground, were several signs.

I started reading them out loud as Phil took out his phone to take pictures. Not out of concern but because he thought they were cool. "Wolfman, the Bearded Lady, Alligator Man, the Amazing Mister Zod, the Queen of the Dead, the World's Shortest Man. Seems more like a freak show."

"Aye, bruther. That it is. Let's get our arses inside." The excitement was evident in his voice. I still hadn't figured out why he was so animated about the show. In my opinion, I was thinking it made fun of Ethereals or whatever truly lay inside. I stood there for a second, thinking about all the times I had more than likely run into people from the other side of things.

"I bet a round of drinks the World's Shortest Man is a Pixie," Petro said, the same excitement in his voice.

I looked over at the old-timey drawing of the Alligator Man, seeing something familiar.

***

"Step right up and leave your inhibitions behind," a skeleton-thin man said in an old-timey show announcer's voice, the megaphone in his hand louder than needed as we marched up.

Walking to the entrance, I held up my arm, showing the VIP bracelet. The man let out a cool, "Ahhh. Do we have a treat for you today . . ." before trailing off as Petro zoomed out from behind me. He had zipped off for a quick bathroom break before we went in. He, of course, had used the VIP toilets. "Oh," was all the man said, the showman expression on his face slightly wavering.

"We still get that treat, bruther," Phil barked, raising his hand too and showing off his bracelet.

Letting out a sigh, the man's eyes lit back up. The average person would have overlooked the brief lapse, but to the enhanced senses coming from the demon side of me, it stood out like a tall man at a dwarf convention.

I looked down, seeing his name etched into a bronze-colored name tag. It read Barnabas. "Barnabas, these two have been beside themselves waiting to check out the show. Where are you from?"

The man grinned. His smile was slightly larger than average, making the expression uncomfortable to look at directly.

"I know who you are. You're that guy who keeps setting things on fire," Barnabas said jokingly, putting his sideshow persona back on fully.

Petro and Phil started laughing, knowing everyone kept recognizing me from the old videos the news kept recycling.

"I get that often," I admitted, swatting at Petro.

"You're the second group of Ethereals to come through the attraction. I hope you enjoy it," Barnabas spoke louder than needed. He wanted others to hear, using us to draw a crowd and more ticket sales. This guy knew what he was doing.

"I'm sure we will," I replied as the thin man leaned in. I could swear a light hint of pepper came from his clothes.

Barnabas's voice changed to a flat, regular tone as he got closer, talking to just the three of us. "I'm sure this isn't anything special to you guys, but please be nice to the folks inside, and I'll throw in a few free T-shirts if you tell others you run into how awesome the show is. Just follow the signs to the attraction you want to see inside."

We all nodded as I looked up to see clouds now covering the once blue sky.

The tent's lobby was just as eclectic as the outside, and the smell of popcorn and dirt filling the air brought back childhood memories. I finally knew why Phil and Petro were so excited to see the show.

"So, what's first, bruthers?"

The three of us looked at the dozen or so signs pointing in various directions down separate hallways leading off from the entrance. Barnabas's voice came booming from behind as he tried to funnel more festival attendees into his tent.

"Let's check out the World's Shortest Man. If memory serves, Petro put up a round of free drinks for the two of us," I said, getting a nod of approval from Phil.

We took a left, walking into a darker than needed, shadowed hallway. A flap to our right and a light signal indicated we were at the right place. Pushing the flap out of the way, the three of us entered the room. The size of the space didn't add up to what I had assumed it would be.

There were five rows of chairs all laid out in a semicircle with a small stage in the center, the back of which led to another section of the tent. The room was also cooler than expected, while a horn and circus music crackled from an old, cheap speaker overhead, letting us know the show was about to start.

The information being piped through the speaker was clearly recorded, letting us know what we were about to see. "You are about to witness the World's Shortest Man. Tato comes to us from the farthest reaches of old Russia."

After another few seconds of music, a young woman sauntered out as a Pixie-sized older man walked onto the stage. Small furniture had been set up for him to use, furthering the spectacle in front of us.

"That's a Pixie, guys!" Petro gasped as Phil and I shook our heads.

"No wings means not a Pixie," I said as the man on the stage got a clear view of Petro.

"Ladies and gentlemen of the audience, it appears we have some special guests. Are you three together?" the small man asked as the young woman walked over, sealing up the entrance for the show to start.

"Aye," Phil bellowed as he raised up a small carton of popcorn.

"Where the hell did you get that?" I asked, more jealous than curious.

"If you got your head out of your arse, you would've seen the cart when we came in," Phil bragged.

I turned around, realizing once again that the room was significantly bigger than I assumed.

The young woman walked by, handing me a carton of popcorn, winking. As soon as it was clear that the room was sealed, the small man onstage took off his jacket, and larger than customary Pixie wings emerged from his back.

"Son of a bitch," Phil said as Petro stuck out his tongue.

"By the gods, another Pixie. Where you from?" the Pixie asked as he landed on the chair Petro was perched in.

The Pixie, while the same height as Petro, was rounder. His cheeks were full, and he had a toothy grin. The man's hair was pitch black and slicked back. Pixies often did this to keep their hair from getting messed up when they flew. His wings looked old, worn, and as if they had seen better days. Petro had explained that taking care of one's wings was the most important thing a Pixie could do. Some of the Pixies on Earth had gotten a little lazy on that front.

"Originally from the Plane, but I work with these lugheads now," Petro said as they shook hands.

"A Pixie from the Plane. You're the one they call the Warrior of the Freeze," the other Pixie said excitedly as Petro pushed what he had of a chest out.

"Mate, don't pump his ego up any bigger than it already is," Phil chided.

"That's me. So your name's Tato?" Petro asked as the

young lady walked up, sitting down as well.

She was beautiful. Her hair was done in a style that looked as if it belonged in the 1950s. Ruby-red lipstick glistened in the dull lighting, drawing attention to her mouth. The woman looked like a pinup girl, and I noticed Phil also staring at her.

"Before your eyes burn a hole in me, boys, my name is Carla," she introduced herself before we focused back on the two Pixies.

"Yup, name's Tato. That's not a stage name either. I'm so excited to meet you. I've heard all about you and your friends. You are kind of a legend these days. Not to mention I've never had a Pixie come to the show before," Tato spit out as fast as he could, his cool, calm demeanor no longer showing. He was clearly a Pixie, and comfortable with talking like one in front of us.

"I wouldn't say legend, unless you were talking about my love life," Petro said as the two Pixies lightly dusted in the chair. Carla rolled her eyes, obviously aware of Pixie humor. The two of them talked for a while before I interjected.

"So, how have things been here?" I asked, figuring we could at least get some information from Tato.

"It's been fun so far. Most of the folks working in the carnival have known each other for years. We all live down in a small city near Tampa. To be honest, some of us are glad for the work. You know things have been a little tight since the Balance for some of us," Tato said.

"Tight?" I asked, genuinely curious.

Carla spoke up. "Ever since the Balance, people have been a little skeptical of our group. Before everything came out in the open, we made a pretty good living on the road working at carnivals and sideshow attractions. A good portion of us worked or work at Disneyland during the off-season. I'm pretty sure you're well aware of that place by now, and what keeps it running. Anyway, our group isn't as special anymore. While it's still exciting to see a Pixie or a shifter, you could just as easily go to a well-known Ethereal hangout and see one without having to pay."

I sat there shaking my head, thinking once again about some of the Balance's intricate details and how they affected everyone. While these carnival workers were obviously a small portion of the magical community, they were still part of it.

"Well," Phil bellowed as he poured the rest of the popcorn into his mouth, crunching on it as he talked. "We'll make sure plenty of folks stop by and see you lot."

"That would be much appreciated." Carla winked at Phil. I had a feeling she was a little bit more than a regular woman.

"Let me ask before we get out of here. Has there been anything odd happening since you guys have been in town?" I asked him in a last effort to get some type of work done.

"Not really. There are one or two new folks here who I haven't met before, but they seem okay." He paused. "Actually, come to think of it, there's one thing," Tato paused thoughtfully, "besides that creepy ass clown fellow. I haven't met the folks who put this together. Apparently, there's some lady from out of town who organized all this. It's just kind of strange that I have yet to meet her."

"Welcome to the age of the Internet," I said, not taking much from the statement. Tato was old-school; the kind of person who liked to do business with a handshake and who clearly let his guard down while talking with people, as he was doing with us. Though to be fair, he had told us he had never had a Pixie come in to see his show before.

Carla stood up, smiling. "Well, gentlemen, it sounds like we have some more visitors coming to see our little show. What Tato is saying, simply put, is that we hope to get more business out of this, and it's nice to know who's signing the checks. Oh, and I won't be around to the Bearded Lady exhibit for about ten minutes," Carla finished grinning while a full beard erupted on her face.

"She's the bloody Bearded Lady!" Phil exclaimed, smiling.

"Sure am, sweetheart," Carla said as she walked us out.

Waiting to come in were roughly a dozen people in their midtwenties, all highly intoxicated. The sounds of burps and various curse words filled the tight walkway.

"Look at those chumps," one of the young men said toward Phil and me, not yet seeing Petro.

"Hey, guys. I noticed a lack of women in your group. None of you were able to get a date for the show, huh?" I said matter-of-factly.

"Watch your mouth, old man," a short, young twenty-something said. It was clear he was the shit talker of the ensemble.

"I'm not a day over thirty," I replied, being truthful. Since my rebirthday a few years back, I had probably only aged a good month. "My buddy Phil here and Petro, on the other hand . . . well, I'm just not sure exactly how damn old they are."

Petro shot out from the opening, having said his good-byes to Tato, and hovered in the air as Phil started glowing a light gray. I let a small shimmer of hellfire begin to emanate slowly from my hands and eyes to top off the spectacle.

The group of young men just stood there at a loss for words. "We-we-we were just messing with you guys," the short man who had yet to show his face stammered from the middle of the group.

We continued walking down the hall as the group flooded into the open room behind us. As the tarp covering the door closed, we all let out a howl of laughter.

"You see the look on those sods' faces?" Phil asked,

laughing.

"I think I got a little whiff of poop from one of them," Petro said, landing on my shoulder. We looked at the next two signs leading off in separate directions, one being toward the Wolfman and the other toward the Bearded Lady whom we had just met.

"Phil, I have to ask. What's up with you and the Bearded Lady?" I asked, wondering why he was so excited to meet her.

"It reminds me of my childhood, bruther. When I was a young lad, my folks always took me to the carnival and local circuses. The one thing I always remembered was the Bearded Lady. I believe it was sometime around the 1940s when my mother became deathly ill. When my dad called for a healer, much like Jenny, a damn Bearded Lady showed up from the carni. When it was all said and done, I learned that they are lower-level healers. All they have to do is go fiddle about with a man with a beard, and boom, there you go, instant face scratchers," Phil said, the memory bringing back good feelings of years long since passed.

"You mean like Jenny and her ever-changing hair color?" I asked, figuring the nostalgia was similar to every time I watched the original *Star Wars* trilogy.

"Yup. Now, let's see . . . Wolfman." Phil pointed to the left again.

We walked up to find another flap with a light and sign stating that the Wolfman was inside. "Hey, boss," Petro started, "it feels like we've been walking around here forever. Am I the only one thinking that?"

"I was about to say the same thing. They must have this place set up like a maze to keep people wandering around longer than needed. I'm surprised they haven't tried to sell us some sodas or merchandise," I said as we strolled into the next room.

This space was different than the last. There were no chairs, only an area to stand. Separating the room in half was a fence, ultimately securing one half of the area from the other. The intent here was clear; make the audience feel as if they were in danger.

"Eww, scary . . ." Petro said as a creature jumped out from behind a curtain with a guttural roar, slamming into the fence, shaking the room.

"Holy hell," Phil let out, spitting out popcorn, having found another container.

The crackling speaker came to life with a recorded message in the same voice as the previous one. "Don't be alarmed. You are safe. For how long, is another question. In front of you is the world-famous and feared Wolfman!"

The creature in front of us was clearly a shifter. Just when I thought it couldn't get any stranger, it did. Another man stepped out from behind the curtain dressed like Indiana Jones, whip in hand, setting up the rest of the show.

"Hey, Al," I greeted as the man with the whip in the ugly green adventurer suit looked up.

"Max," the chunky voice of Al, Hermes's favorite alligator shifter, hissed. Seeing that we were not regulars, the Wolfman jumped down, pushing his will out taking on a more human stance. He was in absolute control of his body, much like Oscar and Al, meaning he was a powerful shifter.

"That was a proper entrance," Phil praised, clapping as the Wolfman took a slight bow. Al also nodded at the others; they had all met on a few occasions.

"Hermes isn't around, is he?" I asked.

Al laughed, the motion looking out of place coming from his longer than usual neck.

"No, I only hang out with the old codger when he's in town. What are you all doing here?" he asked, walking up to the fence with the Wolfman.

"We're here to check out the music show, and we thought we would stop by and see what this was all about," I replied, not lying but also not telling the entire truth.

"So the Council has you checking in on the freaks," Al deadpanned as the Wolfman started to laugh.

I didn't have to answer, seeing as he already had it figured out. After all, he did hang out with a Greek god drinking slushies in his spare time.

"Something like that. We just stopped by to see how things are going," I replied nonchalantly as the smell of popcorn again reached my nose.

The Wolfman finally spoke up as his voice rumbled, full of bass, taking me aback. It wasn't the gravely type, but a deep, strong voice you could feel in your chest. "My name is Lucian. I've heard much about you. What did you think of the entrance?"

Ed, on several occasions, had informed me how cultlike the wolf shifters could be. They absolutely liked to be called Werewolves, and for the most part, the rumors and movies were accurate. Lucian's body was strong and top-heavy, his shoulders doubling the width of the rest of his body. While I knew his face was in public-friendly mode, I could see how the lines could quickly shift, creating a monster. His teeth were clearly in place to tear flesh from bone. That all being said, he was wearing a ragged pair of blue jeans that, while looking old, probably cost a few hundred dollars.

"Well, considering you're only in half badass mode, I'd say you rocked it," I responded as he let out a toothy grin. I was having trouble placing his accent. It was a mix of Polish and some Slavic dialect.

"Thank you. I'm new here, so I'm just getting warmed up. Is there anything we can help you with?" Lucian asked, taking a deep breath, smelling something in the air.

"Everything cool here?" I asked back, leaving it open-ended to see what he said. I already knew Al would play any cards he had close to his chest unless I brought him a slushy.

"I suppose. I'm from overseas and looking to get settled in the States. Al, are you cool?" he deflected, pushing the rest for Al to respond. I had a feeling he was much older and wiser than he was leading us to believe.

"Other than this god-awful outfit, everything's going well. The checks haven't bounced yet, so there's that," Al replied, relaxing slightly as a dull green tint took over his once pale complexion.

"I'm pretty sure the both of you are old enough to be loaded. I will never understand why some of you still do stuff like this. Or work, for that matter. Anyway, we are going to be around for a few days checking out the show. If anything pops up, let us know. I'm only asking because this is the first festival with both Ethereal and regular bands playing," I said, calming the mood.

It was clear the two shifters didn't want to talk about anything other than their little show. Shifters were like that. Not really human, and when in the form of one, still keeping most of their animal characteristics and personalities. This often led to awkward situations when you ran into one, especially when they did something like, say, eat a frog or lick their arms in public to clean themselves.

"We will see you later. It smells like there's a bunch of groups here now. I would recommend coming back later when the crowd dies down and spending more time," Lucian suggested as the three of us agreed.

After several turns and twists, we finally made our way out of the tent, saving the other acts for later. Barnabas was waiting outside when we stepped into the now darkening evening.

"So, gentlemen?" Barnabas prompted, holding a couple of T-shirts in his hand.

"You have some good people in there. It's good to see a familiar face or two," I said. I left out who I knew inside, seeing the man's expression shift slightly. I couldn't place it.

"Oh, you know some of the acts," he asked in the form of a statement. "Well, that just means we are all in good company," he followed up, handing Phil and I a T-shirt.

"No super-extra smalls there?" Petro asked, dusting lightly.

"Here, see if this works." Barnabas handed Petro a small bottle of rum, the type you got on an airplane.

"You're okay in my book," Petro approved, flying back over to my shoulder.

"Here's my number. If you need anything, let me know. We promise to spread the good word," I said, still leaving out who I knew inside.

Once out of earshot, I stopped Phil, making Petro fly down and land on my shoulder. "You guys buying any of that bullshit?" I asked flatly, pulling out the flask in my trench coat. In most other situations, I would look out of place. At this festival, though, I looked above normal, if there was such a thing.

"Ah, bruther, everything seemed to be on the up-and-up," Phil said, grabbing the flask greedily. Truth be told, I had significantly slowed down my intake of libations over the last year.

"I'm thinking more along the lines of the acts we went to see stopping when we walked in. They all knew who we were, and they all wanted to chat. It just seems odd. Not to mention we didn't even see a quarter of the acts. It would have taken us all day to get through there," I said as Petro stopped buzzing his wings.

"Hey, boss. Do you think we somehow got steered away

from the other folks in there? I mean, you're right. There's no way we would have stuck around much longer between all the walking in circles and talking. Of course, you could just be overthinking things again," he said in one rapid thought. While he had considerably slowed down the way he talked, when he had more than one idea, Petro still strung them all together.

"Aye, maybe you are overthinking it. Let's head over to the VIP tent and go talk to the lads before they get onstage," Phil said, taking some of the edge off.

Hell, what was normal, anyway, for a group of Ethereals working in a carnival at a rock festival?

"You guys see a taco truck anywhere?" I asked, taking a deep, clearing breath.

CHAPTER 5

The Show Must Go On . . .

"Just walk in and look to your right. We're at the far end of the bar overlooking the stage," I screamed into the phone before Kim hung up.

Most of the big-ticket bands were set up and playing on the football field inside the stadium. The VIP section was slightly off to the side of the stage and elevated by platforms. They had truly outdone themselves while setting up the rich folks section. I was betting the tickets cost a cool thousand plus bucks.

Women in tight dresses and men with too much cologne and sporting one size too small rock T-shirts for bands they had no clue about, paraded around the section like peacocks. We clearly stuck out like a sore thumb. There were other Mages, and a few Vs we didn't know in the section; however, no Pixies.

"Bruther, is your girlfriend coming?" Phil had downed at least six Vamp Ambers since we'd walked in, all of six minutes ago.

The mood started to shift into party time when the opening act for Planes Drifter walked onstage. "Who the hell is that?" I asked, sipping a Vamp Amber as Petro leaned against a napkin dispenser.

"Some new all-Vampire folk band. They're called The Blood Brood, and the ladies love 'em," Petro replied, his words slowing down.

"Bruther, they sound like a bunch of mating cats that got trapped in a trash bin," Phil said, shaking his head.

The song playing involved the four band members, including an extremely tall woman—well, V—onstage dancing around with keyboard guitars. Loud techno-like drumbeats pulsated in the background as a mix of what I could only describe as Nine Inch Nails and Depeche Mode came screaming out of the loudspeakers.

Turning, all the younger people in the VIP section started to sway to the music's rhythmic beat. I found myself doing the same as Phil looked at me, shaking his head in disapproval.

"Oi, look at that, bruther." Phil pointed, pulling back his hair as a woman dressed in black leather pants and a PD cutoff T-shirt walked in. Her hair was slicked back into a glass-like ponytail, making her ruby-red lips stand out like a light at the end of a dark hallway.

It was, of course, Kim dressed as I had never seen her. "Phil, that's Kim."

"No, it's not . . ." Phil trailed off as she walked closer, smiling. Several other men and women alike gave her glances as she walked by.

"Holy hell, boss. She's proving a point," Petro warned, chuckling.

"Yeah, I think she is," I responded as the rest of the room dissolved and I focused on her. I loved her, and I was pretty sure she cared for me as well. That wasn't the issue. Something was going on, and I had yet to nail it down fully.

"Well, boys, I see it didn't take you three too long to almost drain the bar," Kim greeted with as much sarcasm as she could pull off without being rude. Even if we were having relationship issues, we were all friends, and nothing would change that.

"Hey, you look amazing," I told her, standing up to give her a light hug. Two could play at this game. *Mine*, I thought, truly having no clue what I was doing.

"Thanks. I just thought I would throw on something comfortable," Kim said, giving me a genuine smile. According to Petro's laws of women 101, she liked the attention, which was precisely what I wasn't bringing into the relationship.

"So what was up with the victim?" I asked, trying to change the subject before I stuck my foot in the old proverbial mouth.

This was where the two of us shined our best. Kim leaned over, losing every ounce of cool she had acquired while strutting through the VIP section. "Some rich business owner. It was a literal bloody mess. I took one look at the scene and couldn't tell if it was a bomb or something else which tore the man apart. They found some hair samples and a few other things on-site that the team is sending off to the lab. Till then, it is what it is."

"How did you know it was a man, then?" Petro asked as he slammed another cap full of rum.

"Well, they found his wiener—or what was left of it—stuck on the wall," Kim replied before doing the math of what she had just said.

"Bahahah!" Phil bellowed as Petro and I both spit our drinks out. "You said wiener, lass!"

"Dammit," Kim cursed under her breath as Phil's outburst gained the attention of others close by. She couldn't help herself as she started chuckling lightly.

One of the VIP concierges walked over with a cocktail on a tray. "Excuse me, ma'am, the gentleman at the end of the bar bought you a drink."

I froze, waiting on her response. "You can tell the gentleman that I have more than I can handle with my friends, and that I am fully aware drinks are free here," Kim responded, smirking at me before correcting her expression. She was trying not to have a good time around me and having trouble hiding the fact that she was.

Just as the conversation was about to go stale, a loud drum smacked over the speakers. The Blood Brood had just ended their set.

"I bet John likes that band," I said under my breath as Petro looked up.

"Who?" he asked, motioning for another drink, which consisted of Phil or me waiting on him. The routine was simple: order one cocktail and keep filling his cap.

"Nobody, really, just this V who shows up at FA's every now and then. Scary ass mofo. Anyway, you off the clock?" I finished, asking Kim as she took the now open seat left by Phil going to the bathroom. Her perfume was filling my senses, forcing a broader smile on my face.

"I am . . . hey, look," she started, her eyes wandering, not looking directly at me. It was hard for her to express her feelings, considering she was one of the strongest-willed people I had ever met. "I don't think you and Aslynn have anything going on. And, well, the past is the past. You never judged me because of Neil, and hell, I still judge myself about that one. But this is the closest thing we've had to a real date in months, and I've only been here ten minutes. I need more of this. I didn't want to tell you, but—" Kim was cut off from finishing when a wailing guitar solo erupted from the stage so loud it hushed the entire crowd.

I smiled, looking over. "I'm here and not going anywhere. When this is over, let's grab some food?"

Kim nodded as a sheepish grin crossed her face. It was clear she wanted to talk but had yet to decide on something.

Knight Raider, the guitar player for PD, was warming up the crowd. Shortly thereafter, Kane, the oversized bass player and ogre, thumped several pounding chords, followed by a mathematical drumroll by Jim Smith, drummer and Vamp extraordinaire. It was showtime.

Phil rushed back up to the rail, holding two more beers, as Petro shot up into the air to get a bird's-eye view. That was a good idea. I wondered if they would figure out a way to address Pixies at shows and sporting events in the future.

"Ladies and gentlemen, boys and girls, ghouls and goblins. Well, hopefully no ghouls in the crowd tonight. Welcome to the Dark Carnival," Abby Normal belted out in his smooth rock star voice, chuckling at the end, sounding like a creepy version of Ozzy during "Crazy Train." "Ha, ha, ha, ha."

"This is epic!" I screamed as Kim put her arm around mine, grinning.

"This song and show are dedicated to a true hero. The type of hero who no one knows their name, but their great sacrifices for the greater good are felt. This song is called 'The Gate to Everwhere,'" Abby said as he looked up to the sky then to the ground, saluting.

The song was about Belm, your friendly neighborhood demon and at times greaser-looking son of the Devil, who had sacrificed his life to close a portal to the hellion legions. A light tear almost leaked from my eye as Abby started to sing.

"*If a person doesn't have a grave to talk to in reflection, that person hasn't ever truly . . . respected the dead . . . respected the dead . . .*" Abby growled. He always reminded me of the singer from Pantera, Phil Anselmo, and Robert Smith from The Cure having a singing argument. A little harsh at times with a hell of a lot of melody.

The show flowed like the tide, coming in crashing at times, then receding to utter peace while knowing the waves would come slamming back down. In the middle of the show, PD often took a slight intermission to do a set change on stage. As the music stopped, the crowd dispersed in all directions for more beverages and bathroom breaks. While they could use magic, I was sure they would keep it simple for this show.

"I bet they are having a blast in those box seats up top," I said as Kim nodded her head, agreeing.

"Yeah, I heard they went for around ten thousand a pop, plus a few sponsors," she replied as Phil and Petro headed off to the bar.

"How did you know that?" I wondered why Abby hadn't set us up in one.

"Our victim had one of those executive box suites reserved for tonight. Hang on." She pulled out her phone to send a text to James. "Ahh," she let out lightly, holding the phone up, pointing across the field.

"The box suite with the red tinted glass?" I asked.

Kim squinted, clearly needing glasses. Although to be fair, I did have better than average—or well, human—eyesight.

"I would think they wouldn't have it open tonight. Hold on." She turned to motion for Petro.

"Sup? You need me to get this meathead away from you?" Petro said, raising his eyebrows jokingly while pointing at me.

"Not tonight, hero. Hey, can you fly over to this box suite across the field?" Kim held up her phone.

"What's all this about?" Phil inquired as he walked over, handing me a beer. I held up my hand, getting a sinking feeling in my stomach. Or it could be the nachos we had just eaten.

"Hang on," I said as Petro flew off, zigging and zagging. I swear I heard him singing Dolly Parton's "9 to 5" as he flew off.

The first sign that things were about to go sideways was the clear, straight line of Pixie dust rocketing back toward us. Petro was not taking his time coming back. As he landed, his chest was heaving.

"It's bad. That's blood. I didn't get any closer, but it sounds like something may still be going on in there," Petro spit out.

Phil, Kim, and I looked at each other with the sobering realization that we needed to get our asses in gear. "Dammit!" I exclaimed louder than needed. Kim ran over to a security guard by the entrance while making a call at the same time.

"Phil, how fast does that sober-up potion work?" I asked, pulling out an Evergate stone.

"Ahh, about five minutes at the most. I take it the show's over?" he asked, hoping I would change my mind.

"Yup, it is. Petro, go down to the bands' food trailers and let Trish and Amon know what's up. See that Abby gets this note," I indicated, pulling out a pen and scribbling on one of the napkins.

"I just called James. He's sending a team over. The local security and on-duty police are also heading up. I told everyone to keep it down to avoid the crowd losing it, but I'm pretty sure this entire place is about to turn into a shit show," Kim informed calmly. She was in her element, and she looked way sexy in high heels, leather, and PD T-shirt while doing so.

"We're gating over. Just need to go through the Postern first," I said, willing a gate to open as the crowd in the VIP section all started snapping pictures and walking closer than needed.

"I don't think you guys are in any condition to do anything. Well, maybe Max," Kim said as Petro, Phil, and I all raised the small sober-up potion vials we had with us, downing them at the same time. Petro immediately flew off with my note.

Kim just grinned, shaking her head. "Looks like I'm babysitting tonight, and once again, the evening is a bust," she said as we walked through the gate.

CHAPTER 6

I'm Staying for the Encore

The tart iron tang of blood filled the air, mixing with the smell of freshly cooked food. As Kim, Phil, and I stood in the hallway, an eerie silence occupied the void. The overhead LED lights flickered as a red pool of viscous material seeped out from underneath the door in front of us.

"You guys hear that?" I asked, pointing my finger to my ear, letting them know I was using my heightened senses to pick up on something.

Phil and Kim both shook their heads, pausing as the sound of cracking joints echoed through the empty hallway. As if by design, the pyrotechnic show started then. Flames and fireworks erupted from the stage, followed by a thunderous drumroll and guitar lick.

It had only taken us a few seconds to get across the stadium, and Petro had clearly not made it to his target with my note.

Kim pulled a small pistol out of the clutch purse she held under her arm as Phil started glowing lightly. He was charged up and ready to go, truly not in need of a weapon. It was also clear that the sober-up potion had not taken full hold of his faculties and senses yet.

I took a deep breath, focusing on my right arm as the shimmering red hellfire of Durundle erupted from my hand. As of last year, the sword had melded into my own being. I no longer had to carry the physical form of the sword. I just needed to concentrate and spring the flaming blade to life, having become an extension of my own body.

Two rent-a-cop security guards appeared from the far end of the hallway, taking one look at us before turning and running back through the door.

"Let's get this nonsense over with," Phil said, a stern look on his face.

I nodded toward him. Over the past few years, Phil and I had gotten to know each other very well. When there was an obstacle in the way and I nodded at him, it was a clear message to kick the damn door—or whatever might be in front of us—out of the way.

With a light kick of his foot, the door went flying inward, shattering into dozens of pieces. Kim and I stepped forward from either side of Phil, looking into the blood-soaked room. It looked like something out of a gothic horror movie.

Body parts were strewn in all directions, and blood dripped from the ceiling. Trails of red-and-purple viscous material slid down the walls, generating an even grimmer vision of the violence that had occurred in the room.

Another loud boom echoed, vibrating the space, as more pyrotechnics launched from the stage. The show was back in full swing.

Squatting in the middle of the room was a shirtless man with his back turned toward us. He seemed to be holding a leg or some other large body part. The back of his head moved up and down while his skin flexed from strained jaw muscles. The man was clearly eating whomever he had just killed.

"What the hell," Kim whispered as I quickly moved in

front of her.

"Stand up, and no sudden moves," I ordered as blood dripped down from the ceiling, making my blade sizzle.

The man covered in blood stood up, slowly turning. It was clear he was a Vampire. The crouching nightmare on feet was under the spell of what they called blood rage, a condition which affected Vs when they were exposed to human blood. While it was clear this V was in such a state, he had a blank expression on his face.

"Listen here now. You do what we say, and you make it out of here alive," Phil spoke up as Kim took a step back. She knew the risk of her standing in front of a blood-drunk V.

Before we could move, the V lunged with lightning-quick speed, ramming into Phil, who lodged his fist directly into the V's face. The creature let out a bloodcurdling shriek as he flew backward, the impact hard enough to be felt from across the room. Phil hesitated for a second, shaking his hand to point out that punching a Vampire directly in the face, even with preternatural powers, hurt.

I lunged forward, pulling my arm up, letting the hellfire crackle directly in front of the Vampire's face as he started regaining his faculties. The lights in the room, mixed with the blood and hellfire coming from my arm, caused a rhythmic pulse that, along with the rocking music outside, culminated into an odd club-like display.

The man's chest heaved as strained restraint started showing through his eyes. Kim's voice cut through the noise as she talked to Trish and Petro in the hallway. This distraction was enough to allow the young man to leap through the window in one motion, clearing the entire stadium in one blood-fueled leap.

Unfortunately for the Vampire, in doing so, he had dragged his body from the neck down through my hellfire blade. Wherever the Vampire landed, he would not be alive long. The raging creature had basically cut himself in half trying to escape.

Screams started erupting from directly below the executive suite, as the blood-gorged Vampire had dropped the contents of his stomach on the group directly below. I was betting Petro was about to throw up. Not only did he hate the smell of blood and gore, he especially hated the scent of Vampires; more specifically, dead or dying ones.

The sound and grandeur of the concert below muffled the screams, keeping most of the attention off the box suite.

I turned to see Trish, Kim, Phil, and Petro staring at the room and mess in front of them. In all fairness, I was also staring at the room, the adrenaline having left my body.

"What the hell happened here?" Trish asked while Petro flew out of the room to more than likely throw-up.

"I think we want to know the same thing. I can't stay in here any longer," I said as Kim's phone started chirping.

After everyone quickly agreed, we stepped out into the hall. "I have a callout, and James is diverting forces to help find the V," Kim informed, reading a text.

"Hey, bruther, you better call Frank."

Taking out my phone, I dialed his number. Frank picked up before the first ring was complete. "Hello, this better be good."

"Well, I think you may need to get down here. I'm at the show, and a V just ripped what I believe is a room full of people apart, then took off out a window after being cut pretty much in half," I spit out rapidly

"Huh, well, I guess you actually met my expectations for once. Do I need to get ahold of Davros or Angel?" Frank asked, mixing his jab with a serious question.

The phone hummed as I reflected on the question. In a few short years, Frank had become the head of the CSA for the

Southern US. He was a V and trusted friend, not to mention the first V, to the best of my knowledge, I'd ever met.

"Angel is as far up as I would go for now. Trish and Kim are here, and I'll let you know what else I find. Give James a call. He's heading this way as we speak," I told him as Trish nodded in approval.

"At least there is some adult supervision there. You sound buzzed," Frank said before he hung up the phone. Truth be told, the potion was kicking in, and things were quickly coming into focus. This, of course, only made matters worse. I was pretty sure that Kim and Trish, being sober, saw the room in a different light than I did.

"What did Frank say?" Trish asked as several of the Atheneum marshals walked through the door at the hall's end, Ed and Jenny leading the group. They must have gated-in a team somewhere close by. I was betting this was part of the security plan for the festival.

"Not much. Trish, can you do me a favor and find out who was working the executive suites tonight? Something's not sitting right with me," I admitted as Jenny walked up with her e-meter out.

As it had done with the rest of the group, the sight of the room made Ed and Jenny pause. Jenny lowered the e-meter as her eyes widened.

"What the hell happened here?" she asked, a slight gagging sound coming from her at the end.

"Looks like the CSA must be busy if they are sending out the Artifact Retrieval Team," I said, letting out the lungful of air I had been holding. "Well, the now presumably dead Vampire who just launched himself out of this window was in a blood rage when we got here. I'm not sure how many people all these bits belong to, but it was clear he came through here like a blender."

The sound of more pyrotechnics going off shook the hallway again, lighting up the sky in spectacular fashion. It sounded louder than before as Planes Drifter dug in for some odd solo I had never heard before.

Kim spent a few minutes filling everyone in on the executive suite's deceased owner from earlier in the evening. The one thing everyone agreed on was the scene being no coincidence.

"Right, I see you got ahold of Frank. Perfect," Ed started in his usual cadence. While he wasn't a full CSA member anymore, he was the ranking Council member present and, with that, in charge. "Kim, get your team to secure this location; nobody comes in. Set a glamour so the festivalgoers don't pay us any more attention than they already have. Phil, Jenny, take a few other men to the seats below and get that crowd under control before they spread like wildfire."

"On it. Oh, and we need to take samples of whatever we find. It's important when a V is involved," Jenny added as Kim nodded, agreeing.

"Whatever was in his stomach got dumped on the crowd freaking out," I stated while people with clear orders started shuffling around in all directions. "Petro, did you get my note to the band?"

"Sure did, boss. I ran into Kane. He just grunted and pointed over at all these fireworks lying around. Next thing I know, about a dozen more people are running around setting up more fireworks," Petro said, hovering just close enough to talk.

I nodded to Petro. "It sounds like they set up a little distraction. Hell, I could barely focus with the amount of shit they were lighting off. I bet we hear about that in the papers."

Everyone's phone chimed at the same time with messages from James and Frank. They had found the V and were securing the location.

"They found the bloody bugger," Phil said as he popped an unlit cigarette in his mouth out of habit.

"Sounds like it. I'm going to head over and talk to Abby; I want to catch them when they're coming off stage. Something's not sitting right with me about this whole thing, and I'm sure you guys know that Abby has a knack for figuring things out. A soon as we find out who that was, let me know," I finished while Petro zipped down the hall, leading the way.

"Max," Trish called out, taking a few quick steps to catch up. "When you get done talking to Abby, come by the food trailers. I'll let you know what I find out about the staff."

"Trish, don't you think it's odd we haven't seen anybody else working up here?" I asked as she nodded, agreeing.

***

Petro and I waited in the hallway behind the stage as Planes Drifter completed their set, including the crushing encore of "To the Gates of Hell." If they knew about the chaos that had just transpired out of sight, the band wasn't showing it.

When the band finished walking down the stairs from the stage, Abby motioned the rest of the group to keep going.

"That was a hell of a show. I have a feeling we are going to be banned from ever playing again in Jacksonville. Considering we have four more nights of shows, I have a feeling we're going to be talking to the fire marshal tonight," Abby said, raising his eyebrows, waiting for my explanation of the note Petro had given Kane.

They had let off enough fireworks and pyrotechnics to completely cover the stadium in a layer of hazy smoke and fog. Concertgoers on the field would not be able to see anything past a few rows of seats above their heads in the stands. Unfortunately for the people in the higher rows, they would not be able to see the stage clearly.

Before I walked out of the suite, I had snapped a picture

on my phone. I held it up for Abby. "That's one of the executive suites left of the stage."

"Holy hell, man." Abby blew out a breath. "I saw Jim looking around. I guess this explains it. We figured it wasn't an issue with the regulars here. Is the crowd safe?" he asked in a concerned tone.

"Seems to be. We might have some traumatized regulars, but Jenny is up there sorting them out. I bet she does a mind wipe after talking to them." The conversation with Abby felt familiar, as if it was routine.

"That is if the regular police doesn't show up and . . . never mind," Abby said as the sounds of sirens started filling the air. "The show's over, so most people are leaving. Hold on. I'll calm everyone down."

Abby motioned for a stage tech to bring him a microphone. "Ladies and gentlemen, it's your favorite lead singer. There has been an accident on the grounds. Everything's copacetic now. You know how it goes in rock and roll; someone had too much fun tonight. Please be safe and make a path for the authorities. We will see you tomorrow, and we love you, Jacksonville!" Abby finished in a high singing note straight out of the '80s.

I fell into step behind Abby as we went through the tunnel into the band room. A sign on the door made an unequivocal statement: "Planes Drifter band members only."

"Wow, boss, check this place out!" Petro exclaimed, buzzing off my shoulder to bounce around the room.

The room was as opulent as one would except for a top-tier rock band. Untouched fruit and vegetable trays lay sprawled out on the tables, while large coolers full of drinks of every kind sat at each end of them. A bar sat at the far end of the room, set up for personal use, and if needed, a bartender.

Large, plush chairs and musical instruments sat around

in various locations, having been used for practice. The room smelled like firewood, the scent coming from an incense burner sitting on its own in the corner. I was betting it was spelled.

Another quick glance around explained everything. Two large crates labeled FA's sat in the corner. Kane was pulling out a carton of Onyx cigarettes as Abby motioned for us to sit down.

He grabbed a beer, offering one to me. For once in my life, I passed, since the sober-up potion would only negate the effects in my stomach.

Knight, Jim, and Kane walked over, joining us with concerned looks on their faces. "Spit it out," Kane demanded in his rumbling voice. I had learned last year that he was Mouth's cousin. While Mouth and I were on friendly speaking terms, I hadn't run into him for several months—if not longer—mainly due to me avoiding the Council chambers when at all possible.

I spent the next five minutes filling in the band on the events of the evening. Petro, chewing a mouthful of chips, finished off the story in typical Petro style.

"Then I whooshed down here and gave you guys the note, you know, saving everyone from panicking and probably saving the show. Anyway, then I went and made sure the rest of the team was situated, and here we are."

"I'll give Frank a call in a few," Jim said as Abby leaned forward.

"Max, why are you here telling us all this?" he asked, making a good point. After last year, I had taken some time to look into the band. They had a relatively hidden reputation of helping in sometimes complicated magical issues. It had taken me some time to figure out how they always knew about my misadventures enough to write songs about them.

Abby was on the Senior Council and had worked with Ed

and Jenny on several occasions. The band used its status and ability to have people trust them to get things done, even if not entirely on the up-and-up.

"I was just asking myself the same question. Look, I'm not going to sugarcoat things. I'm fully aware of all your backgrounds. Meaning, I'm sure you would get involved either way, especially as this happened while you were playing. The fact that you all reacted the way you did tells me you know the score when things like this happen. What you guys did was amazing," I said, walking over to the cooler, grabbing a water to help clear what was left of the fog left in my head.

"You didn't answer the man there, rock star. Oh, and if you call us a rock band version of Scooby-Doo, Kane is more than likely not going to appreciate it," Knight warned, kicking his boots on the table, grabbing a smoke from Kane as the band eyed each other, knowing the truth of what I was saying.

"Why did you guys want me to check out the Dark Carnival? Not the name of the festival, but the actual carnival they set up here. I went over and scouted it out earlier, and something seemed a little off." I leaned back. "I'm not saying this is all tied together, but the people in that tent were more than excited to see and talk to us."

The band all looked at Abby as his face went flat. "Ah, yes, that. Well, I would say it's more than a coincidence that Barnabas showed up this morning as well. I found that out prior to starting the show. He saw me and hauled ass in the other direction."

"That guy seemed like a cheesy used car salesman. What's his deal?" I asked as Petro's phone started buzzing.

"I think you need to do some more research. He was one of the original proprietors of the Dark Carnival. Jim, when was he let out of confinement?" Abby asked.

"Five years ago. I believe he was let out on good behavior or something to that effect. I'm not even sure if he's supposed

MAX ABADDON AND THE DARK CARNIVAL

to be doing what he is doing. Hell, who knows. The Council makes no sense half the time," Jim said flatly.

"What was he in for?" Petro asked, flying over to my chair.

"Well, that's up for debate. It was more of an accessory-to-the-crime type of sentence. He actually didn't *do* anything. But other folks said he was working black magic, and the main reason all those people died," Abby replied, grinning.

"I guess you guys left all that out when you asked me to look into it. The team is checking a few things out, and if something comes up, I'll be in touch." I stood up. "Also, I'll see what the marshals say about not shutting this place down, and let you know."

"Well, at least we will have some new songwriting material," Abby said as Petro and I left the room. A stereo being cranked to its maximum volume came from the room as soon as the door closed.

"Is that the spell the incense is letting off?" I asked Petro as we paused.

"Sure is. Anyone outside that room heard the same thing the whole time. Pretty simple yet smart magic, if you ask me."

"Do you have a feeling there's more going on here than we are sober enough to figure out?" I asked Petro, who was standing on a speaker cabinet while he stroked his majestic mustache.

"Yup, there's more shit going on here than in a Burger King bathroom. You sure we want to get involved in this one, boss?"

"I don't think we're going to have a choice. A new key, Jamison back up and running, a mysterious carnival, and whatever the hell that was with the V? I just don't know," I said thoughtfully, pausing.

"Yeah, all these things don't seem to be connected, but

you know how things go. Trish texted. She's leaving for the evening back to FA's, and said you need to stop by tomorrow." Petro looked up, smirking. "What do you say we take some time in the Postern and look at that new key. We still haven't worked with the Mirrorgate other than to gate back and forth from the Everwhere," Petro finished, taking my mind off the night's events.

"Sounds like a plan. I need a break from the past few days, and it looks like everything else is handled at this point. When things like this happen, I keep forgetting it's not always our responsibility to save the world. There's not much else we can get done here."

I pulled out an Evergate stone, walking through to our apartment.

CHAPTER 7

Mo Bo

I thanked Trish as she handed me a cup of Fae honey coffee. Phil had ended up spending the night at the Atheneum, and Petro had been called to help Lacey and Macey go over some evidence they'd found at the stadium, disrupting our plans for the evening. Casey wasn't set to return home for several more days, having gone to visit her family in Savannah.

It had been a long time since it was just me sitting at the bar getting a coffee. Even more striking was its lack of alcohol. The issue with Phil's sober-up potion was that it didn't have a no-hangover guarantee.

"Last night was something else. I heard Ed had to report to the Supreme Council this morning. Just like old times," Trish said as her smile lit up the room.

"Just like old times," I repeated. "So, what did you want to talk about?"

"Oh, it's not me. Amon now demands you talk to him. But first, Max, that was some bad mojo last night. I spoke with the hospitality contractor this morning; the V's name was John Doe. He was apparently a last-minute addition to the team." She waved at Sarah to take care of a few customers who had just walked in.

"John Doe?" I asked sarcastically.

"Vampires, what can I say. But it gets interesting. Listen to this; the service team working the executive floor was called to a quick safety briefing directly before everything went down. We can't verify if John got the message, but he wasn't there. Even better, the management team called the meeting and then didn't show up. They just hung out for thirty minutes smoking and drinking," Trish finished as the smell of fresh seafood wafted from the small food service window that led to the kitchen.

Amon worked in the back and was a well-hidden secret; he was, after all, a hellion general. "Did you get this information to Kim?" I asked, taking a much-needed pull from my coffee.

"Tell you what. I'll give Kim a call to stop by, and you can tell her yourself," she replied winking.

I smiled at Trish as she put her hand on mine, saying everything and nothing simultaneously. Bartenders, at least immortal ones, had a way of doing that.

Trish lifted the end of the bar as I stood up, walking over to the door simply labeled Employee Only.

Behind the entrance was a solid silver and iron door with several intricate-looking locks etched into it. Trish raised her hand, murmuring an invocation as the mechanisms smoothly clicked open one by one.

Warm yet clear light spilled from the kitchen. The rich smell of steak broiled in butter greeted me as I walked in. Trish turned, walking back out to the bar, leaving me on my own.

Tusks protruded from a larger than average maw as rings and various jewels dangling from them clinked. Amon had a large, grossly round belly protruding over his stumpy legs. His eyes looked strangely human, with red pupils slightly shadowed by an overhanging forehead. To top it all off, he had a new apron on that read Kiss the Cook.

Amon rang the order-up bell, setting the steak by the window. "Max, great to see you," he greeted in a rumbling yet articulate voice.

"Same. Plus Trish threatened to kill me if I didn't," I joked as we both laughed, his rumbling voice echoing through the kitchen.

"Garhahah! Sounds about right. Let's go in the back," Amon indicated, wiping his hands off.

His back room hadn't changed much. Deep, rich-colored rugs made from silk hung from the walls and covered the floors as large, overly ornate chairs sat in various locations. He also had a curved copy of the desk I had that was supposedly King Arthur's. I was pretty sure that was an ongoing prank on me.

Also in Amon's back room were two large firepits. One sat in the middle of the room, while the other sat stoically by the back wall with a brick pizza oven built into it. According to others in the know, he had invented pizza.

"What's the good word?" I asked, sitting down in a chair close to the firepit in the center of the room.

"Someone came to talk to me about you a few weeks ago. I figured there would be no better time than now to let you know," Amon said, grabbing two crystal rocks glasses full of whiskey handing me one.

"Was it Tom?" I asked Amon, taking a pull from the exquisitely aged whiskey. For a big, ugly, pig-looking person, he was not only one of the best cooks globally, but also had an exquisite taste in fine liquors.

"I thought that old bird was finally dead," Amon replied, winking at me. I was pretty sure he knew more than I did.

"Something like that. So?" I urged, leaning back in the large, plush chair.

"Why don't you ask him yourself. He never left," Amon said, nodding his head.

Bo walked through the curtain leading off into the back rooms.

I stood up with mixed emotions. The first, as always when seeing a demon, was hesitation, followed by the realization that it had been almost two years since I'd last seen him.

"Hello, darling, miss me?" Bo said in a smooth, gravely yet almost silky voice. This was followed by a disturbingly large smile spreading across his face. He was still wearing round sunglasses; however, they were tinted red. The one thing I noticed immediately was that he had sprung for a new suit.

"Of all the people I thought I would run into today . . ." We shared a firm handshake.

"Well, maybe he will leave now," Amon chuckled. "Ah, I'd be lying if I said I hadn't enjoyed the company. Catching up on old times and all that."

"You two know each other?" I asked, seeing the two men roll their eyes.

"Oh yes. I knew this one when he was a little piggy hellion with a little piggy hellion tail running around all crazy," Bo replied, twirling around. "So, what do you think about the new threads?"

"They look great. Bo, I have more questions than time on my hands," I said, genuinely wanting to catch up. I had, after all, made a promise to find him. Since he was here, did that negate it? Promises, fickle as always.

"Sounds like you have . . . *too much time on your hands*," Bo sang slowly, clapping. I was pretty sure he had just made a Styx joke.

"I can handle that one. Your girlfriend will be just fine," Amon said as the two laughed at an inside joke clearly at my expense.

The mood quickly shifted when Bo sat down. Crossing his legs, he pulled out an Onyx cigarette, lighting it with his finger. "I know you have so many questions. The problem is, I might not have the answers you are looking for." He leaned back.

I reflected on his words, taking in my current surroundings. Shaking the ice in my now empty glass, I stood up as Amon pointed at the large black bottle on the end of the small service bar he had set up.

"I guess we can start with the simple stuff. Why are you here?" I asked, filling my glass then holding out the bottle toward Amon as he reached his glass over. I had forgotten how big the hellion was as a six-foot, massive arm swung in front of me.

"Never saw that one coming. Devin—you remember dear old great-grandpa—sent me here to check up on you. Next thing you know, I got a little sidetracked; well, I was stuck in the Everwhere. Long story short, I finally got ahold of an old friend who brought me over." Bo winked at Amon as the hellion just shook his head.

"How did you get sidetracked in the Everwhere?" I asked, taking a longer than needed pull, creating a slurping noise.

"Apparently, someone took the key we had safely tucked away in the Everstern," Bo said as I rocked on my heels, looking around the room.

"Hmm, interesting. The Everstern?" I asked, playing off the fact that I had taken the key last year when Marlow Goolsby was staring at it.

"Don't be coy. I could smell your overpriced aftershave all over the Mirrorgate. The Everstern is what they call the Postern in the Everwhere. Or Shadow Postern, whatever the flavor of the day is. So, I hung around, reaped some souls and all that good stuff. Next thing you know, I run into Hades. The stories that guy told me would blow your mind," Bo said as a bell chimed, letting Amon know a food order had arrived.

"Let's take this to the food line. Wash your hands in the sink," Amon indicated as I looked at Bo.

Bo must have known what we were about to do, since he was already standing up, heading toward the food prep area. I shuffled around the corner to see Amon standing there with two leather aprons and a beard and hair net for me.

"Are you serious?" I asked as Bo snickered.

"Does he look serious?" Bo said as the two of us cracked a smile.

Amon stood there, letting the joke marinate, looking as if he could take on a small army. The fact that he now had a two-foot-long pitted cleaver hanging off his hip helped.

"You two, garnish and plating," Amon ordered. Bo took position, having done this before.

"Do you think this is a good idea?" I asked, shaking my head. I looked like a dud in my beard and hair net.

"You ever watched *Karate Kid*?" Amon asked while I nodded. "Think of this as waxing the car." Amon picked up a handful of tickets, laughing at his own joke while sticking yellow copies on a sliding rack.

"I'm probably going to slow you down. If you need fire or to steam something, I'm your guy, though," I said, looking at the ingredients and orders.

"Oh, you don't know. How quaint. Time doesn't matter much in this kitchen. It can go as fast or slow as Amon wants. That's kind of his thing," Bo explained, grabbing a couple of hoagie rolls, buttering them up for two separate orders.

"Gods and graves, can this week get any weirder?"

"I have a feeling it's about to," Bo replied as the sound of a cow meeting its end came from the back room, the singing whistle of a blade slicing through the air followed by a wet splat telling me that Amon took the farm-to-table movement way too seriously.

"Does he cook all his meals like this?" I asked as Bo just nodded, handing me the rolls to put in the broiler to brown.

"Getting back to it, Hades made me aware of a few things I needed to discuss with Devin, as you call him. Long story short, instead of just keeping an eye on you, he asked me to see what I can do to help. So if you ask me out of this kitchen, then I can do just that," Bo continued, clearly following some weird, unwritten demon rule I had no clue about.

"I thought you couldn't get involved? Plus, what about them tracking you guys? You remember you can't gate and all that, right?" I said as Amon walked back in with a container full of perfectly sliced, sandwich-thin steaks.

He grunted as he rewashed his hands, followed by slamming the fresh meat on the glowing griddle that looked as if it could forge a sword. It was like watching a surgeon as fat, stubby yet flexible fingers sprinkled spices and herbs on the steak before Amon stopped momentarily. "Do you mind looking the other way?"

Bo took his elongated, razor-sharp index finger and turned my head away. "He's putting the final secret ingredient of his special recipe on the steak, and doesn't want you to know what it is," Bo explained.

The sounds and floral aroma of some type of herb being muddled stopped, and Bo nodded the all-clear to turn back around. My mouth started to water as the buttery smell started coming from the fresh steaks.

"You come around more often, and I may just let you know what that is," Amon tempted, pulling the bread out of the broiler to let it cool and crust over. I looked back over at Bo to continue.

"Oh, right. Remember when you registered me? Of course you do," Bo started, not letting me answer. "From what I can tell, the system somehow thinks I'm not a demon anymore. The surprise will be on them if I ever catch them out on a dark, overcast night."

"What? You would kill whomever?" I asked as Amon shook his head.

"Dear, no. I would scare the crap out of them and get a good laugh. I'm on my best behavior, scout's honor," Bo promised, grabbing some cheese and dropping a basket of fries in grease that was as clear as water.

Bo's best behavior consisted of accidents that may or may not involve brutally tearing bad guys apart. Or anyone, for that matter.

"What do you know about the last few days?" I asked, getting the conversation back on track.

"It looks like Jamison is back on the Plane, and that his sister has been a busy girl. Anyway, what matters isn't who was just killed, but who they were connected to. You find that out, and things may become clearer." Bo pursed his lips. He knew more than he was saying. Demons and their damn code.

"Why not just tell me?" I asked, digging further.

"Oh, that would cost you, young man, and if memory serves, you still owe me dinner. I'm not cheap," Bo replied, smiling. "Tell you what. You let me help you and get out of this kitchen, and I'll let you know. We can work out the rest later."

"This is the kind of shit that drives me up a wall. Okay, you can help, but only if you keep a low profile. I've been off the radar lately and would like to keep it that way. I'm probably somewhere on Darkwater's to-do list of people to get out of the way. He's slowly getting his footing on the Council back. He figured out a way to pin everything on his daughter after last year," I said, figuring I was making a mistake.

In reality, I was happy to see Bo, and wanted to talk to him about Belm if time permitted.

The food had taken well over forty-five minutes to make when Amon finally put the steak on the bread. "Perfect five minutes from ticket to table," he said, putting one plate by the window, ringing the bell, then handing me the other.

It was clear why his food was so good. He made it with time and care. The world in the kitchen moved at a different rate from outside.

"What's this?" I asked as Amon started grinning.

"Your girlfriend ordered a sandwich. You give her that, she may just give you a little something in return." The demon and hellion both made the same damn hip gyration movement as Petro. The mental image now stored permanently in my mind would come back to haunt me later.

"I hate you guys. I really do," I declared, taking off the beard and hair cover as several more tickets spit out of the machine. The two oversized, nightmare-producing products of hell chuckled at my expense.

"We better go before he makes us change one of the kegs. That basement is scarier than Hell," Bo proclaimed. I let that comment slide to the back of my mind for later.

"No time like the present," I said, walking out the door. When I turned to talk with Bo, still holding Kim's lunch plate, he had already vanished. A light smokey haze and the smell of ozone was all that lingered. I wasn't sure if I had just let loose a reasonably polite demon on Earth, or if he had some errands to run first.

Taking a deep breath, I willed my thoughts to project toward a vision of Bo. *"Tonight at 6:00 p.m. My apartment. Don't forget our deal."*

Bo's ghostly voice whispered in my mind, *"Don't get your panties in a wad. I need to go see someone and get some gossip."*

CHAPTER 8

A Murder Like No Other. Except for That Other One.

"**H**ey!" Kim yelled for the third time as I stood there, staring blankly into space.

"Shit," I hissed, not realizing I was doing the head movie-phone thing in the open, probably looking like an idiot. "Order up," I followed, trying to act cool while setting the steak sandwich in front of Kim.

"You made this?" she asked, raising her eyebrows.

"Pretty much," I replied as she squinted her eyes, realizing I was telling the truth to a point. I had, after all, put the hoagie bun in the broiler.

I sat down next to Kim while she started eating her sandwich. The smell of melted cheese accompanied by the rich, hazy aroma of steak made my mouth water. Trish, seeing my condition, quickly stopped by to drop off a Vamp Amber, winking at me.

"Hey, I don't think you'll have to throw another pillow and blanket on the couch. At least for now," I told Trish, referring to Bo.

"It's the livestock I'm more worried about," she said, alluding to Bo more than likely eating entire cows. I was still wondering how fresh the seafood was, and would ask Amon on my next visit. Trish walked off, heading to the kitchen.

"So, Trish had a chance to talk to the people in charge of the service team on the floor of the executive suite. Did she tell you about it?" I asked, forgetting I had barely been in the kitchen for five minutes according to the outside world.

"She said you would fill me in. I just got here, and Trish said you had something to do in the back," Kim answered, taking another mouthful of sandwich. It looked delicious, causing more drool to emanate from the corner of my mouth.

"Apparently, the service team working the executive suites was called to a quick safety meeting, clearing the floor out. When the management team didn't show up, everyone just hung out for thirty minutes. The V's name was . . . drumroll, please . . . John Doe," I revealed sarcastically. Kim paused, letting the new information marinate in her brain.

"Do we know where John came from?" she asked, punching the name into her phone. I glanced down quickly, seeing James's name on the display. The marshals would know.

"Not yet. I figure that damn Transitions Office might come in handy, though. The database is still up to date on names. Plus, we know what his face looked like. I haven't had a chance to send this info to Phil yet," I said, not letting her know with my enhanced vision I could see her texting James the exact same information.

The marshals would have access to the same database, plus regulars were at times significantly more reliable than Mages and the like. Being mortal clearly put a perspective on getting things done promptly. Not to mention they were better at using technology.

Kim's phone dinged with a message after a handful of minutes. "Bingo. It looks like Mr. John Doe's current employer is TDC."

"TDC?" I asked, the acronym sounding like some type of government agency.

"Remind me what college you went to again?" Kim asked jokingly. "The Dark Carnival. According to James's email, he started working there about a month ago when they incorporated the company. There is also a list of about fifteen other organizations tied to it. I'm not a member of the Financial Crimes division, but it looks like these are all shell companies, which is pretty common with temporary festivals and large rock shows."

"Sounds like we might be taking another field trip." I looked down at my castor, getting a gauge on the time.

"It looks like it," Kim agreed as both of our phones chimed and vibrated simultaneously. We both looked up at each other, knowing it couldn't be good.

"Hey." I put my hand on top of hers, holding the phone. "Do you want to talk now?"

"No, I don't think either one of us needs to be distracted for the rest of the afternoon," Kim said as I pulled my hand back, nodding in agreement.

Before looking at the message on my phone, I let Kim's last statement float around in the back of my mind. What she had just said could go two different ways, and until she had made that statement, I had only had positive thoughts about her wanting to talk.

There had been an echo of doubt in her voice. It was almost as if she wanted to kick the can down the road until it went into a storm drain or got ran over by the local bully's bicycle.

***

I arrived at the Atheneum twenty minutes later, Kim driving to the facility while I gated. Another murder had occurred in Jacksonville; this time, a high-powered executive for an insurance company. According to the text we'd received, the body had been left on display. It could only be described as OTN.

"Look at Sleeping Beauty. Glad to see you got to sleep in this morning, bruther," Phil said jokingly, patting me on the back harder than needed. Petro was already there, sifting through evidence from the last crime scene with Macey, Lacey, and Casey. Casey had cut her trip short, returning home early.

I looked around the main entrance of the Atheneum, noticing the lack of people. Admittedly, I had only spent limited amounts of time in the facility's main areas. The place hadn't been this empty since being assigned as a duty station for the regional marshals' team.

James stood at the security entrance installed a few years back looking entirely out of place in the facility's castle-like interior. The large round sphere with jet-black water forcing it to spin on its axis created the familiar hum I was accustomed to. I believe that's what caught my attention. It had been some time since the facility had been peaceful enough for me to hear it.

"It's good to see you two. What's the deal? There's barely anyone here," I said as Petro buzzed over, waiting for me to put my hand out so he could land.

"Aye, it looks like they're moving people and funding around. They're cutting the staff back almost to the way it was when you first joined the team," Phil replied as I noticed Detective Neil walking up behind us.

"That might be for the better. One of the main reasons I stopped coming here was all the damn regulars running around. Not a bad thing, mind you. I was just tired of everybody looking at me like I wasn't supposed to be here. But it still feels like home for some reason," I reflected.

Petro's wings came to an abrupt halt, the slight breeze on my palm stopping.

"Hey, boss, he smells like Phil at 2:00 a.m. on a Saturday after a soccer match," Petro whispered just loud enough for the two of us to hear. Phil shrugged his shoulders, knowing it was the truth.

"Hey, guys, long time no see," Neil greeted, obviously taken aback by the three of us staring at him.

Neil just happened to be Kim's ex-husband. He was a local detective for the Jacksonville Police Department. He was a rude, crude, cursing, drunk, sloppy detective, and if it weren't for the fact he was Kim's ex-husband, we would probably be friends.

"You look like a bloody stray alley cat that just got into a dumpster fight," Phil said, making a good point.

"You smell exactly like what Phil just described as well," Petro added as the three of us stood there, continuing to stare.

"I'm glad to see you guys as well. I got called in last night and still haven't had a chance to go home," Neil explained, pulling his hands out of his pockets, flashing his ID at James.

"We're just messing with you, man," I said as Neil handed me a business card. "Last time somebody gave me a business card, I about had two Amazonian guards kill me. Anyway, why are they pulling you into this mess?"

"Ed called wanting some information on how all these folks are connected. I'll explain when we get inside," Neil huffed.

Ed, Jenny, Frank, Angel, Dr. Freeman, James, Kristi, Kim, and curiously, Leshya were already in the loud room. A few other bootstrap hangers meandered around the hall toward the out-of-place, recently installed vending machines.

"Right," Ed started as we all piled into the actual honest-to-God conference room for once. "We have asked Detective Neil to join us based on recent events. As you are all aware, we've had three highly respected businessmen murdered in the area. Yes, Detective Neil? Before you either explode or cut me off," Ed prompted. He was digging around in his mind.

"Not highly respected. To put it into perspective, Mr. Gool—" Neil was cut off as the group corrected him, knowing I was about to.

"Goolsby," came the chorus, including Angel and Frank.

"Dammit, alright, *Goolsby* won't even do business with these guys," Neil finished. I looked over to see Kim rolling her eyes. She didn't like Neil; at least, not anymore. I had never been made privy to the backstory, but his outward appearance and demeanor made it clear as to why.

"As I was saying," Ed continued. "The body found this morning was left in a clearly OTN-related state. Tony Warrant's body was found naked, sitting in a chair, facing out a window overlooking downtown."

"What's so odd about that?" Phil asked as I squinted my eyes at him, daring him never to do that in front of the living room window.

"His organs were found outside of his body in a bucket. There were no visible signs of entry or exit," Ed explained, the statement sounding familiar.

Petro leaned over from his perch on my shoulder, seeing the thoughtful look on my face. "Sup, boss?" he whispered. In the past, we had talked about using his summoning charm to form a mental link similar to the one I had with demons when around. I would have to look into making that a reality. It would come in handy in moments like these.

"This just sounds familiar," I whispered back as Ed again stopped talking.

"Yes, Max? Something you would like to add," Ed inquired, genuinely curious.

"Isn't that how they found that reporter who taunted Goolsby over his mother's death?" I asked. While this had all been before my time, Phil had told me about his background.

"Aye, something like that. You think he's involved?" Phil asked the room as a whole.

"No," Kim interjected, Angel and Frank nodding in agreement. "He has nothing to gain or lose here. Count him out. It's doubtful it would be worth talking to him on that one count. Plus, this is too visible."

Kim made a solid point, and one I also agreed with. He wouldn't do something so bold and in the open. Time permitting, I would ask about the prior incident. If memory served, he had never been genuinely pegged with the murder. While the rest of the team and I doubted Goolsby's involvement, it couldn't hurt to check in on him either way.

A thought crossed my mind as I reached into my pocket, feeling the business card Neil had given me before coming into the room. *Why did he hand me the business card before we came into the meeting?*

"You want me to go check out the scene?" I asked as Petro shook his head, not approving. Something was bothering me about Neil handing me the card so discreetly. I was starting to think much like the Magical Detention Center I had stumbled across last year, he may be more open-minded than I gave him credit for. Neil knew how to play both sides of the aisle.

"I think we actually have a lead," Phil said. Jenny stopped beating her laptop keyboard like it owed her money as the room turned to look at him.

"I have to hear this one," Angel purred.

"Well, you know that with old Grumpy-Pants Goolsby, the guy was cut open, not sealed up. So I was thinking, maybe they cut the bloke up, then used a healer," Phil started while Jenny nodded. "Then I figured, if they didn't have any organs, they wouldn't be able to heal them."

Jenny spoke up. "I can't believe you actually listened to

my little lesson a few years back. You know, the one where you wondered if you could start a business replacing a regular's liver if they drank too much."

The group chuckled as Phil just grinned. He was proud of his idea. "Aye, it is a grand scheme. I need to be thinking about retirement. Anyhow, when we went to the festival, the Dark Carnival had one of those signs for the old disappearing act," Phil said. Ed, Jenny, and for some reason, Dr. Freeman all shook their heads as if they agreed with something I clearly hadn't picked up on.

"A Spatial Mage," Kristi said, winking at Phil. Kristi was a thin, tall Gate Mage who had become a permanent member of the Atheneum after last year, only to be reassigned to the Dunn in London. Petro and I also suspected she and Phil had some kind of relationship.

"A what?" I asked, my brain not fully taking hold of the concept.

"A Mage who can make things disappear and reappear. Not like a Gate Mage, but they can shift things to another place. Not far in most cases, but enough to move, say, organs. They are not considered strong enough to be full Mages. They used to make the rounds as sideshow attractions. It's sort of like your old sword's sheath in a way," Kristi explained, clearly having talked to Phil before the meeting.

"Sounds like someone needs to talk with the Council," I suggested as Ed and Jenny looked at each other.

"Right, well, I'm afraid this is on us at this point. The Council doesn't deem this serious enough to need additional assets," Ed informed, clearing his throat at the end of his declaration.

After being involved in such large level shit shows, it didn't surprise me that I felt slighted. I hadn't spent much time thinking about the Council in recent times, or on my interest in bringing down Councilman Darkwater. He had been at the center of several of the main issues I had dealt with over the years, including him working to have me *removed* permanently.

Planes Drifter's little stunt had kept the murder off the headlines and, as I sat there thinking, more than likely off the Council's radar. I looked over at Neil. "I'm going to need to ask Kim and Neil to step out for a minute." Kim wrinkled her face. She hadn't seen that coming.

I just needed to kick Neil out of the room without him leaving. "Okay . . ." Neil drawled out. Kim walked by, a scowl forming on her face. I reached out, grabbing her arm, and winked at her as Neil walked out of earshot.

"Hey, just keep him occupied. I'll fill you in shortly. Things might get a little crazy in this room."

Kim winked back, the scowl melting off her face being replaced by a devilish grin. "You owe me," she said, referring to her having to put up with her ex-husband.

"Spit it out, bruther. That was an odd one." Phil put an unlit smoke in his mouth, garnering his usual death stare from Jenny.

Walking over to the blinds, I hit the button, instantly blacking out the room. I could feel Kim shaking her head as she and Neil watched.

"Oh, this is going to be good," Angel said as the oddly quiet Dr. Freeman scooted his seat closer to the wall, away from the table.

"So, we have a visitor. I'm going to be 100 percent transparent. I'm not really sure why he is here, but I don't think any of this is a coincidence," I started while everyone stared at me.

I relaxed my will, pushing my thoughts to Bo. This would give him safe passage into the Atheneum.

With a pop of ozone and overall "*What the hell!*" from the team, Bo winked into existence. He was sitting in a new yet out-of-style leisure suit with his weirdly shaped legs crossed in typical Bo fashion. Topping it off were a pair of white leather loafers gleaming in the light.

"Hello, darlings," Bo greeted, licking his lips.

"Explain," Ed demanded while the others in the room who had yet to meet Bo stared blankly.

"What? No 'Hello, how are you doing, Bo?' Or 'Thanks for eating that dickhead Terrence, Bo'?" he asked, snorting while he talked.

Angel bowed her head lightly while Phil just chuckled. "This shit is about to get interesting."

"Nothing like last time. I'm here on orders," Bo said as Jenny squinted her eyes.

"Whose orders?" she asked as Ed and I looked at each other.

Petro, having been oddly quiet, broke the ice. "The Devil," he interjected matter-of-factly. Dr. Freeman just stared at Bo while Kristi let out a deep breath.

"I wouldn't say that. He's called a lot of things," Bo said, leaning forward, the veins pulsing from his eyes hidden behind a pair of round sunglasses.

"Whatever you call him, we need to understand why you are here," Jenny said. I still wasn't completely clear on his motives.

"With Belm gone—a true act of sacrifice"—Bo made the sign of the cross on his body—"I was asked to pop on over and check up on things. More specifically, Max. I would have been here earlier and probably gone by now, but I got sidetracked on my way here."

Seeing a demon make the sign of the cross was odd, yet it didn't seem to faze anyone else. Over the past couple of years, I'd noticed the line of religious beliefs was as murky as swamp water. After all, Jesus had a taste for beer, and Devin was a reasonably decent business type. It sounded like all these celestials were just doing their jobs at the end of the day. But I still had questions.

"The timing couldn't be any worse," Jenny continued sternly, looking around the room. "Does anyone else know you're here?"

"Of course not. Come to find out, ever since that whole fiasco with the old Transitions Office, I'm in the system. Or something like that." Bo grinned wider, the leathery skin on his face making a stretching sound.

"Right, I wouldn't doubt that," Ed said. "I've heard several other stories about the effects of registrations before they were stopped, or at least corrected. But I'm with Jenny here, Bo. I don't think this is the best time to be running around the area."

"Oh, you mean all those nasty little murders. Are you sure they were all bad murders?" Bo asked, having a moderately reasonable point.

"Yes. No type of murder is justified," I replied, taking back control of the conversation. "Listen, everyone. We all know Bo has a nose for sniffing these kinds of things out. Plus . . . I kind of already made a small deal with him. Bo seems to think the now three murder victims are all connected somehow. If the Council hasn't called anybody in this room by now or nuked the place, we might be all right."

Besides Jenny and Ed, the others in the room seemed to agree with my logic. I grinned, knowing I only half believed what I'd just said. But with Bo here, we might as well see if he could help.

Taking a longer than needed breath, Ed started laying out a plan. "Right. Max, Phil, Petro, and Bo can go back to the festival and check out the person or persons of interest. Angel, can you call the festival security and make sure nobody leaves the property before our team arrives? Dr. Freeman, talk with

Neil and Kim. See if you can find any other connections between our victims, per Bo's comment."

The group slowly started moving as Kim and Neil walked back in. I still needed to talk with Neil about the business card, and wanted to do so privately.

"I just got a message from the local fire marshal," Kim started as Dr. Freeman walked up to Neil, immediately asking him a slurry of questions. "Looks like they are going to allow the festival to continue tomorrow afternoon."

"Meaning we need to get our asses over there and figure out what's going on. I'm not opposed to shutting the carnival piece down, but we need to get all hands on deck," I told her, pulling Kim to the side. "Bo's here and thinks the murder victims are all connected."

Kim paused at my statement. "I have an idea. Let me get the wonder twins over there, and I'll call you later," she said, walking over to Dr. Freeman and Neil.

CHAPTER 9

A View to a Kill

"**B**arnabas, I'm glad you found some time for us," I said sarcastically as Petro, Phil, Bo, and I stood in front of the carnival's ticket booth. Bo had actually showed up on time, allowing us to go over a few different courses of action if things went sideways. Seeing as they usually did, we'd erred on being as unofficially official as possible.

After a little research by Dr. Freeman, it had become clear that Barnabas was an older Mind Mage. Ed had also chimed in that he specialized in projections; of course, not knowing what this meant, Dr. Freeman filled in the blanks. He could use his abilities to manipulate or, better explained, pursue people. After further reflection, we started to think that our path through the tent on our first visit may have been more deliberate than we'd thought.

Workers shuffled around the grounds, prepping for the next day after a "surprise" inspection from the fire marshal. The tent loomed, silhouetted against the dark night sky, as dull yellow lights cast random shadows on the structure, lending to the overall feeling of doom.

"I didn't. Do you have a warrant?" Barnabas asked, razor-sharp in his reply. He knew what had happened and that us coming back to the tent snooping around was probably not a good thing.

"Hello, sunshine," Bo greeted, grinning wide enough to show his second row of teeth. "I heard you put on a jolly good show. Why don't you stop trying to convince me to turn around, and I'll not eat your liver."

It was clear Bo knew the man standing in front of us was trying to get us to leave using his power. The color drained from Barnabas's face as I shrugged. Phil lit up a cigarette, holding out a warrant from the Council. I needed to remind Phil not to crinkle up warrants and cram them in his pocket like loose dollar bills.

I cleared my throat as Phil smoothed out the document. After some shuffling of the paper, it was settled. We were not leaving.

"We have a problem?" I asked.

Barnabas didn't take his eyes off Bo.

"What is that?" he asked, his voice sounding nervous and defeated.

"What? Don't you mean who? How about we use some manners here," I chided, looking over at Bo as he grinned.

"It's alright, Barny old boy. I had a little snack the other day that's kept me full enough," Bo said, licking his lips. "I was joking about the liver. I'm more of a lungs and heart kind of guy."

Bo was good at convincing people he didn't give a damn about them. He did this by letting people know he considered them more of a snack than an issue. The funny thing was, it was mostly true.

Barnabas stood there as Bo reached out, holding a ticket. "One, please."

Without any further thought, the now petrified Mind Mage quickly grabbed it, punching the small paper with a resounding click. "I don't want any trouble. I'm just here to keep things together," Barnabas said, motioning us to the left hallway. We decided to go right.

Even though the festival was shut down for the afternoon, Barnabas was not going to argue with Bo anymore, figuring it would be best for his health.

"Let me guess. You're just doing your job," I replied as Petro dusted lightly, taking off over the man.

"Please go to the left," Barnabas pled as Phil walked up to him, standing so close to the man their noses almost touched.

"Hey, now. I think you need to come with us. You can just walk right beside me. That fella over there with the red suit and crazy teeth gives me the willies," Phil commented loud enough for everyone to hear. Bo just grinned, shrugging at the statement. The four of us made one hell of a team. Never saw that one coming.

"O-okay. After you. I haven't told anyone we have guests," Barny, as he would now be called, said.

"That's the whole point, sunshine." I patted him on the back as Phil lit up a smoke directly in front of the man.

Truth be told, I wasn't getting bad vibes from the guy. I was, however, getting the impression he had more than skeletons in his closet. Well, maybe some of those too.

Petro buzzed a few feet ahead, setting off several of the automatic lights. The illumination they gave off was designed to make the mood more ominous as you walked between attractions. Shuffling noises came from the temporary door at the end of the hallway, as Barny hesitated, his feet shuffling lightly. Bo and I immediately picked up on it.

"Why are you so nervous, and who else is in here that isn't supposed to be?" I asked. Bo turned smiling, the dull glow of the lights reflecting off his teeth. I hadn't noticed it before, but last time I had seen Bo, he had yellow, if not brown, teeth. He must have stopped by the dentist, as they were now snow white, looking more defined and horrific than before.

Seeing that he was cornered, Barny let out a breath. "A lady came here about thirty minutes ago. She paid me two hundred dollars to speak with the Baron La Croix."

"Guess you just left that one out, aye," Phil chided as a loud bang and several odd chirps came from behind the door.

Bo's shoulder rose several inches as Petro flew back to the group. Phil spit out his cigarette, pulling a hammer from his coat. I agreed with his decision. It being close quarters, we needed to keep things simple.

"*Ignis!*" I yelled as the glowing hellfire blade of Durundle erupted from my arm. Several spatters of hellfire dropped to the dirt floor, making a hissing sound.

"Shit, shit, shit," Barny stammered, looking at us. I didn't blame him. You know the old joke; a demon, a Pixie, an Earth Mage, and a mutt all walk into a bar. We looked like a motley crew of all-around *we are going to mess your shit up.*

"Petro?" I asked, seeing if he could tell what was behind door number one.

"I don't know, boss," Petro replied, landing on my shoulder. "There's a lot of magic floating around in there. I can't tell what's what."

That was enough for me. I nodded at Phil as he did his usual job of kicking the flimsy temporary door in, shattering it to pieces.

Barny let out a gasp, as did I for a short second, as several creatures half the size of Petro swarmed into the hallway, attacking us. They were dark gray, with wings much like Petro's. Their pitch-black eyes reflected the light, making them look like a swarm of angry fireflies. It was clear they were trying to rip us to shreds like a flying blender.

"What the hell!" Phil bellowed as Bo started grabbing them by the handful, cramming them in his mouth.

"Omph, vood, aff," Bo growled in response, the mouthful of whatever they were muffling his voice.

Barny let out a scream as several of the creatures darted around him. Petro came barreling out of the sky, sword in hand, slicing through several of the tiny creatures with ease. As soon as his enchanted blade hit them, they disappeared into ash.

Looking over at Phil, I saw him smacking them away with his enhanced strength. I snapped out of it, realizing that a small cut on my face was bleeding. My enchanted coat was keeping most of the damage to a minimum, so I focused.

The creatures were blindly attacking. Several flew into my blade, dissipating instantly in a puff of smoke and whiff of ozone. They almost looked like a school of fish circling in the ocean, all clumping together to form large, dark masses. I lurched forward toward the room, letting my now infused hellfire blade slice through the buzzing creatures.

A loud crack reverberated from behind me as a protection circle flew up around the group, cutting off any of the creatures' reinforcements. That would be Bo doing that little trick. The problem was, the rest would now focus on me. I swung my blade around, pushing a ball of hellfire into my hand while focusing my will on the surrounding area. I was looking for water.

Little wings 101: Petro slowed to a crawl in steam and, in some cases, couldn't fly. I was betting these things would have the same problem. Looking at the far end, a watercooler sat knocked over. "Bingo!"

The water started moving toward my body as I pushed the ball of hellfire at it, creating an immediate hiss that let off a sauna's worth of steam. I had become good at this trick over the past couple of years.

I swung my blade around, catching several more of the tiny insect-like killing machines, as the loud droning sounds of fluttering wings started to thin out. My plan was working.

The taste of blood filled my mouth from a cut some-where on my face as Phil went running by me, cussing loudly.

After a few more seconds, the rest of the group walked in, the steam starting to dissipate. I looked down, seeing a handful of the winged creatures begin to try and take off. *Lord of the River Dance* would have been proud of us as the group, including Barny, started stepping on the remaining pests. I looked up, letting Durundle wink out of existence.

Bo was covered in e-core. A set of wings dangled from the corner of his mouth as he smiled. The creatures dissipated after you killed them, but the ones Bo was eating seemed to stick with him. The feeling of the small insect-like creatures underfoot dissolving into nothing was more than unnerving, throwing off my balance.

After another few minutes, the room was clear. We looked at each other, grimacing.

"Shit, is it that bad, bruther?" Phil asked, looking down at the cuts on his hands.

"Yup," was all I said, wiping the blood off the small cut above my right eye. Petro was winded. You could tell he was used to this type of fighting and was damn good at it. Barny just stood there, staring behind the small curtain at the end of the room.

"Petro?" I prompted, seeing the distant look on his face.

"Yeah, I'm fine, boss," the little warrior answered, wip-ing off his blade before putting it back in its sheath. It was clear that memories of violence long since passed were on his mind.

"Bo, what the hell were those?" I asked as he walked up beside Barny.

"Let me guess, darling. The Baron was into the old Voo-doo." Barny blindly nodded his head. "Max, to answer your question, those were souls that have been sacrificed to Nana

Marinette or Ogun, some rather nasty Voodoo types. Relatively tasty yet have a very distinct flavor. Someone has made a rather unruly deal."

As soon as the words left his mouth, Petro wrinkled his nose. That was always a bad sign. "Boss, I'm not walking over there, but . . ." he trailed off.

"Phil, call Ed. Let him know what happened," I directed.

"On it, bruther," Phil replied, walking into the hallway.

I walked over, seeing the body of who I was guessing was Baron La Croix. At least what was left of him. The scene gave new meaning to the phrase "death by a thousand cuts." The corpse had thousands of small slices all over its body, adding up to a pile of flesh.

"Shit. A possible raging shifter rips a man apart, then a crazy V, and now a damn Voodoo Queen. What's next, Godzilla?" I complained as Bo looked over, wiping his face off with a handkerchief he'd pulled out of his breast pocket.

"You know. Several different cars can have the same driver," Bo said reflectively as Barny started backing off, the gravity of the situation taking hold of his actions.

"Let's just relax there, cowboy. Take a seat by the door," I indicated, walking up to Bo. Phil shuffled in as I threw him a pair of silver-infused cuffs. Barny wasn't going anywhere until I got some answers.

"You said the body had all its organs on the outside. With no signs of entry or exit?" Bo asked in a weird, analyzing tone. He was genuinely curious.

"That's right, nothing," I answered as the smell of iron from all the blood started to permeate the air.

"I don't think the good Baron here could do all that. At least, not from the vibe he's putting off." Bo looked at the body as if he saw something I couldn't.

"Why would you say that?" I asked as Phil finally took

a look at the body, lurching slightly. Petro was still hovering right outside the door.

"He's not got enough Etherium coming from his body to do that type of heavy lifting. This old boy is nothing more than a small-time Spatial Mage. You know, card tricks; what's under the cup; now you see me, now you don't," Bo explained, walking over to the body. Pulling down the curtain, he placed it over the lifeless corpse.

Over the past several years, I had noticed that most demons, at least the few I knew, had some sort of code. It was one of respect. I'd even witnessed them use messages and actions of faith. The worlds were not as separated as organized religion would have one believe. After all, as I'd heard many of them say, *"You have to have faith in something."*

"Here's the problem. That's all fair and good, and I believe you. It's just getting others to believe you, when it's probably better they don't know you are around with all this happening, that's the issue. I'm putting my money on someone setting this guy up. Then . . ." I trailed off, realizing my theory had hit a wall.

"I can tell you that someone used some powerful Voodoo to do this. Do you know why?" Bo spoke loud enough for everyone to hear as he turned toward the center of the room.

"I need to make a call," Barny blurted out, the look of panic starting to take purchase on his face.

"Wrong answer, darling," Bo said, walking over to the man. "Because it's the most obvious type of magic or Voodoo there is. This was clearly a staged act. Many times, people practicing Voodoo have a habit of offing themselves by accident. They have some rather nasty entities."

"Like demons," Phil added, sticking his tongue out, making a good point.

Bo took a deep breath, dropping a black blob on the

ground as once again my favorite little e-core puppy sprang to life. Barny passed out with a resounding thud at this point.

"That bugger pisses on me this time . . ." Phil warned as the puppy looked up at Bo. Bo shrugged, rolling his eyes behind his tinted glasses.

"Okay, he just wanted to say hello," Bo said, pointing at Barny as the e-core puppy trotted over to the man, releasing a torrent of black sludge on his shoes.

With a snap of his fingers, the puppy disappeared. "Party pooper," Bo muttered. Phil couldn't help but grin.

"Phil, by the sounds of the sirens outside, we'll have company soon. I'd like you and Petro to hang out here until everything gets situated. I'll call Kim and see if she can have her contacts get this part of the festival shut down. Permanently. I think they might be able to get away with the rest of the bands, but this sideshow is over," I said as we walked out into the hallway, leaving Barny slumped over, passed out.

"You think that arse had something to do with all this?" Phil asked as Bo handed him one of the pitch-black, tar-smelling cigarettes. Phil wrinkled his nose before finally accepting the cancer-accelerating cigarette of doom.

Petro hovered over, landing on my shoulder, shaking his head. I agreed with him. This guy was a schmuck, a used-car salesman, snake-oil handler, or whatever else you wanted to call him. The one thing he wasn't, was a killer. After all, he could barely handle Bo's presence walking down the hallway, a fact I had taken note of.

"No, Barny's brain locked up when he saw the body, not to mention he passed out when Bo did his little thing," I said as Bo chuckled lightly, lighting his and Phil's cigarettes off his index finger.

"Mate, you're probably right. Once everything gets situated here, I'll shoot you a text. What are you two rocket scientists going to do?" Phil inquired, looking at Bo and me standing there.

What Phil and Petro didn't know was that Bo and I were having a friendly chat in our head movies. Bo'd said he had a pretty good idea of someone who could give us a lead on the Voodoo stuff. He'd also mentioned that it would be for the best if it was only the two of us.

"I have a feeling whoever did this wasn't expecting us to show up as early as we did. There's a piece of the puzzle we're missing. You know, one of those shitty side pieces the same color as the other eight hundred," I said, letting Petro and Phil know without saying that Bo and I had to go on this next journey alone.

In my mind, it was clear. If we hadn't shown up, and more specifically with Bo, the authorities would have pegged the third murder on the good Baron. He, of course, would have then met with an unfortunate accident.

"Do we need to let everybody know that you guys are heading out for a couple of hours?" Petro asked, giving me a light fist bump.

"You know what, partner," I said in a low voice, "I don't technically work for everybody else. According to Ed, this is not completely *official* Council business due to them having other priorities. As old Frankie would say, '*I'm going to do it my way.*'"

As Bo and I walked down the dark corridor, lighting it up as we moved, I could hear Phil and Petro talking to each other with my enhanced preternatural hearing.

"He's getting some balls, that one is. Next thing you know, he's going to be walking around in a loincloth and carrying an axe," Phil joked in a manner only a good friend would.

"This is going to be another crazy one. I'm kinda glad Bo's here," Petro replied in a mutual show of respect.

"Aye, me too. Just don't tell him I said that," he finished, chuckling under his breath.

CHAPTER 10

Mirror, Mirror

"Stars above, if it isn't good old Bobo," Abby Normal said smoothly as he took a seat, crossing his legs, while Bo and I sat on the other side of the table.

"Bobo? You two know each other?" I asked, confused, as Bo slung a small change purse at Abby.

"About time. I never thought you were going to pay up," Abby said, offering me a beer that I, unfortunately, had to turn down.

"Let's just say I got a little sidetracked. You know I would never forget my little ray of sunshine," Bo answered, the two men chuckling at an inside joke.

"Cut that shit out. It's creepy," I said, taking a breath to ask before changing my mind. "You know what? I don't want to know. Where is everyone else?"

"Preoccupied rearranging our stage show to appease the fire marshal." He rolled his eyes, clicking his tongue.

Bo and I just nodded. "Abby, what do you know about Baron La Croix?" I asked flatly.

"Your reputation always precedes you. Straight and to the point. Well, he is a Spatial Mage who has a bad habit of dipping his toes in Voodoo," Abby said, clearly more aware of his surroundings than I often gave him credit for.

"And here I was thinking you said you didn't have time to check it out. What do you know that you're not telling me," I said in a conversational tone, not trying to push any buttons but letting him know we needed more information if he had it.

Abby looked over at Bo. The expression on his face shifted to determined understanding. While he wore the facade of a rock star, I had come to learn that he was significantly more than the persona he showed to the general public. He was intelligent, articulate, and maybe it was just me making a fantasy in my head, but I truly believed the entire band was out kicking ass for the good guys.

"The boys and I did some snooping around after everyone left. Have you gotten all the forensics and workups back from that shit storm in the executive suites?" Abby asked, leaning forward while shaking the now empty highball glass in his hand.

"Not yet. Jenny and Kim said we should get everything back tonight at the latest," I replied, making a mental note to call Kim as soon as we left. I still needed to talk with Neil, and I had a feeling the water was about to become murkier.

"Well, you know how dogs are. They're all nice and cuddly until you throw them a real piece of steak," Abby said as Bo interrupted.

"I love dogs," Bo boomed out of nowhere, settling back down and letting Abby continue.

"As I was saying, as soon as you reach to either pet the dog or take their steak away, your chances of getting bitten increase significantly," Abby finished, raising his eyebrows before leaning back in the chair.

"What the hell is that supposed to mean?" I shook my head as Abby let out a light chuckle.

"Hah . . . well, Max, someone or something had already

painted the walls with blood. When the young V walked in, he lost his mind in a blood rage. Come to find out, the young V had also recently left rehab due to a blood relapse a year ago. He was set up, targeted even. The heart of the matter is, though, he still killed the man at the end of the day," Abby explained as he pointed a finger gun at me, pulling the trigger.

"How do you know this?" I asked inquisitively.

"Frank and Angel stopped by to see Jim. You do know that some Vampires have a special gift; Jim is one of those. They brought him several samples of blood from inside the room. After a few minutes, Jim could tell how old or fresh some of the blood samples were. I don't fully understand it, but he made it very clear that one blood event happened, followed by a pause, then a secondary event," Abby methodically laid out the murder.

"Why would Frank and Angel come to see Jim?" I asked as Bo coughed. One of the small creature's wings flew out of his mouth, turning into dust as it landed on the table.

Abby took a deep breath, clearly about to tell me something that had meaning to him. "Jim was the Vampire who helped Frank get into rehab and linked him up with Ed. I'm not going to tell you the whole backstory, but I'll tell you this. If it weren't for Jim's work, much like this time, they would have excommunicated Frank. Double dead, as it's often put."

"You mean somebody set Frank up?" I would dig into this at a later time.

"Yes," was all Abby said in reply. He did not want to talk about the situation with Frank any further. It was clearly out of respect for the V, allowing him the opportunity to tell his story to me in person.

"Aw, we had a moment," Bo interrupted, grinning. "Where is Maman Brigitte?"

Abby let out a long whistle. "I see. At times I forget the

goddesses often hide from the Above and the Below. While I'm not going to join you on this little trip, I can lead you to her. Max, you can use the Mirrorgate, right?"

That statement took me off guard. "Yeah, I can. Matter of fact, I still have a key I need to figure out."

"Good, let me grab something." He walked over to one of those cheesy rock star mirrors with lights surrounding it. Leaning over, he uncovered another mirror under a cloth. He walked back, setting the small shield-shaped item on the table.

Bo let out a breath. It was clearly made of polished silver with intricate designs bubbling out of the edges, the kind of mirror Vampires couldn't see themselves in, as it was pure silver. Newer mirrors were fair game. It always surprised the general public when they could, in fact, see a Vs reflection. There had even been Vampire detection kits with mirrors sold at cheap gas stations when the big show kicked off. Hey, anything for a buck.

"Are we about to get a lesson in fashion?" I asked jokingly as the expression on Abby's face hardened for a split second. It was enough for me to pick up on. That and Bo letting out a surprised breath told me what was sitting in front of me was important.

"Well . . ." Abby smirked, making fun of my clothes. "Unfortunately not. You will need to bring her a gift. This should suffice."

"Why such a fine artifact?" Bo said, reaching down to touch the mirror. It was clear that he not only knew what this was but that he also wanted it.

"I see you recognize it. Let's just say I don't have any more room for it. I would appreciate you letting Maman Brigitte know where this came from." Abby looked over at me.

"Alright, enough with the mystery. What does it do?" I asked as Bo and Abby enjoyed watching me try and figure it out.

"Oh, Max," Bo started with a drawl. "This mirror allows the person in its possession to see the truth behind the person looking into it. It also, if used to its full potential, can change the appearance of its owner. Mirror, mirror, on the wall, who is —"

"STOP!" Abby bellowed, throwing a cloth over the mirror. "Are you trying to get us all killed?"

"No, I was just going to show Max a little trick," Bo said, smacking Abby on the shoulder. "I'm just bullshitting. I would never call up the mirror directly. You remember the last time someone did that? All those pissed off Dwarfs went on a rampage and, well, you know."

"Let me guess, seven dwarfs?" I chuckled, only stopping after seeing the stone-cold serious expressions on the faces of Bo and Abby.

"Have you been studying history?" Abby asked, an impressed look on his face.

"Sure," I replied, referring to watching the old Disney movie. "Where did this thing come from?" I asked, hitting a nerve with Bo.

"I won it from Bobo here after he lost a rather nasty game of chess," Abby said proudly.

Bo huffed. "What old flappy lips here is saying is that after cheating at a game of chess, he won the opportunity to take one of my prized artifacts. This is what he selected. From what I understand, it spent some time in the evidence room at the Atheneum for nefarious reasons."

"Hardly a prize. More like a burden, which I'm sure Maman Brigitte would love to carry. She stays in the Everwhere to a point. From what I've gathered, once there, you will need to draw this symbol. You know how Voodoo folks and symbols are. Once done, go through the Seekergate, and you should be in front of her lair," Abby explained before standing up. It was time to go.

"How the hell do you know all this?" I was startled by his knowledge of the Postern.

"Bo, probably best if you tell him later," Abby avoided, saluting us as he closed the door. The loud music from the charm inside the room blared what sounded like Mötley Crüe's "Shout at the Devil."

***

Light, snowflake-like particles hung in the air, creating a haze in the Postern. In the Everwhere, the room was opposite to the one back home. Last year we had found the key Tom had lost sitting in the gate, which meant I was now able to gate to the Everwhere from the Postern.

"Hold this." I handed Bo the mirror, pulling out a piece of paper. "I still don't understand why I have to draw this and not just use the symbol."

"Don't ask me. I think Voodoo is the blue light special version of demonology," Bo answered thoughtfully.

I held out the paper Abby gave me, tracing it with the exact design. As soon as the final line was connected, a small pop and whiff of ozone filled the air. Whatever we had done, it was time to go.

"Do you know what that was all about?" I asked, straightening my coat.

He shrugged. "No. So, how do I look?" He pulled on his suit following my lead, dissolving the creases around his arms.

"For a demon, I'd say you're doing pretty good. I didn't see anyone shit themselves today when they saw you. Well, minus Barny," I said sarcastically as Bo just chuckled at me. He was being a smartass.

I walked over to the Seekergate, holding the paper against the door, which dissolved into a shimmering cloud. It was utterly black and void of light on the other side. The majority of the times I used the Seekergate, I could at least see some semblance of light.

As soon as the gate closed behind us, it was clear we were far from home. While swamps in Florida had a particular feel and smell, this one was alien; simply different.

Large roots shot out of the ground, supporting massive trees that disappeared into the black void above us. Unlike other areas in the Everwhere, it was hot and humid, creating a light fog.

Two dull lights radiated from a few hundred feet in front of us, shining like stars being amplified in the dark, humid air. The one thing that took me by surprise was the croaking of frogs. In most circumstances, one would hear a spatter of croaks coming from all directions. Here, it was a constant reverberating hum with no breaks or change in direction.

"*Purrrrreeeeeeeeeee,*" echoed from what I assumed were said frogs with no signs of stopping.

As we took a few steps forward, the house came into clear view. At least as much of it as we could see. If someone had taken the mansion from *The Munster's* TV show, made it a little scarier, then dumped it dead center of a Louisiana swamp, you would have the structure sitting before us.

"Dammit, and here I thought I was a creepy son of a bitch," Bo muttered, looking around as the two dull lights reflected off his round glasses.

"Yeah, I have a bad feeling about this," I agreed in my cheesy Han Solo voice, trying to lighten the mood.

"It all depends on the hopefully cheery disposition Maman Brigitte is in," he breathed out. I noticed he wasn't walking any closer to the stairs leading up to the entrance.

"Hey, that reminds me. What's the deal with Abby knowing so much about the Postern?" I asked, facing Bo.

Bo let out a huffing breath through his nose. "Abby is very old, much like Tom. From what I understand, they're related by marriage and not by blood. What I can tell you is that they grew up together as brothers. Some questions revolve around which one of them was truly supposed to take over the Postern's responsibility. Maybe you should take some time and talk to the two gentlemen about it."

I paused, looking over at Bo. He clearly knew that Tom was alive and well. "Look, I'm not going to ask you how you know, but you obviously have some type of insight into Tom's general disposition. You're well aware that I know he's still alive. The fact that I can even spit those words out proves it. I'm going to tell you this once, Bo." I paused, making sure what I was about to tell him would anchor in his mind. "I don't have to play these games anymore. If you're going to hold back information from me, then I don't need you wasting any more of my time."

"Tsk, tsk." Bo grinned. "You've become quite the man. You've grown, gotten bigger, stronger, and hell, look at that long-ass hair you have. I wouldn't be here if I didn't give a damn about you. The reason why people like Devin, myself, and others consistently seem to be popping up into your life is because we are all connected in some sick way.

"I can assure you I'm not playing any games. If I were to sit here and tell you about all the bull crap, it would take years, if not decades. You need to get that through your thick skull, darling."

I let out a steadying breath, listening to what Bo was telling me. It was true. While I was frequently impatient, Bo had never given me a reason not to trust him. When he did leave out specific facts, it was more than likely because of the damn demon code.

"I just need us to be honest with each other. I'm not sure what the hell's going on right now, and the fact that the Council doesn't want anything to do with it, unless by design, tells me we're on our own. Not to mention that I'm getting very, very tired of surprises. To be honest with you, I don't think there are many more surprises out there for me." I grinned back.

Bo just let out a sigh. It was clear he knew that my last statement about surprises was me doing nothing more than trying to convince myself I had my shit together.

"Let's get this over with," I said, walking up to the door.

CHAPTER 11

Voodoo Vibes

I knocked on the old wooden door. The rap of my knuckles set off a reverberating echo, bouncing back into the dark, heavy outdoor air. Bo and I looked at each other, grimacing.

Looking around the dimly lit entrance, I noticed a pull chain to my right, barely within grasp. Shrugging, I reached up, grabbing the chain, yanking hard as the inner workings of the old-style doorbell chimed and clanked to life. The sound shifted around the entrance as if traveling throughout the building.

"Is there anything here that isn't creepy as hell," I uttered under my breath as the sound of thumping footsteps came from the other side of the door.

The handle clicked and turned as the person on the other side slowly pulled the wooden barrier to the mysterious beyond inward. As was to be expected, the door screeched in desperate need of lubrication. It could have also been the fact that it hadn't been opened in years.

By the time the door stood fully open, the only visible light was that of the two dimly lit bulbs on the front porch. A large black man stood in the opening while the dark void of the house's interior remained shadowy and ominous.

His eyes were stitched shut, and his blotchy head full of hair looked as if it had been in dreadlocks at one point. The man's clothes were just as odd. He was wearing an old-style black tuxedo with long tails going down to the back of his knees. His lack of shoes caught my attention. He also didn't have on a shirt under the open coat, exposing a heavily tattooed chest with several clearly Voodoo-based tattoos plus a few dark, infected-looking brands.

The symbol we had drawn to get to the house was prominently displayed on the man's chest. He was wearing pearly white gloves, which were so clean I doubted they had ever touched anything in the house.

"We are here to see Maman Brigitte, and we come bearing gifts," I said as Bo held up the mirror to show him. The funny thing was, the man clearly didn't have any eyes. I was questioning the entire occasion's sanity.

"Maman Brigitte has been expecting you," the man replied with a thick Haitian accent. "Please follow me closely. Do not look into any of the dark rooms on our way. When you meet the goddess, you can give her your gift, and she will let us all know if you are worthy of her assistance."

The lack of experience I had in the magical world frequently electrified my nerves when I was in a situation I couldn't explain. Even though the Balance and the Accords had taken place, the regular population would never see something like this. I'd learned that the Council and many others in the magical realm—including the Ethereal communities—preferred to stay in the shadows.

The man stood still, blindly staring through us, waiting on a response.

Bo spoke up, knowing the proper etiquette. "We are here in peace. Neither one of us wish to enter this house wearing a false face. Oh, and I just love the tuxedo tails."

I looked over at Bo. He didn't give anything away. The

man in front of us slowly turned without saying a word, lifting his arms above his head with his palms up. At least a dozen candles lit up in the narrow hallway with several doors on either side.

The smell was best described as old stale wood and random spices. Candle wax had dripped on the floor, forming small piles under each sconce. The candles were old, and from what I could tell, made from some type of animal fat. The floor was covered in old creaking wood, letting us know our every move could be heard.

For some reason, as we passed the first set of doors on each side, I felt the urge to look inside.

"Do not look in the rooms," the man repeated, startling me. I looked over at Bo as he tapped the end of his nose, letting me know to listen to the man. Was he a man? Could he be a craft?

I focused on the man's back as odd sounds emanated from the dark voids. I wanted to ask him why they didn't have any doors, but decided to keep my mouth shut. Bo was being very particular about his actions and words. It was rare for him to recommend following the rules.

The hall stretched farther than expected. As we walked further inside the building's heart, the house became alive, more visibly used. The man stopped in front of one of the rooms as light danced off the walls.

Turning, our escort held out one of his pearly white gloved hands, ushering us into the room. Light from the flames inside the fireplace flickered off the walls as shadows moved, the light and shadows dancing with each other, looking alive.

The room was dark with black walls and old, worn, deep-red Persian rugs. Dull, large picture frames hung from the walls. Some frames had nothing but black canvases or simple symbols much like the one we had used to gate here. Curiously shaped red candles sat in dull copper holders, adding to the room's chorus of motion. It felt alive, breathing, and watching.

The centerpiece of the room was a large, overelaborate black leather chair in front of the fireplace. Sitting in that chair was a woman dressed all in black. A veil covered her face, hiding her features. I could make out muted beauty using my heightened eyesight.

Power poured from the woman, the feeling of it radiating, making the hair on my arms stand up. Or it could have just been the fact that the place was creepy as hell.

The woman shuffled in her seat, crossing her legs, the rustling sound of her silk dress overtaking the crackle of the fireplace. "Junior, please leave us," Maman Brigitte purred. Her voice was soft, subtle, yet razor-sharp at the same time.

Bo grinned as we stood there. It was clear he was waiting on the invitation to sit. "Maman Brigitte, we come in peace today with no ill will," Bo greeted, curtsying lightly as he slapped me in the arm to do the same.

The veil in from of her face moved oddly, not lending itself to breathing. "I have been expecting you. Max Abaddon Sand, on the other hand, is a treat. Please sit and have refreshments," Brigitte indicated, motioning us toward two chairs and a table that sat to her right.

I looked over at Bo as he inconspicuously shook his head, saying no to the snacks. The bad thing was, they looked good. A handful of cookies with a crystal decanter full of wine sat just out of arm's reach.

"Thank you for the hospitality. I ate before coming," Bo said, referring to the hundred or so Voodoo bug things he had devoured. He was stating the truth, and Brigitte could tell.

"And you, Max?" she offered, holding out an older, weathered-looking hand. It didn't match the skin showing from her chest, the cut not giving much of anything else away.

"Here on business," I replied as she nodded.

"As I have heard about you," Brigitte said, letting the sentence roll off her tongue. "Why are you both here?"

Bo coughed, followed by a hack, spitting out one of the small winged creatures from the carnival. It flopped on the table, still alive. "How many of those things do you have alive inside you, man?" I asked, not paying attention to Brigitte for a few seconds, stunned by the display of, well . . . grossness.

Brigitte slammed her hand on the table, grabbing the small creature as it let out a welp. "Umph!"

As quickly as Bo regurgitated the creature, Brigitte squeezed it in her hand till it popped, making a sound like a wet balloon bursting. Instead of e-core like back at the tent, blood erupted from the creature, shooting out from the Voodoo Queen's hands.

"Oh, my," Bo let out, leaning back. He clearly knew what that meant, while I just sat there, trying not to vomit.

Brigitte picked up a small bell sitting beside her, ringing it. Junior walked back in. He must have been standing in the hallway. "Yes, my queen," Junior inquired, not acting fazed by the small pile of bloodied bones and flesh Brigitte dropped on the table.

"Get my bowl, please," she requested with a slight accent cutting through. The pleasantries were officially over, and something had piqued her interest.

"Hey, guys," I said as Junior looked at me sternly. "My queen, do you or Bug Breath here mind explaining what just happened?"

Bo let out a chuckle, smiling at me. Junior handed Brigitte a snow-white handkerchief to wipe the blood off her hands before walking out of the room.

"Someone has made a deal, meaning they have an obligation to fulfill. That is, unless they pay the toll," Brigitte explained, leaning over the table.

I just shook my head. Seeing the total lack of understanding in my face, Bo spoke up before I said something in front of the queen I would more than likely regret.

"Whoever made that deal just got a little poke in the side," he said, pointing at the pile of gore. "When we were back home, those devilish little shits were shadows, whispers of will, from whatever made them. Here, they are a part of what made them."

"Here. Where exactly is here?" I asked as Junior returned with a large wooden bowl.

"We are in the twilight," Brigitte answered as she picked up the creature's remains, plopping them in the bowl. Junior handed her a knife and a sizeable yellowish candle. He followed this by pulling a rat out of the inside pocket of his jacket.

Bo rolled his eyes, letting me know we would talk later. "So, you're saying that whoever created those things just got hurt, like a Voodoo doll?" I asked, oblivious to the absurdity of my statement.

Brigitte, Bo, and Junior all let out light chuckles as I smirked. "Child," Brigitte started up as Junior handed her the rat. She was doing some type of spell or enchantment, the sensation of magic growing from the bowl. "As lost as you are here, you see clearly. That's more than a little doll."

After a few more seconds of chuckling at my expense, Junior walked out of the room, dismissed once again.

A puff of smoke and pop of ozone came from the bowl while Brigitte continued grinding the ingredients, the sound of little bones crunching making me uncomfortable.

Brigitte started chanting in a low tone as she pulled out the knife, picking up the large rat. "My blood," the rat started squeaking, knowing its role in the ritual. "My body," she continued, getting louder.

Bo leaned over, "I love a good show." I looked at him, shaking my head.

"My heart, lead me!" Brigitte finished loud enough to take me off guard. With a quick slash of the knife, the rat's blood started to flow into the bowl.

Building to a crescendo, Brigitte started mumbling faster under her breath, only to stop, freezing in place, as green smoke lightly wafted out of the bowl. The smell was something that would keep me from eating anything for the rest of the day.

The once clearly dead rat, upon Brigitte freezing, started moving on the table where she had laid it to rest. She sat there frozen in place as Junior walked in, picking up the now alive rat before leaving the room.

Bo and I had both leaned forward, transfixed on the woman. Brigitte slowly started moving again, waving the smoke from the bowl before looking down. I didn't feel like joining in as Bo leaned further over, also peering down.

My brain finally started to catch up to what I was seeing, and for that matter, where I was. I started thinking about Phil and Petro, wondering what they were doing. I was literally thinking about anything else, trying to take my mind off what I had just witnessed.

"Someone will pay the price for this. Ogun requires much sacrifice," Brigitte said as Bo leaned back, crossing his legs and pulling out an Onyx cigarette before offering one to our host. She waved Bo off, flicking her wrist as the pitch-black, tar-smelling cigarette ignited.

"Thank you, my queen. You are a darling," Bo said, letting out a billowing tower of smoke. The room was already hazy, with Bo's new addition making it dreamlike.

"Who will pay the price?" I asked, bringing the conversation back into focus.

"How many of those creatures did you see?" she asked in return, not answering my question.

"Hundreds. They were flying all over the place. We killed most of them," I replied as Bo leaned back, a puzzled look on his face.

"Much death has, and will come, of this. Every one of these creatures was created via sacrifice." Brigitte leaned back as the veil over her face shifted.

"You mean every single one of those was a person? That what? Was sacrificed?" I asked, seeing the depth of her statement.

"Perhaps, perhaps not. Whoever used these creatures has revenge in their heart," she said, taking a deep breath.

"I get you somehow know we are looking for someone. Can you get us in contact with Ogun or whoever did this?" I asked as Brigitte started laughing.

"Ha, you know not what you ask, child. There is only one reason Boegosh would bring me one of these creatures. Which reminds me." Brigitte looked over at Bo, figuring he knew something I didn't.

"Oh, yes," Bo said, pulling out the covered mirror before setting it on the table, pushing the bowl out of the way.

The woman shuffled her fingers, wringing her hands together.

"We still giving her that? We didn't get anything useful out of this," I said, holding my hand, palm up, in placation.

"Hang on, darling. The show's not over yet." Bo winked.

"Yes, this will do. Very nice; it will look grand hanging over my fireplace," Brigitte muttered before looking me square in the face. "At least you have better manners than your kin. The answer you seek hides in a question."

Truthfully, I was starting to get impatient, and I had a

feeling the other two in the room could tell. "Thank you for taking the time to see us. What's the question?" I asked, leaning back, realizing I was out of my league here.

"There are the manners you need, child. Come here, and I will tell you." Brigitte motioned me over, pointing to her mouth.

I kneeled next to her chair as the smell of frankincense and spices oozing from her skin filled my lungs. She leaned closer as the veil over her face brushed against my ear.

"Blood is not always thicker than water, but flows in the same direction when coming from the same source. Sometimes, only a trickle remains when the journey is over, the rest of the water gone, making the remaining parts strong in current and purpose." The woman pulled me closer, speaking faster as she went. "All roads lead to the same grave when revenge is the deal made. Ask yourself when the time is right, who has the most to gain from revenge, not the loss of the others you are seeing, but the reason they are lost."

On the last word, she let out a frigid breath. It went through my body, feeling as if someone had injected ice water into my veins. Whatever she had done, I had a feeling I would be seeing her again.

Brigitte rang the bell, snapping me out of the daze I was in. I stood up, feeling disoriented, as Bo walked up beside me. "It's time to go, lover boy," he hissed.

He leaned into Brigitte, whispering something into her ear I couldn't make out with my heightened senses. The woman let out a satisfied, "Mmmm," as an odd look of worry took hold of her face.

"Thank you again," I said as Junior started to usher us out the door.

"Max," Brigitte spoke up. I turned in the doorway. "Good people can do bad things to right a wrong. Here, maybe all that is needed is some rotten meat to attract the flies." She walked over and handed me a small, jewel-encrusted golden dagger.

I started to reply but Junior cut me off, stepping between us. We walked a few steps before I turned back, only to see the hall looking the same as the rest. The room we had just left was now pitch black and void of light.

"Do not look into the dark rooms," Junior indicated as he had when we entered. I was sure if I walked back in that room, Brigitte would be gone.

Taking a clearing breath, I started to let the message Brigitte had relayed swim in my head as my hand rubbed the solid hilt of the dagger. I needed to talk with Neil and see if the rest of the group, including Kim, had figured out any connection between the victims.

Walking out the front door, we immediately stepped inside the Postern. I looked over at Bo, who was straightening his shirt. "You think I'll have any luck explaining that one to the others?" I asked, only to turn and find Bo gone, the slight smell of ozone lingering.

CHAPTER 12

The Becoming

"**Y**ou could have called us, boss," Petro chirped while Phil nodded in agreement. After Bo and I had returned from visiting Brigitte, I'd decided to get some rest. I'd also left out that while we had only been gone roughly thirty minutes, eight hours had passed back in the ordinary world.

Wherever it was Brigitte lived, the place ran by its own set of rules. I still wasn't completely sold on it being fully in the Everwhere. Kim, Dr. Freeman, Petro, Frank, Neil, and Phil stared at me as I shrugged. The group was huddled around the dining room table at the Atheneum.

"It was a long night. You know how Bo can be," I said, still not giving the rest of the group what they wanted. There was no way in hell I was going to try and explain Junior, Brigitte, and that big scary-ass house.

Kim squinted her eyes, knowing I wasn't giving out the full story. She also knew I would fill her in later. "Well, while you were out Lord knows where, doing Lord knows what, Dr. Freeman found some possible leads. Also, the carnival is now officially shut down and off-limits to the public. The workers are still allowed to stay on the grounds. They have also been encouraged, after yesterday, not to leave the city." This statement made me pause, changing my read on her squinting at me.

Kim motioned toward Dr. Freeman as he pushed his glasses up. "Yes, thank you, Kim. We did some trace searching of the victims and found some connections, besides last night's addition."

Dr. Freeman was a typical old-school nonmagical professor. He was wearing the usual button-down beige shirt with nonmatching slacks, topped off with beat-up slip-on loafers. The man also had the classic comb-over, and any remaining hair had gone south to form a thick mustache.

The balding man had replaced his old glasses with new designer ones. His frame wasn't full of muscle, but you could tell by looking into his eyes he was bursting with knowledge. He hadn't been involved in most of the Kracken situation, including the death of Ned. It had clearly affected him, since Dr. Freeman had decided to quit his new teaching job and help the team.

Dr. Freeman continued as the room stayed silent. He had come prepared, handing out manila envelopes with pictures and notes. "We have split this into two buckets. First, our three connected main victims, and second, what we believe is an attempt to deflect the focus off the true perpetrators."

"We ever figure out what happened to that first guy?" I asked, raising my hand, not knowing his name and coming across as slightly disconnected from the situation.

Kim nodded at Dr. Freeman. "Yes, we do, and as of this morning, we can confirm that he was torn apart by a shifter. More precisely, a wolf."

"Werewolf, we actually have a Werewolf problem? Did anyone talk with Lucian? That guy was super nice, and I'm fairly certain Al wouldn't be hanging around a problem like that," I said as Phil nodded in agreement.

Frank spoke before anyone else could. "He's missing. We went to get a hair sample and couldn't find him. I talked with Al, and he said the same thing you did. He also mentioned something about an odd vibe in the area before he went missing."

"Dr. Freeman, you mentioned this bucket one thingy, or whatever you call it. So we can confirm that all three of these individuals are somehow connected?" I asked, already knowing the answer to the question.

"As a matter of fact, we do now. At least I think so," Dr. Freeman said as Kim rolled her eyes while the rest of the group just groaned. "We received confirmation that a shifter killed our first victim, now we have one missing. Another had its organs removed, and we have a dead Spatial Mage from the same place as the shifter. It's pretty clear all this is somehow connected."

Dr. Freeman paused as the sounds of shuffling papers from the manila envelopes filled the silence. Taking a deep breath after adjusting in his seat, he started back up. "Here's where it gets interesting. Remember now, we are only talking about bucket number one. Whatever happened to Lucian and whoever else at the Dark Carnival, we need to keep separate. All three of the gentlemen were executives involved in the insurance industry."

"What the shite does that have to do with shite," Phil said, slapping his hands on the table. The papers in front of him went flying in several directions.

One of the main reasons Dr. Freeman usually didn't brief the group was his ability to confuse Phil. While it was funny to watch, it drove Phil crazy to be lectured as if he was one of the professor's students. Not to mention, I was pretty sure Phil was the best C-student the educational system of wherever he had gone to school had to offer.

Ed and Jenny were awkwardly absent from the briefing,

122

leaving Frank to keep the meeting going. "Give the good doctor a chance to finish. Remember, gathering all this information while appearing to remain ambiguous isn't exactly an easy task," he said, taking charge of our motley little crew.

That statement got my attention. "Frank, there's something you want to tell us? Kim?" I asked the two, figuring Petro and Phil would've spilled the beans to me already that there was something to hide.

"Ed may be able to shed more light on that when Davros gets here. Jenny messaged me before you got here, Max. They believe, as do I, that our good old pal Darkwater is keeping an eye on things coming out of here," Frank said cautiously.

"So . . . I get to keep all the crazy shit I just learned to myself?" I asked, drawing it out with a smirk on my face.

"This is going to be great." Petro said, lightly dusting the table. "If things get any weirder around here, they're going to start giving us mandatory drug tests every other day."

The only person in the room who shifted uncomfortably was Neil. I chuckled lightly as Petro's joke lightened the mood in the room.

"All right. Dr. Freeman, sorry we interrupted, please continue. What's the connection, other than our victims sold insurance policies?" I asked as Dr. Freeman cleared his throat.

My interruption hadn't bothered him; in fact, it had given him some time to reorganize his thoughts.

"Saying these gentlemen sold car insurance is the equivalent of inferring Kerry King is a better guitar soloist than Knight Raider," Dr. Freeman surprisingly responded.

"Point taken, Doc," I said. Now he was speaking my language.

"All three of these men were high-level, strategic claim executives tied to the transportation industry. We're talking multimillion, if not billion-dollar policies. The kind of policies small countries sometimes take out. Since the Balance, the way the insurance industry operates has significantly changed, as I'm sure you are all aware. What we hadn't been able to find out was what connected the three men," Dr. Freeman said with finality.

"What about bucket number two?" I asked as Petro echoed what I said.

"Yeah, bucket number two." He was being overly supportive of me, and this was always a bad sign. Either he had taken something apart that I owned or had borrowed an item that I had yet to find missing. I thumped the table with my index finger as he looked back, winking at me.

I shook my head as Kim spoke up. "Max, this is where you can hopefully shed some light on the situation. We can't make heads or tails of what's happened at the Dark Carnival. Honestly, TDC Inc. seems to be aboveboard."

I closed my eyes, gathering my thoughts, leaning back in my chair. If I just blurted out yesterday's events, my level of sobriety might come into question. "After last night, I'd say we can pretty much confirm that Lucian and Baron La Croix were being set up for the murders. Or something like that. The one thing I do know is that whoever killed Baron La Croix used Voodoo," I said, taking stock of the room's reaction.

"I would usually say this is the biggest pile of crap I've ever heard," Neil started, taking a sip of his cooled, room temperature coffee. "But after seeing the condition of the last couple of bodies, I'm not ruling anything out."

"Voodoo," Frank said out loud, letting the words roll off his tongue. It was almost like he was trying to figure something out without getting lost in my statement.

"Voodoo," I repeated back to him. "From what I can tell, someone was using Voodoo to make whatever happened at the carnival seem like an accident. I bet that would have included Lucian if we hadn't shown up. Hell, we could already be too late. We need to find him. Al might know something." The others nodded in agreement.

"We talked with the dead V's boss," Kim started as Frank glared at her. While he couldn't care less about the term, it being used in reference to a dead Vampire hit him. "Vampire's boss," she corrected. "She's sure he wouldn't go into a blood frenzy without being provoked, and I believe her. So that's off the table."

I looked over at Frank, remembering the story about his past. "We will honor his death. As far as I'm concerned, who-ever was in that room was already dead. The blood is not on his hands."

Frank nodded in approval, the rest of the room following suit, grunting in affirmation. Frank reached over, patting my back lightly, smiling a toothy grin. My understanding of V na-ture was clearly appreciated.

"So, we have three men all in the same industry mur-dered in a grizzly manner and left on display for all to see. A group of rejects get set up to take the fall and are also murdered or kidnapped. Then . . ." I trailed off, clicking my tongue off the roof of my mouth in thought. "Someone is trying to force somebody into the open. It sounds like a wicked game of re-venge to me," I stated, remembering Brigitte's message.

"Why would anyone go to all this trouble? Hell, why not just find the bugger then off them," Phil said as Neil shuffled in his seat. My heightened senses were allowing me to again pick up on his unease with the conversation. He knew something.

"Whoever it is must not be easy to find. I'm guessing they're hiding," I said as Kim finished processing my state-ment. I bet she already had the same general idea.

"They are also sending a message," she added.

"What message is that?" Neil finally spoke up, looking as if he was about to fall out. The man must have gone on a bender last night.

"Don't screw with me," was all Kim said as the alarm from the driveway went off.

It had been installed when I first came to the Atheneum, notifying everyone in the dining room when a vehicle pulled up.

"Davros," Frank stated, standing up. "Let's take a break and meet back here in five."

The group started going in several directions, including the kitchen, bathroom, and wherever it was Phil went to smoke these days.

"Neil," I stopped him, lightly grabbing his arm as Petro flew by, saluting me. The little warrior was up to something. "Can we talk for a few in private?"

"Yeah, I was wondering when you were going to ask," he replied as we walked out the door toward the stacks.

As we walked to the double doors, the familiar smell of musty books and centuries of history filled my lungs. The ambient lighting peppering the room was soft and warm, coming from various areas without giving away its location.

The stacks were the size of roughly two football fields, with two other separate parts, one on each side, forming a cross. Overhead, the ceiling went up fifty-plus feet, with a second-floor balcony and a few other small, two-story alcoves in the middle of the stacks protruding above the rest of the room.

There were aisles of books as far left and right as a person could see. Hanging on the walls were tapestries slowly dancing without any wind, same as in the dining room. In between the aisles, glass display cases held different artifacts. At first glance, you would think it was some type of museum. Every time I came in the room, I expected someone in a hat snapping a whip to come around the corner so we could go off on an adventure.

Neil just stared at the room, taking it in. "Is this place, you know . . . magic?" he asked as I motioned him to walk toward the small alcove on the far left wall.

"If you haven't noticed, everything in this building is magic," I replied as we finally got to the small alcove. Four chairs sat around the table, with several old-style, brass reading lamps in the center facing in opposite directions. The three walls had shelves full of what looked like maps.

"A guy could get lost in here," Neil said while he sat down, leaning back, letting out a defeated huff.

"I think they have, if we're being honest. Look, I know you gave this to me for a reason, and that you didn't want the others to have it," I started, garnering Neil's attention as I threw the business card on the table, snapping my finger as two of the lights sprang to life. Even though the alcove was open to the rest of the stacks, the room was small enough to give us any privacy we needed.

"You're not as dumb as you look." Neil sat up straighter in his chair. "So, have you figured it out yet?"

"Figured what out yet? If you haven't noticed, I've been a little busy lately," I said, dropping down in the chair across from him.

"I don't want any trouble. This is my town, and I have to live in it, even if that includes having to deal with all the shit bags that also call it home. I have made it as a homicide detective by keeping my nose out of certain people's business. After last year, I realized I wasn't always going to be able to do so," Neil said with a slight hint of nervousness in his voice.

"You want to sit this one out, don't you?" I asked as Neil pursed his lips, barely nodding his head. A normal person wouldn't have noticed that slight gesture.

"Pretty much. For me to make it on the streets, I need people to be able to trust me. That includes talking to certain individuals who aren't precisely on the Council's or the local government's Christmas card list. I don't mind helping, but I don't need you pulling me through one of those damn gates either, popping out in front of a bunch of people," Neil explained, emphasizing his last sentence.

"All right, I hear you loud and clear. I can also tell you're full of as much manure as Biff's car back in the '50s. You know more than you're telling anyone, and you're going to lay that shit out right now. Here." I tossed him a small vial of Phil's cure-all snake oil for hangovers. "Just take it. It will clear your mind. And before you ask, no, I'm not going to give you a steady supply of the stuff. At least not yet," I finished as we both smirked at each other.

Neil raised his eyebrows, opening the container and sniffing it. "Here goes nothing," he said, taking the contents of the vial down in one pull, making a strange face and slapping his lips together at the end.

After a few moments, Neil sat up straighter, his eyes racing around the alcove, taking everything in. He was awake and hopefully ready to talk.

"This stuff is amazing," Neil said, looking down at his hands before finally resting on me. "I knew one of the victims. He was an informant, and the main reason I knew about Bruce Teach when we first met."

That name took me off guard as thoughts of the prior year started swimming through my head. "Why are you so worried about this then?" I asked, figuring there was more to his story.

"Well, I happened to talk to William Rochester, our first victim, the day before he was torn apart. He wanted to talk about one of his claims but didn't feel comfortable doing it over the phone, so we met in person. Are you familiar with one of the container ships that was lost at sea last year? I believe it was called the *Event Horizon*?" Neil said, sounding razor-sharp for once in his miserable adult life.

"Phew . . ." I let out, drawing out a breath. "I don't like the direction this is going. Let me guess, he was working on the claim for the ship."

"That and all the containers as well. The thing is, he also mentioned Tony Warrant and Ralph Edwards. You know, our other two victims. Those two gentlemen were representing other entities who owned a lot of the cargo, if not all of it." Neil reached out, grabbing the business card and writing something on the back.

"It sounds like you think Bruce Teach might be involved. The Council is still looking for the goon, from what I understand. I'm not sure how many folks they have out there looking for him, but it would make sense," I said thoughtfully.

As soon as the words left my mouth, a sinking feeling slammed into my stomach like a shot of hot sake on an empty stomach. After being demoted last year, Councilman Darkwater had recently been assigned to the field manning committee. This meant he directed and approved the number of assets available for certain operations. Pieces of the puzzle were starting to come together; however, there were still several large gaps.

"That's the part I'm not sure about. By the look on your face, you seem to be running into the same wall as I am," Neil said, still carrying on an actual adult conversation. The guy wasn't half bad when he had his wits about him.

"Yeah, Bruce isn't the kind of guy to do these flashy murders. It almost seems as if somebody is setting him up, or maybe he's the one who's being drawn out into the open." Both of us stared blankly at the business card sitting on the table.

I picked it up, finding an address that Neil had scribbled on the back of William Rochester's card. Even more curious was the odd symbol engraved in the corner. Upon closer inspection, I saw it was a modern version of the skull and bones in some fancy Art Deco form. The design was so subtle I hadn't noticed it before.

Neil stood up, straightening his jacket and shirt. "That address is to the office of the final person involved in the claims. Before you say anything, there's a very good reason that man's probably still alive. But I would bet you a case of whatever potion that was that someone will be visiting him soon."

"Visiting who?" I asked as Neil chuckled.

"The guy's name is Ben Franklin. I'm heading out. I'll reach out to you later," was the last thing Neil said, walking away while I stood there, thinking.

***

"Nice to see you could join us," Ed said as I closed the door. He had shown up with Jenny while I was talking with Neil.

"Where did Neil go?" Kim asked as Davros and Carvel nodded in greeting.

"He got called to go somewhere else. Damn, it looks like the whole crew is here." I grinned, also noticing Angel standing in the corner looking bored.

"Max, so good to see you again," Davros growled as Ed took his seat beside Jenny. "Frank was just filling me in on the situation at the stadium. It sounds like everybody's in full agreement on the lack of motivation from the Vampire side of things. We will still need to do a full investigation. That being said, I have a feeling you have something you want to tell us."

Petro buzzed in from the room's kitchen side, showing up later than I had for once. "Hey, boss, all the girls are down in your lab working on something. I went to go check on things before they caused any trouble," he said, buzzing down, taking his spot in front of me.

Petro had somehow made it back to the apartment, gone to the lab, and come back in a very short amount of time. My guess was he had used the Evergate.

Looking around the room, I noticed Carvel hadn't spoken yet. For someone with an ego as old and large as his, it was rare for the man not to interject his all-knowing effervescent presence. He and I were still on talking terms, and for the most part, good. I'd never gotten the warm, fuzzy feeling that he would be sending me anything for my birthday, but his mother kept sending me pies for saving his life.

"Carvel, it's been a while. I would be curious to hear who bribed you to come here," I greeted as he let a slight grin perk up the left side of his mouth. It was clear he didn't want to be here.

"You know how things are," Carvel replied in his old, just plain annoying voice. "Even though the Council does not believe this situation warrants its involvement, a handful of individuals would at least like to know that you aren't going to set everything on fire this time around."

While he was making light of his visit, his message was loud and clear. The Council wanted to know what was going on, and if we had it under control.

"The Council sends a Supreme member and yourself from the Senior Council for a visit? I'm going to have to call bullshit on this one," I said. Phil let out a chuckle while Ed adjusted himself in his chair. Last year, he had learned that the days of him telling me exactly what to do had long since passed.

While I still respected the man and followed his instructions when we were working on something together, I had made it clear to the others that I had no interest in being the Council's puppet. People like Ed and Jenny, not to mention Phil and the others, had been around for several decades and had already earned a certain level of respect. I, on the other hand, was an anomaly that could play with hellfire. There were more rumors about me than a college cheerleader's locker room.

"Right," Ed interjected, getting to the point. He had clearly been with the two men and Jenny for several hours. "Carvel and Davros are here to make sure things are under control. This also includes some additional help, if needed. Off the books."

After knowing Ed for several years, this was the first time I had ever heard him use that term. It was apparent the Supreme Council had some idea of the situation in Jacksonville.

"Well, ladies and gentle Vs, this is perfect timing. I have a hunch I know who the next victim is." The room went still. You ever say something and look around the room to find everyone's staring at you? Then you feel your face to make sure you don't have anything crazy on you? That was the feeling I was getting.

"You tell them, bruther," Phil piped in. "I'm getting tired of sitting around here playing patty-cakes."

Carvel squinted his eyes, looking at me while doing that weird thing he often did with his nostrils as they flared. It was almost like he was breathing in something.

"I have reason to believe that our next victim is also in the insurance business. That business is handling claims for a certain container ship that everyone in here might be well aware of. The *Event Horizon*," I said as the group continued to stare at me as if I had a horn growing out of my forehead, or one of Phil's world-renowned phallic drawings.

"Dammit, he's doing it again," Ed murmured under his breath, referencing my uncanny ability to walk into a meeting and drop a bunch of truth bombs. Or turds, depending on how you looked at it.

"Anyone in here knows of a gentleman named Ben Franklin?" I asked, not realizing the words coming out of my mouth.

"Dammit," Dr. Freeman said, letting out a slight chuff.

The room again continued to look at me as if I was the village idiot. "Let me guess, *THE* Benjamin Franklin," I said as Phil just nodded his head.

"Well," Ed started with a snarky tone in his voice. "At least we know why he's not dead yet." That was the second person who had stated that about dear old Ben, piquing my curiosity.

"He's a crusty old Mage, isn't he?" I stated shaking my head before echoing Neil's last statement. "Listen, I'm not saying I know everything that's going on. But if I were a betting man, I would put twenty bucks on someone trying to visit him soon."

"Do you think Bruce Teach is behind any of this?" Davros asked smoothly. He, as always, already knew the answer I was going to give.

"Maybe. It's just too exposed, too in the open, and he's been in hiding for a good reason. You know I, and I'm pretty sure a few other people in this room, would really like to kill him and all that jazz. But I think someone's trying to draw him out into the open," I replied as Jenny immediately started pecking away at her keyboard like a chicken in a field of corn.

"Yes, all that jazz," Davros echoed as he looked over at Frank and Carvel.

"All right," Carvel said, annoyed. "Frank, you are good to have one asset. Anything more than that would likely be noticed."

A slight grin formed on my face; they were sticking it to the man. That man being Councilman Darkwater. I picked up on the nuance in his statement. They didn't want anyone else knowing the Council had supplied any additional resources, drawing attention to the situation.

There was more at play here than I'd initially thought,

plus a whole bucket of stinking politics. That being said, any chance I had to screw with Darkwater, or possibly take him out, I would take. Petro, Phil, and I had gotten extremely drunk off tequila one night after reading an email from his office, finally deciding on the fate of his email inbox. We had taken his email address and signed him up on every dating website known to man and mythical creature, with a fake profile and a rather interesting list of likes.

He had apparently not been too thrilled about us putting his personal cell phone number on his profile either. Poor Dark-buns Sixty-Nine, as his profile read.

"Thank you, Carvel. I'm going to ask Two from the Night Stalkers to lend a hand," Frank indicated. Angel shuffled lightly. I was pretty sure by this point she was, in fact, Two. The nameless, faceless, special operations V from hell happened to look great while kicking ass.

"That's settled then," Davros started back up, taking command of the room. "Do we have any idea what you will be doing next?" he inquired, directing the question not at Ed but me.

"The way I see it, we have two options. Go get Ben, whatever the hell that entails, or wait and watch; see if we can flush out whoever is doing this," I replied just as Ed slammed into my thoughts.

"*NO MORE!*" Ed's voice reverberated loud and clear in my head. He didn't want to discuss this any further in front of the present company.

"Anyway, we will figure it out from here and let you know. Well, Ed will let you know," I finished, leaning back in my seat.

"Okay, well, this was nice," Davros said, standing up as the rest of the room followed suit. "If anything changes, please don't hesitate to let me or Carvel know."

I looked over at Phil as he made the motion for grabbing a drink.

CHAPTER 13

To Plan or Not Plan; That Is the Plan

"Well?" I asked as Frank took a pull from his synthetic blood cocktail. It wasn't often that I saw a V drink the stuff. Ever since the Balance, FA's now had a No Regulars ward, meaning other types felt more inclined to relax in the fine establishment.

"Ben's a different kind of Mage," Frank started as Trish dropped off a Neapolitan pizza.

Kim and Frank had decided to tag along for a drink at FA's, the others choosing to stay back and dig into the insurance organizations. Petro had opted to go back to the lab and finish working with the other Pixies, much to my surprise.

"I'm just hearing about Ben Franklin now . . . ?" I drawled out, often forgetting how awkwardly crazy the other side of things could be. I decided to check out a few other key persons from the history books when time permitted.

"Some fires burn bright only to fade with time," Frank replied as he held his glass out to toast. "Don't get your hopes up. Time doesn't treat everyone the way you might think. I'm sure you've noticed that the history of magic and those involved aren't exactly on your local high school's curriculum. I think most of the world is still in denial."

It was odd to hear Frank in a philosophical mood. My understanding words about John Doe's involvement and blame had clearly hit close to home with the V.

"Ahh, bruther, he's an old, washed-up hack. I met him once; total horse's arse. From what I understand, he had his heart broken and all that," Phil said as Kim looked up from her phone. The marshal's office was sending her information on Ben's location.

"Well, it looks like we're in luck. I just got a report that he's not left his property in several weeks, and has been active on social media," Kim informed, taking a sip of her water.

"Social media?" I asked confused, the mental image of the situation not having any luck forming in my head movie. Thankfully, Kim turned her phone around.

"Behold, Ken Ranklin," Kim said, showing us the phone's glowing screen. The picture of a bald man in sweatpants doing yoga was not only weird, but clearly Ben Franklin. He was a social media influencer for elderly fitness as well as an insurance broker.

It was clear why Ben would go under a different name. I still found it odd other historical figures just threw their names out in the open, only to be ignored.

"Does anyone know the guy well enough to keep him from doing whatever it is he does to others when we show up?" I asked, referring back to why he was more than likely still alive.

Frank, picking up on my meaning and also realizing Kim was at a disadvantage, spoke up. "Ben is what we call a Chaos Mage. Most people would know him for his ability to wield electricity. This was mainly done through his true power, which is to manipulate everyday items. I believe he does this through some type of electrostatic energy mixed with Etherium. Petro can probably lay it out better than I can."

"What Frank is trying to say at a third-grade level is that whatever item old Ben charges reacts differently. Kind of like taking a swig from an unlabeled mason jar in Tennessee. You never know what you're going to get. That old codger has it down, though, and knows it full well," Phil explained, seeing everyone looking at him. "What? I used to get bored at the Guild and actually listen in class."

"Here's the deal. I can get into his house—or by the looks of it, estate. I'll chat him up, then if everything is clear, we can gate him back to the Atheneum," I proposed, making the plan sound more straightforward than it actually was.

Frank took a finishing pull from his glass, the thick red synthetic blood clinging to one side. "Two is going to come along for the ride. My understanding is she will be with us shortly."

"Well, no time like the present," I said as Phil shot me a confused glance.

"Bruther, no time for a drink?" he asked as Trish stood there, waiting on my response. She had recently stopped just placing beers in front of me. Truth be told, ever since my body had started changing and things had gotten busy, I had significantly cut back on my intake of booze, much to Phil's dismay. Eating Amon's cooking, yes. Drinking, no.

I thought, taking a deep, centering breath.

"I want to get to Ben before anyone else can. Plus, I'm still trying to figure out if last night truly happened," I finally replied, cracking a smile as Phil waved off Trish while rolling his eyes.

"Well, if you can't beat 'em, join 'em," Phil said as Trish set down two cups of coffee full of Fae honey.

"On the house. If you two stop drinking, though, I may go out of business," she joked, winking at me.

"That's my lass!" Phil bellowed, taking a pull from the togo cup.

"Thanks, Trish. Will you marry me?" I asked as Kim snorted. "What?"

"You can't even get me out on a normal date," she said as Trish smiled, letting out an agreeing chuckle.

"Ha, ha. Laugh it up, ladies. Maybe if the world didn't always need saving, I would step up my game," I replied, smiling at Kim as she beamed back. The happy look on her face was the one I had fallen for. At that moment in time and space, she was content, noticing me looking at her with a longing stare.

Walking over, she put her hand on my arm, nodding at me. "No time like the present," she echoed as I looked around the group.

"Let's head over to my place next door. Frank, let Two know. I don't think we should say anything else till we get out of here," I indicated, noticing the thickening crowd that had started rolling in.

***

"You weren't kidding when you said this was a stupid plan," Two commented flatly. The helmet she was wearing concealed her true identity, slightly modulating her voice.

"I think it was pretty clear from our meeting with everyone. The fewer people know, the better. Who knows, they might have already divined our next moves," I said. "I would like to run this by Ed and Jenny, but I think this is our only shot." Kim nodded.

"To piggyback that," she interjected, "We have a drone in the sky keeping an eye on his estate. He's there, for now, but I agree with Max. The longer we wait, the more time the other side has to plan and act. I wouldn't doubt they already know we are tracking Ben."

The group had adjourned to my office next door. Phil, Petro, and I had taken the time to wall in the windows and section off the front entrance. This allowed for a separation from the front office—which I'd set up—and my main office, which included the lab. A printout of Ben's house lay flat on the desk as Frank leaned over it, marking a few key entry points.

"I almost forgot. We have a lab full of Pixies, unless they took off," I said, reaching under the desk and unlatching the mirrored back to the bar. Sounds of banging immediately echoed up the spiral staircase. In any other building, the room underground would be flooded. The lab, though, was bone dry and still had a fireplace even though there wasn't one above.

"Petro!" I yelled. The banging stopped, followed by the buzzing of four Pixies coming through the small crack in the mirror.

"Hey, boss," Petro greeted, looking as if he had been roasted with a flamethrower.

"Uh, Petro?" I prompted, noticing a small patch of his mustache was missing. It had presumably been burned off.

Casey flew over, cutting off Petro. "We made you something, and the others as well," Casey's strong voice echoed in the still office. Even Two was at a loss for words. Well, she didn't really talk much, so there's that.

"A gift?" I asked as Lacey and Macey zipped off only to reappear with two sets of sunglasses.

"Something you might just need. I heard you could be dealing with Voodoo. My family is from Savannah, and knows a thing or two," Casey explained, her chin raised high, pride showing on her face.

"We'd be honored," I told her, reaching out for a pair. "So, what's the catch?"

"No catch, boss. You put them on and presto! You'll be able to see if anything from the Everwhere or the Otherside is around," Petro said while Casey let him talk before he exploded.

"The Otherside?" I asked as the Pixies landed on the table. Casey walked over to Petro, pulling out a small rag and wiping off his reinforced wings.

"It's a place in the Everwhere that is pretty much the home of Voodoo. It's there but not there. To be honest, I don't really know all the details." She pointed at the sunglasses. "These will help. If you had had these on at the carnival, you would have found the main source of the infestation," Casey said, knowing more about Voodoo than most of the others.

"Infestation?" I asked again, putting on my pair. They were an older style with black plastic rims straight out of the 1950s. I looked around the room, noticing I was the only one putting off a weird glow. "Okay, enough of these for now," I said quickly as Casey spoke back up.

"Yes, the issue with Voodoo is that you can't be very far in order for it to work. I would say whoever manifested those creatures was in the building at the same time. Even more, you would have been able to find the guiding creature. If you kill it, the rest will fall," Casey said with finality.

"Whew," I let out, taking in every word Casey was saying and storing it for later. "Alright, Frank, what's your take on securing the perimeter? Think we could use the Pixies since they're good at sniffing this kind of stuff out?" I asked as Petro interjected.

"Casey can't go. She's—" he started, but cut himself off as the other Pixies stared at him. Casey fluttered her wings, lightly dusting the table.

"Oh, you two need to talk," she said, shaking her head as she took flight. "I'm going to clean things up in the lab. The rest of you can hang up here."

I sat there, thinking about Casey. She had never directly inserted herself into anything right, wrong, or indifferent we did when it came to matters such as this. I always thought she chose to steer clear of all the weird stuff. Of course, "weird" didn't mean much when you were talking about a Pixie married to your Pixie roommate.

Petro just looked up, nodding.

"Okay," I drawled out. "Frank?" I asked as Kim looked over at me, winking.

"Well, with their help, we could secure the perimeter and at least know if something's about to show up. Two and I can wait outside in front of the main house, here," Frank said, pointing at the printout, drawing a small X. "If Petro is up to it," he finished, looking at him.

"I'll be fine. I just need to get cleaned up," Petro answered, always ready to jump in and help.

Kim traced her finger around the outside perimeter of the estate. "Do we know if this wall is warded?"

Two stood up. "I took the liberty of checking before I came, knowing the target. It most certainly is warded; extremely nasty stuff. It is, as of right now, also enchanted with some type of barrier spell. It seems to be very specific. I don't think it will register a regular."

"Typical Mage. Max, how does it go again?" Kim prompted, marking an X by the main drive entrance.

"A bullet is still a bullet," I replied, looking up at Phil. "I say we take the Seekergate right into his front entrance. From there, Petro can tell us where he is. I'd rather Ben finds us in the entrance waiting for him. Do we know anyone who he gets along with?" I was starting to get a bad feeling about old Ben Franklin and his like of unexpected guests.

"No. He's that much of an ass. Probably why nobody has ever mentioned him around you," Frank said, looking over at Two as she nodded in approval. "It's settled then. Max, if you don't mind, we can gate to the Atheneum from here and get the team still assigned there to start tracking in the crucible room."

"I don't know if that's such a good idea. I'm already skeptical that we are not walking into a trap. Let's just keep this with Ed and the others on the dining room team," I said as the rest of the group agreed.

I looked at the knife Maman Brigitte had given me sitting on the shelf. Since returning, I hadn't had time to check it out or look into it. As soon as we got back, I was going to figure out why she had handed it to me.

"I'll go get my beauties ready," Phil said, referring to his fully automatic, 12-gauge, streetsweeper shotguns. Petro had already taken off to get himself put back together. I really needed to talk to the little guy as soon as we had time.

The dining room team was a term dubbed directly after the events with the Soul Dealers. The team included all the people present, Jenny, Ed, James, Dr. Freeman, Leshya, and only a handful of other trusted members. The funny part was that almost everyone reported to a different group or didn't work there. It was a place where trusted companions could talk.

Same as before, when we arrived at the Atheneum, there was an odd lack of ambient noise. We navigated through the front entrance, and from there, it was a straight shot to the dining room. James sat by the crudely installed entrance gate reading a magazine.

"No help tonight?" I asked as Petro landed on the table and the two bumped fists.

"As of this morning, our manning got cut again. It appears a group on the Council has decided this facility either doesn't need security or isn't as important as it once was. I was talking to Mouth earlier. He seems to think someone is doing it on purpose. In my opinion, since the Council finally realized digitizing the entire contents of the stacks is futile, they moved on to bigger and better things. They just transported a bunch of artifacts out of here a few days ago," James said.

It was clear James had sat there by himself with only

his thoughts for company. After a few seconds, his statement started to penetrate into my skull like a good brain freeze after chugging a slushy.

"What was Mouth doing here?" I asked, taking it one step at a time. The rest of the team, minus Petro, headed toward the dining room.

"He had a message for Ed from Carvel. Apparently, he had to give it to him in person. Let me tell you, that ogre was in a foul mood." James sighed.

"Why didn't he call us?" I whispered to myself.

"What was that? Why didn't Ed call you? That's an easy one. As he walked off, he pointed at my phone, took his out of his pocket, and turned it off. Whatever was in that note, it was private," James said, clearly not putting all the pieces together yet. The man was, besides Jenny, the smartest person around. Some would argue that it was Dr. Freeman. However, James was on a whole different level. He'd graduated from M.I.T before he could legally drink or smoke, neither of which he did.

"Hey, boss. I bet that ass clown Darkwater has something to do with this. Isn't he in charge of moving people around?" Petro asked, making one helluva point.

"I've got a bad feeling about this," I said, looking sternly at James. "Look, I think you need to be on your toes and alert. I'll talk to Kim and get some folks down here, but you don't need to be in this facility with only a handful of regulars."

The gravity of my statement clearly passed the smell test as James stood up. He took a few seconds to straighten his shirt and adjust his pistol belt.

"Things are about to get weird, aren't they," James asked in the form of a statement.

Petro, of course, had to make light of James's statement. "Oh yeah, they're going to get freaky," the Pixie replied as he did his extremely off-putting hip gyrations, smoothing his hair back before reaching for his now singed off mustache.

"Let me know what's up before you head out. I'll keep an eye on things. Sarah might stop by as well," James said, giving me a light salute.

I walked into the dining room just in time to hear Darkwater's name rolling off Ed's tongue. We had all come to the same conclusion about the security for the Atheneum.

"Right, let's hear this plan," Ed stated as Frank laid the map of Ben's house flat on the dining room table, reviewing the plans we had made earlier.

"Yes. I see. Hmmm, okay," Ed mumbled throughout Frank's briefing, finally landing on his grunt of approval. Even though I didn't need his go-ahead, I went through the ritual. It calmed my nerves and gave me time to think things out some more, the whole think-things-out-some-more part never really reaching its full potential.

Jenny stood up after hitting the return button on her keyboard hard enough to push the laptop through the table. She had been quiet during Frank's entire briefing. "There's not one damn thing right now that feels right. Dr. Freeman is still trying to figure out what artifacts were taken earlier. There seems to be a delay in getting the transfer paperwork sent back to us. This whole thing stinks of politics. This Voodoo angle doesn't make any sense to me."

Lacey and Macey flew over to Jenny's shoulders, speaking in unison. "We will protect everyone. No need to worry." Their voices sounded like angels singing a chorus in perfect step. I, without hesitation, believed them.

"Hey, we've got these," I said, holding up the glasses, having no clue.

CHAPTER 14

The Slings and Arrows of
Outrageous Fortune, and
Maybe Some Bullets . . .

O n a whim, I grabbed a bottle of water, stuffing it into the inside pocket of my enchanted trench coat, looking around the room. Over the past year, most of my focus had been on using my ability to manipulate water.

While I didn't have the same raw power as when I used hellfire, it had proved useful on more than one occasion. Not to mention, with the explanation about Ben and electricity, I had a feeling it would come in handy.

Everyone stood in the Postern geared up for the afternoon's events. Ed, Dr. Freeman, and Jenny would be staying behind, staffing the crucible room while keeping an eye on things from the sky; Kim had insisted they get one of those fancy drones. While the rest of the Mages and Fae poked fun at the acquisition, it had proven priceless. The magical world often let its ego get in the way of understanding how helpful or deadly technology could be.

The team was outfitted for a fight. Weapons clicked and the buzzing sounds of the Pixies filled the once calm space. Before breaking up our meeting earlier, I had recommended sending out an alert over a few select channels that we would be visiting Ben in the morning. This pretty much guaranteed that whoever was going to make a move on Ben would do it tonight.

"Check it out, boss," Petro said, handing me a small grenade.

"Alright, you got me. What does it do?" I asked, hoping whatever it was didn't go off in my hand.

"It's a whoosh grenade. You throw it up in the air and WHOOSH!" Petro exclaimed, making waving hand motions.

"What he's trying to say is that anything our size flying will find it rather hard to stay airborne. If one of the others throws one, they have to go to ground immediately," Casey again explained in a motherly tone. "Be safe and come back to me. Oh, and make sure Max doesn't die either."

I stood there staring at Casey and Petro. We absolutely needed to chat. I saluted Casey as she continued to tighten straps and hook equipment on the other Pixies.

Phil stood there, chewing an unlit cigarette with a shotgun slung over his back, his Thor wannabe hammer strapped to his side, and two pistols with long clips hanging off his hips.

"Well, I sure wish we had that drink earlier. We make it back in one piece . . . you owe us all a round," Phil declared as Two walked over, taking the cigarette out of his mouth. "Lass?"

"Ben is a little of a health freak. You might not want to light one up in his house. Plus, it's a nasty habit," Two said. The completely blank shield hiding her face gave no signs of emotion.

The body armor the Night Stalkers wore was state-of-the-art reflexive nanotechnology. Or something along those lines. Two sleek, thin pistols sat secured onto the leg sections. When she needed to use them, they simply popped out, no longer being part of the outfit. If she gave the barrel another push down into her shin armor, two six-inch-long silencers attached themselves. Even more impressive were the magazines, which also happened to be part of the armor.

Ed's voice came over the communicators. "Right, there's a report of Ethereal activity two miles away. It's time to move. It may be nothing, but . . ."

"It's game time," Phil finished, using his catchphrase. He, as always, was looking forward to justified violence.

I took a calming breath and let it out before I started talking. "Alright, just as planned. Phil, Petro, and I will use the Seekergate to drop in at the entrance, do a quick sweep of the area, and set up an Evergate stone. Once that's in place, we'll activate it, and the rest of you can come through. From there, you'll go to your designated locations. We'll then come back here and jump over to the main house. Everyone good?" I asked, surprised Frank was letting us go with it.

Kim nodded, still adjusting her rifle. She had remained oddly quiet throughout the conversation.

"Five minutes," Petro said as I cocked my head.

"Five minutes for . . . ?" I prompted as the other Pixies huddled around, exchanging small pieces of paper.

"Well, boss, the ladies and I have a little gentlemen's wager." Petro flew in front of me, forcing me to hold out my hand for him to land.

Two spoke up, much to the surprise of the group. "What's the bet?" She sounded interested.

"We are betting if the plan will last more than five minutes before it all goes to hell. I think we all know things are gonna get crazy tonight. The bet is just how long that takes," Petro explained as Two walked over to Casey, the official bet holder, handing her a crisp $100 bill. I wasn't sure where'd she pulled that from.

"Less than, at four minutes," was all she said as Petro rubbed his hands together.

"Why are you so happy?" I asked.

"I know you too well, boss. I did the point spread too. My guess is under two minutes."

I just nodded my head, agreeing.

I fist-bumped Petro as he took flight while I activated the Seekergate, stepping through into the cool night air.

The sound of cicadas and barking dogs filled the still night. Ben's house was located off the intracoastal, south of J. Turner Butler Boulevard. The estate was on its own, as Ben had evidently purchased the lots surrounding his property, filling them with trees and allowing the swamp to take a portion of the area over.

I looked around, letting my eyes adjust to the dark, seeing how well-manicured the property was.

"This is it. When the others come through, we have to move," I said, setting the Evergate stone on the ground, activating it. Two and Kim stepped through the shimmering wall immediately as Phil, Petro, and I walked back through into the Postern. Turning, I saw Macey and Lacey dart off behind Frank's back as it dissolved into the gate clearly closed from the other side.

Phil quickly slammed a cigarette in his mouth, lighting it, and took a handful of quick puffs as the Seekergate, knowing its new target, sprang back to life.

"Here goes nothing," Petro said, pulling out his sword as he darted through the gate before us. Phil put out his cigarette, grinning.

"Ladies first," he said, gesturing to me as we entered the gate.

The immediate lack of sound took me off guard, and I looked around the dimly lit entrance hall. I had been fully expecting an immediate issue with the homeowner.

"Don't say it, bruther," Phil warned, referring to my favorite Han Solo catchphrase.

"You mean, I have a bad feeling about this? Because I do," I replied as Petro zipped back over to us, having looked around the room.

"Hey, boss, I don't think we should move too much. This place is warded to the heavens above," he said, pointing his sword toward the long hallway going into the inner sanctum of the building.

"Any idea where our target is?" I scanned the room wondering.

Ben's house was not as I'd envisioned it. The place looked as if it was stuck in some odd, early 1990s time warp. Strange blue and purple colors mixed in abnormal patterns adorned the space. Black lacquer furniture with gold trim sat uniformly against the walls, including matching chairs, tables, and weird picture frames.

The floor was a cream color tile covered with a patterned carpet just as 1990s as the furniture. A winding staircase flowed up to a catwalk also leading off into the building.

"Hey, Phil?" I started before Petro could answer. "Let me guess. Ben checked out in the early '90s."

"Yup," was all Phil replied, also taking in the horrific furniture.

"I think he's upstairs. There's some weird magic floating around in here," Petro said, landing on my shoulder.

"Frank, you guys set?" I asked as I looked down at my castor, realizing we were about to hit the two-minute mark. Someone was about to lose money.

"Set and ready. Macey and Lacey are in position. Well, they were. It looks like they are heading this way . . ." Frank trailed off as Ed broke in over the radio.

"Incoming!" he bellowed over the communicators, making me wince.

A loud boom reverberated around the house, disturbing the dust that had been collecting on the picture frames.

"Frank, you good?" I asked as Phil cocked the charging handle on his shotgun.

"Busy; we will be fine for now. I don't think they expected us to be here," Frank replied as the sound of several muffled gunshots from Two's pistols barked in the background.

"They?" I looked at Phil and Petro as a flash of blinding white light interrupted the thought.

"Halt, you are trespassing on my master's property. Identify yourselves or be slain," the high-pitched yet determined voice came from around the room like a surround sound system turned all the way up.

The white light still blinded me as Petro, also not being able to see, slammed into my shoulder.

"Max Abaddon Sand. We're here to help Ben. We are from the Atheneum, and mean you no harm. I give you my word," I said, figuring that whoever I was talking to was more than likely not a regular. Words had meaning and carried weight in the magical and Ethereal worlds.

"Why didn't you just ring the doorbell or call my master, in that case?" an oddly dressed, chubby Pixie wielding a curved sword said, coming into focus as he landed on one of the black lacquered tables.

"Another Pixie!" Petro exclaimed as he flew over, dusting lightly in front of the older, plump version of himself.

"Oh, get that dust off the table," the Pixie scolded, obviously not understanding that the rest of the house needed an army of cleaners.

Another loud crash, followed by a bang, came from outside as something hit the side of the house, sounding as if it had broken into a million pieces. I was betting Macey and

Lacey were out there giving hell to whatever it was. They did, after all, carry some very nasty firepower on them.

Petro looked over as I nodded at him. I would leave the negotiation up to the Pixies.

For those of you not aware of magical or Ethereal customs, anytime one goes into someone's home—not house, but home—uninvited, a slight dance has to occur.

The lore and myths about Vampires having to be asked into one's home was an extension of Fae customs. If a Fae or a V were to enter someone's home without permission, they could become vulnerable. The Fae or V, while still lethal, would just be more prone to end up dead or hurt. Even Jenny had failed to explain the phenomenon. While it didn't pertain to Mages or other Earthborn people, the custom was taken seriously by the magical community.

After a few seconds of low murmuring, Petro buzzed over. "Hey, boss. I'd like to formally introduce you to William." The plump Pixie took flight a little slower than the others, heading over to me. I looked back at Petro to see him making the universal sign for someone who is absolutely crazy.

Phil and I just looked at each other as I held out my hand for the Pixie to land. Unlike Petro, this Pixie was heavy.

"I'd like to welcome you formally to Master Benjamin Franklin's home. King of the Kite, Master of the Double Glasses, an inspiration for the Declaration of Independence, author of "The Drinker's Dictionary" of 1737, and most importantly, Master of the Stairs," William said, taking a slight bow.

Phil just shrugged as I looked over at Petro. He again was making the universal symbol for crazy. "Willy, if you don't mind me calling you that, we don't have a lot of time for pleasantries. I need you to take us to Ben—I mean, your master," I corrected as the sound of orders being given came over the communicator. It was always a sign of respect to provide a Pixie with a name, the symbol much like giving them a gift.

"Okay, all right. Calm down," Willy replied as he raised both his hands into the air. "*Deflecto.*"

There were several subtle pops as the smell of ozone from whatever wards surrounded the entrance dissolved.

"Bruther, we need to get going," Phil urged with seriousness.

"Follow me," Willy indicated, taking off down the hallway.

Petro buzzed over, jumping on my shoulder and whispering in my ear, "He's crazy, boss. Full-on nutjob."

"Yeah, it sounds like it. And it's the crazy ones you need to worry about," I said as Petro nodded his head in agreement.

I was starting to get anxious to know what exactly was going on outside. As in most cases when people are in the heat of battle, radio chatter was nothing more than grunts, groans, screams, and yells of orders that made no sense to anyone other than the ones giving them, often thinking that people can listen and compute them in real time.

We walked up a small set of stairs leading up to a set of intricately carved double doors. The sounds of banging and clanking came from the other side, followed by a proclamation. "Shit!"

"Willy, we don't have a lot of time," I reminded him as Phil turned his back to us at the sounds of something crashing into the building hard enough to break through a wall.

The plump Pixie took off, zipping away. A few seconds later, the sounds of mechanical locks started clicking and clanking to life. As the heavily fortified boarded doors slowly started opening, it was immediately evident that Ben was trying to fit into battle gear that was significantly past its prime. Or more specifically, that didn't have enough notches in the belt to support his rounded figure.

"Master Ben, these people are here from the Atheneum

to help us," Willy informed, flying over to the table and picking up what looked like a small trident.

The three of us just stood there staring at the room. Old suits of armor sat rusting in one corner while axes, swords, and maces adorned the walls. Muskets and other various rifles from decades long since passed—or for that matter, centuries —also dangled at random intervals on hangers.

Topping it all off was a StairMaster exercise machine sitting in the middle of the room, with bandoliers of ammunition hanging off its sides.

"Master of the Stairs . . . ah, the stair master," I huffed under my breath as Phil snickered lightly. Ben literally had an exercise machine in the middle of his honest-to-God armory.

"It's about damn time you got here," Ben huffed, his voice educated, nasal, and generally not sociable. Grabbing a pencil, the man started drawing a notch on his belt while a blue glow emitted from his hand. The man had just drawn an extension for his belt, created out of thin air. Chaos magic was, as described, chaotic. Not to mention incredibly cool looking.

"Look, leave what you have. We've got to get you out of here. There are others outside we need to help," I said as Phil and Petro nodded, agreeing. The sooner we got Ben into the Postern, the faster we could get into the fight with the rest of the team.

The one thing I hadn't noticed immediately was what Ben was wearing. The man had on worn sweatpants, a pair of fuzzy slippers, and a souvenir T-shirt from Chuck E Cheese, not to mention an ammunition belt and a mop handle slung over his back. Upon closer inspection, he also had two small bags of paper clips hanging off his shoulders.

"This is what I get for being sober," Phil complained, shaking his head, also trying to figure out the man standing in front of us. Even though the room was full of weapons, Ben had decided on kitting up with office and cleaning supplies.

After seeing his handiwork with a pencil, I was starting to second-guess how dangerous he could be.

"I, more importantly, *we* are not going anywhere yet. We have to keep this place safe. Plus, if I'm right—which I usually am, mostly—whatever that is outside isn't going to stop until it's destroyed me," Ben said rapidly.

"Sounds like you knew it was coming. Phil, Petro, you guys good?" I asked, seeing Phil nod as Petro spoke up.

"I kinda wish Bo was around," he said, pulling out his sword, letting me know he was also good.

"You know that arrogant, overdressed shit of a demon?" Ben pulled out a handkerchief sneezing into it as his clothes transformed into crisp black fatigues.

"Yup, how do you know Bo?" I asked as more bumbling chatter came over the radio.

"He's in a cell in my basement with some shifter. I think his name is Lucian. I'll deal with them later," he said, finally picking up an old western-style six-shooter.

"I'm not going to ask how you got those two in a cage, but they are on our side. At least for today," I said as Ben guffawed.

"Hah! You're full of surprises. I thought those two had come to kill me. They showed up at my front door, wanting to talk about some artifact I used to have. Well, they are in my dungeon now." Ben shook his head. "William, please release our prison—I mean, guests. Max, I am putting my trust in you."

Willy snapped his fingers. Bo materialized in the middle of the room, holding out his arms with his mouth starting to crack. He did this when he was about to eat someone.

"Bo!" I shouted. He froze, slowly turning around while shifting his jaw back into place.

"Oh, hello, darlings. Are you all here for supper? Here I was, wanting to help someone find something, totally not getting involved, and they go lock me in a dungeon with a dog. Not a bad dog, mind you, but even I have standards as a prisoner. Oh, I get his lungs," Bo croaked as I again held my hands up.

"Everyone chill the hell out—" I started as Lucian ripped the doors off the hinges. He was in full wolf mode, drool falling from his mouth. To paint a clear picture, a shifter in their full form was, in most cases, three to four times larger than the animal they could turn into. Lucian was a beast, his maw large enough to rip a person in half without hesitation.

Phil looked over, barely reaching Lucian's shoulders. "Holy hell!" he barked, that being his only reaction.

The howl Lucian let out was ear-splitting. Ben started reaching into his bag of paper clips, but before he could pull anything out, I lit the room in hellfire, yelling, "*Ignis!*"

"Oh, someone's gone and done it now," Bo said as the room froze. Nothing quite got the attention of others as well as hellfire.

"Yo-yo-you can truly wield hellfire," Ben stuttered. "I thought it was just a rumor."

"Well, chalk that one up as true. Gods and graves, everyone needs to chill the hell out," I said as Lucian bowed his head slightly. Bo was signaling him. It looked as if he had some type of control or way to communicate with the shifter. I was starting to think the two were in cahoots. "There is whatever-the-hell-it-is outside trying to get Ben here. We need Ben in one piece. I'm sure he apologizes for locking you two up." I stared at Ben.

I knew Bo wouldn't move an inch unless an apology was involved. Demons were so damn dramatic.

"I must have made a dreadful mistake—" Ben was interrupted by a loud crash echoing from the main entrance, signaling that someone or something had made it into the house.

Bo took a breath, hearing the noise coming from the front of the house. "Accepted."

"For the love of the gods," Petro chimed in. "My offspring will be here before you all figure out who has the biggest goodies. Whatever it is, it's coming this way!"

Petro's statement caught me off guard. I squinted my eyes, looking at him as he shook his head. Bo and Ben did some kind of awkward handshake followed by grunts of acceptance. It wasn't over between the two.

"William," Ben called out, pulling out a handful of paper clips. "The wards?"

"I reactivated them when we left the entrance; we would already be fighting or gone if not. They have been tripped and breached. We are, I'm afraid, in for a good old-fashioned fisticuffs," Willy informed as I shook my head, hearing his old-timey reference. "I'll stay here and make sure our weapons are secure."

It was clear Willy was more of a lover than a fighter—or eater, by the looks of him. Petro dusted, grabbing a small dagger in his other hand. He was in full dual-wielding, eye-poking mode.

Thinking on my feet, I jumped on the communicator, pushing a little extra will into it to ensure everyone heard the message loud and clear. "Bo and Lucian are here. We are making a stand. Reinforcements are on the way."

"About time," Two replied, sounding winded for once.

Kim followed up as the sounds of her rifle releasing a flurry of death sang in the background. "Roger."

Macey and Lacey flew into the room, a trail of dust following them. "There are hundreds of them. They are like crafts, but not," Macey said as the chubby Pixie zipped over, putting out his hand.

"Hello," Willy greeted smoothly as we all let out a collective groan.

"Hey there, lumpy. Those are my sisters, and I'm pretty sure you don't have a chance. We got this handled," Petro said as Lacey winked at him.

Willy glanced over as Ben pointed toward a hole in the ceiling. The chubby Pixie launched into the dark void.

"We can't tell what they are. You can kill them, but more keep coming. Stars above, you are all here," Macey said, looking at Bo and Lucian, wrinkling her nose.

"Voodoo," I stated bluntly as Phil groaned.

"The glasses, boss!" Petro barked as I reached down, pulling them out. Ben just stood there staring at us. I had to admit, it was probably an odd scene.

"That's right. If you can find one of the guides, you will be able to shut them all down," Macey reminded us. I nodded.

"Or the head of the snake," I added, willing Durundle to spring from my hand. Ever since the sword had melded with my will, I was able to control how it acted. For today, it would be laser-like to avoid collateral damage.

Lucian let out a guttural howl while Bo just shrugged, turning into nightmare fuel in front of the group. Ben gagged slightly.

"It's on!" Phil bellowed, running out into the hallway as Bo and the Pixie crew followed. Lucian looked over, pointing his snout toward his back, huffing.

Without hesitation, I leaped using my enhanced demon-fueled power, landing as gracefully as a roller skater on acid. After a second of adjustment, I grabbed a handful of fur as Lucian launched forward. Looking back, I saw Ben running as fast as the shifter, his shoes glowing blue on the marble floor of the hallway.

The large foyer of the house was in a state of utter disarray. Two was slicing through ghouls with a sword in one hand while releasing laser-like single shots from her pistol with the other.

Frank had an odd trait. Large Wolverine-type claws protruded from his hands as he ripped into the mindless onslaught. I almost panicked before finally seeing Kim behind the second-floor railing, overlooking the swarm and cutting through the remaining ghouls which got past the team.

Lucian and the others were also taking stock of the battle. Phil, as always, dove headfirst into the turmoil.

Kachunk, kachunk, kachunk, echoed from his shotguns as several of the creatures vaporized in front of him. At the same time, the Pixies flew to the ceiling, picking select targets before starting their surgical-like dive-bombing for eyes.

The biggest surprise came from Ben, who jumped over the banister slinging a handful of paper clips. They reshaped, forming burning needles of molten metal, and slammed into a group of ghouls by the front door.

Lucian's back muscles flexed as I patted his fur lightly. The hellfire blade was emitting a red strobing light, getting the attention of the creatures. I scanned the ghouls through the enchanted glasses, seeing two in particular hanging back toward the entrance, not engaging the room.

"There are more flowing into the building," Ed warned over the communicator, looking at the live video feed.

"Yeah, figured that part out," I told Ed as I pointed toward the door when Lucian looked back. "I'm hitting the group at the doors."

"Clearing a path, boss," Petro replied, cussing as he clicked off the communicator. There were at least two hundred of the small-sized ghoulish creatures in the entrance hall.

"You ready to go?" I asked the shifter, who launched through the air slamming headfirst into a small group of ghouls, turning them into piles of gore as they evaporated. The sound of the impact was jarring. A searing pain darted through my calf as Lucian ripped another ghoul in half with his jaws.

Swiping down, the ghoul that had stabbed my leg was already on the ground with a perfectly placed shot between its eyes. Kim was keeping an eye on me. Several more rounds whizzed by, hissing and cracking upon impact in the center of another group.

Petro and Macey flew by at eye-blurring speed, dropping two dissolution grenades which immediately got rid of several ghouls. As soon as the group dissolved, Lucian lurched forward again, turning sideways, allowing me to jump down.

The pain from my leg felt like a jolt of electricity surging through my body. My temper was finally peaking as I swung my hellfire blade around at lightning speed, slicing through several of the ghouls which had just launched toward us.

A crack reverberated as I backed up to Lucian, the both of us taking on the initial push of creatures funneling through the door.

"I need to get to those two taller ones!" I screamed. The noise from the gunfire and fighting was becoming overbearing.

Without hesitation, Lucian barreled to the front entrance like a bulldozer as ghouls went flying through the air, the crunch of the impact sounding like a car crash.

"I guess that works," I murmured as I slung a small ball of hellfire at a group that had turned around, heading back to the entrance. Come to think of it, every ghoul in the room was now turning to protect their masters. They must have realized what we were doing.

"Boss!" Petro came over the radio as the sounds of Phil's shotguns stopped. It was hammer time. Pardon the pun.

The two larger ghouls started pivoting out of the entrance as Lucian turned toward them from outside the house.

The shifter had passed by them, continuing to bulldoze the herd to buy us some time.

The two ghouls moved first, launching spiked projectiles as a group slammed into Lucian while he was distracted. I threw another ball of hellfire; it slammed into the frame of the entrance. Wood flew in several directions and I swung around, finding Two standing there with her back to me, surgically slicing through ghouls.

Seeing the end was near, the two larger ghouls leaped forward as their arms turned into thin piercing spikes. I swung Durundle down, slicing through the arm of the first large ghoul that reached me. The creature reared back, not feeling pain, slamming its other spiked arm at my side, throwing me back several feet.

A howl erupted from outside; Lucian was clearly in distress. The two doorkeepers were on top of me by the time I got to my feet. I took a second, finally seeing the blank, featureless faces of the creatures. They weren't thinking or calculating. These monsters were made for one function only, and that was to kill their target.

Before I could take a full steadying breath, the featureless creatures started swinging their spikes, avoiding my hellfire blade. I pulled my will together, launching a small hellfire ball directly into and through the chest of the already injured ghoul.

The hellfire started burning it from the inside out. While I could launch several rounds of hellfire, I wasn't an endless pit of energy. Throwing everything I had all at once was a bad idea.

Its partner didn't hesitate as the other fell to its knees. The creature slammed into me as I once again flew backward several feet, this time catching myself. To be honest, the demon part of my body was extremely handy in a fight, not to mention the extra few inches of height and extra pounds of muscle it had packed on. I glanced over, seeing the group in the foyer almost cleared out. Then it dawned on me as Lucian let out another howl. He was taking the brunt of the fight outside.

The second ghoul pulled back for another swing as I slammed Durundle through its chest while slinging another ball of hellfire into its head, dissolving the creature's upper half instantly. Unlike the other ghouls, these two didn't dissolve into nothingness.

As if the thought was a light switch, every other creature started combusting, turning into ash. The air filled with gray dust as the team settled into the reality of what had just happened.

The sound of Lucian whimpering drew everyone's attention to the front door as calm finally took hold. Ben was back on the top rail standing over Kim. I looked around the room, conflicted. Something wasn't right. I pulled the glasses off, finally running toward the stairs.

"Petro! Go check on Lucian! Where the hell is Bo?" I yelled as Phil ran out the door after Petro. Two and Frank stood there, looking around the room. Vs had an odd way of reacting to violence. They were scanning for other threats, staying alert, letting the rest of the group reset.

By the time I made it to Kim, the injury on my leg was ensuring I knew it was there. Kim was lying on her back with a small pool of blood coming from under her body. A red hole the size of a golf ball directly above her armored chest plate stained her clothes.

"No, no, no . . ." I said frantically, kneeling down, grabbing Kim's hand.

"Oh, hey. Is it over?" Kim asked, clearly in distress. The touch of her hand was cooling.

"Yeah, it's going to be okay," I said as Ed came over the communicators with an ETA for medical help which primarily consisted of Jenny, one of the best Life Mages in the Southern United States.

"Good. We still going to get that drink later?" Kim asked, not seeing the pool of blood under her body or the wound.

"Sure thing," I replied as a light tear streaked down my face.

"Oh shit, it's bad, isn't it? I can't go out like a bad scene in a cheesy novel," she said, coughing out a light laugh as blood percolated onto her lips.

I looked up to see Ben pulling out a section of his underwear, rolling it into a ball, and cutting it off while blowing on it. Light blue mist flowed from his lips as a loud bang came from outside.

Kim, who was lying at an angle, was able to see what Ben was doing. "He touches me with that, I'm going to kick both of your asses," she warned before her eyes rolled back into her head, passing out.

"Ben," was all I could initially muster as the man leaned over, placing the piece of undergarment on the wound. "You help her, and I promise on my life, you will make it out of this alive."

"That's a rather tall order there, hellfire boy. This will stabilize her," Ben said as the blood under her body started retreating as if it was being sucked back in.

"What the hell?" I asked, confused.

"Magic," was all he replied as he stood, taking a breath while looking around at the wreck of his home.

I started to relax before I realized what was happening outside the front double doors. Frank and Two were standing by Lucian. Angel, who had gone two years without letting us know for sure it was her, had taken off her helmet and was petting the massive wolf, breaking her oath.

Bo also stood by the others with a large gash on his

cheek. Petro zipped over to me as if reading my mind.

"Hey, boss. Is she going to be okay?" he asked, landing on my shoulder, dusting it lightly. His chest was heaving, as he had not landed throughout the battle. For once, Petro had come out of the fight without any injuries.

"Ben here thinks so," I replied as Ben walked down to join the others. "What's going on down there?"

"Lucian isn't going to make it. He killed hundreds of those things before they could get in here, giving you time to..." Petro trailed off, realizing I would carry the weight of Lucian's death.

I sat back, still holding Kim's limp hand. "You did good, kid." I smiled at Petro as he just shook his head.

"Hey, boss, Bo is down there saying something about almost getting the main one. He said he cut her right arm up pretty badly before she just disappeared into thin air," he changed the subject.

"Her? Can you wait here with Kim for a minute?" I requested as Petro buzzed down lightly, taking her hand out of mine. He dusted it slightly as some of her color started to return.

"I got this, boss. I can feel her heart beating," Petro said, reassuring me.

Walking over to Lucian, Angel nodded as Frank shook his head, confirming Lucian was about to take the final trip. Bo and Phil were standing in front of the shifter with their heads hanging low. I often forgot how death, or what the magical community called the final death, affected others.

I reached my hand out, petting the beast's tuft of fur next to his mangled snout. "Can he not shift back?" I asked Bo as he shook his head.

"No, he lost too much power. He will take the journey like this," Bo said solemnly.

"Did you know him?" I asked, understanding the age of most of the other creatures surrounding me.

"Yes, I did. More to the point, Tom did too, as well as Ed. This will not go unnoticed."

Frank walked over. "He's right. Even I had a few run-ins with the big lug. Someone will need to contact his pack."

Looking Lucian in his deep brown eyes, I started talking, not realizing the words coming out of my mouth.

"I didn't get to know you very well, but I wish I had. You are a warrior. I will make this right," I vowed as he let out a calming whimper. It was peaceful and full of accepted understanding. The creature paused, a slight grin perking up the edge of his mouth, before Lucian let out his final breath.

Bo cleared his throat. "Let us pray. May your final journey be swift, and your courage be remembered throughout the years. Your final resting place is yours to choose, as true warriors are not frightened by the unknown. Lucian," Bo finished as the others repeated his name in some type of ritual. The lines of Heaven and Hell again blurred as Bo, a demon, prayed over the fallen warrior.

CHAPTER 15

Puzzle Pieces

"**A**re you sure you don't need me?" I asked Phil as he stood by the door to leave the Postern.

"Aye, it shouldn't take too long. I have a feeling we'll be doing more talking later with Ana, Davros, and Titus. They just want an update. Plus, you need to get Ben here all sorted out," Phil replied as Petro landed on the round table in the middle of the room.

Willy was already sitting there, exhausted from whatever it was he was doing during the fight.

"You mean since Lucian was a possible murder suspect, and the real shitbag escaped," I clarified, referring to whoever the hell it was we were after trying to pin the initial murder on Lucian.

"Something like that," Phil said, not wanting to repeat the statement.

While being a pretty crappy perspective on the situation, it could buy us some much-needed time, plus keep the Council's hands out of things. But if we were pressed to answer truthfully, we would have to. Lucian was a hero, not the murderer of the initial victim.

This, of course, would lead to the situation being escalated. Though it had already deteriorated, a few select members of the Supreme and Senior Council suspected Councilman Darkwater's involvement.

As Phil left, Ben walked to the table where Petro was standing next to Willy. "So, are you going to bother telling me why I'm standing in the middle of the Postern with Tom's grandson?"

"I'm trying to figure that out myself. Well, I'm guessing Bo is still a little aggravated with you somehow locking him up, not to mention Lucian," I said forcefully, making my point. Bo had disappeared as always as soon as more people started arriving.

Ben let out a huff. "I guess you're right. If it weren't for everyone there, I would probably be . . . well, let's just say, not here."

"Tell you what. Let Petro and I ask the questions, and after that, I'll talk to you about anything you want," I compromised, pulling out a few trinkets from my blazer, including the knife Maman Brigitte had given me.

As soon as the jewel-encrusted gold item hit the table, Ben's eyes widened. "Where did you get that?" Ben took a step away from it.

"You know what this is?" I asked as Petro gave me a quick side glance.

"Unfortunately, yes. It was one of the items listed on a recent insurance claim," Ben murmured, taking a closer look around the room.

"Well, boss," Petro started. "It sounds like we have another piece of that puzzle. Why don't you tell us what this knife does? It stinks to high heaven of black magic."

"I know you were on the *Event Horizon* last year. I also happen to know why, and the other proceedings that transpired on that ship," Ben said, giving me a stern look. "Funny thing, the knife was reported to be in the keep of several recently deceased individuals. I never had it, so I'm guessing that was all a rumor. I wonder who put that out there?"

"Okay, now that we have that out of the way. What does the knife do, and what can you tell me about the location of Bruce Teach?" I asked, genuinely curious about what the man knew. It didn't take long to realize he wasn't on the wrong side of things, but it was evident that he was out for himself.

"If you think Bruce had something to do with what just happened, you would be dead wrong. Bruce does his own dirty work. Not to mention, I'm pretty sure I'm somehow working for him through this claim. This leads me to another point. Why does somebody want to kill me?" Ben asked, not giving an inch. He wanted answers, as did I.

"I think someone's trying to flush Bruce out. I'm sure you know about the other deaths—that was evident by the wards and the fact that you were armed to the gills when we showed up," I said. "I have it on pretty good authority that he needs this claim to go through. I never thought in a million years a wizard pirate—or whatever the hell he is—would need money and would try to get it through an insurance claim."

Ben let out a bubbling laugh.

"Bahahah. Dear boy, things of value aren't always money or gold. I'll just leave it at that. The knife is an artifact that supposedly went down with the ship. From what I understand, that knife can cut through reality. I do believe Dr. Freeman works here; you may want to ask him. Long story short, it's one of the few ways to get to the legions, or you-know-who's place, if you know what I'm talking about," Ben said, winking.

After last year's operations in the Everwhere, the majority of things that had occurred were deemed classified by the Council and the civilian government. Ben appeared to be an extremely well-informed senior fitness instructor.

"Okay, I get that piece. I'll buy what you're selling. Someone gave this to me, basically stating it would draw the right people's attention—or wrong, for that matter. Why would Bruce want this knife?" I asked as Willy stood up.

"To release someone, or get to you-know-who," Willy answered, age and wisdom coming through in his words, unlike before.

"Yeah, but—" I started, cutting myself off. I'd never really considered what would happen if I killed someone like Beleth in the Everwhere.

"Oh no, Max. It's not Beleth. I'm afraid he is very dead; you saw to that. He may be in the shadows, but who truly knows. No, you're too busy looking down at the demons. Have you ever looked up at the angels? More specifically, one they call the Angel of Death, Mengele. I'm not so sure that one took the trip. Not to mention Tom," Ben ended in the form of a statement, not a question.

Petro spoke up. "Is you-know-who, you-know-who?"

It was clear I was the odd man out in the conversation. "You-know-who" seemed to represent hundreds of people whose names you didn't exactly want to say out loud, like deities, gods, false gods, and immortal/celestial beings who thought it was funny to show up uninvited.

"That's the one," Willy confirmed as Ben just shrugged.

"Alright! Who is it?" I asked. "You guys do know we are in the Postern. What happens in the Postern, stays in the Postern."

"I would be remiss not to mention that I'm still curious about why we are here. And to answer your question, Hades," Ben said as I let out a whistle. I was still figuring out what was real and what wasn't.

Learning that Hades was, in fact, a real person or whatever, took me off guard. Lana had mentioned him the year prior; I had, as with most things, just filed it away with the rest of the things I couldn't bring myself to comprehend.

"So let me guess, this is another one of those the-world-is-doomed things?" I asked, figuring I needed to use my *oh, shit* meter.

"Hell if I know. I wouldn't think so. You did make a promise to me, and I expect you to keep that," Ben said, clearly ready to end the conversation and ensure his continuing longevity.

"So here's the plan. I'm going to leave you here. More specifically, with the Messenger. I've gotten to know him over the years, and it's about the most secure place I know," I said as Ben nodded.

Petro opened the box sitting on the round table in the center of the room. Inside were several keys lined up on a green piece of felt, with Tom's Postern journal nestled to the side. I picked up the key to the Messengergate as Petro looked at the two other keys sitting there.

I still had to figure out how to use the key that had come out of the broken clock my mom had gifted me on my rebirthday. According to the journal, it had something to do with time, but Tom's writing was vague on this key. I did know it had something to do with the Mirrorgate.

The other key had just been gifted to me by Titania, the Fae Queen. From what I understood, not too many people—or Fae—had ever met her. She stayed on the Plane and didn't take vacations to the other realms.

The key she had gifted me looked very much like the one used for the Planesgate. It would, if the journal was correct, take me to the Plane. It looked simple to use. However, several dozen question marks surrounded the drawing and included notes such as *Not sure how to get back? Where does it come out? Is the location safe? Will this be the same as the Council's Plane's gate? Will I keep my powers?* The list went on enough to tell me he had no clue and wasn't in a rush to find out. The Council, after all, only had one gate that was able to shift to the Plane.

Petro, seeing my lingering thoughts, chimed in. "Hey, boss, when Ben gets set up, we can go check on Kim."

"I was thinking the same thing. Ben, here," I said, handing him a pack of provisions. We also kept several bug-out bags in the Postern for emergencies, which included a few days' supply of food and water. It probably wouldn't be necessary, since the Messenger was a reasonably good host.

"Alright, I'll take your word. I've heard stories about the Messenger. This might be interesting." He looked at me. "Max, I don't know how that knife made its way to you. It was the vessel by which the Thule Society almost released the legions. I'm not a hero—well, not anymore, at least—but that knife . . . it needs to go back to its rightful owner." Ben pointed down.

"Hades, it needs to get back to Hades. I get it. Why can't we just destroy it?" I asked as Willy perked up.

"Good luck with that. Ben here tried to destroy a gate key by tying it onto a kite, trying to get a bolt of lightning to destroy it. Well, you know how the rest of that story goes. Now that key is sitting in that very box of yours," Willy chortled, pointing at the key to the Mirrorgate. The one true path to the Everwhere.

"I'll see what I can do. Look, this has been very interesting, but we need to get moving," I said, activating the gate as it shimmered to life.

After ten minutes of waking up the Messenger and supplying him with a piping hot cup of coffee, Ben and the ancient man were already talking about the best methods of sending letters to the Plane in modern times.

Last year I'd spent several days with the Messenger working out what Plane of existence he precisely occupied. According to the old, dust-covered man, the Messenger Room was very much on Earth, but he had forgotten his name roughly three hundred years ago and the space was so large it disappeared into dark voids on all sides, so I was skeptical.

The Messenger sat at an ancient desk to which he was chained. On the desk sat two boxes: one for incoming messages and one for outgoing. When I'd first arrived in the room, it had not been used in several years. Jamison and I'd thought the man was dead at first glance. But nope, he was alive, and that was where I'd started my super great relationship with Councilman Carvel.

Walking back into the Postern, I closed the gate as Petro turned to face me. "Alright, we seem to be alone for once. What has had you all sideways the last few days?"

"Well, boss. You know that I have a life debt with you and all," Petro started sheepishly, landing on the desk.

"I get that part. Spit it out. You're killing me, smalls," I said, lightening the mood.

Petro rubbed the back of his neck, dusting lightly. "I'm kinda going to have a problem with that moving forward."

"Uh-huh, I see. Okay, so . . ." I drawled out, looking down at my phone as it buzzed.

Petro started spilling his guts in a blast of information, getting higher and faster as he talked. "Casey's with child; pregnant, as you say. I'm pretty sure it's mine, and that means I'll have blood kin to attend to and can't honor my oath to you. I was trying to keep it a secret. I'm not sure why, but I'm going to have to learn how to speak baby and change undergarments and feed it. Oh, and I heard I need to have a party for Casey, and then I have to be home by nine. At least according to the book. Then I might have to take a break from all this!"

I sat there, taking in everything Petro had just said. It was like sitting through a ten-second parenting class. A grin smoothed across my face. I was getting worried Casey was giving him an ultimatum. Come to think about it, I was pretty sure I'd just heard it.

"You are clear and free of your debt to me. Consider it fulfilled, based on saving my life, I don't know, a shit ton of times," I said as the weight of the world lifted from Petro's shoulders. It was the kind of shift that happened after bringing your first girlfriend home and finding out your parents actually liked her.

"So, we're not partners anymore?" Petro asked as a mixed look of excitement and confusion landed on his face.

"Slow down there, old man. You're not getting rid of me that easily. You're stuck with me as a partner until we can't partner anymore. We are unofficially official partners. Hell, we don't really work for the Council anymore unless hired," I said, referring to Abaddon and Associates, AA for short.

AA was our consulting firm, which had pretty much ended up being on full-time retainer for the Council. This, of course, kept us out of the normal realm of rules. What sucked was the fact that I was still a member of the Council, just not working for it most the time, to be clear as mud. Either way, it was a great relationship. But I didn't expect to ride the line between the two much longer. I was getting pulled back in more by the day, since Jenny's castor business had gone belly up.

"Thanks, boss. I guess I was just nervous. You're kind of like the only real family I have here other than the lady Pixies and Phil," Petro said, flying over, forcing me to hold out my hand for him to land. In the Pixie world, this was a sign of trust.

"I'm excited. We just need to make sure Casey is good and gets plenty of rest. Hey, that reminds me," I changed the subject now that the emotional bit was over, "Leshya wanted to talk to me a few days ago. Any idea what that was all about?"

"Oh yeah. I saw her the other day. She was all doom and gloom, then came over and told me the same thing. She needs to talk to you. Honestly, I can barely remember what happened yesterday," Petro said, making a good point.

"Agreed. Everything's been going at the speed of light. Hell, I just got a message that Planes Drifter was postponed again till tomorrow. They want to keep the grounds shut down for one more day. I'm guessing after tonight, the Council will be poking into things more than they are already. I still haven't been able to talk to Phil about all the crap that happened with Maman Brigitte," I said, picking up the jewel-encrusted knife.

"What about Bo?" Petro asked, making another damn good point.

"That's the next thing. He seems to be awfully busy with something other than everything else going on. Bo keeps disappearing as soon as the dust settles. I wish Belm were here to figure out what he is doing. I'll see if I can get Devin's attention. Come to think of it, he's been awfully quiet lately as well," I said as Leshya, having heard her name, walked in through the main door.

Petro and I just stared at her. She moved with ghostlike grace. Leshya was creepy yet beautiful in an innocent way which only a craft, or from what I guessed, a spirit could pull off.

"Hello. I've been wanting to talk with you," Leshya greeted as her hair moved in the still air, much like the tapestries hanging around the Atheneum.

"Where your ears burning . . . never mind, don't answer that. I'm guessing you just heard your name and popped in," I said, wondering how she and others did that.

"I suppose. I'm not really sure. Coming here just felt like the right thing to do," Leshya explained dreamily, holding out a bag clearly labeled Max.

"You brought me a sandwich?" I asked as she nodded. "I could kiss you!" I exclaimed. She stepped back.

"I don't think that would be a good idea. There is enough

for both of you in there. It's your favorite," Leshya said, doing what I considered a smile for her.

"I'm all ears. Things have just been crazy around here." I grabbed one of the chairs leaning against the wall, pulling it over to the table before I opened the bag. My leg was still throbbing, needing a rest. Jenny had been able to get the bleeding to stop, but I was pretty sure as soon as I took the wrap she'd provided off, I wouldn't be able to do much in the way of running. Or walking, for that matter.

The one plus of being a mixed bag of tricks in the gene pool was my uncanny ability to heal at an accelerated rate. Jenny, as well as the others, had made it extremely clear that I needed to keep that little parlor trick to myself.

Inside was a cucumber and cream cheese sandwich with Everything seasoning on it. I never knew I liked these till she made me one. It was a favorite of Tom's.

"I'm sure you are aware the Council came and secured several of the artifacts in the Atheneum," Leshya started, pausing to allow me to respond.

"That's right, I almost forgot about that," I replied, clarifying that I had no idea what had happened and why.

"Well, they only took what they could see." Leshya again paused. I nodded, taking a bite of the sandwich, letting her know to continue.

"They couldn't access the restricted section in the stacks. It made Councilman Darkwater very upset. You remember the one room sticking out in the middle of the floor?" Leshya again paused.

"I do, if memory serves, omphh, ampph," I said, chewing while talking. "Only Tom could get into the main safe, and Ed could access the books in there. Or something like that. Do you think they were looking for something?"

Leshya pointed at the knife still sitting on the table.

"I heard them talking about it. Councilman Carvel was here. He didn't seem happy. I know how that knife got here, you know, before it was given to you." I swore I heard her giggle lightly.

"I think we both know how it got here. I'm starting to think that knife didn't go down with the ship, as Ben mentioned," I said, starting to see a few of the puzzle pieces lining up.

"Ben Franklin?" Leshya asked.

"Yup, that's the one. He's with the Messenger until we figure all this out. I'm sure you heard someone is trying to kill him," I said as Petro grabbed the crust from the second perfectly cut sandwich triangle.

Leshya just scowled. It was clear nobody liked old Ben. "The Council comes from time to time and gathers certain things from here. From what I was told, they are consolidating as many artifacts as possible due to the recent disappearance of several possibly dangerous items. They don't know about the others."

"The others? Tom never really told me what was in the restricted vault," I stated, getting a sinking feeling in my stomach. "They know that Tom is . . . well, you know."

I was starting to think the entire sideshow of taking away some of the artifacts was an excuse to snoop around. Since moving out of the facility, it had become clear that things often shifted around the place.

Leshya just nodded in agreement. This was the first time in years I had had this involved of a chat with her. "If you use that knife, it will get the attention of whoever it is everyone's looking for," she said, picking up the blade before setting it down and grabbing the key Titania gave me.

"These two items are connected by make." Leshya held them both up. She was right. The key and the dagger had the same muted glow of gold, with identical gems inlaid in the handles.

"Great, things keep getting better. Which one of these was in the restricted area?" I asked as Leshya pointed at the knife.

"Someone's been in the vault . . ." I trailed off. Tom had somehow gotten that dagger to Maman Brigitte.

The door at the far end of the restricted area was an old-style safe. It was eight feet high and four feet wide, and I'd never thought about how big the safe was on the inside. I did know the restricted book section was the size of a small house, with shelves at odd angles and locked cases, some glass, some solid iron, and some silver.

"What's behind the door?" Petro cut in. I wanted to know the same thing.

"Treasures beyond your wildest imagination; I think that is how you say it. There is also a gate there. One that is made to keep others out. It was made with that knife," Leshya said as she started to turn.

"Is that all? Can you help us get into the safe?" I asked as she stopped.

"You can get in. Nothing is stopping you now. You just can't get in from here." Leshya turned with finality and continued to walk away.

Petro and I looked at each other at the same time, spitting out something we hadn't considered before. "The Everwhere!"

"Right on, buddy. I keep forgetting that's how Tom got things done most of the time. Look, we need to get focused on who's doing this. I think we know who they are trying to flush out at this point and why. Revenge." I let the word circulate in my mouth before changing the subject.

"Ready to see Kim? I have a hunch. She's being kept at the

Council halls in the medical wing. I didn't even know that was a thing," I finished, finally letting the word revenge settle in my thoughts.

"Sure thing, boss. But I need to check on the missus first, and I'm pretty sure you need to get some rest. Your leg stinks. Whatever they hit you with was full of black magic. Good thing you're mostly immune to it," Petro said, flying into the air while rubbing his now full belly.

"Alright then. First thing in the morning, we gate out," I said, realizing the truth of his statement. I needed to get some rest.

CHAPTER 16

Regrets . . . I Have a Few

"**B**ollocks," Phil said as Jenny huffed loudly.

"I mean it. She doesn't need a bunch of people bothering her. Kim needs to get some rest," Jenny explained as Phil, Petro, and I stood at the door to Kim's room.

The Council's headquarters' hospital wing was just as eclectic and oddly styled as the rest of the sprawling facility. The Council halls' actual location was still up for debate, as you could only gate in and out. Dark solid stone walls set the stage for the rest of the medical wing, which happened to be decked out in modern equipment and lighting. It felt like being in a hi-tech cave underground, the aroma of wet stone overtaking the usual hospital smell.

"Look, at this point, if I don't fill her in on the rest of my evening, I'm likely to need a hospital," I said. Phil and Petro blindly nodded, agreeing.

Jenny let out another huff. "You're probably right. One hour, you three. Oh, and the Council has called a meeting on the events leading up to Kim being here. I think they know Bo is floating around. Phil, Kristi was also looking for you earlier."

I opened the door, finding Kim hooked up to several machines making beeping noises. The good news was that she was sitting up and drinking a juice box.

"Took you guys long enough," Kim said, reaffirming she was in the land of the living.

"What's the word?" I asked, looking around the room for one of those clipboard things doctors always wrote important stuff on. I guess in the magical world, things didn't work like that.

"Well, it seems I'll be here for a few days. Whatever they hit me with was part of one of those creatures—Jenny had some long term for it—but I need to stay here under observation. So?" Kim urged in an aggravated tone. She wanted to know what Ben had to say.

"Looks like the murders, the knife I showed you, an insurance claim from the boat Ned died on, and Ben are all connected to someone out to get Bruce Teach," I said, trying to dumb things down so I could understand them. To be clear, I didn't fully.

"Some lady you mean, boss," Petro corrected, noting what I had told him about Bo's comment.

"That's right. Bo said he went toe to toe with some Voodoo-wielding disguised madwoman who was driving that shit show yesterday. It sounded like it was a stalemate. I haven't seen him since," I said as Kim squinted her eyes.

"I know that look on your face," Kim said accusatorily. "You have an idea of who's behind all this."

I shrugged as Phil and Petro both looked at me. "Do you know, bruther?" Phil asked smoothly.

"Maybe. It's a hunch, or possibly just a scary coincidence. I'm not ready to say anything till I check a few things out," I answered as Kim looked down at my wound.

"I noticed you stepping lightly when you walked in. How's the leg?" she asked, shifting the subject. She would figure out a way to bring it back up in a minute.

"Got hit by the same stuff you did. I'll be fine, just not running any marathons. Hey guys, you mind if I talk to Kim for a few minutes privately?" I said as Phil grinned.

"I need a smoke anyway, and to try and find Kristi. Keep the patty-cakes to a minimum. Let's go, little warrior," he said as Petro hitched a ride on his shoulder.

"Hey, guys," Kim called out to the two as they reached the door. "The person doing this needs to be stopped. It's clear they don't care about collateral damage. Stay focused."

"Yes, ma'am!" Petro exclaimed as the two men saluted her, walking out the door.

"Am I in trouble, or are you about to confess your undying love for me?" Kim said jokingly.

"I'm just worried about you. We never got a chance to talk before last night, and then things got crazy. I don't want to leave things like that," I replied in a hushed tone.

The look on Kim's face said it all. It wasn't a frown but the look of lonely sadness. It was clear things between us had been slipping. I sat there, thinking about how solid they had actually been in the first place. My thoughts must have come across in my expression as well.

"After we get this wrapped up, I'm going to need a break," Kim said, cocking her head to one side. The machine on her right started beeping faster. Her heart rate was up.

I sat there, working to compute what she was saying, looking for clarity. "From me?" I asked, walking closer to the bed.

"Max, this isn't anything to do with you. It's everything. This world, my job . . . well, you to a point. Last year was amazing, but as the days go by, I keep realizing something," Kim admitted as I grabbed her hand lightly, the gesture forcing a smile on her face.

"What, that Phil is an ass?" I said as we both chuckled.

"I've known you for almost four years now. I remember walking into the office and seeing you sitting there, passed out, with chip crumbs all over your shirt. Max, that was roughly four years ago. I'm about to be thirty-five years old, and you've aged what, a few months?" The statement landed on me like a sledgehammer.

She was right. I hadn't put much thought into it. There had been three major events over the past several years which for me seemed like they had just happened yesterday. For Kim, time was marching on. I loved her, and she knew it. But I had taken time for granted. My mother had warned me about time when this had all first started. I decided not to argue the point.

"What are you going to do?" I asked, shifting away from talking her out of whatever she had made her mind up on.

"I'm going to take a leave of absence and spend some time with my parents back home in Colorado. I'll be back, I promise. It's just . . . things are not what they used to be before the Balance. Last night, I realized just how powerful things are in this world. I mean, if you could see yourself through my eyes. You've grown almost six inches and put on pounds of muscle. You can do things I can only imagine. Max, other Mages and Ethereals are scared of you, and the funny thing is you don't even see it. But I don't think it will be long before they try to address that, and I'll be here for you when that time comes," Kim said in a mix of explanation and advice.

"I know. I feel it every time I walk into a room with others. Not the team, just everyone else. Listen, I trust your judgment. I know deep down things are in motion. Get some rest. I'm going to go do what I do best," I said as we both smiled.

"What's that, drink yourself into a stupor and sing old Billy Joel songs? Oh, then figure out the answer to everything once you sober up?" Kim joked. I pulled back, smiling, showing every last tooth in my mouth.

"That's precisely what I'm going to do," I retorted as she

beamed a smile back. "Text me before you leave."

"Oh, once this is all buttoned up, you still owe me dinner before I leave town," Kim declared while I held the smile. Her saying she was leaving again punched me in the gut.

I walked out the door to find the others gone. Standing in the dull glowing light, the realization kicked in that Kim had just put an end to our relationship. At least at this moment of time and space.

Thoughts swirled in my mind of ways to keep Kim from growing old. It was poetic. She was right. I had been blind and naive about the passage of time and the strain on the world around her. While Kim had on a strong face, it was clear she was hurting from the injury.

Since the Balance, there were still people who had yet to meet a Mage or Ethereal. Then there were people like Kim, living in both worlds, not truly having an identity. I then realized I had forgotten she was a regular. The team had grown so accustomed to her being in the fight that we all took it for granted. Dr. Freeman was only allowed to monitor the team when he was involved. He was also a regular, and the team would never put him in harm's way. This would never happen again.

***

"Bruther, there you are. We thought you might have gotten lost," Phil bellowed as I walked into the office of the Artifact Retrieval Team. Ed had been put in charge of it last year as a symbolic slap on the wrist.

I thought it was odd that Ed had not been involved in the removal of several artifacts from the Atheneum. Or had he?

I looked up to see Jenny's face. She already knew. "I just wanted to talk to Kim about a few things. She'll be fine. So, what's up?" I asked quickly.

"Hey, boss." Petro flew over. "The Supreme and Senior

Councils are meeting to discuss what took place last night. Ed and a few others are in there. It's getting a little dicey. You know, certain folks having been there," he said, referring to Frank and Two. Davros and the others had specifically done that without Darkwater's knowledge.

Walking over, Kristi started talking in an official tone. "Darkshit's in there complaining that he was circumnavigated against Council rule. It won't get anywhere, but he is now aware the Supreme Council is watching him."

Kristi had recently been promoted into the Council, but she was still on what was called Junior status, and not privy to certain meetings. The one issue with being at that level was the inability to be on any committees. I also fell into this category.

Me being an independent Mage and what was referred to as a "legacy member" gave me an extra level of clout. Phil had gone through the Guild, and would not be considered for Council appointment. He was more than okay with that.

Being a member of the Guild was much like being a Warrant Officer in the army. You were a member but had your own path. Everyone was always occupied figuring out what exactly you did, or how you fit into the overall scheme of things. It was a good place to be. While Phil had moved out of the Atheneum, he still remained on the payroll. Me, on the other hand, still needed to figure out how to keep the lights on. Though I had yet to pay an electricity bill to date.

"How many people are in there?" I asked, pulling up my pants by the belt loops.

"You're not thinking about going in there, are you?" Phil inquired, grinning.

"Oh, yeah. I'm about to go pee on their little parade," I replied as Phil's grin widened.

Jenny walked over, handing me a folder. "Well, when you

go in, hand this to Ed. We just got this in from the Interpol."

"Interpol?" I opened the folder to see a picture of who appeared to be Bruce Teach and Carol Darkwater.

"Does anyone else know about this?" I asked, seeing the picture on the next page stating Orlando.

"No. From what I understand, they are heading here. Ben just sent this over. It wasn't labeled OTN, but the faces popped up on one of the marshals systems as wanted. This was taken two days ago," Jenny explained as I let out a whistle. This meant things were accelerating faster than I'd thought.

"Hey, in other news, I saw the Planes Drifter show is on for tonight. Does anyone else have a feeling this is a bad idea?" I asked, needing to call Abby.

"My thoughts precisely," Jenny agreed as I tucked the folder under my arm, heading toward the door. Everyone in the room shifted to follow me before I stopped, turning.

"What, bruther? I'm not missing this shit for all the Ambrosia in the world," Phil said while the others nodded.

I pulled out the sunglasses the Pixie crew had made, putting them on and walking out the door. The main chambers were only a short walk away from the office, and Mouth and a handful of others stood outside the main doors. Much to my surprise, this also included Goolsby's accountant.

"Oh, bloody hell," Mouth muttered, grunting as we walked closer. There were a few new faces I didn't recognize, as well as Barny.

The thing with Mouth was that we had come to some sort of weird working respect for each other over the past two years. He hadn't threatened my life in his first sentence, so he was clearly in a mood to talk.

"Mouth, good to see you. It looks like you have babysitting duty tonight," I greeted as Goolsby's accountant, who refused to tell me her name, scowled. Barny just stood there staring at us as Phil slapped him on the back harder than needed.

Mouth grunted. "Ugh, right. Didn't feel like going in there and listening to the bullshit. Don't know about the rest of these." Mouth pointed his large, stubby finger at the others.

"Barny, what's your story?" I asked as he shuffled his feet. The man was nervous about something.

"A bunch of people showed up at TDC and brought me here. Some scary old man named Carvel," Barny replied as Mouth squeezed his fist. While Carvel was a creepy old Mage, he had proven to do the right thing for the most part, not mattering who it may hurt in the process. He had generally passed the smell test. Mouth worked for him, once being his apprentice and now Council understudy.

Long story short, Mouth was protective of the crusty old Mage. "Easy there, big fella. Here, check this out," I said, changing the subject.

I walked up to Mouth, opening the folder where the others couldn't see. "Yeah, things are about to get interesting." Mouth leaned over, getting a closer look at the picture.

"You look stupid in those sunglasses," was all he said in response as I closed the folder. Adjusting my sunglasses, Mouth did the closest thing to a smile he could by raising his eyebrows. Or forehead. It was confusing, since they both ran together.

Goolsby's accountant spoke up sharply. "What's in that folder?"

"This folder?" The sounds of someone getting loud came from inside the main chamber. "Tell me your name, and I'll let you know," I said as Petro buzzed toward the ceiling, going to check out whoever was making all the noise inside.

"Nora," the stern woman replied, adjusting her librarian-style glasses. She was dressed the same as always in a tight-fitting gray long skirt, blouse, and matching blazer. Her hair was up in a bun, with pearl earrings firmly nestled in her ears.

"Nora," I repeated as Jenny and Kristi started looking bored. "Nora, tell you what. I'm a man of my word. Follow us, and I'll show you."

I quickly turned toward the double doors as two well-dressed CSA agents held out their hands.

"We can't let you in unless you are on a committee or a member of the Senior Council and above," the largest of the two men said gruffly. They knew very well who we were and that we—well, Phil—had a habit of not taking kindly to directions. Before I could say another word—or Phil, whom I could feel winding up—the rumble of Mouth's voice cut through the thick fog of dueling egos.

"You'll move out of the way now, or I'll remove the lot of you . . . permanently. That goon of a man in the stupid sunglasses has important information," Mouth said as the other guard spoke into his communicator.

"Goon, really?" I muttered under my breath as the others shrugged. The man put down the communicator, opening the doors.

"I said what I said," Mouth replied, hearing my opinion of his name for me.

"They will allow Max in," the second man told us before Mouth pushed him out of the way. Phil apologized, also sticking his tongue out at the same time. I had a feeling those two agents would be reassigned in the near future, or given a stern talking to.

We would have to remember to speak with Frank and make sure those two didn't get into trouble for doing their jobs. I hated that kind of stuff, but now wasn't the time.

Shuffling into the room, everyone inside went still. Even Phil and Mouth looked slightly sheepish with everyone's eyes burning holes through us. The room, as always, was full of eclectic types and people sitting at odd intervals. Since it wasn't a full session of the Council, the assembly was spread out toward the front. The tall, bald man I liked to call Bull started walking our way.

When he got in front of us, the room erupted in conversation. Titus slammed the gavel down forcefully multiple times, the echo of the wooden instrument making it clear he wasn't happy with the interruption.

"I'm going to have to ask you all to leave. Now," Bull ordered in a very deliberate manner. The room again went silent, apparently waiting for my response. It looked like I was representing the new addition to the party.

"I have something I need to get to Councilman Edward Rose," I said, using Ed's official name, signaling to him it was important. You'd be surprised how calling a friend by their actual full name could garner their attention.

Jenny slipped in quietly, making her way up to the seats. Ed raised a hand, seeking recognition. Titus slammed his gavel down once again as the man's voice echoed throughout the chamber.

"To be clear with everyone in this room. We are having an initial hearing over a situation that has become of great interest to the Council. As a member of this Council, if Max has obtained new information which may affect this conversation, which in turn may change our level of involvement, we need to see it," Titus finished, sitting back down.

I looked over, seeing Davros and Ana both whispering to each other. Darkwater sat stoically as always at his desk, leaning over and speaking with somebody I had not met before. The person he was talking to looked just as bland as the Councilman. I noticed his eyes were slate gray, much like Darkwater's own; they almost glowed. There was still a debate within certain groups on what exactly Councilman Darkwater was. For our team, it was straightforward. He was a regular who had consumed water from the Fountain of Youth, gaining powers.

Bull let out a huff, stomping his foot as he turned. I walked alone as the rest of the group peeled off to seat by the door. The Council halls were much like the House of Commons —or the other way around—with several rows of seats leading up to the eventual ceiling.

"Councilman Sand, this better be good," Ed said, acting as if he was cross with me; I knew better. We had gotten into talking to each other in code throughout the years, and using our actual titles or full names was a clear-cut sign that things were serious. He nodded for me to sit down in the open seat to his right.

I set the manila envelope in front of Ed, letting him open it. I was close enough to clearly see the picture of Bruce and Carol and the accompanying page of notes.

"Shit," Ed said under his breath, raising his hand like a schoolchild in fourth grade who needed to go to the bathroom.

Titus glared at Bull. It was odd to see him in this type of mood. I had a feeling that Two and Frank being involved, plus being found out, had ruffled some feathers. Then again, maybe he was just playing his part. It was very clear we weren't the only ones on the Council who didn't trust Darkwater.

Bull walked up and grabbed the envelope as Ed leaned over. "Why in the hell are you wearing those ridiculous sunglasses?" Ed asked, scribbling down a few words before sliding the note over.

"They want this to happen."

With all the grandstanding and puffing out of chests, I almost forgot I had the sunglasses on. This led me to the purpose of wearing them. I started scanning the crowd. Several familiar faces stared back at me as they usually did, judging, calculating, or just plain trying to figure out what I would do next. What I didn't expect to see was the extremely bright ball of glowing personality at the far end of the room.

Tendrils of silvery smoke floated off the person's body, seeping into everything around them. It was almost as if the silver-like mist were reaching out to other people to either attack or take something away. The glasses had been enchanted by the Pixies to identify whoever was the originator of the Voodoo recently being used.

While I didn't exactly understand how they worked, they had unequivocally accomplished their mission. I couldn't even make out who the person was without removing the sunglasses, it was so obvious.

Ed, sensing what I was doing, nudged me with his elbow. I let out a light whistle as Titus again slammed his gavel down, garnering the group's attention.

As I lowered the sunglasses, the one person I never thought would be involved in this situation stood there smiling at me. A genuine, beaming grin was reaching all corners of their face. While I'd had a hunch, I had been hoping it was just that.

"Son of a bitch," I cursed in such a casually calm manner that several other people around me heard the statement.

"Is there something you would like to add?" Carvel asked, tapping his old, bony fingers on the table as Darkwater leaned over again, talking to the man next to him.

Again, Titus spoke up in his booming voice. "Might I remind everyone *who* is in control of the session? The evidence which was brought to our attention is a picture and some general communications referencing Bruce Teach and his current general proximity to Jacksonville, Florida."

I immediately noticed Titus leaving out the part about Carol Darkwater.

Several people in the room shuffled around. There were

times when I thought the Council halls were somehow around the Jacksonville area, but figured that was pretty much a pipe dream. I was always surprised when people took so much interest in the First Coast area.

I refocused on the situation in front of me, staring at the person looking directly into my eyes. For some reason, the little devil on my right shoulder was telling me to stand up and set the whole damn place on fire. The angel on my left shoulder, however, had different plans for the day.

After everything, the final pieces of the puzzle started to fall into place. The last corner clicked, completing the puzzle. "Revenge," I whispered under my breath, only loud enough for Ed to hear this time.

"I don't want to know. Right now, you need to focus. They have this all figured out but for a few of the key ingredients. You know, like who the hell is doing this," Ed said as I smiled, raising an eyebrow. Ed, seeing this, shook his head.

"You know, don't you. Look, let's see how this plays out first," Ed finished as I leaned over, winking at Darkwater, who was staring at us.

"You think this is pissing off Darkwater? Me leaning over and whispering?" Ed nodded. "Good." I paused for a second before continuing. "I'm not so sure this is all him. I'll just say, I'd like to see how this plays out as well."

Ed stood up, gaining the room's attention. "With this new development, I would like to recommend a team of Night Stalkers, or additional CSA team members, be reassigned to the Atheneum. At least until this is concluded."

Darkwater stood up. "Supreme and fellow Senior Council members. Might I remind everyone that we have other matters that need tending to," he stated. I wasn't sure what else was going on around the globe, but it was clear we weren't the only rodeo in town. It almost seemed like something was deliberately shifting focus.

Ana Vlad spoke up next. "We understand, and will consider the request separately. We will take Councilman Edward Rose's recommendation, and meet privately to go over the request. You will be notified of the outcome from that meeting."

Boom, she had just dropped the hammer on Darkwater, and he sat back down. I glanced back at my target, tracing down to Darkwater. The man had the same smug look on his face as always. It appeared like he was deliberately pushing back, getting sidelined from the conversation. I knew the type. He was, as always, playing a twisted game. Darkwater knew they were after him, and was letting others make the call. Or seem like it. After all, his daughter was involved.

She had tried to kill me once, just saying.

For the next thirty minutes, the group went over the events of the past two weeks. This included actually being asked questions while not hooked up to the truth-teller chair. By the time it was all said and done, the final order of business was announced, and Lorel stood up.

She was the only pure Fae on the Supreme Council, and had been quietly absent last year. The breathtaking, calm, yet powerful woman cleared her throat.

"I would like to announce the reintroduction of Jamison Danann and share my gratitude to the team at the Atheneum and to Max Abaddon Sand," Lorel declared while the room stayed quiet. Over the past three years, I had yet to hear her voice more than a handful of times. The thing was, when she spoke, people listened.

There was a light spatter of applause, mostly coming from the Pixies in the rafters. Jamison walked out of the door leading off into the side meeting chambers, and the group picked up its jubilation. *I guess the apple was the important part, not the farmer who planted it*, I thought, looking over at my newly acquired target for the afternoon. They were still sitting resolute in the fact that I had them dead to rights.

Jamison walked into the middle of the room as Darkwater and several others stood up, marching out of the chambers. It wasn't a rude gesture, just one of indifference. If you've ever been around a political meeting, you know people come and go.

It was then I noticed my target stand up and walk out with the others, the business they were there for completed, and the rest of the session of no consequence. I already knew Jamison would be fine and back to his old I-know-more-than-you ways soon enough.

"Ed, you got this?" I asked, taking a slight bow. The back of my target's head was getting lost in the shuffle.

He looked toward the door, motioning me with his hand to take off. "Don't do anything brash," Ed said as I reached down, whispering, "*Petro*," into the charm around my neck.

"Hey, boss, that was epic! You came in all sunglasses and cool and was like . . ." He squinted his eyes. "You're onto something, aren't you, boss?"

"Do me a favor. Let Phil know I'm going to be offline for a while. Same for you. If I'm in trouble, I'll let you know," I said, moving faster, walking past the main entrance as Mouth chuffed.

"Where you going, bruther?" Phil called out as I pointed toward Petro.

CHAPTER 17

The Tale of Two Faces

"Aslynn!" I shouted, my voice cutting through the crowd as I finally reached the far end of the entrance halls. The area was massive and led off into various sections of the Council grounds. In the center of the room was a giant statue depicting the Great War between the Old Gods and everyone else.

The looming mass of metal and stone was well over three stories tall, demanding your attention.

Moving through the crowd, dozens of other Mages and curiously enough Vs stood in various groups, pointing fingers at each other, more than likely figuring out ways of ending my position on the Council. It had saved my life on more than one occasion, and I was very aware that losing such protection could be lethal. Thus the reason I played the game.

"Max, what a pleasant surprise," Aslynn greeted, standing casually in a long, emerald-green, shimmering dress. She looked amazing and knew it. Her subtle smile took over her previously businesslike expression, Aslynn's shift in attitude showing her lack of comfort in the situation.

"I know you saw me, sunshine. You look amazing," I complimented, seeing how far she would let things go. In all fairness, she had no clue I had her pegged as the person not only guilty of murder but someone with a damn good reason for a nasty case of heartburn over old Brucey boy.

"This old thing. I have a change of clothes in my office," Aslynn said as she threaded her arm through mine. "It's not too far. I have a room in the Fae Council wing. Apparently, it has something to do with legacy children under the employ of the queen. Either way, it's been nice to have the spot to work out of."

We walked in step as I finally took a steadying breath. I needed to talk to her about everything, but not here. While it was evident she was involved, I still wasn't clear on the big picture.

"You want to join me tonight for the show?" I asked, referring to Planes Drifter playing later tonight. Maybe if I could keep her occupied, we could keep the show from turning into a problem. I was reasonably sure Bruce would be making an appearance.

I looked at her eyes, seeing a slight hesitation. Even though she was a full-blooded Fae, the demon part of me was that much faster. Aslynn had plans for the night. If she declined, she knew it would be out of character.

She stopped in the hall in front of the door to the Fae wing. The separate areas were very much like embassies. "Isn't your girlfriend in the hospital?" Aslynn asked, stone-cold.

I at times forgot some Fae, such as Aslynn, were hundreds of years old. The bubbly exterior she often displayed was a mask hiding her true intentions. When I'd first met her, it had been genuine, but things had changed. She had changed—hell, I had changed. The coldness in her tone quickly dispersed when she saw my shock.

"I'm sorry, I didn't mean it like that," Aslynn apologized as her smile lit back up.

"You're right. I just meant that you could join our group,"

I said, quickly scrambling to respond. Her statement had its intended effect, taking me off guard, making me feel bad for asking. My resolve solidified in my mind as visions of Lucian's final breaths filled my thoughts. I wasn't that easily manipulated.

"Ex," I said lightly, as if in passing.

"Ex?" Aslynn replied quickly while she opened the door. The office on the other side was opulent and timeless. Plush purple and green furniture sat methodically in some type of order. The scent of honeysuckle lingered in the air, reminding me of my mother, whom I needed to call as always.

"She kind of broke up with me earlier today when I went to check on her," I said. I wasn't lying to Aslynn, but the reasoning behind the situation wasn't necessary. Mages and Fae were famous for leaving out small yet essential details. Maybe I could use this to my advantage. She would have known if I was lying.

"I see," Aslynn drawled out, tapping her bottom lip. I looked around, noticing the lack of other Fae in the offices.

"Is it normal for no one to be here?" I asked, changing the subject.

"Sometimes. The queen held a meeting yesterday, so I'm sure most of the others are still on the Plane or wherever. I was told to be here instead," Aslynn replied, pursing her lips.

"Tell you what. It sounds like you have other plans. How about we go grab a burger? If you're freed up later, maybe meet the crew at FA's?" I offered, wanting to get Aslynn out into a crowd without making myself look desperate to get her to be at the show, which meant not out blowing things up.

The reason for her actions came into laser-like focus in my mind. That and the vision of Ned being torn apart from the inside out, his face stoic and resolute as he winked out of existence. From what I had been told, a Fae dying in that manner was final. Do not pass GO or the Everwhere.

"You seem to be pretty interested in getting me out for a night on the town. What's really going on?" Aslynn asked, walking into an office, nodding her head for me to follow. She closed the door with a motion of her hand, sauntering over to the desk. "Help me with this."

She motioned me over to assist in unzipping the back of her gown. While she had a head full of blazing red hair, her skin was kissed by the sun, the firm lines of her muscles emphasizing her toned physique.

"Like what you see?" Aslynn asked after I paused in silence. She knew I was taking the curves of her body in. I shook my head, refocusing. What was I doing? Kim was in the hospital, and I was staring at Aslynn's bare skin. She was doing this on purpose.

Without hesitation, I put my arm around her waist, stepping closer. She took a breath in expectation as I clunked the golden dagger on the table with a resounding *thump*.

Talk about a mood killer. Every muscle in Aslynn's body tensed under my light touch as I took a step back, slowly pulling my arm back from her waist.

Have you ever talked to or known someone for what seemed like an eternity, only to have them flip the script on you? The look and tone of Aslynn's voice were almost alien coming from her body as she spoke.

"I would say, 'what a surprise,' but that's to be expected of you." She let her dress hit the floor and turned around.

I looked at her now exposed arm, seeing the wounds put there by Bo during the fight at Ben's house. There was no denying it.

"We need to talk. Just not here," I said, letting a wave of will flow through my body, ensuring I was ready for a fight, err . . . or whatever might happen.

"Oh, we are fine here. This is the equivalent, as I'm sure you know, of an embassy back home for you. Plus, I can assure you, we are completely alone. When did you figure things out? Or have you fully yet?" she purred, reaching for her clothes. While it was clear she was enjoying watching me squirm, it was also evident she didn't know my intent.

"Slowly," I warned, realizing how creepy I sounded. "Just . . . no sudden moves. I need answers, and right now, you're not in the circle of trust. Let's figure out a way to get you back in it before things get crazy."

"Oh, I can assure you they are about to get wild. Max, I mean you no harm. As soon as you started poking around in all this, I knew you would be the one to figure it out, and the one to understand why," Aslynn told me, putting on a T-shirt.

"Revenge, yeah, I get that part. But the innocent people, then Ben? I don't get it," I said as my nerves settled.

"Innocent, those fools? No one is truly innocent; not even you. This is bigger than simple revenge. This attack was not only on my family but the Fae as well." The green in her eyes flared to life while she spoke, the raw emotion and will-power to take revenge for her father unstoppable.

"Then explain it to me. Look, we don't have much time. I need a good reason not to end this here and now," I said, taking control of the situation as she let out a sultry chuckle.

"Hmph. You are not in any position to place demands on me. I work for the queen, and I have her blessing. You want to know what else is going on, Max?" Aslynn asked as if taunting.

I started taking a step as her eyes shifted down to the floor. As soon as I realized what I was standing on, the protective circle sprang to life. She had dialogued me into a trap. I wasn't going anywhere.

After a few raps of my fist against the elastic yet unbreakable barrier, I set my jaw, cocking my head to the side.

"Look, I came here to talk. I'll even take it a step further because I need to understand. I'm the only person here who knows what you've been up to. So cut the bullshit and tell me," I said, gauging if I could reason with her.

An odd thing about being in protective circles with long hair was that it starts floating due to the field's static. I pulled my hair back, realizing I needed to get it cut at some point. Seeing that I wasn't taking her seriously, Aslynn walked toward me, grabbing the knife. She wanted my full attention.

"Oh, are you? I highly doubt that. I haven't exactly been coy about things." She paused in thought. "Okay, I believe you. You're a horrible liar, anyway." She pulled out an Onyx cigarette, lighting it off the outside of the circle.

"Why set up the other people? They didn't have anything to do with this," I demanded, starting at the biggest issue at hand. She was guilty of murder.

"You know that for a fact? I have a strange feeling that if you look into all their backgrounds, including poor Lucian's, you'll find they all have one thing in common," Aslynn said, blowing smoke into the air and pulling out the dagger.

I needed to figure a way out of the circle. In all fairness, even if I was trapped, Aslynn was also doing the exact thing I needed her to: tell me her plan in detail while thinking she was in control. I slowly reached into my enchanted trench coat's side pocket, feeling the smooth Evergate stone between my fingers.

What most people didn't realize was the true power of the Postern and its gates. As long as I had enough room to move, I could gate out of the circle, a feat even a skilled Gate Mage or demon wouldn't be able to pull off. If I had the Seeker-gate figured out in conjunction with the Evergate at the time, things at the Fountain of Youth might have turned out a little less messy.

"They all at one point or the other worked for the Soul

Dealers. Most of those Dark Carnival puppets had some hand in their affairs at one point or the other, except for Barny. That spineless wretch is just trying to stay alive." Aslynn paused, taking another drag.

"Whatever they did in their past doesn't dictate who they are now," I said as she sneered.

"In two hundred years, tell me how much time has passed since Kim dumped you," she said, the statement cutting deep. I knew the truth in her words. Time was in many ways an abstract.

"What about Ben and the others?" I asked as she put her cigarette out on the circle.

"The others were worse. Using money to fulfill Beleth's wishes, covering up drug and soul laundering. Ben, on the other hand, was handed this because he is just that damn good. Bruce cannot get that money or the guarantee of the insurance company to resecure the items lost," Aslynn explained, stepping back over to the desk, putting the knife back down.

"You're telling me that the insurance companies, the ones everyone uses, also go after items lost in a claim? Like a special team?" I sounded stupid. Ordinary folks didn't realize that most crime was held up and supported by regular blue- and white-collar workers at normal everyday companies. You know the old saying, *Follow the money* . . . the rest of the thought winked out of my mind as Aslynn started putting on the rest of her clothes.

"Precisely that. Not to mention they have a contract with the Council. Oh yes, insurance companies are mighty, not only in the regular world. With Ben working the case, he would get not only the settlement but the artifacts too," Aslynn said, shaking her head.

She clearly knew what a wild card the man was. It started to make some sick sense why Aslynn was doing what she was. Not only was she drawing out Bruce Teach, she was also clearing the playing field, dead set on revenge.

Even with that floating through my mind, a few loose ends which I hadn't been able to work out yet still lingered.

"You're not just getting revenge. The queen wants you to prove a point. *Don't play games with the Fae.* She doesn't care what you do or if you get caught doing it because you have a reason," I said as Aslynn grinned, the emotion quickly turning into a scowl. The thought process of the pure Fae was confusing yet logical.

"Ding, ding. We have a winner," she mocked, cocking her head to the side. The conversation was over. It was time to choose. Not only for me, but for her also.

"Wait, something's not adding up. Where does Jamison come into all this? I mean, he has to have some type of hand or play in this. Last I heard, he was back to his normal self, minus some coordination issues," I said, clearly striking a nerve. The look on her face gave away everything.

"Well, that is a rather delicate topic, I'm afraid," Aslynn replied as her gaze went distant in thought.

"The queen is holding your brother till you get the job done as some extra motivation, isn't she?" I pointed out. Over the past couple of years, the calculating way the Fae Court worked had been made very clear. Don't mess with the High Fae courts. Period. Full stop.

Aslynn nodded. "For such a fool, you can be the most perceptive one in the room sometimes." The statement came across as more of a jab at everyone else ignoring her obvious transgressions.

It felt like one of those scenes in an old Spaghetti Western where two people were facing each other, wondering what the other was about to do, or in this situation, say. It was at times like this that I always referred back to those cheesy sales books. The ones which always said, "The person who talks first, loses."

Just for the record, that's some shit advice.

"Okay, now that you have flushed out Bruce, how can *WE* make sure you finish this. Oh, and avoid killing or getting anyone else killed," I said, throwing out an olive branch. It was more like throwing out a telephone pole, considering what I was saying could be regarded as treason or worse.

I had made up my mind.

Sometimes the best method of doing what's right is making sure others don't get hurt, even if it means doing something wrong. I knew Titania would not be as careful. She had targeted Aslynn, from everything I had been told. I cared for Aslynn and her family, more so than she had clearly taken into consideration.

"Interesting thought," she responded as a concentrated look took hold of her face.

"One that would have avoided innocent people getting killed. Look, I want Bruce Teach brought to justice just as mu—" I started, getting cut off in a flurry.

"Dead. The son of a bitch needs to die, and he will," Aslynn declared, throwing out her terms of the negotiation.

"Is anyone else a target?" I asked, the green glow in her eyes starting to calm.

"Carol Darkwater," she replied, clicking her tongue on the roof of her mouth.

"That's going to be problematic. Listen, I'll help you with this, but we need to work together. I can't have the others involved. I made a promise once to your father, and I intend to uphold it," I said, not having told anyone about my conversation with Ned.

It was true. I had made a promise to Ned to help protect his family if anything ever were to happen. The whole thing had seemed silly at the time. Ned had been all, "Be my apprentice, and I'll train you. In return, you must swear to protect my family," or something along those lines. At the time, I didn't realize the weight words held in this world.

"You made that oath to my father? Swear you are speaking the truth," Aslynn ordered, walking closer, her breath making ripples in the protective circle.

"I swear." As soon as the words passed my lips, Aslynn touched the circle, making it wink out of existence in a puff of ozone.

"You know you could have just told me that upfront and avoided all this drama," she rebuked, throwing me the knife.

"That would have taken all the fun out of it," I replied, steadying my voice. In reality, I wanted to get as much information out of her as I could. She was still guilty of murder.

For now, I would figure out a way to bring Bruce Teach to justice. Dealing with Aslynn would be another story for another time. The issue at hand was not getting the others involved. I would have to play this close to my chest. The team would know something was up, and I would use that to my advantage. I would need help, and Petro, as always, would be there for me.

"So you are aware Bruce will be at the show tonight," Aslynn stated.

"I figured as much. First, I need to ask you something. What's up with the Voodoo?" I needed to make sure I wasn't falling into a trap myself.

"A girl never tells all her secrets. Max, some things are just a means to an end. The Fae Court works in mysterious ways, as do we all. I know you visited Maman Brigitte. Let's just say the Queens of Voodoo are at odds with the Soul Dealers. They kind of cut into each other's business. Plus, there was Haiti. You may want to look into that one at some point. They mostly remain neutral, unless called upon. You need not concern yourself with that matter." She was skirting around the issue without lying.

It was so odd hearing the change in her voice and posture. One thing was clear, however. Her dealings with Ogun were not over. Not by a long shot, even if Aslynn thought they were. Though I had the feeling she also knew this, even if she didn't want to believe it.

I had only been with Maman Brigitte for a few minutes and knew there was no closing a marker with her or others from her realm. It might have been my demon senses telling me this, or just knowing the look of a hungry wolf in the woods.

"Do me a favor. Let's go to the show, see what happens without starting a damn riot, and take it from there," I said as Aslynn sighed.

"Well, it looks like you have your date for tonight," she finally said as we both stood there sizing each other up.

No matter the outcome for the evening, I would at least be able to control certain pieces on the chessboard. That all being said, I needed to talk with Phil and Petro. The others would have to wait. Did I mention I still hadn't thought this all the way through yet?

CHAPTER 18

A Night at the Gates of Hell

"I don't know about all this poppycock," Phil said, scratching his face. Over the past year, he had decided to grow his beard lightly back out again. When everyone had started making fun of him, Phil had decided to leave it in a perpetual state of uncertainty.

"Yeah, boss. We like knowing what's going on," Petro chimed in as we sat in our assigned seats in the apartment's office. The sound of wind blowing outside pushing against the windows filled the silence as my two best friends awaited my response.

"I need you both to trust me on this. I'm not saying I have everything nailed down, but if we can get our hands on Brucey boy, the other part of this mess will be somewhat easier to clean up," I said, taking a pull of a Vamp Amber, letting out a sigh.

In defense of the two, I had not come completely clean on who was responsible for the recent string of murders. Checking in on Ben an hour earlier, I had made it a point to let the arrogant old Mage know he was safe. At least from current events. I needed to clarify it didn't include anyone else he may have pissed off, which I was betting included several other people.

"Bruther, we trust you; that's not the spit in the bucket. It's whoever you say is on the hook for all this. I know everyone's expecting the shite to hit the fan tonight. Let's make sure we don't get caught in the splatter," Phil said, grabbing the remote to the radio, turning it on.

An old Moody Blues song started playing, calming the mood. We all started nodding our heads lightly, taking sips of our drinks. Phil and Petro were worried that I wasn't letting them in. It had been some time since I'd held back from the group, and it was clear they were not going to let me off the hook so easily.

"The Council will have plenty of CSA support tonight. We just need to keep an eye out for Bruce, or any other stooges who might pop up. Phil, I'm asking you to keep an eye out for Councilman Darkwater. Trust me, we all know he has his hands in this.

"If we can split our focus, we'll be that much better for it. All I can say is that we don't need to worry about the Voodoo factor. At least, I don't think so. We also need to take a trip to the Everwhere, and I'm starting to think we need to do that sooner than later," I said, refocusing the group.

"Boss, I think you're right. Those Council folks were looking for artifacts, and not only from the *Event Horizon*. From what Leshya said, they were also trying to get into the restricted artifacts vault. Did you get a chance to talk to Abby? Or Bo?" Petro asked, reminding us to keep an eye on the Council.

"It would be nice if this wasn't so complicated. You know, find the bad guy, then stick it to them," I said, taking the final pull of my beer. "I called Abby before you two got here. He's fully aware that things may get a little crazy tonight. I mentioned it might be a good idea to call off the show."

"Well?" Phil urged, also finishing the last of his drink.

"Typical rock star answer. The show must go on," I said in my best impression of Abby. "As for Bo, he's gone off the radar. Tried to get ahold of him earlier. I'm not sure what he's up to, but he always seems to appear when we need a little extra help. To be honest, I would rather not have him involved in this entire situation. Anyway, Aslynn said she was going to join us tonight."

"I agree. That's just one more hand in the cookie jar," Phil said, pausing. "We haven't been out with that lass in some time. I talked with Jamison while you were doing whatever it was you were gallivanting around doing. I'll see if he wants to join us. Since he now has hands again, that bugger went and got a new phone." Phil punched out a text to Jamison.

I stood up, pulling out my service pistol, checking the action and if I indeed had ammunition. Phil and Petro looked at me skeptically. To make my point, I also picked up my short staff and several other small, enchanted items I kept in my desktop drawer.

"Are you going to war, bruther?" Phil asked as I started putting certain items in their assigned pockets on the inside of my enchanted trench coat.

Once upon a time, it used to be a corduroy blazer that fit in rather well at a nice restaurant or a Saturday night on the town. Now, not only was it a form of protection, but it was also large enough to carry and hide a small armory of magical items.

"Maybe. I'm not taking any chances. There's going to be more foxes than hens in the chicken coop tonight. I recommend we all saddle up. The one thing I did happen to accomplish while talking to Abby was acquiring these," I said, holding up three new shiny crew passes.

In most cases, this meant we were going to have a great night full of fun and rock 'n' roll. For tonight, this would get us into the venue via the band's entrance, which in turn would keep us from having to be screened by security for things like liquor or guns.

"You're all over it, boss." Petro buzzed over to the desk and grabbed one of the small laminates made for a Pixie. "I'm going to say before you do: I've got a bad feeling about this."

Petro had used one of my favorite quotes of the immortal smuggler Han Solo.

I grinned as he buzzed down the hall, yelling for Casey. "Phil, if things go sideways tonight, I'm going to need Petro to come with me. No matter what happens, remember I'm one of the good guys."

Phil just huffed out a breath of air and shrugged.

"Bruther, you don't have to explain yourself to me. I know you've got some kind of plan, and even if you mess it all up, we'll figure out a way to make it right." He also stood up, heading to his room.

Since moving into the apartment, the team kept most of its weaponry in the Postern for safekeeping, but Phil still liked to keep some of his items under his pillow. Literally.

"Thanks, I just don't know how things are going to turn out. Hey, I want to give Kim a call and see how she's doing before we head out," I said as Phil disappeared up the stairs.

***

Aslynn walked over as the three of us finally made it through the crew entrance. While we hadn't been given a shakedown, one of the security guards had insisted on confirming with the Planes Drifter management team that we were who we said we were. I kept a mental note to ask Abby later what that was all about.

"Boys, you should see the crowd out there. It's insane. All the bad press about the murders did just what you would expect. Everyone's here to see the show," Aslynn said, winking at me.

"Great," I answered as Petro landed on my shoulder. "I hear the opening act about to start. Let's pop in and see what

Abby and the band are doing."

It was odd how over the last couple of years I had become so well acquainted with a group of people whom, I admit, I was at the creepy fan level of.

Heading toward the trailer set up for the band, Petro leaned into my ear.

"She smells funny, boss; not the bad kind. It's just that something is weird. I want to get closer and see if I can figure it out," Petro whispered before buzzing off my shoulder, heading over to Aslynn's.

I had talked with Petro about paying particular attention to her. The fact of the matter was, I wasn't entirely convinced that when things went sideways, she would hold up her end of the bargain. It's not that I believed she would do it on purpose, but rather out of pure rage and hatred. Aslynn might make a choice she couldn't take back.

As we approached the trailer labeled PD, a crowd of what I liked to call bootstrap hangers and groupies flowed around the area like vultures around fresh roadkill. The sound of the noise-canceling charm blared loud rock music from inside the trailer. In reality, it was usually whisper quiet inside. The band sat around the manicured facility drinking and eating snacks laid out on a table while talking about life or whatever topic, including murder, that might come up.

The man at the door was a familiar face I had noticed on several occasions traveling with the band, first at the ball several years ago—ball which I had avoided every year since—and of course, last week.

"Max, the fellows are waiting for you. Ah, Aslynn. I wasn't expecting you, my lady," the average-sized man said, sounding surprised. What caught me and the others off guard was the slight bow and curtsy.

"Tavares. It's good to see you," Aslynn greeted, holding

out her hand as he grabbed it in one of those annoying, limp wrist handshakes the Fae did.

"Thank you, my lady. Tell the queen I send my regards," Tavares requested, speaking into a microphone poking out of the sleeve of his shirt.

There it was. Tavares was a Fae of some sort, as the interaction confirmed. Aslynn, as a representative of the queen, was not only respected but feared.

"My lady, ohhhh," Phil joked as Aslynn let out a light, bubbling giggle, which she cut off like a light switch as the door opened.

The group of fans outside started pushing on the railing, only to have Tavares turn toward them. Before I could turn to see what he had done to calm the group, the noise disappeared behind the hush of classical music.

Knight Raider sat tuning his guitar without plugging it into an amp, the twang and sound of the strings slapping the frets setting the mood. Looking out of place as always, Bo sat at the end of a long couch, eating cocktail shrimp.

"Hello, darlings. I was wondering when you were going to join the party." Bo smiled, showing off several rows of razor-sharp teeth. He followed this by popping a handful of shrimp into his mouth, tails and all.

"What he meant to say was," Abby interjected, walking in from a small room on the far end of the trailer, "are you ready to get this party started!"

Abby was in his usual rock star mood. Since meeting the band, I'd quickly learned that the preshow warm-up was just as interesting as the show often ended up being. Knight, Kane, and Jim Smith, my favorite Vampire drummer, all let out a collective groan.

"Did I miss something?" I asked as Jim walked over, handing me an official-looking envelope. Petro and Phil took off toward the refreshment table as Bo stood up, walking over to Aslynn and me.

"I can assure you, the fun's not started yet," Bo said as Abby nodded in agreement. He walked up to Aslynn, staring at her through his sunglasses as if he was looking into her soul. "Take a look in the envelope."

I opened the manicured, high-quality paper, mumbling the first few sentences, then reading the important part out loud. "Yada, yada, yada, blah, blah, blah . . . TDC Enterprises, formally owned by B&B LLC, is sponsoring an executive guest who has requested to remain anonymous. The VIP's security detail has the approval to integrate with the stadium's staff during tonight's event. Any issues and/or concerns with the VIP's *forward action response team* must be addressed through Marlow Goolsby's office."

The look on my face gave it away. "It sounds like Bruce is way more organized and in the open than I thought. Plus, the FART? I would think he could come up with a better name for his security detail." I paused as Petro and Phil snickered, letting the other piece of the note sink in about Goolsby. "I knew that sack of horse shi—"

"Oh no, you have it all wrong, man," Abby chimed in. "You know old grumpy Gools. He would never send out an official letter such as this, specifically calling out the old owners of the Dark Carnival, for nothing. Goolsby wanted us to know this."

I let out a breath, grabbing a soda. There would be no drinking shenanigans, as Phil called them, tonight. It was time to focus.

I threw my thoughts out to the group. "So he owns this stadium?" I asked. Everyone in the room other than me seemed to know this fact. "He's been running silent for the past year. Maybe he's trying to clean up his act."

"That wanker? Not a chance. He's probably doing it to

keep his arse out of trouble. Not to mention his reputation," Phil scoffed as Petro flew over to Abby.

"You think Goolsby can help us out here?" Petro asked, landing on the plush couch.

"No, that much I can assure you. He stopped by earlier. His assistant—you know that scary lady, the accountant —handed that letter to me before walking out. Goolsby said he was just checking the place out for later and wouldn't be around. He knows something's coming," Abby warned, belting out a few lines from "Gear Grinder," one of PD's first love songs, afterward.

The old-style phone sitting in the corner started to ring as Knight picked it up. He lifted his finger in the air, making the universal sign for everyone to wrap it up. It was showtime.

I walked over to Bo while the others shuffled out the door. "I'll be out in a minute," I yelled.

"I'll save you a spot, boss!" Petro winked, perching on Aslynn's shoulder for a ride. As the door opened, the roar of the crowd filled the once peaceful trailer.

Abby paused as the last person left. His mannerisms and voice completely changed, becoming dead serious and all business. "Max, watch your ass. The boys are ready in case things take a turn. Bo, don't eat anyone. The last thing we all need is a demon going crazy at one of our shows."

With a salute, Abby walked out. "He's always such a drama queen," Bo said, turning to me. "You know your lady friend there is the one who attacked us?"

"Yeah, I figured that out. That's why she's with us. Listen, I know you want to help, but I don't think you being here is a good thing," I started as Bo cleared his throat.

"It's not always about you, Max. I'm not going to be here much longer, either way. While I am, I would like to reacquire some of the things Beleth and Bruce took from me. I'm not trying to change the subject, but I'm going to change the subject. You know whoever Aslynn made a deal with on the Voodoo side of the veil is going to want to collect soon," Bo said, not giving me a chance to reply before shifting the subject to Aslynn.

"You think she's in trouble?" I asked, still trying to figure this piece of the puzzle out.

"More like everyone else. The Voodoo Kings and Queens collect payment in souls. If I'm right, that means they will collect several, and soon. In most cases, they try to take as much in payment as they can. Now, suppose the one who made the deal doesn't play along or pay the toll . . . well, let's just say, things can become rather biblical." I hadn't been able to talk to Aslynn about the deal she had made. For all I knew, she had made it with Maman Brigitte. Either way, it was time to go.

"Oh, before I forget," Bo said, making a point. Bo reached over, handing me a small printout of the stadium with a section near the executive suites on the opposite side of last week's events circled.

"You know who else likes to collect souls, right?" Bo winked at me from behind his round, tinted glasses.

"Keep your ears on. I'll let you know what happens." I walked out of the trailer as Bo grabbed a final handful of shrimp.

The spatter of a drumroll reverberated loud enough to shake the ground. I could see Phil and the others as Abby's voice came over the loudspeakers.

"Hello, Jacksonville. Are we ready for a night of wonder and amazement?" Abby yelled as the crowd erupted in cheers.

After another spatter of the drums and a deep thump from the base, Knight Raider began the rhythmic crunching high gain of his guitar, starting their first song.

"It took you long enough, bruther," Phil said as Petro

zipped over, landing on my shoulder, nodding his head to the music.

"I wanted to catch up with Bo real quick. I think it's best he sits this one out!" I shouted as Phil tapped his index finger to his nose, agreeing.

I looked over to see Aslynn standing stoically, her eyes dancing around the crowd, looking for any signs of Bruce. While she knew the general location he was supposed to be in, it was clear Aslynn was sizing up any other possible threats.

I found myself doing the same thing, looking over the crowd. It was a typical mix of legitimate metalheads and college kids trying to be cool. Mixed into the crowd were several others, like myself, who had been a fan for decades. The rhythmic jumping and movement of the concertgoers looked like a wave in the ocean as I scanned the upper levels.

Leaning over, I whispered in Aslynn's ear just loud enough for her to hear. "You see anything?"

"No, and that's what worries me. I'm positive he's here somewhere. I can feel it. You notice how all the lights are out in the area he should be in?" Aslynn pointed out as I noticed the same thing.

While it didn't initially stand out, the closer I looked, the more obvious it became. Whoever was in those executive suites didn't want to be seen. I was pretty sure Bruce knew we were here, and what not only ours but the Council's intentions were as well. Bruce had never given me any reason to doubt his intelligence. The gears in the back of my mind started clicking and clanking as I turned back to the stage.

Phil and a couple of college kids in front of us were bumping into each other, looking as if they were about to start a mosh pit. I snickered lightly, figuring it would be a bad idea to do so with the brooding Irishman.

"What's going on, boss? I've seen that look on your face

214

before," Petro said, almost screaming as the band went into the crushing chorus of "Death Walk," one of the band's least politically correct songs.

"Something doesn't feel right. The CSA agents, our team, the extra marshals, and that damn note from Goolsby. This whole thing is starting to feel like a setup," I replied. Petro let his eyes droop. I had just become the afternoon's buzzkill.

We hadn't discussed the possibility of Bruce being aware that we were tracking him or assuming he would be at the concert. Come to think of it, Bo's presence was more telling than I'd thought. I let the jumbled fog that the last few weeks had become, clear in my mind. The sound of the concert and cheering crowd stopped as I focused on one single thought.

Bo wasn't able to get directly involved. If he just happened to be somewhere or sneeze, causing the bad guys to slip and fall, it was considered acceptable by demon code, whatever the hell that was, pun intended. He had, however, told us that Goolsby and others were aware. Bo had also made it clear he couldn't get involved and wouldn't be around much longer. That included tonight.

I snapped out of it, turning around to talk to a now missing Aslynn. "Shit," I cursed loud enough to get Phil's attention.

"What is it, boss?" Petro asked, also seeing my mood shift further south.

"Aslynn took off. Did you see where she went?" I asked as Phil scrunched his face in confusion.

"Why do you care, boss? You guys bumping uglies?" Petro asked, making his ever-famous hip gyrations.

I couldn't keep it from them any longer. "She . . ." I trailed off as the first ball of fire erupted from several of the executive suites. Instead of continuing to play, the band faltered for a second under the blast's shear stress. The band slowly started back up as the crowd near the back figured the explosion wasn't part of the show. Show which they had taken the pyro-technics out of in order to play.

Turning, I could see Abby motioning to someone off stage. As the guitar chugged away, a fire alarm's faint sounds started echoing in the background in time with the music.

"This is it," Phil said, nodding at the entrance to the box seats.

"Yeah. I bet she went that way." As the words left my mouth, a thick fog started pouring out of the already smoking suites.

"Twice in two weeks. This isn't going to go over well, boss," Petro said, launching off my shoulder.

Phil and I bounded down the hall, taking a quick turn only to be met with a group of CSA agents in various stages of pulling weapons out.

"Freeze!" a short, unfamiliar woman screamed, stopping us. "Hands above your head!"

"I don't think that's going to be happening today," I replied, pulling out my Council badge while at the same time putting up a wall of hellfire between us. We didn't have time to see who had a bigger stick.

"They're not going to be happy about that," Phil commented, popping a cigarette in his mouth as we ran in the opposite direction.

We made it back to the field, climbing the stands instead of going through the back way. Looking around, it quickly became evident that the majority of the crowd was a mix of mostly marshals, CSA agents, regular police, and drunk college kids. Oh, and what looked like flying demon cats pouring out of the smoke billowing from the explosion. It appeared that everyone got the memo to be here tonight.

The music stopped, replaced by a general announcement to evacuate the premises in an orderly manner. Abby and the rest of the band had exited the stage and were out of sight.

Phil and I stopped at the top level as a crowd of genuine fans took off in the opposite direction, hindering what looked like a group of marshals. We stood there panting as Petro zipped down between us.

"It's Voodoo, boss. All kinds of things are going on up there. I couldn't get any closer. Aslynn's up there, as well as several Mages and a damn army of crafts. Oh, and the cats. I don't do cats, boss," Petro finished, staring at the swarm diving at the crowd. A layer of smoke had settled over the lower level, making it hard to see what was happening.

Several gunshots rang out, refocusing our progress. I pulled out my pistol, checking the magazine as Phil did the same.

"Bruther, I don't think many regulars are left down there. See that glowing and all those shots? It's a damn war zone," Phil said as Petro pointed toward a door.

The smoke obscuring the scene below looked like heat lightning on a Southern night as bright flashes erupted from various locations. Whatever was happening under the smoke was being generated by Voodoo. That would mean Aslynn had already gone back on her word. All bets were off.

Phil grabbed the locked door handle, ripping it off the frame instead of pushing it in. The sound caught the attention of what looked like another random group of law enforcement who also appeared to be fighting off the nasty-looking flying cats.

"There may be regular folks in there," Phil said, justifying his gentle handling of the solid metal obstacle.

We walked into the hallway as the sound of the chaos outside started to fade. The plush carpet and dull amber lighting told us we were on the right track. It always struck me as odd how rapidly the decor changed in a sports stadium.

"Hey, boss, you notice those cat thingies didn't seem to be interested in us?" Petro asked, buzzing down from the ceiling, making a great point.

"You're right. Come to think of it, they seemed to be messing with people more than anything," I followed up on the thought.

"They're a distraction. Some nutters are letting Voodoo cat lawn darts loose on the crowd to keep them occupied," Phil explained as I held back a grin.

Aslynn, instead of unleashing hell, had set up a distraction. While it wasn't penance for her actions, it was a start. I would hold onto her secret for a while longer.

Knowing that things were looking up for us, a wall of crazy knife-wielding crafts came swarming around the corner. "Not a distraction from those!" I bellowed, "*Ignis!*" as a ball of hellfire erupted from my left hand.

The softball-sized sphere of dripping death rocketed toward the group, exploding in a shower of glowing hellfire. I raised my other hand, squeezing off several rounds of loaded ammunition blindly into the group.

Phil ducked down, firing several rounds as he pulled out his hammer. I would have to ask him later exactly where the hell he had hidden the crushing, blunt instrument of death.

The burning fire and flurry of rounds quickly filled the hall with smoke and the smell of sulfur as a handful of crafts stumbled over the downed lead group. Phil ran forward, slamming several crushing blows into the crafts. I also ran forward, repositioning and letting off another flurry of enchanted bullets.

Several small whistling darts passed overhead as Petro, who had perched on an exit sign, shot several of his dissolution rounds into a small group of crafts bringing up the rear. After a few more seconds of Phil's rhythmic hammer smashing and

Petro and I firing into the group, the immediate fight was over.

"I think that was it for that group," I said louder than needed. The confined space had made the gunshots echo loudly, muffling my hearing, even worse with my senses being supercharged. It would take me a few minutes to get back to normal.

Petro and Phil, on the other hand, didn't have much of an issue with the noise. Phil, being an Earth Mage, was able to control the sound, and Petro . . . well, Petro could just shut his hearing off. He hadn't explained how he did it, and in all honesty, I was jealous of his ability to do so.

"Smells like it, boss. We gave it to 'em," Petro replied, landing on my shoulder, quickly reloading his small rifle while smoothing his mustache.

"I'm not too sure that was the last of them. You lads notice how all the other folks seemed to be coming after us?" Phil asked.

The gears in my head started turning. "Now that you mention it, yeah," I said as the sound of another explosion shook the hall.

I reached into my pocket, pulling out one of the synced, enchanted communicators. Placing it in my ear, I looked over to see Phil and Petro doing the same. We hadn't taken the time to do so when everything went sideways.

"Ed, you there?" I asked as the cool sensation of the communicator linking washed through me.

"What the hell is going on? Why is everyone looking for Aslynn, and more importantly, why are they looking for you?" Ed demanded, confirming what I suspected. "Check your phone."

Looking down, several security pictures of Aslynn with her hands up, summoning the catlike flying creatures, made Ed's questions overly relevant.

There would have to be a way to spin this, I thought, not making a big deal out of the situation.

"I see it. What's the big deal?" I asked, flashing my screen to the others. Petro just sighed while Phil made a screwed up face.

"The entire video should come through shortly. I hope to hell there's a good explanation for this. The footage was immediately sent out to every agency with an acronym. Someone was betting on everyone being there. Look, be careful. We're not sure what's going on yet," Ed explained as static started coming through the communicator.

I reached down, grabbing my ear as the communicator started ringing like a bell. The feeling was similar to someone jumping into your head and slamming a bell with a hammer. Petro and Phil were doing the same thing before the three small communicators tinked on the ground.

"What the hell was that?" Petro complained, holding his ear.

"We've been set up," I replied as I slowly dropped a small round stone on the ground, also pouring a small vial of water I was carrying on the item. Smoke started billowing out of the wet, round stone, covering the hallway in a blinding blanket of fog. I had just activated one of the small spheres Trish had so kindly gifted to me.

"What the bloody hell!" Phil barked as I stood up slowly with Petro on my shoulder, walking down the hall, able to see everything.

CHAPTER 19

By Demons Be Driven

"This better be good, boss," Petro said as we turned the final corner. The fog charm's effects slowly dissipated while sounds of gunfire and shouting echoed off the halls from multiple directions.

Between the distraction from Aslynn, Bruce's crafts, and every person with a badge fighting, the concert had devolved into what I liked to call a soup sandwich.

"Yeah, I keep telling myself that. Aslynn's up here," I said, taking a deep breath. "Petro, I need to keep Phil out of this till it's all sorted out."

"How do you know it's her?" Petro asked, taking flight now that he was able to see again.

"I just do. Listen, things are going to get a little crazy. I didn't think it would go down like this. You good, bruther?" I asked Petro in my best impersonation of Phil.

"I'm all in, boss," he replied as he slapped the charging handle on his rifle. "I knew it was Aslynn, by the way."

Petro never failed to amaze me. People, Ethereals, and Mages alike always downplayed Pixies. They often ignored their keen ability to suss things out. Me, I knew better.

"When did you know?" I backed into a bathroom, avoiding a small group of crafts running down the hall. Once they passed, it would only be a set of stairs to get to Aslynn.

"Technically, after the fight at Ben's. Completely sure, when she showed up. I don't think things are going to end well for her if she keeps throwing around all that Voodoo," Petro replied quickly.

I nodded as we walked up a short flight of stairs to find Aslynn standing over the hole in the wall she had created. Several dead crafts were lying at her feet. It was odd how their bodies had not dissolved into e-core.

"Hey, Aslynn," I barked as loud as I dared to avoid drawing any attention. This was stupid, of course, due to the general tornado of whatever it was Aslynn was spewing out.

"That's not going to do it, boss," Petro said, launching toward her. Sounds of fighting were coming from the other side of the room behind a closed set of double doors.

Much to my surprise, Petro slammed into Aslynn's arm with the point of his sword leading the way. The smoke coming from her started faltering as Petro zipped back out of reach, seeking shelter with me a few steps down from the entrance.

"Aslynn!" I yelled louder. She turned as recognition took hold of her face. I hadn't noticed initially that her feet were a few inches off the ground before she dropped.

The tendrils of smoke slammed back into her body as she held out a hand, looking disoriented. "I'm fine. I just need a second," Aslynn reassured, turning her attention to the noise coming from the other side of the door.

Saying the room was completely destroyed would be an understatement, as Petro and I made our way to Aslynn.

"Look, we don't have a lot of time. I appreciate you not going all crazy while going all crazy," I said sarcastically, helping Aslynn to her feet.

"We were set up," she replied bluntly as we all turned

toward the door. The hums of spells being cast and what sounded like a sword fight were getting closer.

"Ding, ding, we have a winner. The two of us are going to have a nice long chat when and if we make it out of here. We should have known better," I said, reaching into my pocket to pull out an Evergate stone, only to have it flung out of my hand as the double doors went exploding into the room, slamming directly into me.

"Boss!" Petro's voice came loud yet muffled as I pushed myself up. Aslynn was still on her feet, however, holding her head.

Two purple glowing orbs rose from her hands as a shadowed hulking figure whose shoulders reached either side of the double doors came into view.

"The date's over," came Kane's booming voice. He was the bass player for Planes Drifter, an ogre, and more importantly, related to Mouth.

"Aslynn, stand down," I ordered, gasping for air as I got to my feet. I could tell Aslynn was running on pure adrenaline and might not pause to see who she was about to sling a spell at. Abby walked around Kane with a stern yet suave look on his face.

"It's time for an encore," Abby said, smirking.

Kane shook his head, letting out a huff of air. "Don't encourage him," the hulking bass player warned, pointing to Abby.

"So, you guys were just running around the stadium picking fights with random fans?" I asked, still clearing my thoughts.

Jim and Knight Raider came running into the room, having finished off whatever or whoever it was blocking the other hallway. Knight was carrying, of course, a medieval-looking sword, while Jim had a bo-staff.

"We figured you'd be heading this way. Especially after a bunch of crazy video feed and pictures came over the system," Abby explained, dusting himself off. He wasn't carrying a weapon. The sounds of multiple helicopters hovering overhead accompanied by high-powered lights made it clear that the show was officially over.

"What pictures? From what system" I inquired, looking around the floor for the gate stone. Petro, picking up on what I was doing, joined the hunt. We didn't have much time, as it would only be a minute or two before Phil figured out where we were.

Abby spoke up, no longer in rock star mode. "You two need to get out of here. We have a link to the systems in the crucible room back at the Atheneum. We were back in our trailer, and a bunch of video feeds of you and Aslynn walking into the show popped up. Then a bunch of pictures of you two talking back at the Council halls. The one that got our attention was of Aslynn here walking up to the executive suites before she met you; next things you know, there's a big hole in the wall after you two linked up. I know Ned's daughter did this, and to a point why, but I'm not sure why you appear to be helping her. We can figure this out later and how to clean it up. Well, hopefully. Go now."

Petro zipped over, dropping the Evergate stone in my hand as Phil's cussing became clearer from down the stairs. "*Porto*," I barked as a thin portal shimmered to life.

A few seconds later, we were through, and I closed the gate before Phil could make it into the room. The calm coolness of the Postern was a stark contrast to the disaster we had just left.

Before I could say anything, Petro spoke up. "They're going to know we're here, boss."

What I hadn't talked to Petro or anyone else about, was that I had a plan. "Where exactly is here?" I asked, getting confused looks from the others. Walking over to the locked cabinets, I pulled out the purple box Devin had gifted me a couple of years back.

"Aslynn, I'm not going to tell you everything because, after tonight, I'm still on the fence. I'm just not sure what side of it to jump down on yet. This box will lock the Postern and, in effect, make it unavailable. You'll only be able to get in and out by using the gates, and I just happen to have all the ways to do so," I said, leaving out a few minor details Petro was fully aware of, like his brothers still having a stone to the Evergate.

The inside of the entrance door also had the same ornate dragon carved and built onto it. Dark, vacant eyes and an angry mouth sat empty. The mouth hung slightly open, with both fangs missing. I would keep one fang to gain entrance if stuck on the outside, retethering the Postern to a location. It was actually more complicated than that, and I honestly only understood bits and pieces of it after talking it over with Gramps.

"Uh, boss. You sure this is such a good idea?" Petro asked, also knowing my reservations with doing so.

"Yeah. If this works, it may come in handy later. Aslynn, we're going to need to figure out how this knife works, and what we need to do to get Bruce looking for it," I told her, opening the Messengergate. It was also time to give Ben a little fresh air and send him on his way.

We walked in to find Ben and the Messenger sitting at the old desk with a pile of pizza boxes and several empty slushy cups. "Gents, it looks like Hermes must have paid you a visit," I greeted as Ben stood up, looking to be in a good mood.

"That man was *who*?" Ben asked as we made our way to the table.

"Hermes. Look, never mind. It's time to go. I want you to stay at the Atheneum for the next few days till you see me again. Tell Ed, Phil, and Jenny that I'll be back and not to come looking for me. Give Ed this," I requested, handing Ben a sealed letter.

"I guess everyone has a note to hand off," he said, giving me a letter from Hermes.

The Messenger looked up. "People are trying to open gates in here that have not been used in ages. I am, for now, keeping them shut, but I can't do that for long," the old man informed slowly.

"That was going to be my next question. No one can get into the Postern if they didn't come through it to get here, right?" I asked as the man nodded.

"Time to go," I said as I nodded back to the Messenger.

Ben started asking questions as I shuffled him out of the room and into the Atheneum. Voices started echoing from the stacks; a group was heading to the Postern. Closing the entrance, I quickly placed the gems into the face of the dragon facing inward, leaving the fangs out as noted in the journal. Nothing happened.

"Is it supposed to work that way?" Petro asked as Aslynn walked over, examining the head.

"Not work is more like it," she said, placing her hand on the dragon's forehead. "Oh." She backed up. "Put the other fang in, then pull it out."

Following her instructions, I put in the last fang as a sucking whoosh of air swirled around the Postern. My ears popped like being in a plane during a quick descent.

"Grab it quickly!" Aslynn exclaimed as the sound of air grew louder. The dragon's face was starting to move like it was alive and looking for a snack after a long nap.

I quickly pulled the fang out as a pop of ozone knocked me back, the air and pressure immediately stopping.

"What the hell was that?" I barked, looking down at the door handle, only to see it gone.

"I'm not sure, boss, but I don't want to find out. It was like the thing was coming to life," Petro said, buzzing over to the table.

"That's precisely what it was doing. I have a feeling that's not only a lock but a security system, if ever needed. I've never felt magic like that before. It's old, yet familiar," Aslynn trailed off.

I looked down at my phone to see no signal. It had worked. If not, we would have heard knocking at the door by now. Reaching into my pocket, I pulled out the note from Hermes.

"What does it say, boss?" Petro inquired, looking at his phone. This was followed by a slow, drawn out, "Dammit!"

"What?" I asked, seeing the screwed up look on his face.

"I didn't get a chance to let Casey know I wouldn't come home. She's going to be worried sick," Petro replied as I let out a breath.

"Tell you what. We can pop out somewhere long enough for you to send a message. Then we need to leave those in here till we get the rest of this plan sorted out, since they can track us by our phones," I said, placing my phone on the round table in the middle of the room, also grabbing the key to the Mirrorgate.

"What plan is that?" Aslynn asked as I turned the paper around for the others to see. It simply read *Hades*.

I had sent a message to Hermes with a simple question. *Who did the knife truly belong to?* With Hades being the original owner, I had a pretty good idea how to go about finding our way to him. The knife had passed several hands. Bo, Tom, the Thule Society, Bruce, and lastly, Maman Brigitte. The one person who would know how to use the knife was the last person I wanted to sit down and have a hamburger with.

"I'm going to need you guys to sit tight while I go have

a little chat with someone," I said as Petro scrunched his face quizzically.

"Boss, you sure it's a good idea for you to be running around on your own?" he asked, not wanting to be left out.

"Yeah, pretty sure. Take a quick trip so you can reach out to Casey. Don't be long. I'll only be gone a few hours," I said, hoping I was on the right track. Aslynn just shrugged, knowing her options were quickly becoming limited.

CHAPTER 20

The Long Dark Tea Time for the Souls Part II

As always, the beachfront restaurant was moderately crowded. Obvious regulars lined the bar, leaving no room for outsiders, ensuring I would sit at a table. Much to my surprise, the same attractive young hostess nodded at the same corner table as last time, overlooking the ocean.

Even though I had been poisoned by Lilith and her goons last time I was here, I still liked the place. The smell of frying food, ocean, and cold beer reminded me I needed some time off.

"What will you have? The same?" the young woman in shorts about as small as they could make them prodded.

"That will do just fine," I said as she nodded without taking any notes.

As the food arrived, the waitress again smiled with a deceptively innocent grin. "Enjoy, and it's on the house," she said, setting down a glass of draft beer.

The smell of beer, bacon, and cooked beef made my mouth water with every bite. It only took a few minutes to eat as I sat there waiting for whatever spell was in the food to take effect. After five minutes, I motioned the waitress over.

"Is this the same as last time?" I asked as a cool breeze swept across the back of my neck. The young lady stood there looking blankly past me.

"Oh, it is, Max. I just assumed we could be civil this time around," Lilith's voice came as the smell of an Onyx cigarette wafted in front of me.

"That's yet to be determined," I said, the hairs on the back of my neck standing at attention. Grandma sure knew how to make an entrance.

Lilith walked into view and sat across the table, crossing her legs, motioning at the waitress. "Thank you, child. I'll take it from here," she said in a calm, calculating tone.

"So, how does this work? I come in, order a burger, and you get some type of magical alarm letting you know I'm here?" I asked, having come to the beach bar on a hunch and nothing more.

"Let's just say when it comes to family, I have a feel for these types of things. I would be remiss not to ask why you want to have a chat with me. Do consider, there are a lot of people looking for you at the moment," Lilith said, tapping her now human fingers on the table.

Lilith had replaced the one arm she'd lost with a mechanical one. I was partly to blame for the loss of her appendage. Whatever she had done, it was real and back to normal. What truly caught my attention was the golden sash Gramps had also taken from her during the fight at Castle Rock in Antarctica. It was clear the two had been together at some point over the past year.

"How bad is it?" I asked, seeing if she was in the mood to talk.

"Oh, it's bad. I'd be more concerned with the regulars this time around," Lilith replied as the waitress brought over a glass of wine, bowing before leaving.

"Why not the Council?" I asked, pulling out the dagger, setting it on the table.

"Child, you truly think the Council doesn't know what Aslynn's been up to? Or at least a handful of those bloated egomaniacs?" Lilith said indignantly, sipping her wine.

"Pot, kettle, black, Grandma. You don't mind 'Grandma,' right? Grandmother? Grand?" I said, aggravated by the fact that she was always a few steps ahead of not only me but seemingly the rest of the world.

Lilith let out a tight laugh, picking up the knife and running her fingers over the jeweled hilt. "Yes, I'll give you that, child. Tell me a story about a king's castle that still stands, more to the point, one that still has its actual king. Regulars come and go, but the Council . . . let's just say, never underestimate what they do and do not know. Or for that matter, what they allow to go on."

"Fair enough. I'm not here to break bread or work on our relationship. I need answers," I said as Lilith locked her gaze with mine. It felt like she was staring into my soul.

"Oh, you definitely need to work on our relationship. What if I have something you will eventually want and everyone else will need? Huh," Lilith huffed, getting to the point. "The knife has been in many hands lately. It has two functions. I'm sure by now you know it serves as a gate of sorts. It's also a knife."

"How does it work, and where does it go?" I asked, shaking my head, Lilith's attempt at humor falling flat.

"It opens a gate to Hades Keep. That means his personal prison." She leaned back in her chair.

"And it only works from a certain location in the Everwhere?" I continued her thought, already knowing the answer.

"Correct. Now for the interesting part. I don't recommend stabbing anyone with that unless you want to turn them into a spirit set to roam whatever realm the knife deems one suited for," she said. "You know, kind of like that gun you have. Hades himself used to use this on certain types sent to him for judgment.

"Even more interesting, the knife also holds the ability to bring someone back. That part is something I know nothing more about, but I do recognize that is why Bruce wants this particular item." The information she was relaying swam in my mind as the sound of sirens grabbed my attention.

I started thinking about the gate key made from the same material, seemingly part of a set. Truth be told, I had hit a wall on the some of the other gates.

"Let me guess. Gramps gated Mengele to this Keep, didn't he?" I asked, getting a sinking feeling in my stomach.

"Oh, you are just like Tom. To be clear, I would rather Mengele stay right where he is, as should everyone else," Lilith said, looking down at her watch. "Luckily for him, Hades is bound not to interfere."

"About that. Have you been staying clear of the Thule Society and their early retirement plan?" I asked, referencing the large number of goons the team and I had killed. I wasn't proud of the fact, but it was a fact nonetheless.

"I got what I wanted out of that little relationship. One of your esteemed Councilmen has decidedly taken the organization in a new direction." The anger in her voice was close to breaking through.

"Let me guess. You gave Councilman Darkwater powers when you provided him with the liquid from the Fountain of Youth. He became stronger than planned for some unforeseen reason, and then gave you the boot, or at least your plan?" I guessed.

"Watch your tongue, child. I was slaying civilizations

before Christ walked this Earth. Maybe you should be more focused on what exactly they are up to now instead of on what they used to be," Lilith said as the sounds of sirens grew louder. Either I was paranoid or they were heading our way.

"What is this thing you '*got*,'" I inquired, holding my fingers up, making air quotes.

"You're catching on. I thought you'd never ask. Remember the children? Of course you do. Anyway, you know as well as the others that we took several with us. There is one in particular. That one is another thing you should be concerned with," Lilith said, standing up.

"What does that mean?" I asked as she smiled.

"Go to the Keep, give the knife back to its rightful owner, take it off the chessboard or see what Hades says. Either way, it must make its way back," Lilith indicated as blue lights started dancing off the walls.

"That's it? Just turn the knife in like an overdue library book?" I replied, getting agitated at the cryptic messages.

"If you want to get Bruce Teach to show his cards, make it very publicly known you have the knife, even if you don't anymore; I'm sure you'll figure out how to get everyone's attention. Just be careful. He's more than capable, and it's the one thing that can not only bring his father Beleth back but release Mengele as well.

"Oh, and one more thing. Stop being so naive. Certain parties on the Council in high positions are fully aware of what Aslynn is doing, and I would even bet, helping," Lilith said, pointing at the half a dozen squad cars that had just pulled up with lights and sirens blaring.

"What did you and Tom . . ." I started to ask, realizing she was done talking.

Lilith motioned at the knife as she dissolved into dust, floating away in the wind. I looked at the knife, picking it up as a loud, modulated voice came over a megaphone.

"Max Abaddon Sand, come out with your hands up."

"Can't they come up with a better line," I huffed under my breath, shaking my head. I grabbed the knife in one hand and an Evergate stone in the other.

Two things became clear. First, on the beach, there were more public CCTV systems than the average person could imagine videoing you at all times. Secondly, in the span of thirty seconds, a news van had magically appeared.

"How the hell did they get here so fast?" I asked as the waitress walked over and set down the bill, acting as if none of this was happening. "Hey, I thought this was on the house?"

"I called them as soon as you got here, and I changed my mind," the young woman replied as I threw down a twenty.

It was odd how she didn't seem to care about the shit show going on around her. Also, I wasn't sure why I paid the bill. Lilith must be on a budget.

"Here goes nothing," I mumbled again to myself, walking out in front of the bar with my hands up, the knife in clear sight.

"Drop the weapons and put your hands behind your head," the man ordered as I stepped in front of the entrance.

Since the Balance, civilian authorities had to adjust how they approached suspected magical types. It was significantly more complicated than in the past. The thing was, they had always interacted with the magical community. They just never knew it. A purple glow emanated from one of the cars, telling me they had magical deterrent equipment installed, all thanks to Mags-Tech.

Using my heightened vision, I saw the TV crew's cameras focus on me as I activated the Evergate stone behind me, falling back into the gate and closing it before anyone could tell what I had just done.

CHAPTER 21

The Under

"You always know how to stir the pot, don't you," Kim said as I sipped the pitch-black cup of coffee. I had taken a slight detour on my way back, popping in to check on the others before walking right back out to Kim's apartment. She had been released early and was on bed rest for a couple more days.

"We'll see. I don't think this is as bad as it looks, at least for the Council. Bruce and Darkwater set this up. I'm pretty sure it's going to take some patching up, but if everything lines up, I might be able to throw all this right back at them," I replied as Kim winced, sitting up.

"You and your old girlfriend out running around. That didn't take you long," Kim said sarcastically, knowing I had no intention of going late-night barhopping with Aslynn.

"Something like that. You don't have to leave, you know," I said, letting her understand where my head and heart were.

"I do. I need a break from all this. Not you, just this." She waved her arms around.

The smell of lavender and rich coffee filled my nostrils as I took a cleansing breath. I had grown to like her apartment. It felt normal, like old times. No magical gates or Pixie family living in the walls.

"Here." I handed her a folder. Inside was the write-up on Councilman Darkwater's activities over the past three years. "Insurance policy. Don't open it. I mean it. If anyone comes snooping around about Darkwater, well, if you trust them, hand them this."

The one thing I didn't want to do was give too many details to Kim just in case. I had learned Diviners couldn't get information from people if they didn't know it. Prior to heading to the Postern with Aslynn, she had given me some rather damning evidence on Councilman Darkwater.

I was also using this as a possible way out of this mess if needed. With one final pull, I finished my coffee. It was time to go.

"Be safe. Max, you don't always have to try and save the world," Kim added as I opened the gate back to the Postern.

"One step at a time. I already bought the nonrefundable ticket," I said smiling as I walked back.

***

"How's Casey?" I asked as Petro tied a bandanna around his head. Aslynn had the pack she had brought with her open, securing what looked like enchanted charms to her belt.

"She's good. Not super happy I'm going to be gone, but at least I'm not in all kinds of trouble," Petro replied, grinning. "Plus, she gave me this kick-ass bandanna like Rambo wears."

I already knew that Pixies weren't really considered much of a threat. This was, of course, a mistake which had proven to come in handy in multiple occasions. However, the one mistake I had made was exposing Petro to certain movies, *Rambo* being one of them. Other movies such as *Aliens*, *Bloodsport*, and Steven Seagal's all-time classic, *Under Siege*, had proved less problematic than Rambo and his antics as an ex-special forces operator. Petro would literally reenact entire scenes of the movie. Even worse, he would do this in public.

While this mostly consisted of the crowd at FA's, he did one time get a bow and arrow after a cap full of rum before he got shut down by Trish.

"Petro, you aren't bringing the bow, are you?" I asked, looking over at the weapons cabinet, seeing it unlocked.

"Boss," Petro drawled out in his best Sly impersonation. "I'm their worst nightmare; they drew first blood."

"You can't mix quotes," I said as Aslynn cleared her throat.

"You boys done?" she asked, pulling out a potion vial. Taking the liquid down in one pull, Aslynn shuddered as her eyes started glowing green.

"Fairy energy drink?" I asked as she shook her head.

"Something like that, and if you call me a fairy again . . ." Aslynn trailed off, winking at me.

"Boss, Fae aren't exactly the most welcomed creatures down there," Petro explained as I shrugged my shoulders.

"I'm not taking any chances," Aslynn continued. "Out of all the realms and beings, the Fae were particularly cruel during the Great Divide and the war that followed." She slapped a magazine of enhanced bullets into her sleek pistol.

"I have a feeling I should be more worried about this," I said, taking their advice and walking over to the weapons cabinet. Phil's two favorite shotguns hung there, reminding me that I would more than likely owe him several free drinks after this was over if we could pull this off.

The sounds of clicking weapons and dull light reflecting off various pieces of equipment kept us occupied for the next several minutes. I also took a few minutes to explain my meeting with Lilith.

Aslynn, much to my surprise, was in a complete set of

fatigues. Petro was in his usual black and leather miniature SWAT gear. I was in a pair of old blue jeans, a T-shirt, boots, and my ever-trusty trench coat.

While modifying my blazer to reach my knees, I had come to realize that I was a walking cliché when it came to new age Mages. I would keep it simple for this trip: my short staff, service pistol, and a handful of dissolution grenades, which were a newly modified version of the small rounds Petro carried in his rifle.

Jenny, in conjunction with the creative genius of Phil after a liter of whiskey, had come up with the concept. Small round Easter egg–size balls would splatter on impact, dispersing a special solution neutralizing spells and their general magical effects. Long story short, a handful of the small round eggs could take out a wall of crafts. This would have been handy during the concert, or as Petro started calling it, the Farewell Tour.

"Boss, I think we're ready to go," Petro said, breaking the silence as Aslynn pulled out a sleek black wand.

"Yeah, I just hope this moves the needle." I opened the Mirrorgate. "I wonder if old Brucey saw the footage from the beach?"

"Sounds to me like Lilith called them on purpose. I'm more than positive he's trying to figure out where you are as we speak," Aslynn replied, grinning.

"That's the issue. I'm not sure what he's going to do. Let's hurry up. When we get back, we'll ring the dinner bell and play this out on our terms," I said as Aslynn shook her head.

"Wouldn't that be nice," she responded flatly, shaking her head.

"I think we need to take this." I held up the knife. Aslynn grabbed it, pulling it out of its scabbard.

"I would think so," she agreed, stabbing it into the table.

A waft of ozone popped in the air as we all froze.

"I would also think we don't need to mess with this till we know how to use it," I grumbled, putting the knife back in its scabbard before walking through into the Everwhere.

The cool, damp smell of the Atheneum in the Everwhere was more defined than that of its mirrored twin. Small white particles floated in the air as we hopped again through the Seekergate into the stacks. Petro had assumed correctly. If we sealed the Postern from the inside, it would be in the same condition in the Everwhere.

"Damn, this place gets creepier every time we come over," Petro said, staying close instead of his usual scouting runs near the ceiling.

In all honesty, I didn't blame him. The ceiling looked like upside-down pitch-black water shifting and moving above us. Looking at the walls, it was hard to tell when the sides ended and the ceiling took over.

The sounds of clicking and books falling echoed randomly from the thousands of rows of files and various display cases. Dull purple light streamed in at odd angles from random locations, supported by the faint yellow glow of the stacks' ambient lighting.

"How pleasant," Aslynn said quickly, showing she was nervous. I could see the slight shifting of her eyes.

"I'm fairly sure things are only going to get weirder from here," I whispered, turning down a dark row of volumes. "I've always wondered if these are the same books as back home?"

"No, they aren't," Aslynn answered in the same hushed tone. We were trying to take our minds off how unnerving the stacks in the Everwhere were.

After a few more minutes of small talk, we arrived at the riser in the middle of the room. This was home to the restricted section and vault. I reached down, twisting the handle of the door to find it opening.

As the door opened, a whoosh of air flew by, telling us somebody had sealed the room. Walking in, the abnormal pressure and general unease of the rest of the stacks dissipated. Petro zipped over to the far shelf, lighting several candles as I closed the door behind us, locking it.

All three of us let out deep breaths as we relaxed. "I'm pretty sure there's something out there," I said, seeing Aslynn looking around the room. Unlike the artifact cases in the main stacks, the ones here still held some of their treasure. Looking closer, the items were, in fact, not the same as the ones back home.

"I'd bet a bucket of fried bugs on it," Petro agreed, landing on the familiar-looking desk. "Hey, boss? This place is different from everything else."

"Yeah, buddy, I noticed that. If I'm not mistaken, that desk is just like the one Gramps gave me and the one that magically replaced it in his office. It feels different in here too. Not all dreamy, but grounded," I said, walking over to the vault door at the far end of the room.

"Looks like you found another piece of the round table," Aslynn said. "I think you're both right. Something's off in here. The magic smells different. Plus, did you notice the empty cot and small nightstand in the corner?" She pointed, walking up to the vault door.

"I think we have enough life-altering mystery and intrigue for one lifetime. The last thing we need is any other weird shit going on," I said, scanning the door.

Aslynn nodded in agreement, running her hands on the edges of the vault door. She was still giving off nervous energy from our walk through the stacks.

The entrance was much like an old bank vault door. A large ominous pinwheel handle sat offset with a large dial in its center. Intricate metalwork reminding me of the internal kitchen door at FA's adorned the exposed gears and working of the lock's mechanisms.

The door was significantly different, as was the rest of this particular room from the one back home. It felt as if the room was lived in and used regularly.

"Give it a shot, boss. Couldn't screw it up any more than you already have!" Petro exclaimed as I grinned, spinning the handle.

"Oh, you think I screwed this up. I can't wait till you're changing diapers," I said, pointing at Aslynn as she rolled her eyes.

"Diapers? What does that mean? Are they evil?" Petro asked as an echoing click came from the lock.

"You might want to read some more on taking care of a baby," I suggested as I pulled the door open. The mood shifted as chilling air slammed into the room. It wasn't an average gust of wind, but rather a foreboding omen. We stood looking into the black void of the vault, the pitch-black darkness of the space absorbing any struggling glints of light.

I turned to talk as my now visible breath filled the air. "Petro, hey, buddy. I need you to get some light on in there. Throwing hellfire around might not be the best idea."

Petro saluted, zipping off into the dark abyss. While he was brave, he also had an exceptionally keen sense of danger and awareness of his surroundings.

After a few seconds, several flames started breathing to life from the far end of the room. As the size of the vault came into view, Aslynn and I looked at each other quizzically.

"You seeing this?" she asked as we both crept into the room. Petro buzzed down, shaking off the cold while landing on my shoulder after lighting the last hanging lamp.

The room looked to be chiseled out of the cavern. Rocks

with a sheen resembling that of polished coal adorned the ceiling and walls. The cold air muted the smell of ash, furthering the mood-crushing feel of the space.

In the center of the room was a sizeable black arch made out of the same coal-like material. The lack of any furniture—or anything else, for that matter—made it clear this was the gate to Hades Keep.

"How do you think we activate it, boss? You want me to pee on it?" Petro asked as I pulled out the knife.

"I'm guessing it's a knife, so let's cut a path," I said, tracing the outline of the arch before finally stepping back. The three of us paused, waiting for something to happen.

"Well, looks like the boy wonder needs to go back to the drawing board," Aslynn said as I huffed.

As soon as I put the knife back in its scabbard, a dark, black wave flowed through the opening of the arch. "I knew that was going to happen."

Petro and Aslynn groaned as if kickstarting an opera.

"Ladies first," I said as Aslynn disappeared into the void.

***

The change in temperature and general feel of the chamber we had just walked into was staggering. Hot, dry air, much like what I had experienced in Kuwait during my time in the army greeted me like an old friend.

"It's cooking in here, boss!" Petro exclaimed much louder than necessary, making Aslynn and I flinch.

"I think we need to keep a low profile here, buddy. Phewwww." I whistled.

"Little warm for my taste as well," Aslynn agreed, looking around the tight space.

"Not to mentioned cramped. I don't think we could fit many more people in here," I said, pointing at the narrow hallway leading out of the small gate room.

The small cave itself was similar to the prior cavern; however, the stone walls had a bronze, almost gold tint. Ambient lighting emanated from small cracks in the rock. Stepping forward, the hall was just as cramped as the room.

Anyone who had claustrophobia would have already bailed. Only one person at a time could walk down the narrow corridor.

"You think it's safe, boss?" Petro asked, floating in front of us, lightly dusting.

"Not a chance in hell," I replied as Aslynn again groaned.

I stepped forward, scanning the endless void in front of us. The sounds of grinding stone as the path closed behind us made a clear statement. *I know you're here, and you aren't leaving as easily as you came.*

"That answers that," I said as Petro landed on my shoulder. The ceiling was eight feet high at most, adding to the constricting feel of the hall.

"The size of this gate and hall are strategic. Keeps down the number of people, or things, that can pass through," Aslynn said.

I paused, noticing the walkways getting tighter. My shoulders were now lightly brushing the rocky walls.

"It gets any snugger in here, I'm going to have to tighten my belt," I said, also noticing the lack of any echo.

"I'm going to check it out. Hang here," Petro said, darting ahead, a light trail of dust coming from his wings disappearing into the void.

I looked back at Aslynn. "What are you thinking?"

"That we shouldn't be naive. This is Hades's realm. He knows we're here. Since we haven't died yet, chances are he wants to talk," Aslynn stated flatly. Not hearing the playful banter I was used to still made me uncomfortable around her.

"Or play with us," I said as Petro darted out of the pitch-black cone of possible death.

"Well, boss, I think we need to get to the end of this hall as soon as possible. Not sure how it's happening, but the path is close to sealed at the end. It's about another quarter mile," Petro informed, taking a deep breath. He had flown at max speed.

"So . . . we're stuck?" I asked, getting genuinely nervous.

"Not exactly. When I was flying, the walls spread out of my way like a curtain. Weirder than the colorized version of *The Munsters*. It takes some serious mojo to make that happen. It's like this place is alive," Petro said as Aslynn huffed. I nodded in agreement with his assessment and judgment on anything that had been colorized.

"I don't like this. Look down." Aslynn pointed at the grooved scuffs on the stone walkway. Scrape marks adorned either side, confirming that the walkway was opening and closing as we moved forward.

The feeling of claustrophobia started to set in. Without any other words exchanged, we moved forward at a steady mall walker's pace.

By the time a dull, pulsating light informed us our journey was about to end, I was walking sideways with my head turned.

At the exact moment my body was telling me no more, we pushed out into a large, open chamber. Even though we hadn't exerted any energy, the mile walk's mental expenditure had Aslynn and I both breathing heavily.

"You good, boss?" Petro asked, landing on my shoulder, not pausing long enough for me to respond. "I got some good news and some bad news."

"You know to always tell me the good news first so I can

cut it off there," I joked as we smiled at each other. Aslynn didn't argue with my logic.

The room we stood in was roughly the size of a standard grocery store. Small slits like the one we had just squeezed out of, which was now too small to go back through, lined the walls. Overhead, the ceiling was thirty-plus feet tall and looked as if it flared open the further up it went.

"Well, see all those cracks on the side of the walls? Those are ways out," Petro started, pausing to give me a chance to stop him pre–bad news.

"And?" I replied, staring at the far end of the room.

"That." Petro pointed at the massive door.

"Let me guess. It's a door for something that needs all that space to get through. Huuuh." Sighing, I pulled out my short staff. I wasn't going to pick a fight, but I wanted to be ready for one.

"Always the almost smartest human in the group," Petro said, buzzing over to the massive wooden door. "Hang on, boss. Something smells familiar on the other side."

As soon as the words left Petro's mouth, a loud thump, followed by dust jumping from the door's surface, echoed in the room. Someone, or something, was opening it from the other side.

"*IGNIS!*" I yelled as the hellfire blade erupted from my arm. Aslynn, getting the same message, jumped back, pulling out a wand as her eyes started glowing bright green. Petro just floated in front of us, not moving to arm himself. Either he was under some type of spell or trying to figure out what was behind door number one.

I gripped the short staff with my free hand as we backed up to the far wall. The room was empty, giving us no chance of hiding.

Just as the door started to swing open, it stopped. A

small, dark gap at the far end was as far as the door moved.

"Boss, I think we're . . ." Petro trailed off, about to say *good*, when Oscar in his human yet furry form walked from behind the massive wooden door.

On instinct, Aslynn let loose a spell before either of us could stop her. A ball of green plasma flew at Oscar, hissing as it cut through the air.

"No!" I bellowed, releasing the energy from my body and weapons as Oscar jumped several feet across the room, landing as if he had just taken a short skip.

The spell slammed into the black stone wall, sending several small chunks of debris flying in all directions.

Petro flew straight up, avoiding the spatter of stones as Aslynn calmed her breathing, setting her jaw. "Sorry, I just thought it was Cerberus," Aslynn apologized as Oscar licked the back of his hand like a paw.

"Nice to see you as well," Oscar said, finally turning to face Petro and I.

"I've got questions, but now isn't the time. Can we cut out all the trying-to-figure-this-out talk and go directly to you taking us to Hades?" I asked as the bright green glow started to dull in Aslynn's eyes.

"I'd say everyone has questions. Follow me. Drooly face is sleeping, so you don't have to worry about that oversized bag of fleas," Oscar said, referring to Hades's three-headed dog, Cerberus.

"Drooly face?" I asked as we exited through the cracked door, only to have it close behind us. It was as if the place was alive.

"Far right head when facing him. That one drools a lot, so I call him Drooly face, or at least that annoying one," Oscar explained, letting the words roll off his tongue as the significantly larger room on the other side of the massive door came into view.

CHAPTER 22

House Guests

Opulence is a word that always brings to mind wealthy, rich, ornate spaces. When it came to the living and/or working arrangements for demigods and the like, the word's meaning took on a new level of trying to explain the weird shit I was standing there looking at.

The cavern Oscar led us to was a massive, sprawling chamber full of dark, black stone and what appeared to be silver. Columns gilded in shiny, reflective, silver-like material sat at precise intervals holding up a roof that again seemed to disappear into a dark void. Jutting out of these pillars were large torches flickering with an almost bright white flame, giving the room a muted yet angelic feel.

In the center was a sunken area full of ornate couches and a large throne which happened to sit directly in the middle. What absolutely took my and the others' breath away were the massive walls on either side. These looked to have hundreds of frozen sections filled with what appeared to be some type of human or animal. A dull yellow glow made the figures inside stand out as if they had been frozen in amber over thousands of years.

"Well, it's about time!" the loud voice thundered throughout the room. I looked around, not able to pinpoint its origin. Petro pointed to the tall shadow moving closer from the large door across the room.

"Let me guess," I said only loud enough for our group to hear. "Hades."

"Oh yeah, and I think he's been getting things cleaned up in case you showed your face," Oscar shouted, making me wince.

Hades, at first sight, was roughly ten feet tall and built as one would expect a Greek god to be constructed. Chiseled muscle peeked out from under a shiny silver armor. Underneath, the armor, he wore what looked like a Roman-style tunic, with sandals wrapping up to his knees. Hades, Lord of the Underworld, was dressed for either a fight or a party, depending on how you looked at it.

As the man got closer, his sheer mass and size took even Aslynn off guard. Considering she spent a good amount of time around other gods on the Plane, the look on her face was very telling. This guy was not to be taken lightly.

"Max, I've been looking forward to meeting you, young man. And who do we have here?" Hades said, laser focusing on Aslynn.

"Lord Hades, I am Aslynn Danann, daughter of Nuadha Danann. I am here under the queen's direction," Aslynn said. Fae always had an odd way of putting things when posturing around others.

Hades let out a belly laugh that would make Santa proud. "HAHA. The queen. Young one, you have revenge in your eyes, and after what happened to your family, I don't blame you. Tell your queen I send my best wishes. You are free of any obligation while in my Keep. Oh, and I think I have something you may be interested in. Petron, let me see you up close, little warrior."

Hades had used Petro's full name, something not widely

known. Petro zipped off my shoulder to hover in front of the Lord of the Underworld. His hand rested casually on the hilt of his sword, followed by a quick curtsy.

"You know my feelings on this," Petro said in a serious yet respectful tone.

"Of course, as you should. You are my guest here. I have heard many stories about your bravery, little warrior. You have no enemies here," Hades said as I looked over.

"Is there something I need to be aware of?" I asked as Hades motioned us to walk with him. Oscar just rolled his cat-like eyes.

Hades paused. "Of course. I came into this position many moons ago, as I'm sure you know from the magic search boxes you have these days. After the Great War with the Old Gods, I was put in a rather tough spot. With that, I took part in the Pixies' role in the Fae Plane."

"You sent us to a life of servitude," Petro said, still being respectful in his tone.

It started to make sense. Petro had told me about the history of his people, and how they at one time had a Plane or, as they called it, realm of their own.

"I think you need to talk with Fire Hair's queen about that one," Hades said, the hint of finality in his tone telling Petro not to push the topic. His nickname for Aslynn made me raise my eyebrows.

"Hades, Lord Hades, whatever. We're kind of tight on time here," I said, pulling out the knife as the Lord of the Underworld grinned.

"I don't think time truly matters while you're here. I can assure you that Phil and the others haven't even reached the door to the Postern yet," Hades said coolly, inferring time was not relevant in the Underworld.

As we got to the first wall with the odd figures encased in

the amber-like substance, Oscar nudged me. "Pay attention to this."

Hades was about to show off his trophies. "Here in this room are some of my most prized guests in the Underworld. As you know, I have a working relationship with the Under, as you call it, better known as Hell. I manage the in-between, the place of dreams, or better put, nightmares. Here, I keep those who are either not ready to take the final trip or, for lack of a better word, are immortal."

I looked closer at the figure in front of us, squinting my eyes, before quickly jumping back. Aslynn, seeing the same thing, gasped. The tension coming from her was thick enough to feel in the air.

"Why is she here?" I asked, pointing at Maman Brigitte, frozen in time. Her eyes looked as if they were focused on Aslynn, full of hatred.

"Oh, and sometimes for other reasons. I'm sure you know Boegosh. Also, I'm fairly sure Fire Hair is glad to know this one is here," Hades said, winking at Aslynn.

"Why is she here?" Aslynn repeated, echoing my concern. I was aware that Bo had been up to other things while we were busy, and I now had a pretty good understanding what those things had been.

"Bo doesn't like it when people take things from him. As I'm sure you are aware, Tom is alive, and gave the dagger back to Maman Brigitte. From what I understand, she was rather excited to reacquire it until Bo showed up at her front door with Max here. Maman Brigitte is strong in her own right, but Bo can be another level of bad news." Hades paused, putting his hand on the glass-like material.

"I think he wants you to finish the story, boss," Petro said, also taking a closer look.

"She was the one who stole it from Bo originally. Then

it somehow made its way into the hands of the Soul Dealers. Gramps, for some reason I'm not aware of, reacquired it and gave it back to her . . . ?" I said, drawing out the sentence.

"Spot-on, minus a few details and reasons why. The knife was originally part of a set. When the war was over, the knife was sent to the Under and given to Bo to look after. While it was my weapon during the Great War, it was also considered too dangerous to stay near the Everwhere. I agreed to let it go. Too much power in anyone's hands over time never has the planned outcome, no matter how good the intention. Aslynn," Hades started, using her name after seeing his nickname hadn't gone over well.

Aslynn shuffled her feet as I looked down to see the mirror we had given Brigitte leaning against the stone underneath her.

"Your encounter and current debt to a Voodoo bottom-dweller is no coincidence. What I can say is that as long as Brigitte is here, you will be safe from your debt. Ogun is dead. You need to stop using whatever it is he gave you. With his untimely passing, your debt was passed to Brigitte," Hades sternly noted.

"How?" she asked before I could, mild excitement coming through in her voice, sounding as if the weight of the world had been lifted from her shoulders. Well, at least one of them.

"Next time you make a deal, you may want to read the fine print. Maman Brigitte is—well, was—over Ogun. She was his superior, meaning she was responsible for him. She knew and approved of the deal you two made. Before you ask, Ogun came to his mistress's rescue. He tried to, at least. I don't know if you've been around Bo when he's pissed. It's not a pretty sight."

Hades walked toward another section of holding cases.

"What about the mirror?" I asked, wondering if it had a part to play.

"Oh, yes. Bo wanted you to have it. It's none of my concern. I believe he also left a note attached to the back of it," Hades added dismissively as if it didn't matter. The mirror was more vital than I assumed, and this was his way of telling me so.

I started to reflect on our visit to Maman Brigitte as I picked up the mirror and handed it to Oscar. Bo had stated we came in peace. He had also made a point of saying *today*. Come to think of it, directly before leaving, Bo had pulled Brigitte close, whispering something to her as she looked concerned yet content with something. She then had proceeded to give me the knife. Bo had made a deal, or a threat he had carried through with.

"Bo found out about the deal Aslynn made, and was working to help. He knew what was going on all along," I declared as Petro landed on my shoulder.

"That guy never ceases to confuse the hell out of me," Petro said, smiling. This was, in fact, good news. It was one less thing to worry about in the ever-growing pile of problems. I glanced over at Aslynn, noticing the rejuvenated expression on her face.

I cleared my throat again, speaking up. "I still don't get it. Why did Tom give the knife back to Brigitte?"

"He knew the knife came from Brigitte. Tom figured the rest of the Soul Dealers would eventually assume she had it back in her possession. I'm not sure what the rest of his plan was from there, but it appears you, young lady, were part of it. For once, Tom didn't know everything. He wasn't aware Bo was the original owner. Well, after me, that is," Hades said as we stopped in front of another case.

A loud rumbling growl shook the room as Hades grinned. Oscar sighed, turning toward the large double doors at the far end. I started getting an ugly vision in my head of what Gramps may have been responsible for; the deaths of several people. I also started rationalizing what I had heard about most of the people who had been killed due to this situation.

In my mind, I was working to justify that what had occurred had been the lesser of two evils. A handful of individuals with sordid pasts dying, versus thousands. If the Soul Dealers had been able to continue operating, truly innocent people would have died.

"He made sure I somehow linked up with Ogun," Aslynn said with a tinge of vulnerability in her voice.

Hades smiled as he nodded for us to look at the figure encased in the rock wall. Standing there in front of us, frozen in time, was Mengele, the Angel of Death.

"That's the assclown who caused all this!" Petro exclaimed, pulling his sword.

"Calm down. He's not going anywhere," Hades said.

"For now," Oscar added bluntly.

I walked closer again, noticing the alert eyes burning a hole through me. The longer I stared, the more a cold pull started to grow in my chest. Bigger things were at play. Lilith had told me he was here, meaning the lack of surprise was evident on my face. I needed to find out what Gramps had talked to him about.

"Gramps brought him here till he could figure out the next move. The Supreme Council is engaged in this. Are you like Devin? Not able to truly get involved? You're-just-here-doing-your-job type of situation?" I asked in the form of a statement. At the end of the day, it was a big no-no for occupants of the Over and Under to get involved in things on Earth proper.

"You are correct, Max. Some are more flexible than others, but you are correct. Bo, as you call him, was only trying to get his property back. If he just happened to take out the person holding it or responsible for taking the item, that really doesn't break any rules, now does it?" Hades said, grinning.

I liked the Lord of the Underworld, and it was evident after the last few minutes that the others did as well. Or at least felt more at ease. He was there doing his job, not some evil demigod trying to take over the world. *At least for now*, I thought sighing, getting the others' attention.

"I need to get Bruce Teach's attention. I was told using this knife would attract him like a fly on shit. How do we make that happen?" I asked, getting to the point.

"Well, I'm fairly sure you've already done that. I assume you activated the knife on purpose?" Hades said, looking at the four of us.

"Hey, I wasn't with these three," Oscar extricated himself as I started to get a sinking feeling in my stomach for the third time today.

"What do you mean, activated the knife?" I asked as Hades raised a massive eyebrow, taking a deep breath.

"Right before you three showed up, someone used the knife. Maybe to open a gate or to jab it into something? I'm pretty sure wherever the Postern is anchored is where Bruce will be showing up soon. Whatever ward is in place isn't strong enough to hide the blade. It's a celestial item, meaning it follows its own rules," Hades said as several repetitive, thundering thumps echoed throughout the main chamber.

"Oh shit, boss," Petro said, letting off a small cloud of dust.

"Dammit, it's always something. Hell, Aslynn just stabbed the knife into a table, and we opened the gate here. I thought the knife only worked on living creatures? I think I also need to update the notes in the journal. We've got to get back and warn the others," I said, looking around the room for the door we had entered through.

"Calm down. Like I said, while you're in my Keep, time

is of no concern. You might want to take a closer look at that table you just mentioned as well sometime," Hades said with a strained look of concentration on his face.

"So what can you tell us about this knife and what to do with it? I don't think we need to leave here with it," I suggested, looking for a positive response.

"You could leave it here, or you could take it with you and use it. Either way, I'm certain Bruce will be heading toward the Atheneum. What I can tell you is this: if Bruce gets his hands on this knife, there's no telling what he'll do with it. Mengele and Beleth intended to use the knife for significantly nefarious reasons.

"I want to make something clear; the use of this knife, no matter the reasons, has always produced negative consequences. While I can't get directly involved, I can help in other ways. I know, just like I'm sure the rest of you do, that something's coming. Something big, something ancient, and the Thule Society is doing their best to be in its good graces when whatever it is does occur. I believe it was bad enough to make Lilith step away, or manipulate them into changing," Hades said in a fatherly tone.

"Gramps probably thinks there's some good left in her. Maybe so, but she's done enough evil to ever be able to dig herself out," I started, looking at Aslynn. My point was clear; she was getting close to that point as well. "We need to head back. I'm taking this damn knife with me."

"Hey, boss, isn't that a plot of one of those space movies? War . . . Treks, or something like that?" Petro interjected, butchering both names. To be fair, Petro and most other Pixies weren't interested in remembering the movie if it didn't have strong sexual content or something to that effect. This didn't just pertain to the male of the species either.

"As you wish. Oh, it looks like your friend has made it to the door of the Postern. It would be a shame if he missed out on this conversation," Hades said as he reached up, clapping his massive hands. The noise forced me to cover my sensitive ears as the distinct sound of angry Irishman cussing came from a black cloud of smoke several feet away.

"Bloody hell, I'll . . ." Phil trailed off, taking in the scene in front of him. He was clearly disoriented, yet fully understood he wasn't in Kansas anymore.

"Phil, calm down, brother. We got a whole mountain of crap to talk about," I said as Petro zipped forward.

"Not to mention those shitheads are probably heading to the Atheneum as we speak!" Petro barked in a mix of excitement from seeing Phil and, like the rest of us, wanting to get back.

"Calm down, bruther? You tell me to trust you, and then POOF, a cloud of smoke left my arse behind at the stadium. Then I saw some fancy video of you out there having a couple of drinks at the beach. Everyone is looking for the two of you nutters, saying you went all rogue on the team, causing all this hogwash," Phil let out in one heaving breath. "Oh, and who the hell is this?"

I cleared my throat as Phil also noticed Oscar standing behind us. "Phil, Hades, Lord of the Underworld. Hades, this is Phil."

"Whaaa?" Phil guffawed, finally snapping his jaw back shut.

"The in-between, to be more accurate," Hades corrected, smiling at Phil.

"The-wha-urm," Phil stammered as everyone else in the room looked shocked.

"Would you look at that? Phil's out of words for once. Last time that happened, he was locked in one of those porta potties with a gremlin. Remember that? He came out all blue, looking like a Smurf and covered in—" I lightly chuckled, cutting Petro off.

"Yeah, hey, we don't have a lot of time; at least I don't think so," I said, glancing at Hades, who nodded. "I'll explain what I can. I'm still trying to figure it out. Bruce is on his way to the Atheneum."

Phil took a calming breath. "Bruther, this is the craziest shite I've seen in a long time. Hades, uh, where's your dog?"

Like the others, Phil was very aware of Cerberus from our prior trips into the Everwhere and the stories. It was a good question. I had a feeling he had been making the thumping noise.

"He's excited about something. I need to let him out shortly," Hades said knowingly.

"What does that mean?" Aslynn asked as Oscar walked into the middle of the group.

"That means something in the Everwhere is not where it's supposed to be. If I were a betting cat, I would say something is looking for you back at the Shadow Atheneum," Oscar said, contributing to the growing pile of problems.

"And here I was thinking things were getting easier." I glanced up at Hades. "Think you can wait till we leave to let him out of his cage?"

Hades, picking up on my intention, knew I wasn't trying to get him involved but rather giving him an out. What I wasn't sure about was the condition of the Atheneum back home. From what I gathered, we wouldn't have long to prepare for unwanted houseguests.

"Of course. I'll wait for a few to ensure your safe passage," Hades agreed. He was starting to speak less and less, telling me it was time to go.

"Phil, who else is back at the Atheneum?" I asked, taking stock of what we had at hand. The issue was that upon our arrival back home, there was a good chance the civilian authorities would be waiting for Aslynn and me. If this was the case, they would also be greeted by a ravenous army of whatever the hell it was Bruce was about to throw at us. I started clicking my tongue on the roof of my mouth.

"A handful of marshals, James, Jenny with the girls, Ed, and I do believe some of the civilian police were heading our way," Phil replied, a slight note of worry in his voice.

"I don't think it's going to be enough firepower even for us. We've all seen what kind of shitstorm Bruce and the others can come up with. We need a solid plan," I said, open for ideas.

"What about Bo?" Phil asked, but I shook my head.

"He's out. I'm pretty sure he's already in some kind of trouble for what he's done up to this point. I just wish Bo had told me. We won't have a lot of time when we get back. I hate this crap; knowing what's about to happen," I huffed as the gears in my head started to turn.

"Hey, boss, what about that pretty lady Lana? She's still running around the Everwhere if she's back on the clock. You know, all sexy loincloth and that crazy bow. She was like, bam, whoosh—" Petro started before Hades cut him off.

"I do believe, as of a few minutes ago, Lana has become rather busy. She is indeed at the Shadow Atheneum, as you call it," Hades said. His eyes looked distant, as if seeing everything and nothing all at once. He was, after all, a god.

"Why am I starting to think that our walk through the stacks isn't going to be as easy as it was last time. Phil, before we head back, I will walk you through most of what's happened. It will help in case questions come up when we get back. Hades, if you were going to kick us out of here because we had overstayed our welcome, how much time do you think we would have?" I asked, figuring again it was all about playing the word game.

"I have some things to attend to. I would recommend

you lot head back down to the gate in no later than thirty minutes. Cerberus is a good dog; he can wait," Hades said as he walked toward the center of the massive room, sitting down on the throne. "Oh, and Max, don't forget to make sure I or Bo get the knife back. After all, you haven't returned it yet, have you? I'm not so concerned about the key. I think that mirror will also help at some point. Try looking at your reflection in the Postern."

"Dammit," Oscar purred, standing in the middle of the group and looking at Phil, Petro, Aslynn, and myself. "I'm guessing you guys are counting me with this team. I need to check on a few things first, so I'll follow you."

"Yup," was all I replied as the group laid out everything that had happened since the concert.

The one big plus from our trip to Hades Keep was learning several valuable yet disjointed pieces of a substantially larger puzzle. Bruce was now on the move in the open. Tom was very involved in what was going on. Aslynn might just make it through the evening. And I had another clue to unlocking more of the Postern's mysteries. That being said, I still had questions about Gramps and what he was doing with Lilith.

CHAPTER 23

Lizards O' Doom

"**D**ammit, bruther, this place is more packed than a toilet at Taco Bell," Phil complained as we finally made our way down one of the claustrophobic hallways from hell.

"I'm just glad Petro hasn't had any of those aforementioned tacos," I added as Petro snorted. The little warrior's digestive system and the magical fast-food taco mecca of the gods didn't jive. Pixie gas was a whole other level of things I could have lived without before coming into the magical world.

Ever been driving down the road and think you smell a skunk? You very well may have crossed paths with a gassy Pixie.

"Everyone ready? It's not that far, but we have to work our way through the stacks. If Lana's out there, chances are she knows we came through the restricted area. I have a feeling that might have been her stuff. Petro, get to the Postern as soon as you can. The rest of us will move as a group. If things go south, well . . . run," I indicated, not even convincing myself as I activated the gate.

***

Petro flew to the vault door as Lana stood there looking pissed. "What did you do?" she demanded in her blunt yet feminine voice.

"Great to see you too, lass," Phil said, stepping forward.

"It's always something with you. There are a dozen hellions and what I'm guessing is a lizard of some type running around out there."

A loud thumping noise vibrated the room.

"I think we may also have a new pet," I said, trying to gauge Lana's reaction.

Aslynn walked out of the gate last as Lana grabbed the hilt of her sword. "Alright, ladies, calm down. I don't know what happened between you two, but we need to work together," I said as a loud crash echoed from outside the main room.

"Good luck with that one, bruther. Fae and Elves don't exactly get along too well," Phil explained as I noticed the unease in Aslynn's posture.

"Lana, Aslynn is under my protection. I am fulfilling a promise to her father. If you work with us and allow safe passage, I'll be in your debt," I said as Petro let out a whistle.

"I accept," Lana agreed, walking forward, holding out her hand to Aslynn. The air stilled as Aslynn reached out and the two grabbed each other's wrists in some odd warrior-type sign of respect.

"Okey dokey. Now, can we get the hell out of here?" Phil asked while we walked into the restricted area's main room.

Lana handed Phil a spear as I took a deep breath before opening the door. The immediate sounds of chaos-driven violence filled the usually hushed stacks in the Everwhere. Petro darted out of the room and up at lightning-quick speed.

"Let's move," I whispered as the group exited the restricted area alcove, only to be met with what looked like a spell being cast across the shelves of books in front of us.

"Who the bloody hell are they firing those spells at?" Phil boomed louder than necessary as the hairs on the back of my neck stood on end.

"They're trying to locate us. Let's go left and then cut behind the alcove," Lana indicated, taking the lead with her bow at the ready. Turning the corner, a loud crash echoed through the massive room, accompanied by the howl of a rather large dog. Hades had let Cerberus out. According to Oscar, only one of the heads was rather outspoken, leaving one to drool, and the other to generally rip things to shreds.

Before we turned the next corner, a hellion slammed through a row of shelves, sending books flying in all directions. The creature was mindlessly running through the rows looking for us. Lana raised her bow, loosening two arrows before I could react.

"*IGNIS!*" I yelled, bringing my hellfire blade to life as Phil launched himself forward before I could even let off a ball of hellfire. He was clearly taking out his pent-up frustration from the past two days on the hellion unfortunately standing in front of us.

The creature, slowly realizing it had made a poor choice, looked down, seeing the two arrows sticking out of its gut. "Raghhh," the hellion barked, lurching forward and colliding with Phil head-on as Lana launched another arrow into its leg.

The crackle of bones crushing under Phil's full-on attack, as well as the spear ramming through its body, froze the hellion in place. Its eyes glossed over as we all paused, realization in its stare that we were the last things it would ever see.

Phil pulled the spear out as I walked up to deliver a finishing blow, slicing the creature's head off. The smell of seared, rotten meat made me want to gag. Aslynn stood staring as the three of us turned around. She was in over her head, the stark reality of the situation landing on her like a ton of bricks. Not only had she been used but she was also expendable.

"Hang here for a second. Let me check around the corner," I indicated, lightly jogging ahead of the group as several loud crashes emanated from the area we had just left.

I focused my sight on the misty, dark far end of the stacks. The row I had just left opened up to a large aisle leading off into the distance. Movement caught my attention as I squinted my eyes, asking them for more.

The floating, snow-like particles in the air swished in several directions as a scraping sound mixed with clicking made itself known. The loud crashing noises had concealed the latest addition to the party.

"What the hell . . ." I drawled out, turning back as I launched a ball of hellfire into the darkness. Lurching forward at superhuman speeds, I turned the corner to find the group staring at me. There was no way in Hades Keep I was slowing down.

"Big lizard! Sharp teeth! Looks pissed!" I screamed as the rest of the team, picking up on my mood and the high-pitched screech coming from the monster, joined in behind me.

The timing was perfect, as the rest of the shelves exploded in a flurry of papers. The sound of Lana shooting several arrows whistled through the air as I turned back toward the far wall and subsequent group of hellions. It was the most direct and quickest path to the Postern.

Sensing, or rather hearing our approach, three hellions lumbered from behind a pillar, pulling back what appeared to be axes. I lashed out with my arms, yelling, "*EJECTUS!*" as a wall of tendrilled hellfire flew from my hands with no real organization, shotgun blasting the three hellions.

One thing about hellions was that they were one of the few beings impervious to hellfire. While it still made for a bad day, it was the equivalent of hitting them with a hot taser. The exciting thing about this, however, was that this rule didn't apply while in the Everwhere.

The hellions staggered, letting out guttural howls. The blast had landed spatters of hellfire on their now melting faces as they clawed to put themselves back together.

"Keep going!" Aslynn barked as the sounds of her wand casting spells filled my ears.

Much to my surprise, Phil went running past me. His legs were a blur of silver mist, his body charged to move in front of the team. Phil had done this before. I was almost certain he was getting a good position to sling a kill shot at the lizard o' doom.

"In front of me!" I yelled over the almost deafening bangs drawing closer. "Keep running straight. When you get to the far end, turn right. Petro will be there." I would give Phil as much time as needed for him to figure out how to stop or, at least, slow down the creature.

Lana ran by, nodding in understanding. I often forgot that we had been in substantially worse situations than the current one. At least I hoped. She was a warrior and knew we were setting something up.

"Alright, let's see if you like this," I hissed under my breath, pulling out my pistol and emptying the entire magazine of enchanted ammunition while also slinging a ball of hellfire at it. The wall of sound and fire stopped the creature only long enough for me to realize I had just pissed it off even more.

My feet pounded on the dark marble floor as I slid into the far wall, not making the turn. "Get down, bruther!" Phil yelled as the lizard charged forward, opening its mouth to enjoy its dinner.

I ducked as an almost undetectable whistling "Whoosh!" passed overhead. The *shing* sound of a razor-sharp object slicing through wet flesh forced me to look up.

The lizard stood there, frozen in place. Phil's spear had ripped through the creature when it opened its mouth, leaving it vulnerable. The lizard o' doom was trying to figure a way to get out of its current situation just as Aslynn launched a rocket-fast ball of green plasma from her wand directly down its exposed throat.

Spells cast from a wand had the weird sound of a flushing toilet which made me smile every time. The grin on my face was short-lived, though, as the creature's internal guts erupted from its pinned mouth directly where I was lying.

The group paused, looking at me as I slapped as much of the gore off my body as possible. Lana walked over. "I may have been incorrect."

"About, thppt, pof?" I asked, spitting whatever disgusting viscous material had made its way on my face and into my mouth.

"Two lizards," Lana replied as two more hellions trotted out from a distant aisle of books, followed by the familiar clicking of massive monster lizard claws. They had followed the sounds of the fight.

Hellions, while lethal and fully capable of destroying small armies, were also relatively bad at running. Short, stubby, overly muscular legs supported their large, fat torsos, making them do an odd trot-like shuffle. This, of course, was offset by the fact that they could launch themselves through the air, as the two in front of us just had.

"You mates go. I'll take care of these ruffians!" Phil declared, rolling up his sleeves reaching into the melting lizard, pulling out his spear just in time to counter one of the cleavers the lead hellion was swinging.

I pulled up my right hand, letting loose a small laser-like ball of hellfire into the second hellion. He, assuming it was a he, just stared blankly at me. I had used a good amount of energy already, and was not only focusing my attacks, but what energy I had left in my reserves. There was possibly a more significant fight ahead.

The sounds of metal meeting its equivalent tinged, growing louder. Phil and the other hellion were in a heated game of back-and-forth with their weapons.

I looked over as the hellion standing in front of me just grunted. "Shhh, hush," I said as the large monster started to sway.

This was the first time I had used my combustion hellfire spell on a living, or not so living being. The intent was simple; the results, not so much. Launch a small, concentrated hellfire projectile into an object—or for this event, hellion. As the tight projectile enters whatever it was aimed at, drop your focus, allowing it to blossom uninhibited from the inside.

My primary practice subject for this trick had been trees. I had it down to a science. After some time, I could fire one of these spells at a tree, and it would immediately burn from the inside out. The entire process was fascinating. One minute, the tree was there. The next, it would cave in on itself with little to no warning.

The hellion raised the cleaver over its head to deal a death blow. Phil moved quickly, his body driven by the Etherium coursing through his body, and dropped to one knee, thrusting the staff upward through the chin and brain of the beast. After a second's pause, the hellion's blade clattered to the ground as Phil stood up, his spear still lodged through its skull.

"Behind you!" Phil exclaimed as I turned to see smoke coming out of the hellion's nose, ears, mouth, eyes, and I guessed, its belly button.

"Smokey here, he's long gone. What did you call them? Ruffians?" I asked as a grin erupted from Phil's face.

"I missed you, bruther," Phil said as the hellion behind me finally burst into flames.

"Ditto. We got to go. Time's ticking since we left," I said as Petro flew around the corner.

"It's locked, boss! Remember? From the inside!" Petro said while Phil snorted.

"Oh, yeah." I pulled out one of the Evergate stones from the Postern in the Everwhere. "Don't tell the ladies," I said, grimacing.

I walked up, activating the gate directly in front of the door, trying to play it off. As always, I was significantly less smooth than I gave myself credit for as Lana and Aslynn just shook their heads.

Truth be told, we needed to clear the hellions out. I still wasn't clear on how things or destruction in the Everwhere could affect the normal Plane.

CHAPTER 24

The Big Bad Wolf

I picked up my phone, seeing dozens of messages, and of course, pictures of Phil's middle finger sent before Hades had brought him to the Underworld party. I wasn't precisely sure how my phone had received the messages.

My only guess was the signal had reached the device when one of the gates had been opened, since the Postern was still locked from the inside. I focused, pushing out my thoughts to reach Ed.

After a few seconds of trying, it was clear the enchanted security system also blocked out mind magic, and with that, I assumed, any tracking or divination.

"Hey, boss, either you're trying to poop or making a phone call in your head," Petro said as he flew to the weapons rack. Phil was pulling out his shotguns, talking to them as if they were long-lost star-crossed lovers reunited.

"I was trying to reach out to Ed. Whatever this dragon guard thingy does, it's more than just physical," I informed as Aslynn looked at her phone, pursing her lips.

"Well, I can state that we're about to get some company. That is, per my last few messages before being shut out of the system. Councilman Darkwater sent a large group of CSA agents and Night Stalkers to chase a rogue pack of Werewolves

269

in Australia. You know, the exact opposite side of the Earth," Aslynn huffed. While this was bad news, distance wasn't always a significant factor in the magical community.

The civilian world had also been allowed the use of a handful of registered gates. That being said, I understood that Goolsby sold black market Mags-Tech gear to regulars, including the authorities; stuff the Council generally wanted out of the hands of others. I was actually surprised the Order Society had kept under the radar over the past year.

I nodded at Phil as I reached into the locker, pulling out the Judge. After a few seconds of checking the weapon, I walked to the door, no longer wanting to prolong the inevitable.

"I'm good. I got my babies all loaded and ready for a night out on the town," Phil said, seeing I was about to shut down the dragon ward.

"Drinks are on you later, boss!" Petro exclaimed, holding his dissolution rifle.

Taking a deep breath, I flexed my hand in preparation to ignite my hellfire sword, and opened the door.

"Well, that was uneventful," Phil stated as the eerie sound of silence greeted us.

"Yeah, I don't know what's worse. Petro, get to the others and tell them to meet us in the dining room. We're right behind you," I said, stepping out, looking around the stacks. Compared to its shadow in the Everwhere, the space was as immaculate and calmly eclectic as a magical library could be.

I reached down, grabbing my phone before punching several buttons in quick succession. Detective Neil picked up.

"It's your dime," was all he said, followed by the sound of cigarette smoke being exhaled and blown over the phone.

"I'm guessing you know the score. I'm also guessing you have folks either almost here or already on the property. Can you buy us some time?" I asked and stated at the same time.

"Oh, they're here. Correction, I'm here. The issue is we can't exactly find *here*. We've been driving around for the past thirty minutes. Guessing the wards are all activated? Expecting company?" Neil said tightly.

He was in a vehicle with someone else and didn't want them knowing it was me on the other line. *Note to self, only mess with Neil half the time, not all the time.*

"Look, I can't explain, but things aren't what they appear. Bruce and Carol Darkwater are heading this way, and I'm guessing they aren't coming alone. You need to get your men out of here, or let me see if I can get Ed to shut the wards down for a few minutes," I said as Neil paused.

"Jake, stop the vehicle," Neil ordered after a few moments to whoever was carting his more than likely hungover or drunk self around.

"You won't regret this," I said, figuring the civilian police would be able to help until we figured out what was about to land on our laps.

"Oh, I already am." He hung up.

Petro came flying toward our group as we turned to the exit of the stacks. "Everyone's in there, boss, and they say there are hundreds of things heading our way. Oh, yeah, and Ed seems pretty pissed at you."

"Things?" I asked, picking up my pace to a light jog as the others followed.

As we got to the dining room door, I looked back, seeing the expression on Aslynn's face. She was concerned about what I would do with the knowledge of her being responsible for directly killing several people and Mages.

The door slid open to show Ed, Jenny with the girls, James, and a handful of others standing around the table, staring at a large tablet. Leshya was standing in the corner with a blank look on her face. As the room turned, they took in the motley crew I had assembled one by one.

It was very evident they had not spent much time around a female warrior Elf from the Everwhere, but they mostly stared a hole through Aslynn and me.

"Hey, guys, someone call a taxi?" I asked, my attempt at humor falling flat. Whatever it was they were looking at was serious.

"Max, we will talk about this later, if there is a later. You two," Ed started in the tight, commanding tone he used when things were going south, pointing at Aslynn and I. "You two have a lot of explaining to do, but right now, we need all hands on deck. Here, look at this."

For the first time I could remember, Ed didn't know everything going on, and it reflected in his posture and tone.

He motioned us over to the table as I remembered Neil and the police driving around the property. "Oh, can you lift the special ward long enough to let Neil and whomever he has with him in?"

Jenny looked up, walking toward the door. "On it." While the wards were magical, they were controlled and powered from the crucible room.

She stopped directly in front of me, taking a deep breath. "I'm glad you're here, but you need to clean up whatever mess it is you're involved in." She grabbed my arm, giving it a light squeeze, before continuing on her way out.

I looked down at my watch as the driveway alarm installed a couple of years ago chimed. The wards were down, and reinforcements had arrived. What the others didn't know was that I had also sent out another request for backup.

"Petro," I said, leaning over the table as Ed pointed to several large white blotches on the map overlay of the surrounding area.

"Yeah, boss?"

"Can you check on plan B?" I asked as Oscar, who had decided to show up out of nowhere, hacked up what sounded like a hair ball.

"Oh, yeah, baby," Petro said, zipping off back toward the Postern.

The team at the Atheneum had grown used to Oscar. Even though he was still unnerving at best, I knew as well as the others that we needed him.

"You good?" I asked Oscar as he licked the back of his hand.

"Making room for later," Oscar purred, smiling as his fangs glistened in the light.

"Max, if you're finished," Ed prompted, going into *oh shit* mode once again. "These represent some type of magical signal. It could be a Mage or Ethereal or, well, anything. They'll be here in a few minutes. The outer wards will keep them on the perimeter for a few minutes at best. We need to funnel whatever this may be into the main entrance. From there, we might have a chance."

"Isn't the Council sending anyone?" I asked, knowing the answer was probably not good.

"Not this time, I'm afraid. Whatever is going on in Australia is big. It was, of course, set up to be. I'm going to personally melt Darkwater's brain and make him shit it out," Ed growled as I let out a whistle. Ed was pissed; not the type which forced you to fight and take unwarranted risks. He was the kind of angry which made you see red.

"The others know something's up. I've already talked to Frank. He's trying to get Davros to cut them loose, but that's going to take some time," James said, looking over at the five other marshals in the room. I recognized their faces, but not by name.

"I'm not buying any of this bullshit. The Supreme Council knows what's going on and what's at stake. We are once again doing their dirty laundry without getting their hands dirty," I said, realizing Oscar was again gone.

The rest of the room grunted and nodded in agreement. Even Lana joined in.

"Where did Oscar go?" Ed asked. I shrugged. "I don't have time to babysit, and we need him." It was clear Ed was about to boil over.

Neil walked in, letting out a belch. "Oh shit, this isn't good," he said, seeing the state of everyone in the room. I hadn't realized it yet, but the others were locked and loaded. Phil was standing at the door with two large, fully automatic streetsweeper shotguns. Oh, and there was a battle Elf; I kept forgetting how out of place Lana looked.

"How many officers did you bring with you?" I asked as another alarm rang. This was a new one, and it sounded substantially more ominous than the doorbell.

"By the looks of this, not enough. We came to take Max and Aslynn in. The Council agreed, so here we are," Neil said as Ed shook his head.

"Right, let me guess who authorized that." Ed gritted his teeth.

I walked over, standing in front of Neil. "I get why, and appreciate you taking the lead on coming in. I have a feeling the Council, more specifically Darkwater, will not be doing any more official business. He only sent out what he thought would get everyone pointing fingers my way. Nothing solid," I said, reaching for my phone and tapping out a message to Kim telling her to send the package I had left. She replied with a frowny face. She knew this meant things weren't good.

Just as Ed was about to dole out orders, Treek, Bosley, Gran, and a handful of other Pixies came screaming into the dining room with Petro in tow. He was now painted red, as were his brothers and the handful of other Pixies.

Macey and Lacey jumped off the table. "Hooray! The heroes are here!"

"We are here to save the day," Bosley said rhythmically, pulling out his sword.

Treek landed by the tablet. "Let me at them. I'll gouge their eyes out!"

Gran, Petro's third brother, coolly pulled a small toothpick out of his mouth. "Is the Elf single?"

Much to my surprise, Lana looked as if she was blushing, letting out a slight grin. I mouthed, "WTF," to Phil, who shrugged.

Petro landed on the table, the still wet red paint glistening over his regular body armor. "Well, boss. Plan B is a go, baby," he said, doing his hip gyration as the others joined in. The girls landed by the group as Bosley winked at them. Pixies, what can I say . . .

The utter ridiculousness of the scene forced a momentary grin on Ed's face.

For the next couple of minutes, Ed laid out the plan. Funnel everything into the main entrance hall and stand our ground till reinforcements hopefully arrived. We might even be able to thwart the attack entirely. If things got too rough, it would be up to me to get everyone out of the facility. This would involve them letting down all the wards, which according to Ed, would be a significantly emotional event.

"Neil, keep your folks as far back as you can," I said as a sound resembling thunder strong enough to feel in one's feet rumbled throughout the Atheneum. Bruce and his goons were knocking at the door. "Not by the hair of my chinny chin," I whispered as Petro and crew took off toward the entrance.

"Max, you couldn't be any more correct. It will not take

long for that much power to break through. We figured they got someone inside the Atheneum and set a damper or some kind of two-way field to allow them in. Jenny thinks they did it when the Council came in and removed some of the artifacts," Ed said. His demeanor was more centered than before, knowing that raging violence was about to occur.

"How do you know?" I asked as Phil and Lana walked out. Aslynn was hanging back. It was clear she didn't want to get out of earshot of me.

"When everything happened at the stadium, Jenny checked all the wards. Something was off. Like I said, muffling their output. I trust you, Max, but we need to get some things sorted when this is over," Ed said as I nodded in agreement.

Walking out into the main hall, I saw Phil moving several concrete barriers back from the entrance station set up when James had first started working security.

"Where's Petro and his gang?" I asked as Jenny walked behind the newly placed barriers.

"They went outside to scout what it is we are about to deal with. I'm going to keep an eye on our backs," she replied, smiling.

"Why are you smiling?" I asked, pulling my short staff out. Truth be told, I felt drained from our previous encounter.

"I don't think we will have to hold for too long. I'm with you; the Council knows. All they need is a reason to show up, then they can play dumb; they want to look like heroes. While you and the others were at the festival working things out, they were sitting idle.

"Since the civilian authorities are now involved, they want a scapegoat in case things go bad. We, and more specifically you, are that scapegoat. Whoever set that explosion off at the stadium and threw all that Voodoo around is who they truly want to get their hands on. The video feed and pictures only allow one to assume you and Aslynn had a part to play. With Darkwater spinning the whole thing, it didn't take long for his goons to take the bait. You know the shitty part, Max? I think the Supreme and Senior Council are embarrassed they didn't get this worked out first," Jenny said reflectively.

As I have stated on several occasions, she was one of the most intelligent people I had ever met. Jenny was also insightful. Since she and Ed had come out as a couple, Jenny also tended to show her more thoughtful side, not always basing everything on science. Which, of course, was ironic for a Mage.

"More big angry dogs!" Petro barked, flying at max speed. The other Pixies were taking positions at random intervals overhead, showing their comfort with fighting. I looked up, seeing Gran winking at Lana.

"Slow down. More dogs? Like Cerberus?" I asked as he finally hooked a clean breath.

"Werewolves, dozens of them," Petro clarified, buzzing up overhead.

"Bruther, I thought those were supposed to, you know, be in Australia?" Phil said as the gravity of what Bruce was throwing at us hit like a piano on a coyote.

"This is the bullshit game Darkwater's playing. Right problem, wrong place. Ed?" I yelled.

Ed's voice popped into my head. *"This is bad. I just sent a message to Frank. It will take them some time, but they are going to divert back here."*

"How do you know this?"

"I don't. Educated guess," Ed finished, hanging up the headphone.

The snarls and growls of what I supposed were Werewolves reached my ears before the initial sight of shiny, elongated fangs came into view, followed by the smell.

Stained glass and fragments of the massive wooden

front door exploded under the pressure of large, clawed paws and hulking forms, the initial vision of horror solidifying my resolve as I forced my will into my hands. While I didn't look back, I could feel the hesitation from the regular cops Neil had with him.

As the thought crossed my mind, rounds exploded from their guns, cutting through the air. The sounds of bullets hitting flesh increased as Phil's shotguns joined the metal chorus of general death. Petro and the other Pixies held back, knowing most people's initial instinct with a gun was to shoot it as rapidly as possible.

Before the second onslaught of bullets found their targets, an unnatural wall of smoke instantly erupted between our team and the Werewolves. The billowing, gray smoke additionally muffled the Weres movements.

Our team paused as the noises stopped. "I don't like this," Lana said. I nodded.

There are a few things worse than being attacked by a pack of ravenous Werewolves: Godzilla, angry gods, super big ass scary monsters, a cut bleeding in a room full of hungry adolescent Vs, nuclear war, giant spiders, and the list goes on. Today, this list would forever be updated to one thing: Werewolves with guns.

Glowing red bullets erupted from the cloud of smoke, forcing everyone to the ground. Petro and the other Pixies launched further up as the sound of a muffled grunt echoed behind me.

The thump of Lana loosening several arrows whistled by, allowing me to launch a handful of small hellfire balls into the blurry smoke.

A whelp announced one of our attacks had landed. This, of course, motivated the rest of the team to start firing again as the Weres joined in the back-and-forth.

My military-trained mind started to recognize a disturbing pattern. The attackers pushed us to attack, seeing our footing inside the Atheneum. This was followed by a smoke screen and covering fire. The Weres were repositioning, if they hadn't already. What made matters worse was the realization that the east wing of the house would lead them to the back entrance of the stacks and the crucible room in a roundabout way.

"They're distracting us. We need to split up!" I barked as Aslynn fired an odd silver mist from her wand into the middle of the room. The smoke started retreating from the corners of the entrance, shrinking in on itself and directly into Aslynn's mist.

"Me and the boys will hold it down here. We won't be any good moving around those things. Leave us as much firepower as you can," Neil said, holding his pistol over the concrete barrier, firing a handful of rounds while looking at me. He had also picked up on the move, and was keeping the rhythm of our defensive posture fluid.

I looked behind Neil, seeing a downed officer. He was still alive and breathing, with Jenny leaning over him, pushing her healing energy over his body. Taking stock of the surroundings, it was clear that as long as the group had ammunition and the ability to cast spells, the long corridor leading away from the entrance was a perfect defensive position.

The large hallway was set up like a funnel, or as we called it in the army, a kill box. It was mostly secured, and before the Weres could get to the group, they would be torn to shreds by the enchanted ammunition and whatever else the others could throw at them.

Petro zipped down with the rest of the Pixies. "We're coming with you, boss!"

The other Pixies all had various stabby-looking weapons drawn. They were effectively a flying miniature blender, bringing new meaning to the term *death by a thousand cuts.*

"Perfect. Aslynn, you're coming with me," I said, since she was a full-blooded Fae and lethal on the worst of days. Not to mention I wanted to keep an eye on her.

With Lana, Phil, and Ed staying, the police team would have more than enough support for the time being while we kept the other Weres from flanking the group, which, of course, could be problematic.

I nodded to Phil as he stood, firing both his shotguns at their full cyclic rate. The Weres, now partially visible, were obviously distracting our team, buying time. An echo of snarling growls confirmed Phil had more than likely just pissed off some of the attacking beasts.

A handful of Weres leaned over the far wall, returning fire, as Aslynn, the Pixies, and I rammed through the door of the crucible room, sprinting toward the back exit which led in a handful of directions.

"Petro, which way are they coming from?" I asked, working to ensure we didn't miss the oncoming onslaught.

Treek darted forward a few feet, smelling the air. Petro tapped his nose, letting me know his brother was better at the whole bloodhound routine.

"One floor up. They seem to be moving slowly," Treek said, not knowing the entire layout of the house.

I looked over at Aslynn. "There's a set of double doors at the far end. I'm betting they're warded."

Treek shook his head. "Nope, there's someone, well, something else up there. I can't figure out what it is, but it smells like clay and sunshine?" Treek looked confused as Petro grimaced.

"Petro, for the rest of the afternoon, you're more than welcome to tell me the bad news first," I said, closing the door to the crucible room behind us, melting the lock just in case. It would buy the others time if we didn't stop the other Weres.

"It's Leshya. She's trying to help, boss. We need to get to her," Petro said as I got my body in motion, leaping several of the spiraling stairs at a time.

One thing I often ignored was just how much my body had changed since turning thirty. I now stood roughly six foot six and weighed in at a muscled two hundred and thirty pounds. In my own right, I was now a reasonably useful wrecking ball. It had only dawned on me over the last year that when I walked into a room, people often stopped and reconsidered making smart-ass comments about my hair or drinking habits.

And I was now, in effect, priming myself to go toe to toe against a massive, snarling shifter.

The sounds of fighting started as soon as we rounded the corner and exited the stairwell. A loud crash, followed by an echoing boom down the hallway, told us Leshya was holding her ground.

Much like the corridor downstairs, the long, narrow pathway in front of us had the same funneling effect. It was slowing the Weres down, forcing them to focus their attacks instead of surrounding their prey. The more I thought about it, the more it became clear that the Atheneum itself had been designed to withstand an attack from outside forces.

Rainbow-colored flares erupted in front of Leshya, who we could now see. She was firing some type of spell at the door, which had long since disintegrated.

"Petro!" I barked, pointing toward Leshya, also letting her know we were there. A flurry of wings and multiple trails of Pixie dust streamed overhead, looking like fireworks trailing off into a dark night sky. The eye-gouging blender of death was on the offensive.

The quarters were too tight for me to sling any real hell-fire, so I pulled out my short staff and pistol, running forward as Aslynn came up beside me with her wand fully charged. A muted glow emanated from her hand surrounding the intricately carved weapon.

With the dust and spells now dissipating, I could see the hulking mass in front of us. It was the first time I had gotten a full view of one of the beasts. It stood well over seven feet tall, with muscles in places I didn't know existed. Even though they considered themselves Werewolves, they were still shifters, able to manifest their form in different manners to scare the ever-living shit out of people.

Its eyes were what took me off guard as Leshya pulled back while the Pixies darted in and out around the creature's head, causing it to swat blindly in the air. They had landed their target, blinding the Werewolf. The problematic part was the two other hulking masses right behind who had just joined the fight.

"Leshya, get behind us!" I barked as Aslynn and I took firm stances. There was nowhere to hide or seek cover. This was going to be a one-on-one fight.

I nodded at Aslynn as we picked our targets. She would go after the Were on the right, and I would go after the one on the left, while the Pixies kept the one in the middle occupied.

Running forward, it was clear Petro and the gang were paying attention, as the Pixies all flew at the beast's head at one time, forcing it to the ground. I leaped over the feet of the middle Were as my target realized that I was, in fact, making the dumbest possible move in the history of man: I was running straight toward a snarling Werewolf. The beast hadn't expected me to have the balls to do so, the expression on its face giving everything away.

"*IGNIS!*" I yelled, letting off a couple of small volleys from my pistol as the beast jumped back several feet into the larger, more open room beyond.

I was laser focused, not paying attention to the fact that I had just ignited my hellfire blade with my pistol in the same hand, and it melted into a pile of molten metal. The red-hot material hissed on the floor and walls, spattering in front of me like a shotgun blast at close range.

The small laser light show distracted the beast long enough for me to get within swinging range of my sword. It swiped its elongated arm, slamming me against the wall hard enough to cave it in, pushing me into the other room. The sounds of Aslynn firing spells from her wand cut through the echoing ringing in my ears.

As if straight out of a movie, instead of attacking, the beast stood in front of me, letting out a guttural howl. It was showing its dominance. I leaned on my elbow, pushing myself up, launching directly into the creature once again.

The hellfire from my blade had caught the side of the wall I had gone through on fire. Good news was the blade was still in front of me as it seared through the Werewolf's chest right as it locked its massive claws on my shoulders, pinning my arms.

"Arggh!" I bellowed as the beast started to squeeze, making me feel like a car in a junkyard compactor. The Were's razor-sharp claws started sinking deep into my upper torso. I felt blood shooting from the punctures. Gazing into the beast's eyes, it opened its massive jaws, preparing to take a killing bite.

While I couldn't move my arms, I still had my hellfire blade firmly seated inside its body. The fact that it hadn't dropped to the ground yet told me how strong the beast was.

I started seeing stars as the muscles flexed on the Were's neck, getting ready to strike. The one thing about having my enhanced abilities was that while I couldn't slow time down, I was able to focus at laser speeds, making it seem as if the beast was moving slowly.

On instinct, much like the trick with the tree, I released the energy in my hand, and the hellfire that was once a focused blade took on a mind of its own. The released energy immediately spread throughout the inside of the beast like blood pumping through its veins.

I looked into the creature's eyes as traces of hellfire zipped under its skin in all directions. The Were's now snarling open mouth revealed a glowing light coming from its throat, as if about to throw up fire.

That was the last thing the beast did before dropping me to the ground and grabbing its own body as one of its knees combusted into flames, tumbling the Were to the carpeted floor in a muffled thump.

I paused, taking in the violence in front of me as a large chunk of its neck turned into nothing, forcing its oversized head to topple to one side. It was over. I shuffled my feet backward, pushing myself against the far wall before looking to my left, realizing there was still a fight going on.

Leshya and Aslynn were at one side of the hall, shooting spells at a Were as it held up what looked like a shield. Some shifters also had magical abilities to shoot spells and cast enchantments.

Taking stock, I quickly realized the second Were was down on the ground, still holding its head, unseeing. Its clawed hands were bloodied, looking like pieces of raw meat. The Pixies were slicing the beast to death.

I slowly stood up and dusted myself off, shaking the remaining stars out of my vision from almost being squeezed to death. Blood ran down my shoulders and chest, making me wince as I rolled my arms back, resetting myself. Pushing my will back into my right arm, I whispered, *"Ignis,"* not wanting to draw the attention of the others.

Nothing happened. I looked down at my hand and squeezed my fist again, trying to will the blade of the once glorious Durundle to life. Again, nothing happened. I turned to the beast lying in a pile of smoking fur. Had I done something I wasn't supposed to, or had I simply exerted too much energy over the past couple of days.

Refocusing, I pulled out the Judge, firing at the Were the Pixies had been fighting on the ground. The beast shattered into glowing embers. It had been judged. The loud boom of the gun overtook the sounds of the spells the others were casting. The Pixies, sensing this, darted over to me as one of Aslynn's spells the Were had dodged flew by my head.

I only had a handful of rounds left and would use them sparingly. Slamming the weapon back in its holster, I formed a ball of hellfire in my hand, slamming it directly into the back of the Were in front of us. I could still do at least this much with whatever remaining power was in my body.

Leshya and Aslynn had the beast so occupied, it never saw the attack from its rear coming. It had hesitated slightly when I fired the Judge, but with all of us pressuring the Werewolf, the beast had made its choice, focusing on the targets in front.

As the beast let out a guttural howl, clawing at its melting skin, Leshya slashed the beast with what looked like a rainbow-colored lasso. Simultaneously, Aslynn planted one of her green plasma balls directly into its face, immediately evaporating any distinguishing features and dropping the creature to the ground.

The fight was over; at least the one in front of us. Destruction, small fires, and the stench of burning hair filled the hallway as I walked over to the two women. I turned away from the still masses of what once were living, breathing creatures. Smoke started to fill the hall, and the concern of the fire spreading began to grow. I hadn't focused enough.

"Petro, you guys think you can get those flames out?" I asked as the group saluted, taking off down the hall. Pixie dust was a fantastic thing. It would often affect things as willed by the Pixie. In this case, we needed them to be mini fire extinguishers.

I turned to Leshya while she stared at the chaos. Her face had four deep, distinct slash marks running from her hairline to the bottom of her jaw.

"Leshya, are you okay?" I asked as she just pointed at my own wounds.

"I'm fine. That was rather easy," she replied, her words floating off.

Aslynn squinted her eyes. "She's right. Those were scouts. In human form, they would barely be able to buy a beer," Aslynn said, taking stock of herself and adjusting her belt.

The problem with getting too many sinking feelings in your stomach was that your body eventually started to ignore them and everything else around. I paused, holding my finger in front of my mouth, telling the others to be silent.

"I could hear the gunfire when we got up here, dammit!" I cursed as Petro flew over, seeing my change in mood.

"Boss?" he asked as the rest of the Pixies came closer. Lacey and Macey looked around, also getting a feel for what else was going on in the building.

"This was a diversion. We need to get back downstairs now!" I yelled as blood ran down my arms, finally reaching my hands. My immediate thought was that I was sweating.

"We don't even know if they're still alive," Aslynn said, lowering her voice after realizing what she had said out loud.

"No, they would be tearing the rest of the house apart. Bruce is here for the dagger. That son of a bitch is smart. We should have just stayed with the others," I chided myself, wiping my hands on my coat.

Leshya snapped out of her trance, clearing her throat. "The others are downstairs and appear to be subdued. There are more people here, not just the Weres."

"Bruce and Carol are here. Aslynn, Petro, you guys up for

another fight?" I asked, getting the thumbs-up from everyone.

"Yeah, boss, but I don't think you are. Have you looked in a mirror lately?" Petro winced. The smell was more than likely about to make him sick.

"Petro, I need you to find out how much longer reinforcements are going to be. Try to reach Frank. I'm pretty sure at least Angel is heading our way," I said, forming some sort of plan.

"You think this is a good idea? I still have the charm Ogun gave me," Aslynn offered, pulling out a silver necklace from around her neck.

"That's the last thing we need. It would . . . well, let's just say there are certain parts of this that the others still don't know about.

"We had a hard enough time with these three Weres. I'm sure we're not going to do any better downstairs. Bruce will know we're stalling—" as the word *stalling* swept across my lips, Bruce's demanding, pirate-like voice echoed throughout the building.

"Max, I know you're home. I have your friends down here. They are relatively unharmed . . . for now. Come downstairs, bring the dagger, and we can talk this out. No one needs to get hurt any more than they already are."

He was using some type of charm to boost his voice throughout the facility. I paused, taking a calming breath.

"Oh," Bruce continued. "You have two minutes. No stalling for backup."

"Petro, see what you can find out. He just wants to talk with me. Aslynn, here," I said, handing her the knife. "Stay in the crucible room. If I call you to come out, do so. It may buy us a minute or two once he realizes I don't have the knife on me."

It was simple. The plan was not really a plan, just a way to buy some time. I would make sure we used every second in our trip back. Leshya would stay with Aslynn in case the others started showing up. Petro and the other Pixies would head outside and work to get ahold of Frank. If I said "hellfire" out loud, they would swoop in to help.

There was no more time to plan as we walked down the stairs.

CHAPTER 25

Cat Scratch Fever

"Stay in the break room and don't move," I indicated as Aslynn paused by the door, both of us noticing the smell of briny salt water in the air.

I walked over to the sink, rinsing the blood off my hands and face. My hands had a slight tremor in them from a mix of overexertion and just plain nerves.

Leshya walked over, handing me a towel. "I have a feeling things are going to work out," she said in an odd yet soothing tone.

"I hope so. Stay here and help in case things get dicey." I handed her the towel back.

Aslynn paused, grabbing my arm lightly. "Thank you," she said, leaning on her tiptoes to kiss me lightly on the cheek.

"Thank me later. I'm still not sure how this is going to play out," I replied, looking at my feet to avoid eye contact before walking out of the break room and into the crucible room.

As was to be expected, a hulking shadow covered the door leading into the main hall where we had left the others, the smell of the ocean getting stronger as I approached.

The security glass on the door to the crucible room exploded inward as a massive, hairy, clawed fist pulled back. The sound of groaning metal as the door was finally pulled off its hinges signified to everyone my location was no longer a secret.

"Bruce, tell your dog to calm down and back up. I'm coming out!" I yelled, amplifying my voice.

The Were was significantly larger than the ones earlier, and as it stood up, I could only see its chest in the doorway stepping out of view. Behind were the officers Neil had brought with him and Ed and Jenny. All of them had their hands tied behind their backs and seemed unconscious. I immediately noticed the absence of both Phil and Neil.

"No sudden moves. Step out with your arms above your head, slowly," the gurgling, underwater-sounding voice of Carol Darkwater said flatly. There was something in the way she spoke. It was as if she wasn't human; at least not anymore.

I cleared the doorway to see the worst possible scenario. There were at least ten more of the larger Werewolves standing around at odd intervals, and Bruce Teach sat astride one of the giant lizards we had run into in the Everwhere. But more off-putting of all was the appearance of Carol Darkwater.

When I had last run into her, it was clear she had gained some type of magical power. Now, it appeared the shift had become physical. She was an odd shade of greenish blue, with not only her two arms coming from her body but several tentacles flowing from her back with suckers identical to those of an octopus. Her face was sharpened, and water seemed to weep from her eyes and mouth. She was no longer human, but a monster. Carol was the source of the ocean smell.

After scanning the threat, my attention was caught by the sight of Phil being held by two of the Weres initially out of my view. Directly in front of him was the limp, bloodied body of Detective Neil. I quickly focused on his figure with no luck. I couldn't tell if he was still breathing.

Phil strained against his captors as spittle fell from his

gagged mouth. A flurry of cussing was being lost in time, never to be heard. He was not easily subdued, and thinking about it, I had yet to see him incapacitated beyond being a little light on his feet after a late night at FA's.

"Everyone calm down. I think we've all had a long enough day," I calmly said, seeing if Bruce would take the bait and buy us some time.

"Oh, don't worry. Your little friends outside were able to contact the others. Unfortunately, they have run into a little detour. They will make it here eventually," Bruce assured, jumping off the lizard in one dramatic leap. "It's been a while, Max. Let's cut to the chase. Where's the knife?"

"I have it. That's a fact. The issue is, I don't have it on my person at this exact moment." I paused. Every second and minute counted. Besides, I wasn't lying. Bruce looked over at one of the more humanoid Weres. It nodded. It could sense if I was telling the truth.

"I will need you to go get it. Or else I'll start killing these people and things you call friends one at a time. I'll start by pulling the arms off your good pal Phil here," Bruce threatened as the Werewolf holding him flexed. Phil's joints produced a cracking sound, making me grimace.

"Stop!" I barked, taking another quick, desperate look around the room. Something was off. Something new, something that hadn't been here when I left. "I left it in the other room. Let me get it," I followed, figuring a significant emotional event, be it good or bad, was about to occur in the hallway.

Sitting resolute, as if part of the entrance to the stacks, were two concrete lions. One had a rather familiar bloody handprint on it. Ordius the Keeper was here. My mind raced, finally figuring it out, as the roar of a rather large, angry tabby cat now turned battle beast echoed through the air.

The ears on the sides of the Weres' heads all pinned back

at once as the two holding Phil dropped him immediately on instinct. More significant threats were around.

Bruce, seemingly unfazed, threw a small dagger at Phil, which buried itself in his back. He froze immediately, no longer fighting. "I'm growing impatient. Carol, go with Max, get the knife. If he doesn't give it to you within two minutes, kill him. Take Ming with you," Bruce said with finality.

One of the larger Weres whom I assumed was Ming turned, lowering his head and walking toward the mangled opening to the crucible room. I turned, nodding for her to follow. Bruce had no idea the level of *oh shit* that was in the hallway with him and the others. Carol's smell filled my lungs as the sound of Ming's heavy steps replaced the sounds echoing in the hallway.

Carol walked up beside me, her breathing sounding taxed and garbled, as if she were breathing water. She paused before I stepped into the hallway that led toward the break room.

"Your friend out there is dying. That dagger has poison from my body in it. I, and I alone, can ensure he makes it." Carol paused, taking another gurgling breath. "Ming, if Max moves other than to get the knife, tear him apart."

The statement was final, with no room for interpretation. Knowing that Oscar had gone for help allowed me to focus on the situation at hand. All I had to do was ensure neither of the monsters that had walked into the crucible room left.

"It's in the break room. Nothing fancy. I have someone watching it," I said as one of Carol's tentacles lashed forward, slamming into the wall.

"I guess you can be reasoned with. I've heard about your weakness toward your companions. We stand by our word. Give us the knife, and we will leave," Carol stated flatly again, taking another breath. The sound of water dripping on the floor dug into my thoughts.

Words meant something in this world. They held power, and in many cases, were to be taken literally. Carol hadn't been as specific as Bruce. She had simply stated that once she got the knife, they would be leaving. It was clear I was not supposed to leave the room alive.

"Aslynn," I shouted as an odd hush filled the room. "It's okay, come out with the knife. If we do so, they will leave," I deadpanned, figuring she would understand the situation.

"The Fae is here? With you?" Carol asked skeptically. She was aware of what Aslynn was capable of and what she had done searching for her and Bruce.

Aslynn walked out holding the knife in her hand, strolling toward us from the far end of the hall.

"Stop. Max, you go get the dagger and bring it to me," Carol ordered, not taking any chances. She knew being in tight quarters with a full-blooded Fae could be problematic. The entire evening was turning into one giant game of chess.

"I'm going to walk down that hall and get the knife. I promise I'll give it to you," I said, nodding my head as Carol smirked approvingly. Ming huffed so hard I could feel the breeze and stench of his breath on my back. As soon as I returned from that hallway, both of them were going to kill me.

I walked forward slowly, buying as much time as possible. Before reaching Aslynn, I quickly noticed Leshya, Petro, and the other Pixies leaning against the conference room wall. They weren't flying to prevent the Were from hearing them.

"No talking. And hurry up; you have forty-five seconds," Carol said, moving away from the hallway opening.

Aslynn handed me the knife, the look of pure hatred from seeing Carol burning through her body. I shook my head not to move as I turned slowly, walking back toward the open room and possibly my last chance to fight.

The sound of muffled howling and general chaos erupted from the hallway, catching Carol's and the massive Werewolf's attention. Ordius was making his presence known.

Carol hissed, a gurgling slop of water falling onto the floor. "Go see what's going on, and kill the others," she barked, turning back toward me as I reached the end of the hallway.

One of Carol's tentacles shot forward in a frantic lunge. I dodged the strike, sliding on the wet floor and using the momentum to push myself forward past her. Ming turned to face me as the sound of Aslynn casting a spell echoed down the hall. In a few seconds, violence had erupted in the room. The fight was on.

I collected a ball of hellfire in my hand as the sound of Petro shouting, "CHARGE!" also joined the soundtrack of violence. Pushing my will, the baseball-sized orb of hellfire launched toward Ming, smacking his body with little to no effect.

The shifter lashed out with one of his clawed hands, forcing me to duck as he pulled out an off-looking gun with the other, firing a round directly into my chest. I flew back, almost knocking into one of Carol's now occupied poisonous tentacles. The Pixies were slicing and working on keeping the odd appendages occupied while Aslynn did the rest.

I started getting up, noticing the smell of burning flesh coming from my chest. Leaving me no time to think, Ming leaped forward, slamming down in front of me as I again pulled my will together and pushed out another small blast of hellfire. The shot landed in the beast's face long enough for me to pull out the Judge. Not having Durundle was taking its toll.

The round slammed out of the weapon with a loud, thundering roar as Ming leaped into the air, crashing through the glass wall of what once was Phil's office. I quickly swung around, pulling the trigger again as Ming launched himself a second sooner than I could react, even with my heightened senses. This time, the hulking mass slammed through the glass into the communications room.

Sparks flew as a small flame started on the far end. The massive monitors on the walls sparked, blinking out of existence. Making matters worse, an actual sprinkler system started shooting water into the room.

Ming let out a roar as I looked down the barrel, having him dead to rights. "Die, you son of a bitch," I growled, the symbolism of the statement not lost on me, as the gun clicked. I was out of ammunition, not landing the other two shots.

I let out a huff, still not able to get on my feet. Ming launched forward with his maw fully extended. I dropped the Judge in slow motion, leaving my arm up. There was no more time for tricks, no more time to grab another charm, no more weapons at the ready. I didn't blink as the Judge clattered to the floor. Water splashed as every other sound stopped.

As Ming's jaws surrounded my extended arm, I screamed at the top of my lungs, filling my body with all the pent-up rage and frustration of the past few days.

"*IGNIS!*"

All the lies, all the deceit, all the pain my friends had felt. I put every part of my being into my hand as my hellfire blade sprang to life, ripping through the Werewolf's head as his teeth shredded into my arm.

I pulled my arm up, cutting the rest of the now dead shifter's head in half. While this had only taken a millisecond, the rest of Ming's body was still in motion as it slammed into me at full force, driving me across the floor, through the wall, and into Ed's office.

Gasping, I started to move my body, ensuring it was still, in fact, all in one piece. The Were must have weighed four to five hundred pounds, making it almost impossible to move. Just as I was about to relax my body and accept my fate, the large mass was no longer there. Looking up, I saw Leshya standing beside me with her ghostlike hand outstretched.

"I think you have better things to be doing other than napping," she said, pulling me to my unsteady feet.

I couldn't get any words out as I rested my mangled hand on her shoulder. Leshya pointed toward Carol. "The water is making her stronger. Maybe you can help with that," she suggested, handing me a small potion.

"Is this what I think it is?" My chest was heaving as loud crashes sent vibrations through the building from the hall.

"I won't tell if you don't," she said again, grinning her odd, flat smile. Without hesitation, as I often did with potions or, well, anything else with alcohol in it, I bottomed up the concoction. As a side note, I really needed a stiff drink.

Energy shot through my veins, making me gasp, the pain of the multiple injuries on my body taking a back seat. I would pay the toll later. My eyes came into laser focus as I started to take stock of the room.

Most of the Pixies were still fighting. Petro and Bosley flew in a circle overhead, darting in and out, attacking. Aslynn looked injured, yet still slinging spells. She was moving like a ballet dancer on stage.

I looked at the floor then over at Carol, figuring out the best way to attack, when it suddenly dawned on me. She needed water to survive, or at least to use her powers.

A devilish grin spread across my face as I took a step forward. Even though my senses had been dulled from the pain, my body was clearly in a state of disrepair.

"Hey, Carol, I got your knife!" I yelled, only catching a bit of her attention. She was focused on the fight in front of her, and about to win, by the looks of it. Carol knew this. I was betting she also knew I was a mess.

"Die!" she yelled as all her tentacles flew forward at Aslynn.

"*AQUAS!*" I yelled, holding out my hands, one pointing toward Carol and the other toward me.

Sensing the attack, her tentacles slammed to an abrupt halt and shifted course as a sphere reflecting all the water around Carol sprang to life.

Carol turned, now focused on me, and took a step forward as I let my will flow into my other hand. Water started pouring out of her mouth, nose, and ears.

"No! What are yo—gurgleeguff," Carol screamed, her body starting to go limp. Her once menacing tentacles started dropping, still moving in a life-preserving effort. I looked her square in the eye, taking a few more steps into the offices' central room. The look on her face was one of panic, almost like a person drowning underwater.

Before either of us could move or say another word, Aslynn shot forward, taking advantage of the confusion, slamming her wand into Carol's chest.

Carol's face turned to see Aslynn's. The two women stared at each other for a brief second before Aslynn yelled, "*ERUPTO!*"

Chunks of green flesh and waves of water shot out from the center of the room as my bubble winked out of existence. The sound of water splashing the floor from the sprinklers took over the once loud battle. Aslynn stood frozen, her hand still out, her wand nothing more than splinters.

Petro flew over. "Boss, you okay? You look like hell! Oh good, you're still walking. I got to take care of the others. Treek is hurt bad. We need to get him out of here," Petro said at lightning-fast speed after I nodded at him. I was still short of words.

Leshya slowly followed behind as he flew away, disappearing into the dark hallway leading under the Atheneum. The fire in the communications room made the water in the room shimmer as I walked up to Aslynn, grabbing the hand with the wand in it.

"Hey, it's over for her," I said as she let the remaining piece of wand splash on the floor. "We still have to get to the others."

The stark realization that the fight wasn't over poured over both our bodies. She relaxed her shoulders. Shouting and several howls started coming into focus from the hallway, telling us the team was back in the fight.

"I just . . . I thought it would feel different," Aslynn said as a thought crossed my mind.

"Do you still have that charm Ogun gave you?" I asked in a hushed tone.

"This damn thing? I don't need it anymore. I've done enough damage," she said, handing me the necklace.

I walked over to what was left of the top part of Carol's deformed body, trying not to gag as I placed the necklace around her neck. Looking down, I also picked up a small vial of what I guessed was the antidote to her poison tucked into a pouch on her belt. She had inadvertently patted it when informing me she had it.

"What are you doing that for?" Aslynn asked, turning toward the main hall and the growing sounds of gunfire.

"The way I see it, the Council will still be looking for whoever was responsible for the deaths. Those will still be on your conscience, but when they check out this body, they'll find the charm and link her to them, more than likely. Even if they know it's a plant, it'll give them an easy way out to explain everything, even the concert. We can work around the pictures and videos. That being said, you're still not in the clear with me, though," I said, breaking more laws and rules than I had time to add up.

Aslynn lowered her eyes in understanding. My debt to

her father was paid. She would be responsible for her actions from here on out, even if they included what she had done.

"Let's get out there and finish this," I said as we walked into the main hallway.

Looking around, it was evident that Ordius and Oscar had joined the fight. Several Werewolves lay ripped to pieces where they had been standing before I left. Neil was still lying on the ground, not moving. I saw Phil leaning up against the wall with one of his shotguns in his lap. Further down the hall, several of the officers, James, Ed, Jenny, and I assumed Ordius and Oscar were still fighting.

"Phil, how you holding up, brother?" I asked, pulling out the antidote and putting it to his lips. "Bottoms up."

Phil took the potion, wincing as his eyebrows reached the top of his forehead. Whatever it was didn't taste good.

"Gahh, oof, what is that? I've had better days, bruther. Not too sure I'm going to be able to move. See that hairy bag of bones over there? Old Betsy here sent him on a proper ride when Ordius showed up. Neil . . ." Phil pursed his lips before shaking his head. He was clearly, for the first time since I'd met him, genuinely hurt.

I glanced over as Aslynn leaned over Detective Neil, looking up. The message was clear. He hadn't made it through the initial fight.

"Dammit. Look, I'm going to end this shit right here, right now. I'm going to need you to stay put," I said as Phil winked at me.

"I'll just stay right here and hold down the fort," Phil huffed as Aslynn walked over.

"What are you going to do?" she asked, kneeling beside Phil and handing him a small flask full of whiskey.

"You had that the whole time and didn't offer me any?" I asked indignantly as Phil stuck his tongue out.

"You didn't look like you needed it yet," Aslynn replied, nodding down the hall.

"I don't know," I said, getting back on my feet. Aslynn started to stand as Ed's voice pierced my thoughts.

"*He's going to gate—*" was the last thing Ed relayed in my thoughts before a bright flash of blinding light took over my body.

I blinked, seeing purple and yellow flashes before my eyes settled on the dulling colors of the Everwhere. Tiny speckles of dust floated in front of me as Bruce turned the massive lizard he was riding around. It let out a hiss that gained in volume as it traveled down the gloomy hallway.

Bruce had gated us both to the Everwhere.

The sounds of crashing and what might be fire coming from the shadow stacks behind me snapped me back into the present. Whatever had been going on in there when we gated back to Earth was still going on.

"Give me the knife, and this will all be over," Bruce said in a relatively calm voice. He was covered in scrapes, including a river of blood flowing from a wound on his side. Bruce was dressed in odd leather armor that was a mix of, you guessed it, pirate attire and new, flashy fatigues. Two pistols stuck out from the belt on his waist as the handle of a cutlass peeked out from his hip.

"If not?" I asked, taking stock of my energy levels. I looked down at my castor, only seeing a light red coloring on the watch's face. While I still had some reserves of energy, I would be hard-pressed to keep it up.

"Ah, stalling again, postponing the inevitable. It was clever of you to bring a guardian with you. I must admit I didn't see that one coming. He's quite busy, so I don't think we will hear much from him again," Bruce said, bringing the giant lizard to a halt before sliding off its back. While most people would think he was exposing himself, I knew better. He had just doubled his odds if he attacked me.

"Is he dead?" I asked, figuring he would tell me.

"Ordius, no. That would be a rather adventurous task I'm not up to at the moment. You only met a portion of the pack. I sent the rest toward downtown Saint Augustine. As you know, he's bound to protect the city, so *poof*, he had better things to do," Bruce explained, holding out his hand while cocking his head sideways.

"Yeah, that's going to be a no from me, dawg," I replied in my best Randy Jackson voice as I leaped back several feet to better position myself away from the lizard, not to mention closer to the stacks. If Cerberus was still in there, he would at least help with the lizard situation.

"So be it." Bruce pulled out his pistols, firing several rounds in quick succession as I again jumped in the opposite direction. The bullets tore into the walls, sending chunks of plaster hissing through the air.

I reached up, firing a small ball of hellfire not at Bruce, but rather at the lizard as it lurched forward. Again, I leaped through the air, pushing the potion and my body to its limits. The lizard crashed into the double doors to the shadow stacks. It started pulling its stuck head and legs out, swinging its tail wildly in the air, hoping to strike me.

I pulled up, holding my short staff, firing the stunning spell as Bruce raised his hands, throwing up what looked like a shield. The spell reflected off, dissipating as it winked out of existence.

The crunch of the lizard's head being bitten off by what I assumed was Cerberus froze us both in place as the visible part of the creature's body went limp.

"You'll pay for that!" Bruce bellowed, pulling out his cutlass before lunging forward.

I gritted my teeth, yelling, "*IGNIS.*" My hellfire sword once again sprang to life just in time to catch the soul sword. Unlike other swords—or much of anything, really—a soul sword was enchanted and one of the few items which could withstand hellfire.

We exchanged blows as Bruce moved at lightning speeds. For his size and build, Bruce Teach's movements were unnatural.

Pulling back, Bruce swung down, slicing the already damaged upper part of my arm. The pain shot through my body like ice water being pumped into my veins, the enchanted blade's effects not fully realized due to the cut not going all the way through.

I pulled back to release a ball of hellfire when Bruce, moving faster than I could react, pulled up one of his pistols, shooting me in the leg. My calf disintegrated in a shower of blood and muscle as I dropped to my knees, letting out a howl of both pain and anger.

The hellfire blade winked out of existence as all my energy poured back into my damaged body. My physical being had reached the point where, no matter how strong the potion, I could no longer keep moving. A loud bark vibrated the floor as the sounds of Cerberus ending the life of another giant lizard stilled the air.

Bruce paused, looking at me from several feet away. "It didn't have to end like this, Max. When I'm done here, I'll make sure your friends die as slowly as possible. That includes that woman of yours," Bruce gloated as I lay there.

"Go to hell," I spit out, gritting my teeth as waves of pain rocketed through my body.

"Oh yes. When I do go to Hell, I plan on making some changes," Bruce replied, walking closer and kicking my staff out of reach.

"They won't stop coming after you," I said, trying to put the pieces of my body back together, focusing on getting one last push of energy. If I wasn't going to make it out of here, neither was Bruce.

After all the training and talking with Jenny, Tom, Bo, Belm, and everyone else, I was fairly sure I could go supernova. Meaning, if I could muster enough energy, I could release hellfire from my inner being. This, of course, meant disintegrating myself in the process.

"Oh, you still have some fight left in you," Bruce mocked, prodding me with the end of his cutlass. I looked down to see the sheath of the dagger poking out from my belt. "If you think your grandfather Tom is going to avenge your death, I don't think that will happen. He's too busy out there trying to figure out a way back to Terrum."

My face went blank hearing this. I had never truly figured out what Gramps was trying to do. "Why does he want to go there?" I asked, my genuine want to know the truth showing.

"My God. You don't know. I'm sure you know he went back to that harlot Lilith, thinking he could save her and your daughter. My boy, he's trying to reach the Old Gods," Bruce said, leaving a hell of a lot of room for interpretation. He was playing with me. He had to be. My daughter? I didn't have a daughter.

Bruce raised an eyebrow, seeing my response to his words. I could hear him tightening his grip on the hilt of his blade.

While I was sure some of what he'd just told me was the truth, Gramps had a habit of making people think and know exactly what he wanted them to. If I made it out of here alive, I would figure the rest out. I needed to know what he was talking about.

The conversation I had had with Lilith flashed through

my mind faster than a beat of my heart. I needed to live. I had to live. I would live.

"I'm going to need that knife now," Bruce said as I unhooked my belt with my nonmangled arm.

I pushed myself back against the wall, sitting up slightly as the horror of my leg finally registered. A light tear streaked down my cheek, making a path through the contrasting dust and blood.

Bruce looked down, seeing the scabbard. Satisfied, he grinned as gold teeth glinted in the ambient lighting.

Much to my surprise, Bruce walked past my belt, standing directly in front of me. I had hoped he would bend over to pick it up. I had one final charm at my disposal. If he had picked it up, he would have been slammed with a stunning grenade. While it also would have knocked me out, it would have bought me time.

"I'm not going to take any chances with you. It's nothing personal." Bruce swung his cutlass as I used the last bit of energy left in my body to dodge right, rolling to my side.

I looked up to see Bruce slowly turning around, his sword clattering to the ground.

"What have you done," he demanded under his breath as if he were talking to someone far away.

"Tell Devin I said hello," I replied as I rolled onto my elbow, pulling the dagger out of Bruce's foot.

An odd black void started growing under his feet while I scrambled backward. Whatever it was, I didn't want it anywhere near me. I gave up any dignity I had left and rolled several times, finally coming to a stop when I slammed into the still tail of the dead lizard.

My chest heaved with exertion as I watched Bruce look at his feet, still staring as if he was looking at something not there. Several dark, clawed hands started pulling at his legs as

Bruce began to slowly melt into the floor. Sounds of screaming and anguish erupted from the floor as Bruce's head finally disappeared in a swarm of claws and darkness.

Just as quickly as the hole in the floor opened, it closed. Silence engulfed my mind as everything around me started to fade. I whispered, "Daughter," as my eyes closed and darkness filled my body.

CHAPTER 26

Hospital Bills . . .

S ounds started to reverberate in my mind as the echoes of beeping and other mechanical apparatuses pinged and whooshed. Was I dead? Was I still in the Everwhere? My mind started racing, not allowing my body to function.

"Why the hell do you wankers keep bringing me applesauce and no damn roast!" Phil bellowed. I was sure at that point I was either in Hell and Phil was being tortured, or we were in a hospital.

"Oh, so you want more applesauce? I'll make sure the cafeteria knows," a stern male voice cut through Phil's tirade.

"And send one of the lady nurses in next time. I don't know what we did to get Mongo the Beastmaster as a nurse," Phil chided as the sound of something being pulled off his skin ripped through the air.

"You son of a bitch!" Phil yelled, his tone pleading this time.

"I'll make sure to send that lady nurse in," the male nurse said, chuckling under his breath as the door clicked shut.

"Gods and graves, is he gone yet?" I whispered, my mouth dry from the breathing tube jammed up my nose.

"What's this! Bruther! You're awake!" Phil bellowed

again louder than needed, making my head throb. "Male nurse fella!"

"No, I'm fine. By the sounds of it, I don't need him pulling out anything stuck in my body," I said as my eyes opened, focusing on the bright overhead LED lights.

"That git keeps bringing me applesauce in a bowl. He's messing with me for sure. That's a sauce for a roast, not a damn soup. I'll find out why, if it's the last thing I do in here," Phil vowed as I coughed out a laugh.

"Phil, I'm fairly certain in the amount of time you've lived in the States, you've had to eat applesauce at least once. It's hospital food 101. I couldn't tell you a time I was in a medical facility and didn't get a bowl of the stuff," I said, blinking my eyes. I reached up, slowly pulling out the tube in my nose.

"What kind of sorcery is that? Tease an injured man like that. I want a roast; been wanting one since yesterday," Phil grumbled as I finally shifted my head over to see him.

"Yesterday? How long have we been here? What happened?" I asked, finally regaining my train of thought. My chest started to heave as pain shot through my body.

"Calm down, bruther. We've been here a couple of days. I don't know all of it, but Ed can fill you in on most of what happened." The sounds of electric gears whirred as I pushed the button on the side of the bed.

"My entire body hurts," I complained as visions of my leg flashed before my eyes. Looking down, all I could see was a blanket and a large square cast around my foot sticking out at the end.

"You were all banged up, worse than me. Bruther, I think you're going to be out of commission for a while. The good news is, we got them," Phil said, smirking.

"Got them?" I asked, still foggy on some of the details.

"Yeah. Lana brought you back. She said something about

that Hades fella, then you sending Bruce to Hell or something. They also found Carol's body. Whatever you and Aslynn did to her, there wasn't much left. From what Jenny told me when she stopped by earlier, they found a strong Voodoo charm on her body. I'm guessing they're testing it now, but they are pretty sure it's a match. Oh, and someone released the whole kit and caboodle on Councilman—well, no longer Councilman—Darkwater. They're going after him," Phil said as I let out a breath that felt like I'd been holding for weeks.

"Has anyone seen Aslynn?" I asked as Phil shuffled in his bed.

"Phew, I'm not your damn maid, bruther. No clue," Phil huffed as he looked down at the bowl of applesauce.

Reaching down, I grabbed for Petro's now missing charm. "Shit, do they have our stuff stored somewhere?" Phil stared at me.

"Bruther, you must have really banged your old noggin. You were barely alive when Lana found you. From what I heard, about everything you had was either broken or gone," he replied, picking up the buzzer by the bed, smacking the red button at the top several times.

"This better be good," the male nurse wearing a name tag simply reading *Ernie* said before looking over at me.

"Look who's back from the dead. Hopefully you got better manners than your friend here," Ernie said, walking over while scribbling something on a notepad.

"If you bring him some roast, I bet he'll calm down. Hey, did my phone or a small chain necklace with an old-looking coin on it make the trip with me?" I asked as Ernie smiled.

"No, and no. There was one of those little people who showed up threatening to take out one of my eyes if I didn't call him when you woke up," he replied, shaking his head and grinning.

MAX ABADDON AND THE DARK CARNIVAL

"He's serious about the eye thing, you know," I informed him as Ernie's grin faded away.

"I figured. I'll give him a call." He turned to Phil. "Tell you what. You promise to stop yelling at me, and I'll see what I can do about a roast. This isn't one of those fancy magic hospitals; they didn't think Max here would survive the trip. I'm still not really sure how all of this stuff works, but you have basically done several months of healing in a couple of days," Ernie said, pulling out his cell phone before punching in a number written on his tablet.

He put it on speakerphone just as Petro's voice screeched out of it like it was a fast-food ordering booth. "Is he awake? I can hear him breathing. Max!" Petro exclaimed, clearly taking off without telling Ernie he was hanging up, or actually hanging up.

Within thirty seconds, Petro zipped through the door. "Boss! You're awake, thank the stars above. I was so worried. Casey made you some bug snacks, but I left them. Everyone was worried about you, but I wasn't. Now we can go to the movies and get dinner and drinks and—" Petro started spouting as I cut him off.

"It's good to see you, buddy. How're your brothers?" I asked as Petro shook his head.

"My brothers are fine; Treek is still a little banged up. We lost two of the other Pixies who volunteered to help. Lacey also got her wing damaged. She's going to be like me," Petro said, sadness in his voice as he flexed his mechanically modified wing.

I looked around the room as my mind kept racing, finally remembering Neil's body lying on the ground. "What happened with Neil?" I asked, already knowing the answer.

"He didn't make it, bruther. You know, he ended up not being such an arse," Phil said under his breath. For Phil, this was a compliment and show of respect. The man had sacrificed his life to help, and in many ways, probably saved mine. I would ensure his actions would not be forgotten.

The sounds of a woman telling off another nurse made their way into the room.

"I don't care. I'm going into that room." Kim's voice carried through, talking to a losing orderly.

"Ma'am, you're supposed to be on bed rest," the young woman said as Ernie's shoulders slumped.

"What is it with you people, or whatever," Ernie sighed, setting down the clipboard. "It's okay, let her in. They'll burn the damn building down if we don't," Ernie finished under his breath, recognizing Max from the videos on the five o'clock news.

I honestly liked the young man. He was taking this all in stride. Kim rolled her wheelchair into the room, almost leaping out of it as she got close to my bed.

"Get a room," Phil said, realizing we were already in one.

"I'm here, I'm here . . . aren't you supposed to still be on bed rest?" I asked as she hugged me. I could feel the tears start to form on her eyes without even looking. Her breath caught as she pulled away, leaning back in her wheelchair.

"I needed to see you with my own eyes. I got a room here this morning," Kim said, a vulnerability I hadn't heard before coming through in her voice.

"I'm sorry," I replied as Petro took off, landing on Phil's dinner tray.

"Yuck," was all Petro said as Ernie walked out of the room, slamming the door behind him.

"Kim, I'm sorry about Neil," I started, knowing even though she hated him, at one point, she had loved him. An old drill sergeant of mine had once told me, *"If you love someone once, you love them just a little bit forever. Except for your girlfriend's boyfriend. She'll love all that guy forever."*

"It's okay. I think in some way he made up for all the shitty stuff he did." Kim grinned, her eyes distant.

"He did, and then some. Look, I'm not sure any of us would be here if he hadn't shown up," I said, taking a wheezing breath as my ribs protested.

"Damn right, bruther. We'll lay a drink out for him at the bar from now on," Phil declared, jabbing his spoon at the spilled applesauce on his tray.

"So, when are you leaving?" I asked Kim as she set her jaw.

"Leaving? After that shit show? I don't think so." I smiled. This was the best thing I had heard in weeks. "Not so fast, lover boy. There are going to be some changes around here."

Phil, Petro, and I all let out groans at the same time, me with a smile on my face. Kim winked, turning her wheelchair around, pushing herself out of the room.

CHAPTER 27

Promises

"Another round?" Trish asked, setting several ice-cold bottles of Vamp Amber on the table. After another three weeks in the hospital, much to Ernie's chagrin, Phil and I had finally been released. Kim had also finally come off bed rest.

Ed, Abby, Jenny, Frank, Angel, and the rest of the Pixie crew had all joined the three newly released, moderately healed members of society. James was also with the team, but he was sitting at the bar with his new fiancée, Sarah, whom according to Gramps would become problematic at some point.

Dr. Freeman had taken a leave of absence that, from what I understood, started right before everything went down at the Atheneum. There was more to that story. Also joining the crew was Abby, looking as rock star as ever.

Phil's injuries had left him with several scars on his arms, and one that went from his hairline to his chin, cutting through his eye, which made him look even more badass than before.

Kim was still wearing a cast and was on sabbatical, whatever that meant. The week prior, she had turned in her badge and resigned from her position on the Council. While I believed this to be temporary, it had been her one condition for staying. I'd even joked with her that I had an opening at AAs.

I, on the other hand, was another story. Besides finding out I may have a daughter, the right arm that I had conveniently jammed into the mouth of a raging Werewolf would be a road map of scars and ridges leading all the way to my hand. If it weren't for my pride and overall lack of need for a year-round Luke Skywalker costume, I would wear a glove. Jenny had told me the scarring would eventually fade, if she took an educated guess based on my lineage.

My leg hadn't been so lucky. Another odd Soul Dealer weapon had been used to shoot off my entire calf. This, in turn, had been fixed by a group of highly skilled Dwarfs and Jenny. Ernie, the male nurse, had taken a particular disliking to the smelling, short, drunk, angry group.

Much like Lilith's arm, my calf was now an odd mix of steampunk-looking biomechanical gears and actual flesh. I had stopped asking when even Jenny started grimacing. It was all packaged together neatly and reasonably inconspicuously.

The power of Dwarfs and their craftsmanship was not only a thing of legend, but now proven fact. It had taken only a handful of days to get used to my latest addition. They had even added a few upgrades to it, giving it a very similar function to a castor.

Others in the group had various scars, burns, and bruises; however, they had fared better than the three amigos.

"Thanks, Trish," I said as she winked at me, the smell of food wafting over from the kitchen. "Tell Amon I'll pop back and see him later."

"He'll like that. I think he's back there making you all some pizzas," Trish said, walking back to the bar.

"Right," Ed started, sounding much more like his usual self. "What happened next, Abby?"

"Next thing you know, man, all these big ass lizards

show up out of nowhere. If it weren't for Knight, Kane, and Jim, you probably would have been dealing with a bunch more of those nasty creatures. I think Kane ate one of those damn things," Abby finished, describing what had happened as they were leaving Jacksonville.

"So let me get this straight. You just happened to all be driving through Saint Augustine, leaving town, and ran into a bunch of raging lizards?" Phil asked as Petro buzzed over beside me.

"Yeah, man, groovy for sure," Abby replied as we all grinned. Phil wasn't up to date that Planes Drifter was a little more than they appeared to be.

"It's like a damn episode of *Scooby-Doo* with you lot," Phil said, raising his glass.

"What's up?" I asked Petro under my breath as the rest continued to tell stories about their part in the fight.

"You might need to use the bathroom," Petro whispered, nodding toward the back hall. It had become a tradition that after something significant happened, I would go to the lavatory and more than likely run into the Devil, a demon, or some other sordid figure. The far end stall in Trish's bathroom was some type of gate to somewhere I had yet to figure out and she had yet to tell me.

I huffed, standing up. "I'll be back," I excused myself from the table. One of the TVs Trish had installed around the bar started announcing a breaking news report.

Without even entering a stall, I looked around the bathroom. "I'm here," I said as the door on the far end clicked open, sending the scent of strong pepper through the small space.

"Maxxx," Devin hissed. Another sound came from behind him.

"Isn't there a more dignified way to get here?" Bo complained, walking out behind Devin, waving. He was wearing lacy, old-timey white gloves. Again, his sense of fashion was either way out of place or the next big thing.

"You two weren't doing anything funny in there, were you?" I asked jokingly while they looked at each other, not getting it. I still let out a snort.

"It looks like you are doing well. I meant to come see you earlier, but other things have been keeping my attention," Devin said. I stood there, wondering why both of them wanted to talk to me.

"Why not just pop in when I'm somewhere else or not having a good time?" I asked as Devin set his flat smile.

"The Atheneum has been partially destroyed, last I heard a few weeks ago. Plus I wanted to drop a little something off," Devin said as I just shook my head. He clearly didn't understand toilet humor.

I hadn't been back to the Atheneum yet. I'd heard that it was left in bad shape. It must have been worse than I suspected. Come to think of it, Aslynn, the Pixies, and I alone had demolished a good piece of the new offices and upstairs east wing.

"Alright. Bo, Devin, you know the drill. What's up? I'm not having an hour-long meeting in here; that includes moving forward as well. You're more than capable of showing up elsewhere," I informed the two as someone tried to open the bathroom door behind me. I was guessing Devin was ensuring it would stay closed.

"Of course. Here," Devin said, handing me a letter. "Tom has cleared his last marker with me. He wanted me to give you this letter."

I reached out, grabbing the clearly open envelope. "Of course you would read it. Alright, I get why you're here. Bo? You?"

"Yes, well, darling, I might have overstepped my bounds

a little bit. With that, I've been given what you call community service. Devin has instructed me to hang around here, without getting involved in any nonsense, and help you work on the other gates in the Postern," Bo said, grinning his overly broad, nightmarish smile.

"I'm not sure that's a punishment, but sure, I could use the help. Plus the Council has been asking about the Postern a good bit lately. Where are you staying?" I asked as he put his hands out. The Atheneum was on its last leg, having had a large portion of it damaged or completely destroyed in the fighting. I was supposed to go with the team and walk through the property the next day.

"Amon was looking for a roommate, so I'll be staying here," Bo informed, about to explode with excitement.

"Look, I get it, Devin. Bo is one of the only demons you trust since Belm is gone. Let me read this letter and go from there. I'm still working out some of the shit that hit the fan over the past couple of months," I said, pocketing the letter.

"Max, before I go. A storm is coming, one that will not lend shelter. You've proven yourself in my eyes and that of your enemies, which I promise you have. Just remember, things aren't always as they seem. Oh, and take the queen up on her offer and pay her a visit. I'm curious to hear what she has to say," Devin said before turning to leave; he was done talking. The door clicked shut behind him.

Bo stood there, rocking on his toes, not talking.

"Jesus, okay, you can join us for a drink," I said as he winced at the J-man's name.

I walked out and sat next to a smiling Kim. "So?"

"So, Bo has decided to join us for a drink." We both grinned. She had heard all my stories about Devin and his bathroom meetings. We had figured there was something about the room that made it Devin's new go-to.

The group hadn't grown comfortable with Bo. Since Abby and he had been friends for what I guessed were centuries, it made his introductions to those who had not met him yet less dramatic.

"Hello, darlings!" Bo greeted, clapping his hands. He was being theatrical, taking a seat next to Abby.

"Bo, do you know where Aslynn is?" I asked. The group turned, everyone wondering the same thing.

"Right, that's a good question. I sort of figured you might have seen her," Ed said, cocking his head sideways as Jenny wrapped her arm around him.

"I'm not too sure about that. After she was cleared due to Carol being to blame for all the tomfoolery, I believe she headed back to the Plane to spend some time with Jamison," Bo answered as Trish set a glass of milk in front of him.

Truth be told, I was reasonably sure everyone had their suspicions about Aslynn being involved in the murders. It had also come to light that the victims mostly all had less than stellar backgrounds, much like she had mentioned, with a few of them being wanted. Lucian, however, was the unforgivable death.

I had kept my promise to her father, and to her. But if she stepped out of line again, it would be a different story.

"Well, at least we can take some of the chess pieces off the board," I said as Trish turned up the TV as a reporter started talking.

Angel looked up. "Yes, but we're still playing the same game."

The group nodded in agreement, taking pulls from their drinks.

"What's that lady saying?" Petro asked as Casey slowly flew over. She was due next month and looked as if she could give birth at any moment.

"I'm not sure. Something about a magic misfire in Chicago. I'll make a few calls and see what happened." Trish turned the TV back down, smiling.

The group started talking again as I looked over at Kim, the various conversations and stories being told giving us a minute to focus.

"We need to talk. I have something I need to tell you," I started, wanting to relay what Bruce had told me, and my overall gut feeling about the situation.

"If you're going to ask me to marry you, the answer is no. A date, yes," Kim said, pausing as she smiled. The look on her face melted when she saw the concern in my expression. "Sure, let's go to the bar. I need to stretch my legs anyway."

"Kim and Maxy, sitting in a tree, k-i-s-s-i-n-g," Phil rhymed as I gave him the universal finger sign for friendship.

"Last I heard, your girlfriend was hanging around Knight Raider after the concert," Kim jabbed, smirking, referring to the visibly absent Kristi.

"What's this bollocks?" Phil said, looking over at Abby.

We finally made our way to the bar, taking a seat as Sarah brought over fresh beers.

"Is that true what you said about Kristi?" I asked, surprised by the news. Kristi was a strong Gate Mage whom Phil had spent more than his fair share of time around. She had also been reassigned to a British gate detail with none other than Inspector Richard Holder, Dick Holder for short.

Sitting at the bar, the jukebox was more pronounced as "Riders on the Storm" by The Doors started playing subtly in the background.

"No, but I did talk to her the other day, and he needs to call her. Maybe that will get his juices flowing. Now, talk to me," Kim prompted, taking a pull from the bottle as I watched her lips.

318

"I don't know how to say this, so I'm just going to lay it out there. One of the last things Bruce said before whatever the hell happened to him was that . . ." I paused, taking a pull. "According to Bruce, I have a daughter."

Kim's eyebrows scrunched together as she set her beer down. "Are you okay?"

"Am I okay? Did you just hear what I said?" I asked, confused by her response.

Kim put her hand on mine, leaning forward. "You do know I was married before we met. Hell, there's so much shit about me you don't know that would make you think twice about sitting here. Listen, I don't know what this is all about or what it means, but we will figure it out together, alright?" Kim promised, the smile again taking its rightful place on her face.

"I'm not asking for anything, or for you to help. I just need someone to understand. There's more. Tom and Lilith are involved somehow," I continued. Her smile again faltered. She knew the implications of what I was saying.

"Good God, Max. You sure know how to keep things interesting, if anything. What do you say we go check on the kids? They've missed their uncle Max, last time I heard. Something's telling me that's important," Kim finished as we both took finishing pulls of our beers while staring off into nothingness.

We stood up to rejoin the group. At the end of the bar, much to my surprise, was an odd-looking, long-haired, blandly dressed gentleman. J-man, as Phil called him, saluted me with his beer. I turned, walking with Kim back to our friends.

EPILOGUE

*Tom and a Mysterious Figure
in a Cave on the Plane.*

"Will it work?" Tom asked as the cloaked woman lifted a finger. Tom was sitting at a stone table in a manicured cave deep inside one of the forge mountains on the Plane.

"Work, yes. The way you want it to, no," the scratchy voice replied, tapping a skeletal, almost transparent finger on the table.

Tom pondered as the hood over the woman's head shifted. "Is there any other way to safely hide the child from Lilith?"

"Perhaps, but as soon as she uses her power, Lilith will be the least of your worries," the mysterious figure replied while a cool breeze swept across the room.

"You of all beings know what's at stake here. Tell me, and I'll ensure you get what you are asking for," Tom said as the shadow of Chloe pulled her hood back.

Tom knew what Chloe wanted. He was one of the few necromancers with the actual ability to wield the magic necessary to bring her apparitional body back. With the Soul Dealers out of the picture, Chloe's options had become limited.

"I have nothing left to lose," Chloe said. The sounds of an incoming storm starting to echo off the cave walls.

"Perhaps. Listen, I'm probably the only other person who

knows what you have truly sacrificed. Well . . . besides your sister Sarah. The trip to London. I know Max was not supposed to leave that park. I also know he was not supposed to leave Riverplace Tower.

"At the Fountain of Youth, you killed Jayal, effectively saving the lives of the entire team and my grandson, allowing them to gate out. You, and you alone, knew what Max had given you with that bracelet, and ensured it made it into the circle, and it was you, and you alone, who convinced Lilith and the others to focus on the secondary route, thinning out their numbers," Tom said, detailing Chloe's true betrayal working alongside Tom.

"What difference does it make?" Chloe asked as she stared into the distance.

"All the difference in this world and the next. We also don't want to forget how you ensured Ed was only injured in the woods in Georgia when you could have killed him. You then knowingly took a direct hit from Max in the process to divert Lilith again." Tom paused, taking a deep breath, knowing the rest of the story.

Lilith had figured out Chloe's constant yet subtle attempts to stop her. This was the reason the Thule Society had sent her to die at the Devil's Castle. While they hadn't known the depths of the betrayal, they had known she wanted her daughter and a way to escape. Chloe had craftily diverted their assumptions of a mother's love for her child.

"Max has to know," Chloe pleaded, her voice getting weaker and more distant with regret.

"When the time comes, he will. He still doesn't remember the night you were together. I promise, you will have your day in the sun," Tom said, knowing the crushing agony Chloe was in. This was the reason Max had felt so conflicted with Chloe when she took the final journey while in his arms, again, lies and deceit changing reality.

She had worked with Tom the entire time to help in the battle not only against the Old Gods, but those in the wrong. Chloe loved him Max. And the night they had been together before destroying the Fountain of Youth had been forever wiped from his memory.

"But the child . . ." Chloe followed, the pain in her voice unfathomable.

"Neither you nor I could have predicted what events Lilith had put into motion, or why. I'm trying," Tom said, feeling as if all the centuries of his life were crashing down on him like waves on a beach.

The two sat there in silence, knowing Chloe would have to get back before someone noticed she was gone.

◆ ◆ ◆

Thule Society Meeting Chambers

"What the hell happened!" Darkwater yelled, raising his voice as Lilith held up her hand.

"We all need to remain calm," Lilith said, smiling at the group sitting around the large oval table.

"I don't want to hear anything from you," a large, hulking figure spat out, pointing at Lilith. "She is a traitor. She left, then when everything goes sideways, she just shows up. The only reason she is here is because of the event in Chicago. She should be dealt with," the man followed, pulling out a dull cleaver.

"Enough," Darkwater ordered as the figure, losing control of his body, slowly started moving the cleaver toward his own neck.

After a few seconds of silence, the sound of metal cleanly slicing through flesh cut through the room, followed by the echo of blood splattering on the table in front of the once hulking man.

"We all understand things have changed since Mengele and Beleth are no longer here. Things have progressed ever since I had to leave the Council. Now that I am out of the shadows, we need to take a new path forward. The path that Lilith started. Does anyone else have an issue with this?" Darkwater asked as fury raged behind his cold black eyes.

The death of his daughter had solidified his resolve. He would not only end the Council but those surrounding it.

Lilith had played the Thule Society all along to get what she wanted. Ending Mengele, Bruce, and Darkwater's daughter had been nothing more than another calculated plan, like weakening the very people surrounding Max. The thought planted firm roots in Lilith's mind as she leaned back.

"Mengele and his Soul Dealers were just one part of the Thule Society. They were the old ways. They were misguided and unprepared. We will flourish in the new order," Lilith purred as the rest of the room silently nodded in acceptance.

"What about the deal with the Old Gods?" an older voice spoke up.

ACKNOWLEDGMENTS

Who would have ever thought we would be four books down in the world of Max Abaddon!

Hopefully, everyone's enjoying the ride and starting to see the big picture. Yes, Chloe and Max had a child. Remember, not everything is always as it seems, or at least how they re-member it . . .

A few folks I'd like to give a shout-out:

Hunter Blain (okayest author of the Preternatural Chronicles). Man, thanks for the guidance earlier on. John On! Drinks on me.

Luke Daniels and team. Thank you for taking the time to bring Max's world to life. You are a master of the craft. I always used to say it would be amazing to work with you one day, and here we are.

To everyone who has supported Max Abaddon through books 1–3, cheers! Book four, can you believe it?

To my family, my wife, and two sons. This book is part of my legacy to you. When I am but a memory in time, you will always be able to pick this book up and remember what a nerd I really was and, well, still am...and will probably be some more. Then when you think I'm done, I'll pop up again being even more of a nerd.

BOOKS BY THIS AUTHOR

Max Abaddon And The Will

Book 1 of the Max Abaddon Series

Max Abaddon And The Purity Law

Book 2 of the Max Abaddon Series

Max Abaddon And The Ghost And The Grave

Book 2.5 of the Max Abaddon Series

Max Abaddon And The Gate To Everwhere

Book 3 of the Max Abaddon Series

Max Abaddon And The Dark Carnival

Book 4 of the Max Abaddon Series

Sheltered: Part 1 Of The Sinking Man Series

Book 1 of the Sinking Man Series

Awakened: Part 2 Of The Sinking Man Series

Book 2 of the Sinking Man Series